# "Sir, *where* are my clothes?"

Logan suppressed a smile. "My aunt Mary Rosa undressed you, then spread your clothes out to dry in the kitchen," he explained, admiring her calm, considering that she found herself more naked than not, and with a stranger.

"Then we are not alone here?" Katherine asked in a formal, polite tone.

"Unfortunately, no," he teased, liking the way the color rose in her creamy white cheeks. "However—" he lifted an appreciative eyebrow " —if I had known I'd be having such lovely company, I would have locked Mary Rosa in her room."

"Mr. McCloud, are you always this forward?"

He gave her question brief consideration. "I prefer to think I'm direct."

"Some people might call it arrogant," she said flatly.

Logan had never known a woman to work so hard at putting a man off. It made him all the more determined not to give in.

Dear Reader,

Thanks to the success of our March Madness promotion during 1992 featuring four brand-new authors, we are very pleased to be able to, once again, introduce you to a month's worth of talented newcomers as we celebrate first-time authors with our 1993 March Madness promotion.

*Teller of Tales* by Laurel Ames. When free-spirited Jenner Page captures the eye of the bored nobleman, Lord Raines, their reckless affair causes a scandal that Regency London is likely never to forget, or forgive.

*Riverbend* by Mary McBride. Despite their differences, Lee Kincannon and the fiesty Jessamine Dade seem destined to cross paths at every turn, but the jaded gambler still can't believe that fate has finally dealt him a winning hand.

*Snow Angel* by Susan Amarillas. Katherine Thorn never expected to find herself stranded at the ranch of her unfriendly neighbor during a Wyoming blizzard, and she was even more surprised to discover that Logan McCloud was definitely not the man she thought he was.

*Romance of the Rose* by Claire Delacroix. Though Armand d'Avigny vowed that he would never again allow the lovely Alexandria de Fontaine to be taken from his side, Alex knew that as long as her enemy remained alive she would never be safe—even in the arms of the powerful knight.

We hope that you enjoy every one of these exciting books, and we look forward to bringing you more titles from these authors in the upcoming year.

Sincerely,

Tracy Farrell
Senior Editor

# Snow Angel

## SUSAN AMARILLAS

**Harlequin Books**

TORONTO • NEW YORK • LONDON
AMSTERDAM • PARIS • SYDNEY • HAMBURG
STOCKHOLM • ATHENS • TOKYO • MILAN
MADRID • WARSAW • BUDAPEST • AUCKLAND

Harlequin Historicals first edition March 1993

ISBN 0-373-28765-8

SNOW ANGEL

## SUSAN AMARILLAS

was born and raised in Maryland and moved to California when she married. She quickly discovered her love of the high desert country—she says it was as if she were "coming home." When she's not writing, she and her husband love to travel the back roads of the West, visiting ghost towns and little museums, and always coming home with an armload of books.

For the cowboy in my life, who never gave up—
no matter how rough the trail

I love you, Tom

# Chapter One

*Wyoming, 1881*

Katherine knew she had made a serious error in judgment.

Bending low against her mare's slender neck, she tried to shield herself from the frigid north wind that numbed her cheeks and brought painful tears to her eyes. She should have turned back sooner, she told herself as another gust of icy snow swirled around her, turned back while she still had time.

With aching fingers, Katherine pulled her cold-stiffened rain slicker more tightly around her, though it offered little protection over the lightweight wool riding skirt and cotton blouse she wore.

By force of will, she tried to stop the tremors that racked her body, but it was a futile effort. Leaning forward, she ran her gloved hand along the snow-caked neck of the sturdy little sorrel. "We'll make it, Sunrise," she said firmly. The words were lost on another gust of wind.

She glanced at the gray-black sky. God, how she hated the wind. *Don't think about it. Keep going.* Over and over she recited the words in her mind until her panic eased.

Katherine could have kicked herself for her foolishness. The last few days had been warm for March—too warm, her mother had said. But Katherine's eagerness to go into town had pushed all thoughts of the unseasonable weather from her mind. She'd seen the ominous clouds draped low on the horizon when she left Clearwater for home; she never imagined they were snow clouds. In Philadelphia, such clouds meant rain and her slicker would have been enough, but here, the cold seeped into her skin, making it ache.

The wind died down for a moment and she looked out over the treeless terrain. Snow collected on her lashes. She swiped at it with her sleeve, then blinked and looked again. The road and the few landmarks were all gone. White...everywhere was white. The force of the storm had driven her off into unknown directions, and she knew she could be miles from her family's sheep ranch. *Keep going. Don't panic.* She recited the litany once more and ignored the sudden pounding of her heart.

Deceptively delicate flakes lashed against her unprotected face like a thousand tiny knives. Her whole body shook until she wondered if she could stay in the saddle.

Flexing her gloved hands, she winced at the pain in her fingers. How could it get this cold so quickly? She had to find shelter—soon!

Pulling her horse to a halt at the top of a small rise, she stood up in the stirrups. Shielding her eyes, she searched for some landmark, someplace where they could wait out the storm.

She found it.

To her left, maybe a quarter mile away, a light flickered. She spurred Sunrise forward. The mare stumbled in the deep snow before finding her footing, and Katherine clutched the saddle horn to keep from falling. Caution, she chided herself. More carefully, she rode across the icy white plains toward the beacon of light. She was determined to make it.

Katherine Alicia Thorn was not a quitter.

She rode down a small slope, nearly colliding with a white wooden fence that was almost invisible in the falling snow. Keeping the light in sight, she traveled beside the barrier and turned through an open gate flanked by stone pillars. Finally, she came to a stop.

The sprawling log-and-stone ranch house stood like a citadel against the force of the storm. Snow drifted high around one corner and lay heavy on the roof. Smoke rose defiantly from the chimney against an angry wind.

Katherine stared at the smooth pine door, her limbs refusing to move, her mind numb. Odd, she thought, how it didn't seem quite as cold now. If she could sleep, just for a bit, she'd be able to think better. Her eyelids fluttered closed.

Sunrise gave a violent shake against the cold, jolting Katherine awake. With her last bit of strength, she dismounted. She forced her painfully stiff legs to carry her across the ice-covered planks of the porch to the door. Leaning against the frame, she knocked once. The stabbing pain from that simple act ricocheted up her arm, and she moaned out loud.

The door swung open. A man's tall form filled the doorway, his face cast in shadows.

"C-caught in storm," she managed through chattering teeth.

"My God, woman!" The man wrapped a strong arm around her shoulder and helped her inside. Exhaustion took the last of her strength and Katherine sagged against him. A swirl of snow filled the entrance before the man kicked the door closed with his booted foot.

Katherine felt herself being drawn out of her warm and blissful sleep by a painful tingling sensation in her legs. She squirmed. The tingling persisted. She opened her eyes and gave a cry of surprise when she saw a man kneeling at her feet. He held her left leg in one hand and was slowly rubbing her bare calf. She wiggled her toes, felt them brush against warm flesh and realized her foot was inside the man's woolen shirt.

"How are you feeling?" he asked, not looking up. He calmly removed her left foot from his shirt and lowered it to the quilt. Never hesitating, he picked up her right foot and repeated the procedure.

A hurried glance told her she was sitting on a pallet of quilts in front of a huge stone fireplace. The crackling flames radiated heat and provided enough light to show her she was alone with this stranger.

Katherine sat bolt upright. The red woolen blankets that had been covering her dropped to her lap, revealing her white flannel camisole.

"What the devil do you think you're doing?" she demanded, her heart pounding. She tried to pull her leg from his grasp, but the stranger tightened his grip. "Stop that." She wiggled that foot in turn and felt the hair on his chest tickle the bottom of her toes. Her eyes widened in panic. "I said stop that right now!"

"Not yet, your skin's still too cold," he replied while his hand continued its provocative path to her knee. "Do you feel any tingling yet?" He looked into her face.

Katherine's gaze was transfixed by a pair of coal black eyes framed by long black lashes. Her breath caught in her throat, the sharp retort unspoken. Dark hair, dark as the sky at midnight, curled slightly around his ears and over his collar. He had a straight nose, high cheekbones and a square jaw shadowed by a day's growth of beard.

But it was his mouth that held her attention. His bottom lip was full and his top lip almost invisible behind the neatly trimmed black mustache. Though mustaches were the vogue, his seemed appropriate, regardless of style. It softened his angular features while remaining uniquely masculine.

The stranger smiled at her, an easy, relaxed smile, while his gaze slowly swept over her. She felt indignant and excited, and something else, she realized with a start. As she continued to stare into his black, liquid eyes, she felt unexplainably safe.

"I said, do you feel any tingling yet?" he repeated, a slight trace of amusement in his deep voice.

"Yes…no. I mean, stop doing that!" She pulled her foot free of his grasp and covered it with one of the red blankets. He chuckled.

When he stood and began tucking his navy wool shirt into the waist of his well-tailored tan trousers, she looked away. It was then she noticed she was clad only in her undergarments, and she snatched the soft blankets up around her shoulders. She glared at the man standing before her. "Where are—"

"Feeling warmer?" he asked, with a wicked glint in his eyes.

Tantalizing little sparks of heat skittered along her nerve endings. She looked at him sharply. "I'd be warmer with my clothes."

He merely chuckled again. "They're still too wet." He stepped to the hearth and tossed another log on the fire, then sucked his fingers where the flames had touched them.

Katherine twisted to face him, the blankets draped around her like a flowing red cape. "Wet or not, they'll have to do," she told him curtly, more curtly than she had intended. He had, after all, saved her life, and she was grateful. But he was doing something unfamiliar to her senses and she felt out of control. Not a pleasant feeling for a woman who'd spent the last four years of her life caring for an invalid aunt and running a successful millinery business in Philadelphia.

If he was offended by her tone he didn't show it. If anything, he seemed more amused. His smile broadened. "We'll talk about it as soon as I've made us a drink guaranteed to chase away the remaining chill." He started toward a doorway at the far side of the room, his boots thudding on the bare planked floor.

Katherine tried to control the temper that got her into trouble so often, especially when dealing with arrogant men. And this one topped the list.

"What about Sunrise?" she called after him.

He glanced back over his shoulder. "What?"

"Sunrise, my horse," she explained.

He nodded with understanding. "Taken care of. Don't worry." He disappeared into the other room.

The wind made a low moaning sound across the porch. The large parlor windows rattled and the front door creaked. In a heartbeat, everything else was forgotten. Katherine's gaze became riveted to the oak door. The firelight cast flickering shadows on the walls, adding to the eerie spell. Her hands trembled as an unfounded childhood fear came back to haunt her like a ghost from the grave. The moaning increased a little, then died away. It was almost as if the wind were laughing, telling her that it had found her hiding place.

"Here, drink this."

Katherine looked at him in surprise. She hadn't been aware that he had returned. Without speaking, she reached out from the blankets to accept one of the delicate white china cups. Her hand shook and the cup teetered precariously in the saucer.

"What's wrong?" the man asked.

A long, breathless whistle traveled across the front of the house and Katherine flinched, again nearly spilling the contents of her cup.

He glanced in the direction of the sound. "It's just the wind," he said, seating himself at one end of the brown leather sofa. "It gets caught under the eaves."

"It sounds worse inside than it does out there."

"I know...almost human sometimes." He slumped back and the smooth leather creaked under his shifting weight. "You haven't tried the drink yet," he reminded her. "It's an old family recipe."

Cautiously, listening for the wind, Katherine lifted the cup to her lips and took a small swallow. Her eyes opened wide as the alcohol-laced liquid hit the back of her throat and burned a path to her stomach. She choked. "I don't drink spirits, Mr...."

"McCloud. Logan McCloud." His smile revealed a slash of even white teeth behind his ebony mustache. "Allow me to offer you the hospitality of the Double Four."

Katherine paused, then lowered the cup to her lap. *Logan McCloud.* One of the largest cattle ranchers in Wyoming. If memory served her correctly, and she was sure it did, he was also the head of the Cattlemen's Association, which had tried on several occasions to convince her father to move on. Now here she was in the devil's den. She looked at him through lowered lashes. He was as handsome as the devil, she'd give him that. She lifted the cup to her lips once more, deciding she needed some of the liquid courage.

"Just sip it." He gestured with his cup. "Slowly. If that doesn't warm you, then we'll just have to try something else." Amusement shone in his dark eyes.

It was a blatantly suggestive remark and Katherine should have been angry. But he said it with such charm, she was tempted to smile. She didn't. "Now, Mr. McCloud, about my clothes—"

"And your name?" He gazed at her over the rim of his cup.

"Why do you keep changing the subject?" The man exasperated her to the extreme.

"Am I?" He gave a small shrug. "I thought we were in the middle of introductions."

"I'm Katherine Thorn." She said it like a challenge.

Logan's smile faded and a stillness came over his face. "Thorn?" he muttered.

"Yes, Mr. McCloud." Her chin came up a little. "We raise sheep."

There. It was said. Let him make of it what he would.

A muscle flexed in his jaw. Katherine waited while he absorbed this information. Her brother, Daniel, had painted McCloud as a villain, possibly even involved with her father's murder. She found that difficult to believe. The man who had rescued her hardly seemed a cold-blooded killer, and Daniel was prone to the brashness peculiar to fifteen-year-olds.

Logan lifted an eyebrow. "Then Charles Thorn was...?"

"My father," she supplied.

The day was full of surprises, Logan thought. He hadn't even known Thorn had a daughter. An image of Thorn's scowling face came to mind. The last time Logan had seen him, they'd had an argument over the fences. The man had died—been shot—four weeks ago.

The marshal had come up from Cheyenne, but Logan didn't hold out much hope of the lawman finding the killer. Thorn was the only sheep rancher in the middle of cattle country. Between the damned sheep muddying water holes and then the damned barbed wire fences, anybody within a hundred square miles might have pulled the trigger.

"I heard your father had died. I'm truly sorry for your loss, Katherine," he said sincerely. The lady met his gaze directly.

"It was not a loss, as you put it. It was murder, Mr. McCloud," she corrected him with a deliberate tone. Her expression was tight when she asked, "They still hang murderers in this territory, don't they?"

"Depends..."

She shot him a questioning look.

"Depends on who gets to him first, the law or the family."

She favored him with a trace of a smile that did little to counteract the cold, hard look in her eyes. "I'll keep that in mind."

Logan studied her for a long moment. Her adamant tone surprised and concerned him. He was tempted to pursue the matter, then changed his mind.

"Why haven't we met before?" he asked, deciding the present was much more pleasant than talk of death.

"I've been living in Philadelphia the last four years."

Logan was only half listening. Her voice had a throaty rasp, warm and rich, and it heated his blood like fine French brandy. He knew he was staring, but couldn't seem to stop. She had the biggest, bluest eyes he'd ever seen. They almost overpowered the delicate features of her face.

She was something, all right, sitting there with tousled hair and rosy cheeks, the way a woman looks when she just wakes up or has just made love. He shifted a little, surprised that his body responded so quickly to the thought. Of course, when he made love to a woman she never glared at him as if he were her mortal enemy.

His lips turned up in a lazy smile. "Will you be staying long?" he asked, surprised at how much he hoped she would be.

"We'll be staying *permanently*." Katherine squared her shoulders, put the saucer on the floor next to her and adjusted the blanket around her. "Mr. McCloud—"

"Logan," he corrected.

"Mister McCloud," she continued coolly, "I am grateful to you for your hospitality. However..." She gave an exasperated sigh. "Did you undress...? Sir, *where* are my clothes?"

Logan suppressed a smile. "My aunt Mary Rosa undressed you, then spread your clothes out to dry in the kitchen," he explained, admiring her calm, considering that she'd found herself more naked than not, and with a stranger.

"You said your aunt?"

He nodded.

"Then we are not alone here?"

"Unfortunately, no," he teased, liking the way the color rose in her creamy white cheeks. "Once we knew you were going to be all right, Mary Rosa went on to bed. There was no sense both of us staying up. However—" he lifted an appreciative eyebrow "—if I had known I'd be having such lovely company, I would have locked Mary Rosa in her room."

"Mr. McCloud, are you always this forward?" Katherine asked in a formal, polite tone.

He gave her question brief consideration. "I prefer to think I'm direct."

"Some people might call it arrogant," she said flatly.

Logan laughed. He'd never known a woman to work so hard at putting a man off. It made him all the more determined not to give in.

Katherine untangled her feet from the blankets, preparing to stand. "Right now, I've got to get home. My family will be worried sick."

Logan drained his cup. The china clattered when he put it down on the carved cherry side table. He glanced toward the camelback clock on the mantle. "Considering it's well past midnight and the storm shows no sign of letting up, you'll have to be my guest for the night."

Katherine looked at him, hoping to find a way around the truth of his words, hating to put her family through more worry. In the end she conceded, "I guess you're right...and thank you... for everything."

Suddenly, the low, steady roar of the wind changed, reminding Katherine of its presence. A large gust hit the front of the house like the fist of some unseen giant demanding entrance. The sound propelled her to her feet, the blanket pulling tightly around her neck. Her terrified gaze riveted on the creaking front door. *Wind.* The sound of it, the force of it, seemed to wrap around her, penetrating every pore until there was no escape.

She stood frozen to the spot. Every muscle in her body tensed, waiting for the monster to knock again.

"Katherine?" Logan asked softly, coming to stand beside her. She felt his hand grasp her trembling shoulder.

Turning her head, she looked at him with fearful eyes. "I *hate* the wind," she said angrily, defiantly, as if by saying it she could scare the wind away.

He brushed the hair back from her face with the edge of his hand and gave a reassuring smile. "Don't be afraid.

Come on, sit here.'' Logan motioned toward the sofa. "I'll get you a robe.'' He started for the hallway, then turned back. "I'll just be a minute.''

Katherine nodded, but her attention was fixed on the side of the house where the wind had found some small wooden object to lift and bang against the wall like a bad-tempered child with a new toy. Each sharp knock vibrated through her body, irritating nerves still raw from the day's ordeal.

Logan returned a few minutes later carrying a maroon-colored woolen robe. "Here, I think this should do for now.''

Katherine reached from between the blankets to accept the robe, and Logan turned his back while she put it on. Even on her five-feet-seven-inch frame the garment was much too big, but the material did feel soft and sensuous against her skin. Pine soap and the unique fragrance of a man's cologne filled her nostrils as she tied the sash around her waist. "Thanks,'' she muttered.

"My pleasure,'' Logan replied as he sat on the floor and relaxed against the sofa.

Relaxed was not what Katherine was feeling. She perched on the edge of her seat, her rigid posture the envy of any military cadet. Her hands rested in her lap, the fingers so tightly interlaced that the knuckles were white. She hated being like this, especially in front of a stranger. But wind was one fear she'd never been able to conquer.

The windows rattled with the force of the storm. She jerked at the sharp sound.

Logan reached up and enfolded her icy hands in his warm fingers. Katherine forced a ghost of a smile as she looked down at his compassionate expression.

"What were you doing out in this storm, anyway?'' he asked, his hands still covering hers.

"I was in town taking care of some errands. I shouldn't have stayed so long. I thought those were rain clouds.'' The fear and anxiety of the last few hours could no longer be controlled and she began to shiver. "I thought I could make it home. The wind blew so hard. Suddenly everything was covered in snow. I couldn't find my way.'' Tears slid down her cheeks.

Quickly, Logan was beside her and she was enclosed in his strong embrace. For once Katherine didn't want to be strong. She gave in to her need to be comforted and laid her cheek against his chest. The steady beating of his heart soothed her nerves.

''Until I saw your light, I wasn't sure if I would make it. I got so cold, and I couldn't...'' Her words were muffled against his shoulder.

''It's all right. Shh...shh.'' He rocked her as he would a frightened child. ''You're safe. I'll take care of you.''

It didn't occur to her to question his words. She believed him. Her shivering lessened.

''I'm not usually like this.'' She wiped at the tears with the backs of her hands. ''Just give me a minute.''

''Katherine, that's a helluva storm blowing out there, but you kept your head. Men have died in less, so you have nothing to feel bad about.'' His voice was quiet, calming.

He continued to hold her, his hand gently rubbing up and down her arm as her head rested against his shoulder. When the tears slowed, she looked up into his face, only inches from hers. She could feel his warm breath on her cheek, see the flames of the fire reflected in his eyes. His hand lightly caressed her tear-moistened skin.

''Angel,'' he whispered, and her skin tingled as if she'd been caressed by a warm summer breeze.

Held transfixed by his heated gaze, Katherine couldn't move, didn't want to, she realized. He touched the pad of one finger to her trembling bottom lip. Her breathing became ragged. He lowered his head a fraction of an inch.

Blessed reality struck and Katherine looked away, though she couldn't bring herself to give up the comfort of having his arms around her. She felt him take a deep breath. When she looked at him again, he smiled at her; a gentle, relaxed smile that soothed and warmed her all at once. Still holding her, he leaned back against the sofa.

"Don't be afraid," he murmured against her hair, and she wondered if he was referring to the storm or him.

## Chapter Two

Katherine's eyes opened, then closed again as she attempted to enjoy the last moments of drowsy half sleep. She snuggled lower on the soft leather of the sofa, pulled the blanket a little more tightly under her chin and turned toward the heat of the fire. She wanted to sleep, but her empty stomach wouldn't let her. The tantalizing aroma of fried ham and brewing coffee filled the air. As she patted her stomach to still its grumbling, her fingers caressed an unfamiliar woolen fabric instead of her usual flannel gown.

Her eyes flew open and she looked around the room, her heart beating quickly. Where was she? Her gaze stopped on the fireplace where pine logs crackled and popped, sending cascades of multi-colored sparks up the stone chimney.

Suddenly, memories of last night came rushing back and her face grew hot. Katherine watched the flames, remembering similar flames reflected in Logan's eyes. His gaze had held her suspended in time, shutting out everything around her.

Why, she'd almost let a complete stranger kiss her. He'd wanted to kiss her, she was sure of that, even if she wasn't sure why she'd almost let him. She shook her head in disbelief. Exhaustion, she reasoned. She'd been tired and afraid. Anyone might have behaved strangely under the circumstances. Today she was recovered. Today she was in control.

Standing, she turned her back to the fire and really looked at the parlor in the gray morning light. The pine-planked floors and paneled walls gleamed. The dark browns and greens of the furniture were definitely a man's strong taste, but they were softened by cut-crystal lamps and carved side tables. It was a beautiful room, she decided, down to the heavy white lace curtains covering the front windows.

Looking through them, she could see the storm continuing its rampage. At least in the light of day it didn't seem quite so fierce. Even the wind's howling seemed less threatening. Still, she hugged herself against the shiver that traveled through her body as she thought of her mother and brother.

*Please God, let my family be safe.* This uncivilized country had taken her father and left her filled with an aching emptiness. She refused to let it take more.

If only she could have convinced Daniel and her mother to return with her to Philadelphia. The brick house and hat shop that Katherine had inherited when Aunt Martha died would have provided them with a comfortable place to live and an adequate income.

Katherine had great plans for the shop. She'd worked in it when she'd first gone to Philadelphia four years ago. As Aunt Martha's health declined, Katherine had taken over. With planning and innovation, she'd nearly doubled the business. She thought herself lucky to have found her special niche in life at only nineteen years of age.

Yet she understood Daniel's refusal to leave the ranch. After all, Papa had spent the last five years of his life on the Bar T and only recently had things finally moved into the black. To sell it would mean turning her back on all he'd worked for, on the home and future he'd dreamed of giving his family. She wouldn't destroy his legacy.

Anger and grim determination welled up in her as she thought of the coward who had coldly, heartlessly, killed her father. Not to rob him; Lord knew he had nothing to steal. No, someone had deliberately set out to kill Charles Thorn.

She was sure of it, just as she was sure that that someone lived here in Clearwater.

Tears slipped down her cheeks. Angrily, she swiped at them with the back of her hand. There was no more time for tears, she chided herself. There was too much to do.

The first order of business was to learn all she could to keep the ranch running. Her mother, quiet, kind woman that she was, just wasn't forceful enough to manage a ranch. Daniel, for all his youthful enthusiasm, didn't have the skill. There was no one among the ranch hands to take over, and trying to hire someone would not only be an added expense, it would be next to impossible.

So it fell to her and the skills she had acquired running her own business. While ranching and millinery were hardly the same, she did have experience in making decisions and dealing with suppliers and purchasers, bankers and attorneys.

In a year, maybe two, Daniel would be able to take over and she could return to Philadelphia and the life she'd made for herself there. She would hold on to that dream in the months to come.

Hushed voices sounded from beyond the doorway near the back of the parlor. Glancing in that direction, she heard the familiar clank of a stove lid being dropped into place. Her empty stomach growled once again. She gathered up the hem of the robe and walked noiselessly across the room.

As she stopped, unnoticed on the threshold of the large kitchen, she saw Logan standing at the window, his back turned to her. His forest green shirt was pulled tightly across his broad shoulders, and his black wool trousers fit snugly around his long legs. She watched as he reached behind his neck and rubbed a shoulder muscle.

Near the wood stove, a woman leaned down to slide a pan of biscuits into the oven. She was fair-skinned, with graying black hair held in a coiled bun on top of her head. When she straightened abruptly, Katherine noted the woman was barely five feet tall.

"Good morning." Katherine smiled nervously, uncertain of her reception now that they knew who she was.

Logan turned to face her. His smile was immediate and devastating. He was clean shaven, except, of course, for his mustache. His dark wavy hair looked damp and freshly brushed, yet a few stray curls teased the tops of his ears.

When she looked at him, a tantalizing knot of excitement formed low in her stomach. It was irritating that he could affect her so with only a smile.

She tore her gaze away.

The woman wiped her hands on the stark white apron she wore over her blue wool dress. "Good morning to you." She smiled broadly and hurried forward to take Katherine's arm. "Please, come in and sit down." She gestured toward one of the spindle-back chairs around a worn pine table. "How are you feeling?" she asked, the smile replaced with a look of concern. "You had us worried for a while last night."

"I'm—" Katherine began.

"My goodness, your feet are bare."

Katherine looked down to see the robe had fallen away from her feet.

"You shouldn't be walking around here like that. This floor is too cold. Logan, get a pair of socks for Miss Thorn," the woman instructed without missing a beat.

"My pleasure." Logan strode out of the room.

"Please, I'm fine." Uncomfortable with all the attention, Katherine tucked the robe under her feet. "See."

The woman frowned. "Socks will be better."

Logan returned, carrying a pair of heavy white socks.

Before Katherine could stop the woman, she pulled the robe free and tugged the socks onto her feet. Satisfied, she grinned at Katherine; not just a polite little smile, but the sincere kind that made tiny lines crinkle around her clear blue eyes. Katherine couldn't help grinning right back.

Logan laughed. "This whirlwind of energy is Mary Rosa," he said, as he affectionately hugged the petite woman to his side. "She's my aunt, housekeeper and the best cook in Laramie County. This poor bachelor couldn't possibly survive without her."

"Ha!" Mary Rosa slapped playfully at Logan's hand. "It's long past time you had a wife to cook for you and I had some more nieces and nephews."

"Now, Mary Rosa, you know I'd get married in a minute if I could only find a girl as pretty as you!"

Katherine grinned as she watched the two people so obviously fond of each other.

"He's such a rascal," Mary Rosa said through her laughter. "Don't you listen to him, Miss Thorn."

"Please, call me Katherine."

"Thank you, Katherine." She nodded. "It'll be awhile before the biscuits are done. Then I'll cook up some eggs. Would you like tea or coffee?"

"Coffee, please." Katherine started to get up, but Mary Rosa placed a firm hand on Katherine's shoulder.

"Nope. First-time visitors are always guests. Next time you come, I'll expect you to make yourself at home."

With a swirl of blue wool, Mary Rosa walked to the cupboard. She stood on tiptoe and stretched toward the bottom shelf. "This kitchen was surely planned by a man," she complained.

"I don't see any problem." Logan's expression was the picture of innocence as he reached up with ease and handed her a cup.

She scowled and snatched the cup from his hand. "Go sit down. You're always underfoot."

In two easy steps, he moved to the table and sat down in a chair across from Katherine. The traces of a grin lingered behind his mustache. He held a half-full mug lightly between his fingers.

"I was going to put you in the guest room, but you were sleeping so peacefully I hated to wake you. I hope the sofa wasn't too uncomfortable. We usually treat company better." He leaned forward. "Especially the beautiful ones," he added for her ears only.

Katherine felt the color rise in her face. Before she could respond, Mary Rosa joined them at the table.

"This'll get your heart pumping," Mary Rosa announced, pushing the steaming mug toward Katherine.

The wind made a low moaning sound and Katherine flinched.

"Lord, I'm tired of winter." Mary Rosa sighed and glanced toward the window. "I like summer better. Warm weather, and I can be out in my garden."

"Speaking of warm, I think I'll check on that water I started to heat. It should be about ready." Logan walked toward the parlor doorway.

Mary Rosa gave a small wave of acknowledgement before taking another sip from her mug. "We thought a hot bath would help to chase away the cold," she offered without being asked.

"Oh, no. Please. That's too much trouble."

"No trouble at all." Mary Rosa leaned forward and in a conspiratorial whisper added, "I made Logan do all the work." She chuckled.

Katherine laughed, enjoying the woman's delightful company. "I really want to thank you—both of you—for everything." She wrapped her fingers around the mug, letting the warmth permeate her hands.

"I'm just glad we were here."

Katherine nodded her agreement. "I wish there was some way to let my family know I am all right."

"I know, dear. It's times like these I wish we had Mr. Bell's newfangled telephone invention." She gave Katherine's hand a pat. "Please try not to fret. It won't do a bit of good, you know. Your family's been in Wyoming for a while. They understand the winter storms. I'm sure they'll wait until the snow stops before they start a search, and by then you'll be on your way.

"In the meantime," Mary Rosa announced, setting her cup down, "let's get you to that bath." Her chair made a scraping sound as she pushed back from the table. "By the time you're finished, I'll have a nice big breakfast waiting. We'll have you fixed up in no time.''

Katherine followed Mary Rosa through the parlor, then down a wide hallway. They passed one set of closed doors she supposed opened to bedrooms and stopped at another door a few feet farther on.

Mary Rosa turned the shiny brass knob. ''Here we are.'' She pushed open the door. The well-appointed room was cozy and warm from a wood stove and the steaming water. Katherine's gaze quickly took in the carved dressing table with beveled mirror and cut-glass lamps. The royal blue upholstered bench matched the draperies, which were drawn across the window.

Her face lit up. ''This is wonderful,'' she exclaimed softly, focusing her attention on the large copper tub that Logan was filling. ''I've never seen anything like it in my life.''

''My mother suggested we build the room.'' Logan placed the empty water container on the floor with a hollow thump. ''Actually, insisted may be closer to it. She says just because she has to live in the wilderness every summer, is no reason to do without the comforts she enjoys in Cheyenne.''

''I think I'd like your mother,'' Katherine answered with a smile.

''Well, we McClouds are a likable bunch,'' Logan replied with a wink that only Katherine saw. He started toward the door. ''I'll be in the kitchen if you need me,'' he finished before pulling the door closed behind him.

''Your clothes are there on the bench.''

''What?'' Katherine's thoughts had been on the man who just left. He was entirely too familiar, entirely too at ease with her. She was entirely too intrigued.

She pulled her gaze from the door and looked at the freshly pressed skirt and top. ''Thank you, Mary Rosa. I really didn't expect . . . well, I don't know what I did expect, actually. I mean, my family being sheep ranchers and Mr. McCloud being a cattleman . . .''

"You're a guest in this house." Mary Rosa reached into the pine cabinet and took out a fluffy white bath towel.

"Not an invited guest," Katherine prompted.

"It doesn't make a bit of difference." Logan's aunt put the towel on the dressing table. Turning, she leaned back against the edge. "You're here and welcome."

"I know there's been trouble with some of the cattle ranchers."

"True."

Katherine hesitated to say more, although she wondered if Logan was involved.

Mary Rosa looked up with an indulgent smile, as if she sensed Katherine's thoughts. "Logan is a good man." There was an unmistakable note of pride in her voice. "If I had a son, I'd want him to be just like Logan. Now, your bath is getting..." She sniffed the air and looked startled. "My biscuits!" Mary Rosa rushed from the room, closing the door with a bang.

Katherine couldn't help chuckling. She eyed the tub, which seemed to beckon her. After removing Logan's robe and her undergarments, she stepped into the steaming water, feeling the warmth seep into every pore. Her sore, tense muscles relaxed and she stretched her slim frame in the heated water.

Heaven, she thought.

Logan set the pan of golden biscuits on the table as Mary Rosa rushed into the kitchen. She pressed her hands to her heaving chest and took a deep breath.

"Thank you."

He grinned. "You're welcome."

The kitchen door creaked from the cold as it opened and a gust of snow-laden wind filled the room. Pete, the Double Four foreman, shouldered the door closed behind him and slapped his hat on his leg to free it of snow. Then he pulled off his fur-lined gloves and ran one hand through his straight brown hair. "Must be close on to thirty below out there." He shrugged out of his plaid wool jacket and hung it by the door.

Mary Rosa scowled and tapped her foot.

Pete glanced at the snow already starting to melt on the floor. "Sorry about the mess."

"There's no sorry to it," Mary Rosa snapped. "Just clean it up. There's a cloth in the basket under the bench."

Hurriedly, Pete obliged. Two steps toward the stove he stopped. "Why, Logan," he murmured, his slow Texas drawl evident even after eleven years in Wyoming, "if I'd known you was baking biscuits I'd a been over sooner." Pete's eyes danced with amusement and he clamped his lips tightly together to keep from laughing.

Logan took the teasing good-naturedly. "Pete, you better be careful," he replied as he filled two cups with coffee. "If you insult Aunt Mary Rosa's cooking she'll run you out of here, blizzard or not." He handed one of the cups to Pete, who had joined him at the stove.

"Those biscuits are for company," Mary Rosa announced, shaking one finger in Pete's direction.

"You mean you ain't gonna give me even one?" Pete asked with his best sad-little-boy expression.

Mary Rosa propped her balled fists on her narrow waist. "If you want biscuits, go ask Cookie to make some."

"You wouldn't really want me to get poisoned eatin' ol' Cookie's biscuits, now would ya, Rosebud?"

"I told you not to call me that!" She glared at Pete, then pulled a small basket with some cleaning rags and furniture wax from under the sink. Tucking the basket against her ribs, she turned with a flounce and bustled off.

Pete and Logan waited until she was out of ear-shot before they let go with their laughter.

"I sure do love a high-spirited woman." Pete shook his head, a smile lingering at the corners of his mouth.

The icy snow made a sharp sound as the wind drove it against the kitchen window. Both men's expressions turned serious at the reminder.

"This storm is going to play hell with the cattle," Logan commented in a quiet tone that showed the frustration he felt.

Pete nodded. "If it keeps up, the herd could drift a hundred miles by the time it's over."

Logan straddled a chair, his forearms resting on the top rung of the back. "There's no way to tell if this will last a day or a week."

"I know, and there ain't nothin' a body can do. Them cattle will turn their backs to the storm and drift south till the wind stops—or they drop dead." Pete moved closer to the window and lifted the curtain to look out. "If they bunch up in the gullies southeast of here, we stand to lose a lot of them." He let the curtain fall back into place. "Sure hate to think of Slim out riding the line in this mess. Course, he'd just say it was part of the job."

"Well, you Texas boys never were known for your good sense," Logan replied, trying to ease the tension. There was nothing he could do for men or cattle out in the storm.

Pete brightened a little at the teasing. "What's good sense got to do with anything? If we had good sense we wouldn't be punching cows for a living, that's for damn sure. We'd be living the good life, working in some nice warm store." His ever-present spurs jingled as he walked across the room. "Or better yet, some nice warm saloon."

He pulled out the chair across from Logan and sat down.

Logan rested his chin on the back of the chair and stared past his friend toward the window. "You know you wouldn't last a week cooped up in a store."

"Well, I might just give it a try. In the meantime, do you suppose I could have me a couple of them biscuits? They sure do smell good." Pete reached across the table and slid the pan closer. "Did I hear Mary Rosa say these were for company?" He helped himself to two biscuits.

"Yes."

"I noticed a little sorrel in the barn this morning when I was checkin' on that thoroughbred mare you brought from back East." Pete heaped butter and jam on a biscuit.

"How's the mare doing?" Logan asked, avoiding the first comment. "Is she showing any signs of labor?"

"Not yet."

"I'll be out to the barn later to check on her."

Pete finished off the biscuit in two large bites. "About the sorrel?"

"Yes?"

Pete halted his coffee cup halfway to his mouth. "Look, if you don't want me to know, just say so."

"Thorn," Logan said flatly.

Pete replaced his cup on the table. "What?"

"Katherine Thorn. That's who the sorrel belongs to."

"You mean Bar T? That Thorn?"

"Yes."

"What was Thorn's missus doing out in the storm?"

"It's not his wife. It's his daughter."

"I didn't know he had a daughter." Pete's curiosity was piqued. "What's she like?"

Logan looked at Pete. "Extraordinary."

"I see what you mean."

Logan's glance followed the direction of Pete's stare.

Katherine stood in the doorway. She was dressed in the same clothes she'd been wearing when she arrived, and yet she didn't seem the same woman he'd held on his shoulder most of last night.

Maybe it was the way her waist-length hair was pulled back in a tight braid or the way her high-collared blouse gave her a keep-your-distance appearance. He was almost ready to believe he'd been mistaken about her when his gaze drifted down to the riding skirt that he'd hardly noticed when she'd arrived.

He'd never seen anything like it, except maybe the polonaise skating pants some women in the East were wearing. He knew for a fact she wasn't wearing any petticoats, so the pleats lay flat across her belly and hugged her hips, and the way the skirt divided between her legs...well, it was damned provocative.

*Ah, sweet Katherine, which is it, angel or seductress?* A grin spread slowly across his face at the prospect of finding out.

Pete coughed loudly and brought Logan out of his musing.

He shot Pete a glance, then stood. "Please, Miss Thorn, forgive my bad manners." He pulled out an empty chair. "Won't you join us?"

Katherine's mouth curved up in an uncertain smile. "I'm interrupting. I'll wait in the parlor while you finish your business."

"We were just talking," Logan assured her. "Please..."

He watched Katherine cross the room with long, graceful strides. "Thank you." She nodded politely when Logan helped her with the chair.

"My pleasure," he replied. His words were formal, his tone was amused. "Miss Thorn," he continued, "may I present Pete Watkins, my foreman."

"Ma'am." Pete promptly acknowledged her with a nod.

"Mr. Watkins."

Katherine sat on the edge of her chair, hands folded in her lap. Outside, the wind rattled the wooden shingles on the roof. She looked toward the sound.

"I don't believe I've seen you around before, ma'am," Pete remarked.

"No, Mr. Watkins, I've been living in Philadelphia."

Pete's expression grew serious. "Condolences on the death of your pa."

"Thank you. You're kind."

Pete smiled. "Who wouldn't be nice to a lovely lady?"

Logan frowned, not liking the way his friend was settling in so comfortably. Pete's big, friendly grin and Texas drawl made it easy for him to charm the ladies. Saloon girl or preacher's daughter, it made no difference. Logan usually thought it funny. Not this time.

"I don't suppose you've had a chance to look around much," Pete continued. "I sure am sorry your first taste of Wyoming was so sour. But when the weather clears up a bit, you'll see it's right purty."

"I'm sure you're right, Mr. Watkins. And I'm looking forward to it."

Pete twisted a little in his chair and faced Katherine more directly. "There's fine hunting—antelope and deer." His mouth turned down in a frown. "Course you're not interested in that, though." He brightened. "There's some good spots for fishin'. Nope." He shook his head. "That won't do, either."

"Actually, I like to fish," Katherine offered sweetly.

A big grin slashed across Pete's weathered face. "Well, that settles it, then. As soon as the weather warms, we'll just see about gettin' us some fish."

"Pete," Logan interrupted, trying to sound less annoyed than he felt, "don't you have some work that needs looking after?"

"Nope. Not right now." He never even looked in Logan's direction.

"I thought you were going to check on that mare," Logan snapped.

"I checked on her before I came in." Pete looked puzzled. "I told you that."

Logan's chair scraped on the pine planks as he slid back from the kitchen table. "That was a while ago. Check on her again." He stood, expecting Pete to take the hint and do the same.

He didn't.

Someone knocked at the kitchen door.

"Now what?" Logan sighed in frustration and rolled his eyes heavenward. Wasn't he ever going to be alone with this woman?

"Come in!" he shouted, in a voice so loud and angry it didn't seem to come from him at all. He ignored the stares from Pete and Katherine.

The door slammed open and Shorty, one of the hands, stomped in. "Pete, you better come. Dan's out in the barn and got hisself bit by that horse of his. Looks like he might need some sewing."

Pete grumbled under his breath before he went to retrieve his coat from the wall. "Well, Miss Thorn, it's been a real pleasure." He buttoned his coat. "I hope to see you again before you leave." He took two steps toward the door, then stopped. His spurs jingled as he turned around. "Don't you go forgetting about that fishin' trip now." He slapped his well-worn hat onto his head and touched one finger to the brim in a salute.

Katherine smiled back at him. "It was nice meeting you, Mr. Watkins. And I won't forget."

Pete shuffled his feet, then turned and made a beeline for the door, pushing the ranch hand out before him.

"Well, alone at last," Logan muttered before he turned to Katherine.

"What?" She looked puzzled.

"I asked if you were hungry," he lied.

"Yes, actually, I am."

Logan made his way around the worn kitchen table and headed for the stove. "I think we can take care of that problem in a hurry." His cheerfulness was returning.

From the warming shelf over the stove he lifted down a white china platter covered with a calico napkin and placed it on the table in front of Katherine. He removed the napkin to reveal fried ham, sausage and potatoes. "Mary Rosa said she'd stir up some eggs when you're ready."

"Goodness, no." Katherine stared at the huge dish of food. "This is more than enough. Aren't you going to eat?" she asked, noticing only one place had been set.

"I already did. But I'll keep you company, if that's all right."

"Of course."

The delicious smells stirred her appetite and Katherine helped herself to some ham and potatoes. She enjoyed the food, and tried not to notice the way Logan watched her, which was impossible. When she couldn't stand it a minute longer, she shot him a cold glance and was rewarded with a breathtaking smile that made a knot form in her stomach.

Their silent stare lengthened as his presence, so dark and masculine, seemed to invade her senses. There was a definite gleam in his eyes as his gaze traveled downward, stopping on her breasts, then drifted back to her face. He had a sensuous way about him that made her uncomfortable, but she refused to let him know it.

Fortunately, Mary Rosa chose that moment to march into the kitchen, breaking the spell. Katherine looked at the little woman. Only her face and the hem of her dress were visible behind the arm load of linens she carried.

"Did you have breakfast, Katherine?" Mary Rosa crossed the room and dropped the laundry on the floor near the back door. "Yes, I see you did," she commented, glancing at the empty plate. "Now, you two go on out of here. I have work to do." She gently ushered Katherine toward the doorway. "Come on, Logan, you, too."

"Please, let me help you," Katherine insisted. "I'm not used to being waited on."

The woman flashed Katherine a smile. "This won't take me long at all. Later I'm going to make a cake. You could help me with that, if you're inclined, and we can visit."

Logan came up behind Katherine and placed his hand naturally on the small of her back. "Come on." He urged her through the doorway. "Aunt Mary Rosa doesn't like having anybody in her kitchen when she's working. Besides, if she gets mad, I'll never get that cake."

He escorted Katherine to the parlor and motioned for her to sit on the leather sofa. Katherine decided she would be more comfortable in the green, high-backed chair. Maybe *safer* was a more accurate word.

Logan stood in front of the fireplace, one shoulder leaning against the heavy pine mantle, his arms draped casually across his chest. The only sound in the room was the crackle of the fire and the eerie howl of the wind.

"By the way," he commented nonchalantly, "I liked it better down."

"What?" Katherine looked up, puzzled.

"Your hair. I like it better down." He lifted an appreciative eyebrow. "Like last night, soft and flowing around your bare shoulders." His mouth slanted up in a smile.

Katherine self-consciously touched the back of her neck. She felt foolish. Abruptly, she stood and walked to the dropleaf table behind the sofa. She could feel his gaze follow her. When she glanced back at him, his smile had broadened into a lazy grin that was so teasing, so charming, so totally male, that she felt a knot of excitement form in her abdomen. He was doing it again. Annoyed, she searched for a safer topic. "You have a beautiful home."

"Thank you. My mother is the decorator." He gestured toward a portrait on the back wall. "Although I manage to get my way, now and then."

She had the feeling he got his way a lot—and probably in more than just decorating. Katherine went to stand in front of the portrait of the dark-haired beauty.

"It was painted just before she married my father," Logan volunteered, then moved over to sit on the sofa.

She gestured toward the tintypes displayed in silver frames on the mantle. "Are those your family?"

"Yes."

She walked forward to take a closer look.

"The one on the left is my younger sister, Cassie, and her husband, John, on their wedding day. They live in San Francisco. My mother's there now. Cassie is due to have her second child and Mother is there to help." He crossed his leg, one booted foot resting on the opposite knee. "Personally, I think Mother just needed an excuse to spend some time in San Francisco and spoil my nephew rotten in the process.''

''A grandmother's prerogative.'' Katherine laughed, then picked up another tintype. The carved silver frame felt cold against her fingers. ''And this one? Is it your mother and father?''

''Yes. My father died almost eight years ago.''

She studied more closely the tall, fair-haired man in range clothes standing beside a petite woman, elegantly dressed. Warm, happy faces looked out at her. A nice family, she thought; like her own. At that moment she missed them terribly, especially her father. She didn't even have a tintype of him to keep, only his memory in her heart.

Logan's voice interrupted her thoughts. ''So, tell me, Katherine, why were you in Philadelphia instead of here?''

''I was living with my father's sister. She was in poor health and needed someone to look after her and keep her small hat shop going. I was the logical choice—the only choice,'' she amended. ''She died . . . recently. So now it's Daniel, Mama and me.''

''It's been a sad year for you, hasn't it, Angel?'' he asked with genuine kindness in his voice.

''Yes,'' she murmured, feeling the hurt well up inside her.

He walked over, took the picture from her and replaced it on the mantle. ''So much sadness.''

Crooking one finger under her chin, he lifted her face until she looked into his bottomless eyes. He pushed an imaginary wisp of hair away from her face and his touch left a tingling sensation in its place. Katherine's control was slipping away and she couldn't seem to move. Her breath came in shallow gulps.

His gaze rested on her lips. His voice was a husky whisper. ''Who shares your sadness, Angel?''

She knew the answer—no one. She was by choice a private person not given to sharing her feelings.

Logan seemed to sense that much too easily. His outstretched hand rested on the heavy pine mantle, only inches from her. His handsome face filled her field of vision.

She felt surrounded, overwhelmed by the sheer presence of him. A pleasant shiver traveled up her spine again and shot out along her nerve endings.

*Stop this—now!* The words echoed in her brain but her body refused to obey, to deny the nearness of him. Oddly, she felt as if she were about to embark on some great discovery—one not to be missed.

Far away a door slammed, then another, then Mary Rosa's high-pitched voice raised in a chorus of "Sweet By and By" drifted into the room.

The tune was so off-key, the words so jumbled, that it was impossible not to notice. Reason got a fingerhold in Katherine's brain and she took a step back, then another, and she drew in a lung full of cool air.

She stepped around him and walked to the window. Looking out for a moment, she tried to force her breathing to return to normal. She suddenly wanted to put some distance between them. A great deal of distance.

"The storm appears to be lessening." She managed to sound calmer than she felt.

"I thought it was just getting started," he corrected.

She turned back toward him with a questioning stare.

His familiar smile was back. "If you mean the one outside..." He gave a small shrug, then sank down on the sofa. "Well, the wind has let up some."

"I think I could go home today," she told him directly.

Logan sat straighter. "Not a good idea."

"The storm has let up—you said so yourself. One of your men could take me."

"When the snow stops."

"It doesn't look bad out there right now and the ranch is only a couple of hours from here," she pressed, as anxiety overcame good judgment.

Logan frowned. "Maybe you don't realize it, but a couple of hours on a clear, sunny day can be six or seven hours slogging through that stuff out there. If you flounder in a drift or misread what few landmarks there are, you could wander in the wrong direction for hours before you get turned back around."

"But I think—"

Logan stood up, his eyes sparking with anger. "Woman, aren't you listening to anything I'm saying? There's a blizzard going on out there. You almost died in it last night." As quickly as it had come, the anger was gone, replaced with an amused glint. "Or don't you want to remember last night? I remember *every* detail."

Katherine turned an icy stare on him. "How dare—"

"What's going on here?" Mary Rosa interrupted their argument. She looked from Logan to Katherine and back to Logan.

"Nothing. We were just discussing the weather," he answered with a grin.

Katherine watched Logan turn on his heel and saunter from the room. The man was insufferable. A few minutes later they heard the bang of the back door.

Mary Rosa turned toward Katherine. "What's come over him?"

# Chapter Three

Logan stepped out on the back porch, still buttoning his sheepskin jacket. He chuckled to himself. The lady had a look that would stop a man cold—*if* he'd let her. This man wouldn't, though why, he wasn't quite sure. Maybe her holding back so much simply brought out a greed in him to test and tease and touch, to see what she was trying so hard to hide. *Lady, I think you've met your match.*

A smile lingered on his lips as he stepped off the porch. The wind tugged at the brim of his black hat and he pulled it lower. He didn't use his gloves, just shoved his hands in his pockets, leaned into the blizzard and trudged the three hundred yards to the large log bunkhouse.

Smoke curled from the stacks at each end of the building. The half-dozen windows across the front were partly covered with ice as cold outside competed with heat inside.

Logan brushed loose snow from his trouser legs and stamped his feet on the front stoop before he walked inside.

The large open room was filled with rows of bunks that could bed sixty men in peak season. Ropes and clothes hung randomly from pegs on the wall. Several men were sleeping; others were sitting at tables playing cards and talking. The scent of cigarette smoke and unwashed bodies filled the air. The foreman's room was near the door. Logan checked there first. Empty. He flipped down his jacket collar as he turned to scan the long room.

Spotting Pete sitting at a table against the wall, Logan made his way down the long center aisle between the two rows of bunks. A couple of men waved and nodded. As Logan approached the table where Pete sat, a loud peal of laughter drew his attention to a group sitting on two bunks nearby.

"Well, least ways not everybody's sufferin' from the cold," a heavyset cowhand with a broken-toothed grin was saying to the group. "I heard the boss has got him a sheep-rancher's daughter to keep him warm under the covers."

The man's smile disappeared as Logan grabbed the cowboy's rumpled shirtfront and slammed him against the wall. All sound in the room ceased.

Logan's eyes narrowed and his voice was deadly quiet when he spoke. "Mister, you're new here, so let me tell you there are two things I can't abide, snakes and whining dogs. You are fast becoming both. The *lady* is a guest in my home. If I ever hear you or anyone else mention her name anywhere except in church, you'll answer to me."

The man swallowed hard and shifted his eyes around the room as though looking for help.

"Do you understand?" Logan ground out, never releasing his hold.

"Yes." The man's voice cracked slightly.

Letting go of the cowhand's shirtfront, Logan stepped back. He felt a hand on his shoulder and turned, his fists ready, only to look into Pete's questioning stare.

"What's goin' on?"

"Nothing. I was looking for you." Logan shouldered past his old friend and headed toward the door.

Pete grabbed his coat and hat off a wall peg.

"Arrogant whelp," the cowhand pronounced loudly, now that Logan was outside. He rubbed his throat, then straightened his wrinkled shirt. "That boy better watch his step around me."

Several men looked around with incredulous expressions. For all his good humor, Pete knew Logan McCloud was not a man to cross. He was faster with a gun than anyone ought to be and not above making his own law.

Pete turned to face the loud-mouthed cowhand, his expression hard. "Mister, that 'boy' don't make idle threats. Consider yourself warned."

He slammed out the door and caught up with Logan a few steps off the porch. For a moment neither man spoke.

A cold swirl of wind whipped around the two of them. Logan flipped up his collar against the snow. "Some of your men don't know when to keep their mouths shut." Logan scowled. "I don't like hearing a lady's name being thrown around."

"I didn't hear. I'll send him packing."

Logan shook his head. "Never mind. Just keep an eye on him. I think he understands my rules better now."

"Yes." A big grin crossed Pete's face. "You do have a way of getting folks' attention." He slapped his arms across his chest to ward off the cold. "Was there some reason you was lookin' for me?"

"I want you to come up to the office at three this afternoon. We need to go over plans for the roundup. Bring Ralph and Bill with you. Oh, better bring Cookie, too." Logan took two steps toward the barn. "Come on." He gestured with his gloved hand. "Let's check on the mare one more time. I don't want to take any chances."

They entered the barn together and went to the foaling stall. The wind whistled around the eaves, bringing nervous snorts from several of the horses.

Pulling off his gloves, Logan ran a hand along the side of the expectant mare in a soothing gesture before checking under her tail. He walked around the other side of the horse and stopped near Pete. "Soon," he predicted softly.

Logan moved around the mare and began to rub her nose and speak in a soothing tone. "You're going to be just fine, aren't you, little lady?'' He rubbed her neck. ''No trouble at all.''

''I have a feelin' this little lady ain't gonna be nearly so much trouble as the one in the house,'' Pete offered with mock consideration.

Logan shot him a warning glance. ''I can handle trouble,'' he promptly replied, then he strode out of the stall.

Pete followed Logan out and closed the gate, the metal latch dropping with a clink. ''See you at three.'' He walked back the other way.

It was past noon and Logan sat in his office going over some ledgers. But his mind was on Katherine Thorn. She had burst into his life out of a blizzard like a spring flower bursts through the snow, bringing color and sunshine to a cold, gray world. Extraordinary—that's what he had told Pete and that was what she was. He closed the book and drummed his fingers on the rough surface. A small voice of reason said, *Leave it alone.*

Alone. The word lingered in his mind. He'd been feeling alone a lot lately. Oh sure, there was always family, and occasionally a lady to help pass the time. He'd inherited his father's charm. At least that's what Mother always said, and she should know, he thought with a chuckle.

It had caused quite a scandal when the daughter of one of New Orleans's richest Creole families married a Texas cowboy. Together they'd come to Wyoming. He could remember Pa saying that Mother was his princess, that it was a man's job to protect a woman, care for her, make life as easy as possible. That's why Pa had built this unlikely house in the middle of range country, and later the big one in Cheyenne.

Logan slouched in his comfortable chair and let his thoughts roam back through the years. Jason McCloud's pampered son, some had said when he'd hit adolescence. Logan didn't mind. It wasn't true, and anyone who knew Jas McCloud knew he'd insisted on a day's work for a day's pay. Thirty dollars a month and board had been the going wage. Logan had been fourteen that first payday. Lord, he'd been proud enough to bust.

The wind's mournful moan drew his attention and he pushed back from the desk. The heels of his boots echoed on the bare floor as he went to the stove in the corner. Grabbing up a pine log from the box under the window, he tossed it onto the fire, then banged the stove door closed. A chill permeated the air and he rubbed his hands together.

Winter. Maybe that's where the loneliness came from. He'd gone to boarding school in the winter and he'd hated it. But he'd never complained. It had been important to his parents.

And it was just about this time of year when the telegram had come to him at Harvard saying Jason McCloud had been killed in a wagon accident. Logan had left for home that day to take care of his mother and sister and to run the ranch.

That had been eight years ago. Now he was twenty-eight. Mother spent most of her time at their house in Cheyenne. She had turned out to be quite the civic leader, much to some men's irritation. He chuckled.

His baby sister was married. And by the look of it when he'd seen Cassie a year ago, she was extremely happy. He was glad for her because she'd found someone to share her dreams with, someone to love, someone extraordinary.

Extraordinary.

Logan started pacing. A vision of Katherine filled his mind. Flashing, bright blue eyes and that incredible mane of hair, the kind a man wanted to run his fingers through, bury his face in.

He dropped into his chair. He thought about her attitude that morning, distant and controlled—he had wanted to challenge her. Last night, when her defenses had been down, her eyes filled with tears—he had wanted to protect her. She stirred his blood faster than any woman he could remember.

*Find someone else,* the voice of reason urged. This wasn't going to be simple.

Simple be damned. He'd deal with the problems of the Bar T when he had to. Hell, the sheep ranch had no business being in this part of the territory. He'd been trying to buy them out for two years, but that damn fool Thorn had been stubborn to the core and had refused to discuss any sale.

Everything was different now that Thorn was dead. It was ridiculous to think that a young woman and her kid brother would really be able to keep the place going, no matter how good their intentions. He'd offer them twice what the place was worth, and once he pointed out the obvious problems, they'd accept his offer.

In the meantime, he was going to enjoy getting to know the lady and he didn't want to rush it. Anticipation was part of the pleasure.

Muffled voices and the stomp of men's boots on the porch brought Logan out of his reverie. He looked toward the side entrance to his office.

"Come on in, boys," he called before they knocked.

The four men filed into the office and hung their coats on pegs near the stove. Pete and two of the men seated themselves on the leather-upholstered chairs in front of the desk. Cookie remained standing, rubbing his arthritic hands together near the warmth of the stove.

"As soon as the snow stops," Logan announced, "I want the men in the saddle." His thoughts immediately shifted to work and he glanced around the room to make sure he had everyone's attention.

"The cattle will have drifted south and east." Logan went to a large map on the wall. The men came to stand behind him. "Divide the hands into two groups. I want one group to go with Cookie to set up a base camp here." Logan pointed to a place on the map.

"Chuck wagon's ready. The boys put runners on her this mornin'," Cookie confirmed.

"Pete, I gave you instructions a couple of days ago." Logan paused, got an affirmative nod from Pete, then continued; "Ralph, you'll be in charge of the base camp group. Better take Quarternight and Johnson with you. You'll need them to start breaking the horse herd."

The next two hours were spent reviewing stock requirements, compiling supply lists and organizing work assignments for the roundup that would be necessary to recover the herd. That done, the conversation drifted to small talk.

George spoke up. "I was workin' a ranch down in the panhandle a few years back when a blizzard hit. When it was over, seven thousand head had walked right off a forty-foot cliff." He shifted a wad of chewing tobacco from one side of his chubby face to the other. "We had to burn the carcasses. Thought I never would get the stink of rottin' flesh outa my nose."

The men were suddenly silent, each aware of the terrible consequences of a blizzard. Outside, the wind swirled, picking up icy crystals to hurl against the window. Pete and Ralph winced at the sound.

"Well, it won't hurt my feelin's any if some of them sheep wander over a cliff," Ralph remarked. He shifted his lanky frame to a more comfortable position in the chair. "I don't mind saying I hate sheep."

Pete glanced around. "A month ago somebody hated sheep enough to plug ol' Thorn right through the heart."

Logan sat on the edge of his desk, both feet resting on the floor. "You boys wouldn't by chance have heard anything about that, now would you?"

"Nope," Ralph offered quickly, and the others agreed. "Boss, if we knew something, we'd tell ya." His shaggy brows came together. "Can't fault a man for killing in self-defense, but cold-blooded killing makes a body nervous."

"True enough," Logan confirmed. He didn't think any of his regular men were involved. Still, they'd hired a lot of hands recently in anticipation of the spring roundup, and men did talk over a drink or two. If there was anything going on, he wanted to know.

"Who pulled the trigger is a real mystery." Pete stood and pushed his hat back slightly on his head. "That barbwire fence Thorn put up didn't help tempers none."

"Man would have to be crazy to go fencing open range," Cookie chimed in. "Don't care if the land did belong to him. Open range is open range." He let fly a stream of tobacco juice that sailed through the open door of the stove.

Pete eyed Logan with a thoughtful expression. "You know, some of the ranchers are saying it's no loss—Thorn being dead, I mean. Can't say as I blame them." He shoved his hands into his back pockets.

"I *understand* their feelings, but I don't like it. Someone just couldn't leave bad enough alone and had to go stir things up." Logan frowned. Hell, there'd been no love lost between him and Thorn, but Logan hadn't killed him. "If the family stays, we could be looking at a range war."

Katherine stood outside the partly open door to Logan's office. Mary Rosa had asked her to tell Logan supper was ready. She'd been about to knock when she heard voices.

At the mention of a range war her blood turned colder than the storm outside.

She knocked once. "Supper," she called in a loud voice. Not waiting for an answer, she turned and walked back toward the kitchen. Had she misjudged these people?

She hugged herself against the deadly chill that passed through her. She and Logan had argued earlier, but he hadn't seemed cruel. She paused halfway down the hall. Deep in thought, she didn't hear the office door open or Logan's booted steps echoing on the bare floor.

"Katherine."

She jumped at hearing his voice so close behind her. Turning abruptly, she bumped into his hard chest. His arms went around her, and her heart slammed against her ribs as the full length of his body molded to hers.

Logan dropped his hands and stepped back. "I didn't mean to startle you. I wanted to talk about this morning."

"This morning?" she repeated, still dazed by the revelation she had just overheard.

"I didn't want you to think I was insensitive to your worry about your family. It's just that the storm has settled in and the thought of you out in it when we have a choice seemed, well, unnecessary. I promise I'll get you home the moment it's safe to travel. Just trust me."

Her mind was spinning. "Trust you! You're planning a range war and you stand here talking about trust."

Logan glanced over his shoulder toward the office door, then turned back to her with a knowing look in his eyes.

"If you're going to eavesdrop, you really should try to listen to the whole conversation. I've been trying to prevent one, not start it."

She looked into his face for the deceit she knew would be there. It wasn't. Instead she saw a gentle smile and caring concern in his dark eyes. One thing she did trust was her own instincts, and right now they said he was telling the truth.

She sighed with relief. "I didn't mean to listen," she offered by way of an apology. "The door was open and I couldn't help hearing."

"I know." He placed one hand on her shoulder.

She felt the warmth of his touch penetrate the thin fabric of her blouse and travel along her nerve endings like lightning. His hand slid down her arm and he took her hand in his. Very slowly, his eyes never leaving hers, he lifted her hand toward his mouth. The air around them was suddenly charged with anticipation.

Lightly, his mouth touched her knuckles. His mustache felt feather soft against her skin, his lips moist and warm. When she looked up, his gaze was heated.

"Kat," he murmured.

She felt lightning strike a second time.

# Chapter Four

It took a few minutes for Logan to realize the persistent tapping was someone at his bedroom door. A hurried glance at the watch on his bed table told him it was nearly dawn. He sat up and reached for his robe, when he heard a muffled voice through the door.

"It's me," Pete called in a hushed whisper. "You alone in there? I could come back."

Logan scowled. Ignoring his robe, he walked naked to the door and jerked it open. "Of course I'm alone." He stared into Pete's smirking face. "What are you, the dean of boys? I haven't had bed check since I was in school." Completely unembarrassed, Logan stepped back and allowed Pete to enter. "If I did have someone in here, I would have shot you for interrupting."

Pete seemed to find that amusing and Logan's scowl deepened. He hated mornings anyway, and this one in particular, since he'd only had about two hours' sleep. That is, if you could call dreaming about eyes the color of summer sky and skin the texture of fresh cream, sleeping.

A clump of snow slipped from Pete's jacket and landed with a splat, spraying Logan's bare toes. He plunked down on the bed and wiped his foot with a corner of the bed cover.

"Maybe I'll just shoot you anyway," Logan snapped. That's how it had always been with them—teasing and harassing.

The first time Logan met Pete, he hadn't been too auspicious. Logan had just landed face down in the dirt after being thrown from a particularly ornery bronc. Looking up, he'd heard Pete say, "Pardner, you ain't never gonna break that critter if you keep nappin' down there." Then he'd offered Logan a smile and a hand up.

"I wasn't napping," Logan had answered, "just giving him a breather so he'd have a fighting chance." Both men had laughed, and it had been like that between them ever since.

Logan knew a lot about cattle and horses; Pete knew more. Together they had worked, laughed and occasionally fought to make the Double Four the biggest ranch in the territory. Through it all they'd become trusted friends.

Pete understood that and so only laughed at his boss's threats. "You're getting lazy. It's an hour till sunup. Any decent cattleman is up and movin' by now." He raked Logan with an appraising stare, then shook his head woefully. "Yup, soft. Definitely soft."

Logan hurled a pillow in Pete's direction, which he deftly caught.

"Why the hell..." Logan halted. He knew he was grouchy as a bear, but he also realized something must be wrong for Pete to come looking for him. "Has the storm stopped?"

Pete tossed the pillow back on the bed. "Naw. Looks like you was right about that mare, though. She's gonna foal purty quick."

"Figures." Logan ran the palm of his hand over his face trying to wipe the sleep away. He grabbed his clothes from the wardrobe and threw them on the bed. Shoving his legs into the denim pants, he mumbled, "Why the hell is it always in the middle of the night?"

"It's not the middle of the night," Pete corrected with a smirk. "Besides, she's a female and they're a contrary bunch, no matter what the breeding."

"True." The bed creaked as Logan sat on the edge again. "How's she doing?" he asked, tugging on a worn brown boot.

"Well, I wish she'd held off a couple more weeks, but she appears to be okay."

Logan stamped on the other boot and immediately adjusted his pant legs over the top. "All we can do is take it like it comes." Tucking his black shirt into his denim trousers, he rose and raked his hands through his sleep-tousled hair. "Let's go. My coat's in the kitchen."

Pausing by the stove, he took a minute to get some coffee going. "I think we're going to need this," he predicted. Lifting his coat from the peg, he buttoned it hastily and they headed for the barn.

The path the ranch hands had dug earlier was only partially visible. Logan squinted as swirling snow lashed against his face, numbing his cheeks. He mumbled a few choice curses under his breath.

Once inside the barn, they hurried down the long row of stalls to a particularly large one used for foaling. He found the mare lying on her side on a bed of straw, her eyes wide, her nostrils flared. A grunt sounded with each breath.

Around them other horses snorted and pawed the ground in their stalls, seeming to sense the mare's anxiety.

Logan's brows knitted together. "I don't like the look of her. Something's wrong or soon will be." He jerked off his gloves and ran a gentle hand along the horse's heaving side. "How long has she been like this?"

"Not long. She was up when I come to get you." Pete eyed the mare and frowned.

Logan looked back at his friend. "Better get some hot water from the house—"

"I know, towels and soap." Pete was already moving. The barn door banged shut behind him.

Outside the wind ripped at the shingles on the roof, making a sharp clack. The mare snorted in agitation. "Don't you worry, girl," Logan said, his tone calm. He stroked her neck, hoping his touch would soothe her.

A short time later, Pete slammed the barn door again. "Saw Mary Rosa." With a thud he put down the gray metal tub of water on a nearby bench. "I had my hands full so she said she'd bring us the coffee."

"Okay."

Glancing at Logan, Pete asked, "How do you want to do this?"

"Let's try to get her on her feet. If something is wrong, maybe it'll help."

Pete looked skeptical but agreed. He bent and braced both hands on the mare's back, while Logan grabbed hold of the halter.

"Ready," Pete called.

"Come on, little lady," Logan coaxed, tugging gently but firmly on the leather straps. "Up you go."

Pete leaned his whole weight into the task. "It ain't no use, Logan. She ain't budging."

"I know." Logan ran a hand through his hair in frustration. Mentally he reviewed his choices. There weren't many. He'd wait a bit longer, he decided, before taking drastic steps.

Several times over the next half hour he consulted his pocket watch. Five more minutes, he decided finally, and closed the lid with a snap. Five more minutes was all he'd wait. He could almost hear the minutes tick by. He paced the six long steps across the stall and back. The mare grunted in complaint. Then the foal's foot appeared—but only one. The horse's legs flailed wildly with each contraction.

"Damn!" Logan muttered, his eyes narrowed to slits. "The other foot's twisted back and unless I can get it moved, we're gonna lose both of them."

Katherine thumped the feather pillow with her fist. The storm that Logan created in her mind matched the one that continued full force outside. She would not think about *him*. She would not think about laughing dark eyes deep enough to drown in, or smiles that sent her pulse racing. She would not wonder if the lips that had caressed the back of her hand so softly would feel the same against her mouth.

A warm, languid feeling formed low in her abdomen. Defiantly ignoring her body's reaction, she rolled onto her stomach and willed herself to go back to sleep.

Noises in the hallway caused her to turn over again. She listened for a moment, trying to hear above the roar of the wind. No, she must have been mistaken.

After staring at the ceiling for a while, she admitted that all attempts at sleep were useless. The fire in the small stove was almost out and the chill air on her face told her there was only one thing to do. Throwing back the quilts, she sprang from the bed in one hurried motion. Goose bumps covered every inch of her flesh while she dressed in record time.

It couldn't be more than an hour until dawn, she thought as she headed for the kitchen and the perpetual warmth that waited there. She'd surprise her hosts by getting coffee started and biscuit dough made.

Her boots made a light tapping on the bare floor as she walked through the parlor. The dim light of a kerosene lamp illuminated the kitchen entrance as she entered the room.

She stopped short. "Mary Rosa. Do you always get up this early?" She glanced toward the window, confirming the predawn hour.

Mary Rosa shook her head and covered a sleepy yawn with the back of her hand. "Not if I can help it." She pulled the navy wool robe she wore more tightly across her chest. "I heard the men moving around out here. I knew I'd best get up and take care of things or I'd find an awful mess."

Katherine frowned. "Is something wrong? Is someone sick?"

"Oh, no." Mary Rosa stretched and lifted down two gray metal mugs from the cupboard. "Seems that thoroughbred mare decided to go into labor a while ago. Logan and Pete went out to make sure she's doing okay.''

Taking two red-and-white checked towels from under the counter Mary Rosa wrapped them around the coffeepot. "I was just going to put on some clothes and take this out to them. You want to come?''

"Why don't you let me take that? I'm already dressed and there's no sense in both of us going out there—unless, of course, you especially wanted to go.''

"Not particularly," Mary Rosa replied with a casual wave of her hand. "But I don't want to send you out in this blizzard, either.''

"I'd be glad to help. It's the least I can do after all you've done for me. Besides, I wouldn't mind seeing the new foal. Really.'' Excitement bubbled up in her at the prospect of witnessing the miracle of new life. Katherine took her slicker down from the wall peg, anxious to be on her way.

"Goodness, girl. That wouldn't keep a flea warm on the Fourth of July.'' Mary Rosa walked over and tugged down Logan's capote. "Here, this is more like it.'' The hem lay on the floor while she held the overcoat open for Katherine to slip into. "I can't have you freezing out there.''

The garment hung in folds on Katherine's slender frame. Only the tips of her fingers peeked out from the ends of the chocolate brown sleeves. "I'll just drop off the coffee and come straight back and help with breakfast.''

"You sure about this?'' Mary Rosa asked once more.

"Sure.''

Wrapping the coat across her chest, Katherine reached out for the coffeepot and mugs. She walked slowly to the back door. In the heavy coat, slow was all she could manage.

The bottom of the coat dragged on the snow as she trudged the few hundred yards to the barn. Glancing at the eastern horizon, she saw the first gray streaks of dawn breaking through the night sky. The wind seemed a little lighter, but the temperature felt more like the North Pole in December than Wyoming in March.

With only one hand free, it took her a minute to manipulate the door latch. The soft whinny of a horse greeted her arrival. The sweet smell of fresh hay, leather and the acrid aroma of horses filled the air.

Stamping off the snow, she glanced at the straw-covered floor and the row of at least twenty raw wood stalls. The sound of Logan's voice drew her to the far end of the structure. Several horses peered at her, their breaths pale gray in the chill air. She made her way down the center aisle following the sound of Logan's voice.

"Talk to her, Pete. Try to keep her from thrashing around."

Katherine could tell by Logan's tone that something was wrong. She stopped at the open gate. Pete held the mare's head cradled in his lap as he stroked her neck and murmured reassuring words to her.

Logan cast a hasty glance in Katherine's direction. His expression was grim. "Just put it anywhere," he said with a cursory nod when he spotted the bundle she carried. He yanked his gloves and hat off with quick, sharp motions and tossed them onto the fresh straw in the corner.

Katherine's gaze shifted from Logan to Pete and back again. "Is there a problem?"

"Yes." Logan fumbled with the wooden buttons on his jacket, then rolled his eyes heavenward. "Since I'm going to have to do this, would a little warm weather have been too much to ask for?"

Gritting his teeth, he stripped off his jacket and shirt. The cold air against his bare chest sent a giant shiver through his body. He went to the tub of water and, grabbing the soap, lathered his hands and arms to the shoulders.

Katherine stood motionless by the gate. She'd never seen a horse born before, but she knew this wasn't normal. She suddenly feared for the mare and the unborn foal. "What's wrong? Can I help?"

"Foal's twisted," Pete answered, concern obvious in his voice.

"I'll be damned if I'm going to lose these two." Logan looked at Katherine once more. "This is going to be... unpleasant. I don't think you'll want to watch."

"I'll stay, if it's all the same to you," she replied in a quiet but firm tone.

"Suit yourself."

Behind him, the mare snorted, Katherine could tell each contraction was causing the horse more pain.

Logan stretched out on his belly on the floor of the stall. The fresh straw cushioned his bare chest. Slowly, carefully, he inserted his hand into the mare's birth canal.

"Take it easy, Mama." He rubbed his free hand on the mare's hind quarter in a soothing gesture. "You're going to be just fine." His tone was hushed.

Katherine winced at his task. She'd seen a calf born once when she was a little girl, but it had been over in minutes and had required no human help.

She was riveted by the scene before her. The muscles of Logan's broad back flexed tightly and he stretched to reach farther, his arm disappearing beyond the elbow. "Slow, that's it girl." He kept talking, soothing the nervous animal, but the mare's hind feet suddenly jerked back.

"Look out!" Katherine cried, and Logan rolled out of the way of flying hooves.

Back in position, he asked Pete, "How's she doing?"

"Getting a mite fidgety, as you just noticed."

Logan mumbled his understanding. "I won't hurt you, girl. I'm gonna help you. Just take it easy."

Fascinated, Katherine watched as Logan struggled with gentle determination to save both animals. His cheek rested on the mare's hindquarter as he carefully repeated the procedure. She could see the muscles of his jaw clench as he strained not to rush. Every bit of energy was focused on his task.

"Got it," he announced triumphantly.

His whole body tensed with the effort. Every muscle in Katherine's body did, too, as if she could somehow help by doing so. She saw his eyes slam shut, then open suddenly as he withdrew his arm and the foal's other foot. He sat back on his haunches, his eyes narrowed, his mouth drawn in a tight line.

The mare grunted again. Immediately, Katherine saw the foal's dark nose appear. The mare gave a final push. With a little more help from Logan, a shiny black foal lay wide-eyed on the floor of the stall.

"We did it," Logan announced grinning.

"Son of a bitch, you did! She's a beauty, that's for damned sure." Pete laughed, then looked sheepish. "Sorry, ma'am. No offense."

"None taken, Mr. Watkins."

The mare stood and eyed the new foal. A while later, the foal struggled to her feet and Logan said, "Come on, Mama, it's time to meet your daughter." The men herded the unsteady little horse for the clean-up process that would bond the two together.

Katherine saw laughter dance in Logan's eyes. A proud boyish grin covered his face. She was grinning like a kid on Christmas morning herself. Pure joy, and Logan had made it happen.

It was, she realized, another side to Logan's personality. Behind the charming rogue was a determined, caring, gentle man she hadn't seen before.

Still beaming, Logan said, "It's the start of a new blood line. In five years, well..." He shrugged as he glanced around the barn. His grin grew a touch bigger all the same.

"I've never seen anything so incredible. What you did was wonderful," Katherine exclaimed softly. "And *she's* wonderful!"

"Wonderful," Logan agreed, his gaze fixed on the rosy-cheeked lady a few feet away.

"You two can stand out here admirin' good horseflesh if you like," Pete interjected. "Me, I'm goin' in the house and get warm."

Logan regained his composure. Bare chested and badly in need of washing, he strode toward the tub of water. "I'll wash up and we'll be right in." He was pleased when Katherine didn't object to waiting with him.

"See ya inside, then." Pete touched two fingers to the brim of his hat. Spurs jingling, he left by the door at the far end of the barn.

"It won't take me long to get cleaned up," Logan commented to Katherine, who stood, unmoving, watching the foal and mother. He saw the emotions play across her face. Her eyes were bright, her laughter deep and warm at each unsteady action of the pair.

She sent his heart and thoughts racing. Strong enough to make it through a blizzard and proud enough to tell him her name like a challenge. Now, warm and still like a woman waiting to be loved—by him. The stirring in his loins confirmed his thoughts.

Telling himself he was too old for rampaging schoolboy lust, he turned away and scooped up a couple of handfuls of cold water from the tub. He deftly worked up a lather over his arms and upper torso. There was no painless way to rinse. Gritting his teeth, he submerged his arms to the shoulders in the now frigid water, then splashed great amounts on his chest and face. In the brisk air his teeth chattered so loudly, he was sure the sound would scare the animals.

"Damn! It's cold!" Tossing his wet hair back, he grabbed for a towel and briskly rubbed his face. When he lowered the cloth, he looked straight into the eyes of trouble. They were a lush, dark blue, and looking directly at him.

His heart slammed against his ribs, the towel suspended in midmotion. A heat wave must have come through in the last sixty seconds, because he sure wasn't cold anymore. He didn't move. He didn't want to break the magical spell that engulfed him.

Katherine *wanted* to move, but didn't have the strength. Good Lord, what was the matter with her? She'd been watching the foal, until she heard the splash of water and heard Logan's playful groan.

Of course, she realized he was shirtless. She'd seen the play of muscles stretch across his back, hadn't she? But watching the birth had so absorbed her thoughts, she hadn't registered the fact that Logan was half-naked and heart-stoppingly handsome.

A warm blush traveled up her neck. She was staring right at his chest and the moist black hairs that arched over each nipple.

Her gaze flicked up to his face and the small drops of water clinging to his mustache. His tongue came out and licked at the moisture. Her eyes followed his movements and sparks shot along nerve endings from her nose to her toes.

But it was the wicked look in his bottomless dark eyes that was almost her undoing—hot enough to melt all the snow in Wyoming. Her knees had certainly turned to water. It wasn't fair that he could do that with only a look. With more strength than she thought she had, she tore her gaze away. It took two tries before she could get her voice to function. "What are you going to name the foal?" she asked, searching for a distraction—any distraction.

"You choose."

Out of the corner of her eye, she saw him put on his wool shirt, button it, then shrug on his jacket. She took a deep breath and let it out slowly, then took several steps back toward the gate.

"I think I'd call her Storm." She glanced at the baby horse, then back to Logan. "She's black like a thunder-cloud, and with those legs she'll be fast as lightning."

She laughed at her little joke; a deep, enticing laugh that clung to Logan like morning mist to the pines. His throat convulsed sharply.

"What do you think?" she prompted.

*I think I want you so bad it's making me crazy.*

"Perfect," he replied instead, eyeing the washtub. If he didn't get this desire under control, he'd have to pour the cold water over his head. That image helped—a little.

Katherine stepped out into the center aisle and looked down the row of stalls. "Where's Sunrise?" she called, trying to break the spell he wove much too easily around her. She started off in search of the sturdy little sorrel that had brought her to safety.

Logan closed the gate to the foaling stall and followed. His footsteps were muffled in the hay-strewn floor. "She's over here," he said, indicating the fifth stall from the end. Just then the little filly's white face appeared over the gate.

"There you are, Sunrise," Katherine exclaimed, hurrying forward. She rubbed the mare's nose affectionately. "How are you, girl?" The horse's ears twitched at the sound of Katherine's voice. "Yes, I missed you, too," she crooned. "We'll be going home soon."

"Well, maybe not for a day or two," Logan added. The thought of her leaving didn't settle well with him, although she would leave—later, much later, if the storm gods were in his favor.

The horse nudged Katherine's shoulder. "Sorry, girl, I don't have any treat for you today." She looked over at Logan who was leaning casually against a post.

It was hopeless. She was drowning in the depths of his eyes and couldn't look away. Nervousness kept her talking. Those devilish black eyes of his kept on watching.

"I've been spoiling Sunrise, I'm afraid. I usually give her a piece of carrot or rock sugar." Her mouth turned up in a tentative smile.

Still watching her, he shoved his hand into the pocket of his sheepskin jacket. A moment later he held his balled fist out to her. "Anything to please a lady," he commented.

With uncertainty, she reached toward him. His warm fingers lightly skimmed the sensitive skin of her palm and her pulse took off like a stampede. When he lifted his hand away, a piece of rock sugar dropped into her palm.

Katherine's eyes widened in surprise. "Why, thank you, kind sir." Her tone was playful. So was her smile.

Desire shot through him like quicksilver. He thought about the cold water in the washtub and decided it wouldn't even begin to cool him down.

"You know," he said softly, "you're beautiful." His gaze never wavered when he reached for her face. His voice was hushed. "What else makes you smile, sweet Katherine?"

She looked alarmed, like he'd just asked for her deepest secret. Maybe he had. The backs of his knuckles brushed across her cheek before he pushed the hood of the capote away from her upturned face.

He cupped one side of her chin in his hand. "You haven't got any idea what you do to me," he said, chuckling a little behind his mustache, "have you?"

Katherine shook her head, certain she couldn't speak. His thumb played across her bottom lip. A hot liquid rush centered itself low in her belly. She felt his breath mingle with hers. Logan's handsome face filled her vision. His head dropped closer.

"Logan, please..."

"I want to, Angel."

His lips brushed across hers in a feather touch that sent sparks skimming through her. A moment later, his mouth covered hers and every nerve in her body went off like a skyrocket. Her body responded in ways her mind would never have imagined.

The kiss turned more demanding as he slanted his mouth across hers. She grabbed the lapels of his jacket and hung on. Her bones had turned to applesauce about ten seconds ago.

The world spun away and she didn't even notice. It could have come to an end and she wouldn't have cared. The wild desire that was heating her blood blocked out all but the man holding her in his arms.

She arched toward him, wanting to feel his strength. When his tongue teased her lips, it seemed the most natural thing in the world to open to him.

The instant his tongue touched hers the impossible happened—her desire doubled. She heard him groan, a husky animal sound that came from deep down inside him.

Logan felt her stiffen a little at the invasion of his tongue. He tightened his possessive grip on her shoulders while his tongue laved at the tender inside of her mouth. She tasted sweet and smelled like roses.

Logan's body tensed with urgency while his mind flashed images of wild honey hair, soft flesh and long legs. God, he loved long-legged women. His hand drifted lower, splaying around her thigh.

Damn these heavy coats, anyway. More than anything else he wanted to get through all the layers of cloth and...

Instantly, everything changed. This was Katherine. *Your angel, remember? Not one of Saturday's girls,* his conscience chided. What was he going to do, take her here in the hay like an animal?

The answer pounded in his brain. Exactly!

He trailed tiny kisses along her jaw and nipped at the tender skin behind her ear. "Woman, you sure know how to heat a man up."

His words shocked her and gave reality a chance to flutter in her mind. Still in his embrace, she filled her lungs with blessed cold air.

Even so, it took a full ten seconds before her breathing returned to normal. The world filled in around her—the nickering of the horses in the stalls, the smell of fresh hay, the feel of Logan's arms around her.

Oh God, what was she doing? She pushed at his chest. He didn't seem to notice. He stood there, holding her, his chin nestled against the top of her head in a natural way that made her anxious.

She pushed at him again. "Let me go," she added for emphasis.

He released her and stepped back. "Kat—"

"No." She shook her head and refused to acknowledge the tingling that coursed down her legs.

This could not be happening. She wouldn't let it happen! She had plans—the ranch, returning to Philadelphia, to civilization and her business. Nowhere did her plans include a handsome stranger with hypnotic eyes.

She took a purposeful step back.

"Now, you just stop..." Her voice was a shaky whisper.

"What's the matter? Don't you like being kissed?"

"I like it just fine," she answered, knowing no one had ever kissed her like that, as if he were staking a claim. "However, a gentleman usually asks permission first." She made a show of straightening her coat.

Logan's full laughter sounded through the cavernous barn. His eyes sparked with a devilish glint. "Lady, the way you've been looking at me the last twenty minutes was all the permission I needed."

Katherine's anger boiled over. "Why, you arrogant... Don't you dare insinuate that I led you on!"

Logan's mouth turned up in a lopsided grin. "Like I said earlier, you sure do heat a man to boiling."

"Then stay the devil away from me and we'll have no further problems!" she said sharply. With a groan of frustration, she turned on her heels and stormed from the barn.

Logan watched her go. A smile lingered on his lips, but inside his mouth he could taste her. He took a deep breath, then another.

The lady needed to be kissed. She liked it, too, he decided smugly. His smile returned as he followed her back to the house.

# Chapter Five

When Logan came into the kitchen, he'd tried to talk to her. Katherine had made it clear that she wasn't interested in talk or *anything* else.

Right after lunch, he'd gone into his office and she hadn't seen him since. And that was just fine. Imagine, him telling her she'd led him on. Her fingers clenched into tight fists. The man was insufferable.

When Mary Rosa asked for help hanging some new kitchen curtains, Katherine agreed, glad for the opportunity to concentrate on something—someone—else.

The sky blue curtains made a cheery addition to the kitchen, and once they were in place, Mary Rosa decided a break was in order. They settled in for a visit over tea. Mary Rosa poured while Katherine served the cinnamon cake left over from yesterday.

"This is delicious," Katherine pronounced as she swallowed a bite. "I hope you'll give me the recipe to take home to Mama."

"Glad to," Mary Rosa responded, obviously pleased by the praise. "I have to admit, I do enjoy cooking. 'Course, the only one around here who appreciates it is Logan. Those mangy galoots they call cowboys aren't interested in anything unless they can rope it and brand it, or shoot it and eat it."

Katherine chuckled at Mary Rosa's description of the proud, profane men who spent their lives working cattle or horses. Or sheep, she amended to herself.

Outside, the wind rattled the back windows and both women glanced in the direction of the sound. The tea sloshed in Katherine's cup and she dabbed at the small spill with her calico napkin.

Mary Rosa gave a huge sigh. "Lord, this storm is gonna last forever, it seems," she commented to no one in particular. "It's the worst one this year, and it's been a bad year." She sipped cautiously at her steaming brew. "All of the ranchers have suffered something awful." She glanced over to Katherine. "How's your family managing . . . with your pa gone, I mean. They holdin' up all right?"

"Like you said, we're managing." Katherine wasn't trying to be evasive, but considering it was only four weeks since her father had died, it was all she could say. When she went home, she'd take a close look at the books and have a planning meeting with Daniel and her mother. "How about the Double Four?"

Mary Rosa took another bite of cake and washed it down with tea. "Well, the losses have been high. No use saying it isn't so. Fortunately, the Double Four is a large spread and we can handle the strain a little better than some."

"Better than who?" Katherine hadn't met her neighbors. Perhaps now was as good a time as any to start learning about them. After all, one of them could very well be her father's killer.

"Well, Bromley and Morris, they're your neighbors to the west, and Statler over at the Flying W." Mary Rosa pushed a stray wisp of hair back into the coil on top of her head. She refilled her white porcelain cup with tea, then did the same for Katherine. "They all have small places. None bigger than twenty thousand head. A couple, Bromley and Morris, have lost nearly a quarter of their herds. Statler is doing a bit better. We won't know for sure until spring branding."

Katherine stared into her drink while she absorbed this information. She'd have to ask Daniel about the ranchers. Of course, just because someone was having a tough time, didn't make him a murderer.

"Why do the ranchers have to hate the Bar T so much?" she mumbled, thinking about the tiny ranch with its four thousand sheep.

"It has caused some consternation from time to time."

Katherine replaced her cup in the saucer, her interest sparked. "How much trouble, Mary Rosa?"

The woman looked at her for a long moment and Katherine thought perhaps she wasn't going to answer.

"Please, Mary Rosa," she encouraged in an earnest tone, "I need to know what I'm up against."

"Well, Katherine, I'll tell you straight, cause I don't think it does a body good to be skirting the truth. Your pa came here, bought the land straight out and made his home. Far as I know, he never asked for any help, and there's not a man for a hundred miles that could fault him for that."

Katherine felt pride swell inside her at this praise of her father. She'd always known he was a good man, but it was gratifying to know someone else had realized what a special person he was.

"But..." Katherine prompted, sensing there was more.

Mary Rosa toyed with her cup a moment, then looked up. "But your pa was stubborn. When he put up those fences, it was like pouring salt on a open wound. Just about every cattleman from here to Cheyenne was up in arms."

"But why? He only fenced what was his."

Mary Rosa gave a shrug. "Yes, but it had always been open range. Your father didn't want to understand how things were done here, and I fear that was the cause of his demise."

Katherine got up slowly and walked toward the sink. She toyed absently with the tiny button at the high collar of her shirt while she tried to comprehend Mary Rosa's evaluation. "Are you saying that because my father wouldn't knuckle under, it was all right for someone to kill him?'' She turned and looked with an unwavering stare at Mary Rosa.

"Goodness, no." The woman hurried over to Katherine. "I'm saying this winter's been exceptionally bad. Frustrations are high, tempers are short and there was no way to fight—no *one* to fight. So when your pa put up the fences, it gave them something to hate, something to strike out at."

Katherine didn't understand. How could she? It was all so useless, so wasted. Her father was dead. She hadn't even seen him before he died. She'd been robbed of the chance to tell him goodbye, to say she loved him one last time. Swallowing the lump in her throat, she asked the question she had been dreading. "Mary Rosa, do you know who killed my father?"

"No, Katherine, I don't. If I did, I'd tell the marshal straight-out. I find it hard to believe it was someone I know and so I keep telling myself it had to be some stranger."

Katherine gave the woman a hug. "Thanks for being honest with me." While she didn't agree about a stranger being responsible, she understood Mary Rosa's difficulty in believing it was a trusted friend.

The two women embraced for a moment longer, then parted, each with a reassuring smile for the other. Mary Rosa pulled a large white handkerchief from her pocket and blew her nose.

"Must be all this cold weather," she said gruffly, then hurried back to the table and began gathering the dishes.

Katherine smiled at the tiny woman's need to perpetuate her tough demeanor. Turning away, Katherine walked toward the kitchen door, needing a moment to regain her own composure. She opened the door slightly for a breath of cold, fresh air.

"It's stopped," she muttered. She turned back toward Mary Rosa and repeated, "It's stopped, Mary Rosa. The storm has stopped." She pulled the door open a little further and looked out, just to be sure. Her breath came in icy white puffs, and she wrapped her arms across her chest for warmth.

It was true. The storm was over. The howling winds, the whirling snow—all gone, as unexpectedly as it had started. Thick gray clouds lingered overhead, blocking the late afternoon sun.

Mary Rosa joined her in the doorway. "Thank the good Lord."

Katherine gazed out across the yard in the direction of the barn. A huge drift of snow lay deep around the structure and nearly covered one section of the corral fence. The treeless area was draped in murky white like an unbleached bed sheet. "It's beautiful," Katherine commented softly, not wanting to disturb the eerie silence.

"It really is something, isn't it?" Mary Rosa agreed.

Katherine's mouth curved up in a smile. "I can go home now," she said simply.

"Yes, you can."

"No. You can't." Logan's voice startled them and they both jumped.

Katherine spun around to face him. He had changed clothes from the denims he'd worn that morning to a forest green wool shirt and dark brown trousers. Her eyes narrowed and she regarded him carefully.

"Let's talk," was all he said.

She drew herself up to her full height. There'd be no surprises—no repeat of this morning's mistake. "All right."

"Not here," he corrected, ignoring his aunt's interest. "In my office."

"If you like," she responded with more calm than she felt. He stepped aside and allowed her to lead the way.

Past the bedrooms, at the end of the hallway, she pushed open the solid pine door and walked into the office.

So this was the inner sanctum, she thought, glancing around the room. The well-used mahogany desk and raw log walls were what she would have imagined. The bookcase filled with leather-bound volumes seemed appropriate. She wasn't so sure about the large gun rack near one window. Logan was the kind of man who commanded respect and attention without a weapon.

Like the man, the room was dark and pleasing. The kind of room that lulled you into feeling relaxed much too easily. Her resolve stiffened.

"Please . . ." Logan gestured toward one of a half-dozen chairs spaced between the desk and the cast-iron stove, and he watched as she sat in the chair farthest from him. So, he thought, annoyed, that's how it's going to be.

He perched on the edge of the desk, one booted foot resting on the bare plank floor, the other swinging back and forth. "When I saw the snow had stopped, I thought I'd better talk to you. It might be just a lull, you know. If that's the case, it could start up again any time. I won't let you leave just yet."

Katherine pivoted toward him, determined not to lose her temper at his autocratic attitude. Her expression was schooled, her tone calm. "I appreciate your generous hospitality. You've tried to make me feel . . . welcome."

"Sounds like I haven't succeeded," he replied, with a mock frown that immediately turned into a lazy smile. "Should I have done more?"

The teasing Logan was back, the one that was too charming, too familiar and much too dangerous to her plans. Hoping to think better on her feet, Katherine rose and walked over to peruse the books that covered one wall. Absently, she selected a volume and flipped it open. Poetry. Keats, of all things. The man was an enigma.

She closed the book with a snap and replaced it on the shelf, then glanced at Logan, who was watching her. They were both adults. They were both thinking about that morning. Why not be direct? "The sooner I leave, the better it will be. For both of us."

"You really are afraid of me, aren't you?" There was a distinct note of smugness in his voice.

She shot him a defiant look. "Not at all."

"Are you still upset about this morning?" He lifted a questioning brow. "Because I kissed you, I mean?"

*Because you're cattle and I'm sheep. Because you're opposed to everything I want and because every time you look at me I go up in flames.* "I see no reason to go looking for problems."

Amusement danced in his dark eyes. "It was only a kiss. How big a problem can that be? Surely, you've been kissed before."

"Many times. Of course," she answered lightly with a casual wave of her hand. Honesty had its limits. She wasn't about to tell him her experience consisted of two very quick, very bland good-night kisses from polite young men. Nothing like the heated possession of Logan's mouth on hers. Her gaze flicked to his lips as the memory came flooding back with electric clarity.

His head tipped to one side and he eyed her intently before answering, "Of course."

Sable eyes locked with royal blue. This morning's kiss had affected Logan more than he cared to admit. Her lips had been soft and pliant against his mouth. She had leaned into him like she was welcoming him home, drugging his senses so fast he'd nearly lost all control. That was a startling admission for a man with his experience.

Desire stirred and he shifted uncomfortably. He saw her cross the room in a few long, graceful strides. The riding skirt clearly defined her figure. She sat on the edge of a chair and crossed her booted feet demurely at the ankle.

"My family will be worried," she remarked, not wishing to continue on the path their discussion was taking them. "Just as I'm worried about them."

"I understand. But they'll be a lot more upset to learn you survived the blizzard only to die in a drift somewhere." Logan thrust his hands into his trouser pockets. "Besides, it'll be dark in a couple of hours. I'll take you home myself tomorrow if the storm hasn't returned."

She glanced at the window. "I guess you're right. It would be wise to wait—but only until tomorrow."

"Tomorrow," he agreed, pleased she hadn't been more stubborn. He stepped around the desk and sat in his chair. "What are your plans when you get home?"

"Simple, really. I'll do whatever it takes to keep the ranch running until Daniel is experienced enough to take over. I may have spent the last four years in Philadelphia, but I'm not afraid of hard work, or getting my hands dirty."

He admired her determination, but what she was planning was impossible. Ranch life was hard on women. She'd throw herself into the work and age ten years in one in the process. He'd seen it a hundred times before.

"Is that it?" He couldn't keep the incredulity out of his voice.

"I see no need for further explanation."

"Why not?" He shrugged. "Maybe you can change my mind about the wisdom of a sheep ranch smack in the middle of cattle country."

Katherine shot him a skeptical look. She doubted that Logan McCloud changed his mind, ever, about anything—unless he wanted to. But there was something in those black eyes of his that made her forget the doubt. If there was a chance she could convince him—well, it might make things much easier. She decided to try.

"My parents had a small farm in Virginia, which they lost when . . . never mind why, they just did. They spent the next two years working wherever and at whatever they could until they'd managed to save a little money."

"That must have been very hard for your mother."

"Very hard." She swallowed down the thick lump that formed in her throat every time she thought just *how* hard. Working on other people's farms. Mama cooking, Papa helping with the harvest. Every night Mama would count the money in the mason jar and plan for the time when they'd have their own place. Their bedtime stories had been about a house of their own with red-checked curtains at the windows and a room for each of them. Papa had kept his word. She'd keep hers to her family.

"We moved West and they found this place for sale. The man who owned it—"

"Eddington," Logan interjected.

"That's the one. He said he didn't want much for it, something about another investment coming in. Anyway, he helped my father get a bank loan."

"So I heard—too late," he muttered under his breath.

"Cattle were out of the question because of the expense and the *competition*." She emphasized the last word for his benefit. "Papa knew a little about sheep because we always had a few on the farm in Virginia."

Logan looked at her sitting there all stiff-backed with pride. She was doing her best to be self-composed and detached. But she was in over her head.

Perhaps this was the time to make another offer for the land. Perhaps she would see reason where her father hadn't.

"I imagine you'd like to see things easier for your mother and brother. I'd like to help."

She eyed him suspiciously. "Why do I find that hard to believe?"

He shrugged off her sarcasm. "I would be interested in buying the ranch. I'd give you a good price, certainly above the market value."

"Why so generous?"

"I'm not being generous. It's no secret that I wanted the land. I had my lawyers contact your father, but he refused to sell."

"My father was a determined man."

"There is a difference between determination and foolishness." His tone was sharp.

"I see." Her eyes glittered with controlled temper. "My father—my *family* is foolish. I guess that means I'm foolish, too!" Katherine walked to his desk and braced both hands on the scarred surface. "When we get through the spring lambing and the shearing, then we'll see who's a fool.''

"You don't know the first thing about sheep ranching," he said patiently.

Katherine's glare never wavered. "You weren't born knowing about cattle ranching, but you learned. So can I."

Logan stood and mirrored her stance from the other side of the desk. "Not fast enough, woman. You're courting disaster. If you sell—"

"Sell my family out, you mean!"

"I'm suggesting that you use good sense. This is a tough part of the country. It's unforgiving." His black eyes snapped with anger. "The foolish ones don't survive and they don't deserve to."

"McCloud, who do you think you are to say who deserves to stay and who doesn't? We may not be the biggest ranching outfit in this county," she said, her voice dripping with sarcasm as she raked him with her gaze, "but we are every bit as good as you—you, you cowboy!"

Katherine turned on her heel and strode out of the room, shutting the door firmly behind her.

Logan dropped down in his chair. Damn the woman, he thought. He offered to help by buying the ranch and what did she do? She called him names. Cowboy, no less! Well, he was a cowboy, dammit, but she said it like it ought to be a hanging offense.

Logan ran his palm across his face in an effort to calm himself. It must be cabin fever, snow blindness, lack of female companionship—something. Why else would he have ever been attracted to her?

Well, if she wanted to go home so badly, by God, he'd take her. Tomorrow. Hell, he'd take her home tonight, snow or no snow.

He started for the door. She was the most infuriating, hot-tempered— He pulled the door open and stopped. Sweet-tasting, intriguing, arousing . . .

He stood poised in the doorway, one hand on the brass doorknob, the other gripping the pine frame.

"Damn," he said out loud, realizing the path his thoughts had taken. His chin dropped to his chest and he took a deep breath.

The woman drove him to the brink of distraction. He should walk away but in two days' time she'd gotten in his blood like no other woman ever had.

Katherine threw herself down on the double bed and buried her face in the multicolored patchwork quilt. The soft fabric wadded in her clenched fists.

"Who does he think he is?" she ranted to the empty room. She got up and paced across the floor, her boots tapping a steady rhythm on the polished pine.

The nerve of the man! Talking about who deserves to stay and who doesn't. Who died and left him king of Wyoming? He probably thinks he *is* king. Born with everything anyone could want right at his fingertips.

A tapping on the door brought her back from her thoughts.

"Go away!" she ordered, thinking it was Logan.

"I'm sorry, I didn't mean to disturb you," a female voice answered.

Katherine hurried to the door. "Oh, Mary Rosa, I didn't mean to shout at you."

The tiny woman looked at Katherine for a long moment. "What's wrong?"

"Nothing's wrong. Really," she added when Mary Rosa looked skeptical. "I suddenly have a very bad headache." A raven-haired devil of a headache, she thought.

Mary Rosa's brows knitted with concern. "Oh dear. I'll get a powder for you to take. Won't take a minute and—"

"Please, don't bother," Katherine entreated, "I'll just lie down for a while and rest. A little nap and I'll be good as new."

"Well, okay, but if you change your mind, just holler." Mary Rosa gave Katherine a kindly pat on the arm. "I'll check on you around suppertime."

Later, Katherine declined Mary Rosa's offer of the evening meal, choosing instead to remain in her room. She stretched out on the bed. Her lack of sleep the night before, coupled with her anger, had left her exhausted, and she drifted off to sleep.

When she awoke the room was dark, except for one candle that burned on the four-drawer mahogany chest by the window. A fire glowed in the stove. Mary Rosa, Katherine thought. She was grateful for the kindness.

A quick check at the window told her it was late. She rubbed the sleep from her eyes and decided to change into her borrowed flannel nightdress. That done, she was about to climb under the covers when she remembered she hadn't eaten anything since noon. Maybe there were some biscuits left from dinner. If not, at least a cup of tea would help.

Katherine opened the bedroom door and checked that no one was moving about. Assured that all was silent, she stepped out into the hall, her bare toes curling briefly against the cold floor. Hurrying through the parlor, she went straight to the kitchen.

A small kerosene lamp burned low on the pine table. She heated some water and set a pot of tea to brew. There were some biscuits on a plate in the warming oven and Katherine ate one while the tea finished steeping. Licking her fingers clean of crumbs, she poured the tea and headed back to her bedroom. The fire was low in the parlor fireplace, casting eerie shadows in the otherwise unlighted room.

"Did you find everything you wanted?"

Startled, she spun around. The cup and saucer dropped from her trembling fingers and shattered.

"Don't move," Logan commanded, stepping out of the shadows toward her.

"Now look what I've done." Instinctively, she bent down and started picking up the broken pieces. How could she have been so clumsy? China was expensive. China this delicate was dear. "Don't worry, I'll replace the cup, if you'll tell me where—ouch!" She pulled back as a sharp edge sliced into her fingertips.

China crunched under Logan's boot heel. "Well, at least you're consistent—stubborn, no matter what."

Before she realized what he was about, Logan scooped her up in his strong arms. It seemed so natural to loop her arms around his neck. His hair brushed the sensitive skin on the back of her hand. She fought the impulse to lace her fingers in the silken threads.

The heat of his body penetrated the flannel of her nightdress. She stiffened, trying to avoid contact with him and slow the frantic beating of her heart. It was no use. His hands intimately cradled her at her thigh and ribs.

A lush, warm feeling started low in her belly and spread slowly in every direction.

Logan turned his head. Her delicate face, only a kiss away, filled his vision. His mouth went dry and he took a deep, ragged breath as he put her down, none too gently, on the sofa.

She twisted around and started to stand. "I'm sorry about breaking the china. I'll—"

"I don't care about the cup." He ignored her effort to rise. Instead, he took her hand in his to examine the cut that glistened bright red on the tips of three fingers. "I care about you."

She snapped her head around to find Logan gazing at her, the familiar smile gone, replaced with a look so intent it made her stomach do funny flip-flops.

Logan dropped down on one knee in front of her and told himself not to think about the way her hair caught the firelight or how it draped enticingly over her shoulders, inviting his touch.

Frowning, he held her hand up, checking to make sure there were no bits of china in the cut, then pressed a handkerchief to the wound.

"Make a fist and stay put while I get something to clean up the rest of this mess," he ordered.

She complied.

"How does it feel now?" he asked a few minutes later. He sopped up the spilled tea and broken china with a kitchen towel and deposited it on the stone hearth.

"Fine."

"Let me take a look. It's not bleeding." He dabbed at the spot once. "It'll be fine."

"Didn't I just say that?" Katherine commented with a touch of arrogance.

Logan straightened abruptly. "I bow to your superior knowledge for the second time today."

The camelback clock on the mantle softly chimed eleven. He glanced at it before he went to the table by the window and poured himself a whiskey.

Katherine's eyes narrowed and she clenched her jaw as she struggled to contain her temper. The man was overbearing, sarcastic. She wasn't going to stay here and go through this again. Two steps toward the fire, she stopped.

"I'm going back to my room. I'll be ready to leave at first light. I trust that will be convenient for you."

At the sound of her voice, Logan turned. The vision before him took his breath away. She stood with her back to the fire, her hands balled into her waist. The pink nightgown was pulled tightly across her flat belly and outlined her firm, high breasts—just right to fit a man's hand, he noticed with pleasure. She glared at him, daring him to challenge her, totally unaware of the image she presented.

The thought crossed his mind that he really hadn't been angry before she walked into the room, except perhaps at himself.

In fact, he'd been staring into the flames for the last hour thinking about the lady. He'd thought about the way her eyes had flashed like sapphires when she'd stormed out of his office today. He'd also thought about the way her eyes grew dark and lazy when he'd kissed her this morning. After that, all his senses had sprung to life. He could almost feel her ivory skin, like satin against his fingertips. Hear her moan when his tongue slipped into her mouth; taste the sweet honey of her. He'd just about decided he would have to take a late-night walk in the snow to cool off when she'd entered the room.

"Good night, Mr. McCloud."

It took only a heartbeat for the words to register. "Katherine, wait," he demanded gently, trying to sound less urgent than he felt.

She turned warily and looked at him. He was staring at her with unconcealed interest, and she suddenly felt exposed, naked. Glancing down at the pink flannel fabric of the nightdress, she realized she nearly was. Embarrassed, she moved two steps to the side and shielded herself behind the high-backed chair.

"Don't go," he encouraged softly.

"Why not?"

"I want..." *To take you in my arms and lose myself in you,* he thought to say, but didn't. In a voice that was husky and rich with promise, he said simply, "Stay."

# Chapter Six

It was absurd, totally irrational, the way that one word and his mere presence reached inside her and started a sudden spiraling warmth that overpowered all other feelings.

Katherine crossed her arms in a protective gesture. "Logan," she said wearily, "I don't want to fight anymore. It's obvious we aren't going to change each other's mind about the Bar T, so let's just avoid trouble."

He regarded her carefully, thoughtfully. For a moment his smile was a trace smaller, his expression a little more serious. "How about a truce?"

She sensed the change in him, his mood, his demeanor. These elusive, brief insights into another side of him intrigued her. A deeper, caring side that he kept to himself, hidden behind a wall of teasing wit and heart-melting smiles.

It was the chance to know more that made her say, "Truce."

He grinned his familiar grin, then strolled back to the liquor table. "Would you like something?" He gestured toward the crystal decanters while glancing over his shoulder at her. "I think sherry would be appropriate." Not waiting for her agreement, he filled a small glass. "It's my mother's favorite. I think you'll enjoy the taste."

She watched him walk toward her, a dark shadow moving in the dimly lit room. He held out the small glass filled with rich hazel liquid. The delicate crystal made an odd contrast to his work-roughened hands.

Their fingers brushed as she accepted the offering, and she could feel the warmth of his skin against hers. His fingers seemed to linger for a moment, testing. She made the mistake of looking into his beautiful ebony eyes. The man had a way of touching her with his gaze that sent shivers skimming along her skin, like snowflakes in a spiraling wind.

"Why don't we sit down?" he suggested with a nod before sinking down on the sofa.

Katherine watched the leather flex and give under his weight, and the wool of his shirt pull tight across his broad chest. For a moment, visions of his chest, bare and dripping with water, assaulted her senses. She remembered wanting to touch its mat of coal black hair, and wondered if it would be soft or coarse beneath her fingers. Oh, Lord! What was the matter with her?

She was clearly courting trouble. Yet, she needed to understand this attraction she felt. All afternoon she'd denied the warmth that filled her every time he got close. Now she was determined to prove, once and for all, that she was impervious to Logan McCloud's enticement.

Sipping the sweet liquor, she looked at Logan reclining casually on the sofa, waiting. *Well, what's it going to be?* her mind chided. *Stay,* another part of her answered firmly.

She snatched up the oversized green shawl that Mary Rosa had left on the chair. Draping it over her shoulders, she stepped around the chair and sat down. With her legs curled under her and the wrap spread over most of her lap, only her bare toes showed below the hem of her nightgown.

The air around them was suddenly very still. The aroma of pine filled the air as a log snapped in the fireplace.

Katherine let her fingers trace the tiny leaf pattern cut in the glass she held while she leaned her head back against the soft fabric of the chair. The sherry and the silence worked their magic and she felt the stiffness ease from her shoulders.

Logan's movement caught her attention. She watched him walk to the hearth and adjust the half-burned logs with the soot-blackened poker.

"Since we've agreed to a truce," he commented when he turned back to face her, "we need to establish terms."

She straightened just a little at his suggestion. "Like what?" she inquired. A feeling of suspicion made her stomach flutter. She reminded herself that she was a businesswoman, experienced in dealing with autocratic men. Of course, it was a little difficult to maintain an air of aloof dignity when she was wearing only a nightgown. But her chin came up a fraction just the same.

He sat down on the edge of the stone hearth and gave no indication of being the least impressed with her wary stare. His tone was confident. "I think we should say cattle and sheep, ranches and families, are forbidden topics."

She relaxed. "I will if you will."

He flashed an infectious grin full of roguish charm and dimples and mustache. "Angel, it's guaranteed."

It was the darn dimples that got her. She was powerless to stop the smile that pulled up the corners of her mouth.

Logan moved back to the sofa and this time sat at the end closest to her. He rested one booted foot on the opposite knee, his fingers wrapped around his ankle. "Perhaps it's safe to ask what you like to do for fun?"

"Fun?" she repeated with a small shrug. "I'm a little old to be playing with dolls or at hide-and-seek."

Logan chuckled. "Oh, I don't know, hide-and-seek can be quite exciting ... especially in a hayloft."

He gave her a wink and a lopsided half smile that made her heart beat a little faster.

"You're very sure of yourself, Mr. McCloud."

Logan slouched lower on the sofa, legs crossed at the ankles, his glass resting on his chest. "About some things, yes, I'm sure."

It could have been a challenge or it could have been a promise. Either way, his words, his nearness, made her fingers tremble ever so slightly. She glanced at him to see if he'd noticed. Apparently not. He appeared relaxed, more relaxed than she was, she thought, watching the way he turned the glass in his hands.

He had wonderful hands, she remembered—gentle hands. Hands that had soothed her that first night, stroked her hair, caressed her cheek. A pleasant warmth started building inside her. Taking a calming sip of liquid courage, she focused on the topic at hand. "When you aren't playing in haylofts, what do you like to do?"

A log snapped in two and tumbled in the fireplace, rolling dangerously near the edge. A small puff of gray ash and smoke settled on the hearth. Logan rose and deftly adjusted the logs more securely.

He glanced over his shoulder at her while he worked. "I hunt sometimes, over near the Yellowstone." His tone was suddenly husky. "You know, there's a lake over there that's the exact color of your eyes."

He rose and leaned one shoulder casually against the pine mantle, looking more handsome at that moment than any man Katherine had ever seen. She lifted her glass to her lips before noticing it was empty.

He refilled it. "To keep the chill off," he commented to when she sent him a questioning look.

He took a sip of his whiskey and licked the glistening drops from the ends of his mustache. Muscles tightened in her abdomen as she watched the seemingly natural act. She was *not* attracted to the man standing a scant three feet away, she told herself firmly. And she was *not* curious about the sizzling sensations caused by his kiss that morning.

Logan's deep voice interrupted her thoughts. "So tell me, do you miss the city?"

"What? Oh, very much. Philadelphia is a wonderful place, with its museums, parks, shops...law and order," she couldn't resist adding.

He ignored the jibe. "You're anxious to return then?"

"Yes. I had to close my millinery shop and I miss it."

"A woman in business is unusual. Especially one so young." And beautiful, he thought to say, but didn't.

"Perhaps," she conceded, "but times are changing, some say women all over the country will soon have the vote just as they do here in Wyoming."

He chuckled. "Then there's something about Wyoming you like, after all."

She gave a small laugh. "Okay, you've got me."

*Not yet, but soon.* Katherine finished the last of her sherry. She was feeling warm and very, very relaxed. Her head rested against the back of the chair. "In another month or so the trees will be budding in the park near where I lived. Aunt Martha and I used to go there sometimes on summer evenings. That was before she became bedridden, of course. After that, well, it was impossible to leave her."

Logan frowned. At a time when most girls were going to parties and dances, she had been valiantly trying to care for a dying woman while managing a business. The image didn't sit well with him.

"Your family expected a lot from you," he said flatly as he sat down on the floor near her chair.

"Family is the most important thing. And you're breaking our truce," she reminded him.

"Sorry," he mumbled.

He glanced at her. Katherine, in his aunt's green cashmere shawl and bathed in firelight, was more enticing than any woman he'd ever known. Reaching out, he touched her hand where it rested on her knee.

Katherine looked down at the way his long tan fingers curled around her smaller ones. She started to pull away when his grip tightened ever so slightly, but that lazy, lopsided grin of his was her undoing. She relented.

Logan made small circles on the back of her hand with his thumb. "You have beautiful hands." He wondered how they would feel against the bare skin of his chest, or back, or... "This isn't Philadelphia and we don't have a band, but I can provide some music," he told her, his voice just a little rough.

Her eyes widened in surprise. "Really? I love music. I always wished I could play the piano."

In one easy motion Logan stood and moved to the mahogany sideboard near the back of the parlor. He returned carrying a large wooden music box, which he sat on the floor near Katherine's feet. The metal crank turned easily, clicking like a clock running too fast. When he lifted the carved cherry lid, the strains of a Strauss waltz carried forth.

With great formality, Logan extended his hand. "May I have this dance, Miss Thorn?"

Katherine tried to strike a haughty pose and pushed her loose hair back behind her shoulder. "Why sir, have we been properly introduced?"

With ease, Logan formally bowed. Though it didn't fit with his casual attire, she loved the gesture just the same.

Logan then made a great show of clearing his throat. "Allow me. I am Logan McCloud and I've been admiring you across the dance floor all evening." He made a sweeping gesture around the room.

"You mean the parlor?"

Their little game changed as quickly as it started. She was acutely aware of her state of dress, or more precisely, undress. She sat a little straighter.

"Come on, sweet Katherine, just put your hand in mine."

The warmth of his voice, the easy way he spoke her name . . . well, it seemed so natural to place her hand in his. His dark gaze held her spellbound and she was gently pulled into his strong arms. The scent of pine and wool and a uniqueness that was Logan filled her nostrils. It was just a dance, nothing more—no need to get in a dither. Katherine rose on her bare toes and slid her hand around Logan's neck. She positioned herself as far from him as possible, without leaving the room all together, that is. Slowly, carefully, they turned to the enticing rhythm of "The Blue Danube" waltz.

The flames in the fireplace radiated warmth, but it was nothing compared to what Logan's touch sent coursing through her. His hand rested near the small of her back and she felt the searing heat of it through the flannel of her nightgown. A delicious shiver rippled up her spine.

"Not so stiff, Angel," he encouraged with his usual roguish charm. "I promise I won't step on your toes." He chuckled, then pulled her closer until her breasts were pressed against his chest.

That was Logan's second mistake. The first had been asking her to dance. He knew he shouldn't touch her. He'd promised himself he wouldn't, not after the way his body had reacted to the feel of her in his arms that morning.

Looking down into her face as they moved, he knew he was in serious trouble. He had as much chance of not touching her as he had of drawing to an inside straight— maybe less.

She molded to him easily, as if she were made to fit. All day long, erotic fantasies had paraded through his brain, all of them involving Katherine naked and in his arms. While she wasn't naked now, she was damn close. It was a start.

Desire, clear and hot, pounded through his blood. His hands ached to caress her. What would she do if he cupped her breast in his hand, teasing the nipple to a hard peak? Would she give in to the pleasure? Would she let him show her all they could give each other?

He stopped dancing. The only rhythm he was thinking about was very ancient, and very demanding.

Their gazes found each other. Silence stretched between them, ripe with anticipation.

Transfixed, Katherine watched him lift her hand to his lips, then kiss and suck the tip of each finger. Her whole body trembled.

He placed her hand on his chest and she could feel the heavy beating of his heart beneath her palm. Her other hand rested on the broad plane of his shoulder.

"It appears the music has stopped," he commented softly.

"It's a lovely song," she answered, her voice just a little breathless.

He pulled her hair over her shoulder and she watched as he let the strands slide slowly through his fingers.

"You're quite a woman, Katherine Thorn." His tone was hushed.

With a light touch, he arranged her hair across her breasts. Unfamiliar sensations rushed through her when the back of his hand brushed against her nipple.

She was tempted to flinch, to turn away. But every cell in her body was inflamed by the sheer closeness of him. Every muscle tightened in expectation.

His fingers drifted to her throat, then curled around to massage the muscles at the back of her neck.

"We're good together, Katherine." Logan looked at her, drowning in the depths of her midnight blue eyes. He traced the edge of her jaw with the tip of one finger.

Katherine took a deep breath, ignored the warm shiver that moved up her spine and returned his gaze. "Perhaps we are," she admitted grudgingly, "here and now." She forced herself to shrug. "We dance well together, anyway." The man had a way of soothing and enticing that was hard to resist. Yet she knew she must. "If we had met under other circumstances...well, that doesn't matter now. We don't see things the same."

"Oh, we're different, I'll give you that."

His finger continued its maddeningly sensual path along the side of her neck, making it impossible for her to think let alone speak.

"They say," Logan continued, "opposites attract. I think it's true. What do you think, Angel?"

"Logan, the kiss today was as much my wish as yours, I've come to realize."

"How understanding of you." He grinned.

His palm cupped the side of her face and she leaned into it, for a moment enjoying the gentleness of his touch.

"Nevertheless—" Katherine straightened abruptly, "—I can't let it happen again. When I leave tomorrow, I'll return to my world and you to yours. It's better if we leave well enough alone."

She saw him arch one dark brow in surprise, but he didn't argue the point.

Feeling suddenly confident, she stepped away and started toward the guest room. Pausing after a few steps, she glanced back over her shoulder. "After tomorrow, I doubt we'll see each other again soon." She gave him a small smile. "Good night, Logan. And thank you...for everything," she added.

"Katherine," he called softly. "I'll have Cookie take you home on the wagon tomorrow. It'll be more comfortable, and I can trust him to get you there safe and sound."

She nodded her agreement then continued down the hall. "Good night, sweet Katherine." He watched her step into the bedroom and heard the soft click as she closed the door.

*Your world. My world. Sometimes worlds collide and, Angel, the results can be glorious.*

# Chapter Seven

Early morning sun glinted off the snow with a harsh, near-blinding light. Logan adjusted his wide-brimmed trail hat lower on his forehead. No help. "Damn," he muttered. He pulled his glove off and tucked it under his chap-covered thigh, and rubbed his tired eyes.

He glanced over at Pete, riding beside him. "At this rate, it's a toss-up who'll go blind first, me or old Joker here." He affectionately patted the neck of his Appaloosa.

Pete nodded. "Know what ya mean."

They rode in silence for a while. The ice-crusted snow crunched beneath the horses' hooves. The occasional snorting of a horse or the jingle of a bridle was the only other sound.

Logan twisted in the saddle, the stiff leather creaking in protest. He put all his weight on one stirrup for a minute and scanned the terrain behind them, looking past the forty or so Double Four cowboys and the dozen packhorses. Grim-faced, the men followed, saying little. They, too, searched the white-frosted terrain for the thousands of cattle they knew were out there—somewhere.

Nothing.

Logan settled back. Katherine was gone. Only a couple of hours ago he'd lifted her up on the seat of the chuck wagon and tucked the buffalo robe around her.

He'd wanted to escort her back to the Bar T, but knew he couldn't. He had work to do and she'd be comfortable on the wagon.

The wind tugged at his hat and he settled it more firmly on his head. Instinctively, he hunched his shoulders against the cold that seeped in around the up-turned collar and cuffs of his sheepskin jacket. At least sheep were good for one thing, he mused, although he doubted Katherine would agree.

She'd practically drowned in the plaid wool jacket he had insisted she put on this morning. As he'd expected, she'd argued with him about wearing it. He'd argued right back that she couldn't go riding across Wyoming in the middle of winter in nothing but that damned oil slicker.

A smile tugged up one corner of his mouth. The woman was unique. She was all fire and temper one minute, gentle and soft the next. Just when he thought he was getting ahead of her, she'd go and surprise him.

She was a challenge. And Logan liked a challenge. It got his blood up, made things exciting. And it made winning all the sweeter. His smile turned into a full grin.

He took a couple of deep breaths of freezing cold air.

"Rider coming in," Pete commented.

Logan fixed his attention on the man, who was slumped in the saddle and moving slowly in their general direction. "Looks like Slim's big chestnut gelding," he commented, half to Pete and half to himself.

"Yep."

Logan tucked his thumb and index finger in the corners of his mouth and gave a loud, shrill whistle. Horse and rider stopped. The man straightened, waved and turned toward them.

"Howdy, boss," Slim called as he neared the group a few minutes later.

Logan shook his head at the picture Slim made. Unlike usual cowboy humor, which gave men nicknames that were the opposite of their image, the name in this case fit perfectly.

"I know I shouldn't ask this, but where the hell have you been?" He glanced at the ice-crusted buffalo coat that Slim was submerged in.

"Why, I been out doing the job you pay me thirty dollars a month for." He sat up a little straighter in the saddle. "Me and ol' Buck here been following them beeves, of course."

"Where'd you leave 'em?" Pete asked.

"'Bout half a day's ride. Down near Hazard Bluffs," Slim responded in a hushed tone.

Logan frowned. "Damn." He thought about the series of bluffs, some twenty feet high. In the middle of a snowstorm, cattle would walk right off the edge and kill themselves—or have to be killed.

A knot formed in his gut. "How bad?"

Slim shook his head. Loose snow shifted from his hat brim onto his shoulders. "Can't tell for sure. There was no way I could turn 'em without getting myself in a fix."

"I know. There was nothing you could do."

There was nothing anyone could do.

By the time the wagon pulled into the yard at the Bar T, it was noon. Katherine was cold and tired and grateful that she'd given in when Logan insisted she not ride her horse.

The harness jingled on the double team of workhorses as the wagon slid to a stop by the porch of the clapboard house. Smoke drifted gently from the stone chimney. Someone had shoveled the snow from the front door and made a path to the barn. Probably her brother, Daniel, or a couple of the hands.

Cookie told one of the men to put Sunrise in the barn, then he helped Katherine down.

Anxious to see her mother, she quickly thanked Cookie and the two outriders. She turned just as the door swung open. Sarah Thorn rushed out, a smile beaming on her thin face.

"Katherine!" she shouted joyfully. "Thank God, you're all right."

"Mama!" Katherine cried, hugging her mother. "It's good to see you."

"You're home." Sarah's chin quivered. Tears slid down her wind-chilled cheeks and she looked toward heaven for a moment then hugged her daughter again.

"Oh, Katherine, I was so worried, but you're home. . . ."

She pulled back, grinned, swiped at her eyes with the sleeve of her dress and embraced Katherine once more, just for good measure.

Suddenly, Sarah remembered they weren't alone and she turned a grateful smile on the men who'd brought her daughter home.

"Won't you come in?" she called to them as she tucked a strand of graying blond hair back in the bun at the nape of her neck. She slipped her hand around Katherine's. "There's coffee fresh made, and I could heat some antelope stew."

Katherine echoed the sentiments. "Yes, Cookie, please do. All of you must be cold."

"Thank you, ma'am."

"Kind a ya, ma'am."

The men spoke almost in unison.

Cookie tipped his hat politely, revealing his balding scalp. "Yes, indeed, that's right kind of ya, ma'am, but we got to get going. We've got to get camp set up by nightfall and there's a lot to do. We sure do thank you for the invite."

He stepped on the wagon runners and climbed up on the high-perched seat. Picking up the reins, he called, "Gid up," to the team.

Sarah and Katherine called "thank you" and waved as Cookie and the men rode out of the yard.

Now that Sarah had her daughter back, safe and all in one piece, she looked her over with a mother's appraising stare.

"Katherine, are you *sure* you're all right?" she questioned again. "Where have you been?"

Katherine chuckled. "I'm fine. Come on, let's get in the house. It's too cold to be standing out here and I've got so much to tell you."

Arms still wrapped around each other, they grinned as they tried to wedge through the doorway of the small cabin at the same time. Closing the door, Sarah smiled. "I see someone was kind enough to loan you a coat."

"Yes," Katherine said, tossing it on the sun-faded blue divan near the window.

Sarah didn't press the issue. She couldn't resist giving Katherine a rib-crushing hug. "Lord, it's good to have you home. I don't mind telling you I was scared. And Daniel was beside himself with worry."

Katherine's voice was hushed. "I'm sorry, Mama, to put you through more hurt, but there was no way I could get word to you that I was all right."

Sarah nodded. "I know, dear. I'm not complaining. You're home. That's all I care about, except..." Sarah's voice trailed off as she went to the kitchen and poured two steaming mugs of coffee. Carrying them to the square kitchen table, she asked, "What happened?"

Dragging out two wooden chairs from the table, they sat side by side so they could both keep their backs to the welcome fire in the stone fireplace. Katherine quickly related how she had been caught in the storm and rescued by Logan.

"Logan McCloud," Sarah repeated, unable to keep the shock from her voice. Her eyes opened wide. "You mean those were Double Four ranch hands who brought you home?"

"Yes, they—"

"My goodness, Katherine, I never suspected..." Sarah got up. For a moment she stared into the crackling fire. "Of all the people in the world... Logan McCloud." She shook her head, then looked at Katherine. "Are you absolutely certain you are . . . unhurt?"

Katherine's head came up with a start. The wooden chair creaked as she twisted to face her mother. "Yes, Mama. The McClouds were very kind."

"Hard to believe," Sarah replied, clearly dismayed. "Of course, I'm eternally grateful, but I never would have believed it if you weren't telling me. After all, Logan McCloud has wanted us gone for years. Your father said McCloud wasn't always too polite in the asking."

Now it was Katherine's turn to look surprised. "You mean he was violent? Did he threaten Papa?"

"No, I don't think things ever went that far. I wasn't there, of course. Your father liked to handle business privately. But I think the words got hot and heavy a few times." Sarah's lips turned up in a small smile. "Your Papa always could hold his own in a fight—Irish temper."

"True enough." Katherine smiled too. There was no denying her father was all Irish, with auburn hair, green eyes and temper enough to take on any three Englishmen. Yet he had never raised his hand to his family. He'd worked hard and been a good provider. Just glancing around the room, she could feel his presence. He'd built the third bedroom on the house, enlarged the kitchen and made half the furniture with his own hands.

And now, in the second it took for someone to pull a trigger, everything had changed.

Pain, fresh and raw, welled up inside her, and anger. She hadn't seen her father since the family had come to visit her in Philadelphia two years ago. Now she'd never see him again.

She should have been here when he died.

He shouldn't have died at all!

Now there were only the three of them left in the world to look after each other. Sweet, kind Mama was strong in her own unique way, but running a ranch and bossing a crew of men wasn't something she could handle. No, if they were going to keep the Bar T going, it was up to Katherine and her little brother.

Which reminded her. "Mama, is Daniel out with the flock?"

"He left early this morning with one of the hands to go to town." Sarah's thin fingers curled around the top rung of the chair. "We thought maybe you got stuck there. He'll be glad to find you home."

About midafternoon, Daniel stamped into the house. The frown on his young face quickly changed to a smile when he saw Katherine standing at the kitchen sink doing the dishes.

"Sis!" he shouted, racing across the room. Snow slipped from the legs of his denim pants and spattered on the floor. He nearly slid to a halt. "We thought . . . well I just came from town and no one had seen you and I . . ."

He enveloped his sister in a hug, then suddenly stiffened and stepped back. He made a great show of clearing his throat and straightening the front of his navy wool jacket. He cleared his throat again and tried not to look embarrassed at his uninhibited show of affection. "Where have you *been?*"

Katherine smiled and returned the hug. So what if he squirmed a little? It was a big sister's job to make little brothers uncomfortable.

"Daniel, I missed you, too." She raked him with her gaze. "You'd better get out of those wet things."

"Never mind me," he returned, while shrugging out of his jacket. He tossed it carelessly over the edge of the sink. "What happened to you?" He wrapped his hands around the mug of steaming coffee Sarah handed him, then sank down on the closest chair.

Katherine talked while Daniel sipped. She was two minutes into her story when—

"The Double Four!" Daniel shot to his feet in one angry motion. "You were at McCloud's for the last three days?"

Sarah glanced up from her place at the table. "Daniel, don't shout at your sister."

Daniel sent her a hard look as he paced away. His hands curled into fists. "My God, sis, how could you even stand to be around them? And especially Logan McCloud?" Just saying the bastard's name left a bad taste in his mouth.

"Daniel, they saved my life. They were very nice."

"Nice! Nice!" His tone was incredulous. He gripped the top rung of his chair so hard, the edges dug into his palms. "McCloud probably killed Papa and you sit there and say he was 'nice.' Maybe you'd like to invite him to tea?"

"Maybe I would." Katherine glared back with defiance. Her temper was no less Irish than her brother's. "The McClouds *were* nice to me and I'm not going to say it was different just to please you."

"Please me? I—"

"Stop it, you two," Sarah ordered looking first at one then the other. "I won't have you fighting."

"Daniel," Katherine said with as much calmness as she could muster, "you're going to have a hard time convincing me the man who offered me the hospitality of his home is the kind of man who'd shoot an unarmed man in the back." She shook her head, certain of her judgment.

A look of disbelief crossed Daniel's face and he made a sound of disgust. "Sure. Next you'll be telling me you believe in Santa Claus." He snatched up his coffee mug and stomped to the sink. The cup made a soft thud against the galvanized metal when he plunged it into the soapy water. Hands braced on the edge of the sink, Daniel stared down into the murky depths.

Standing near the table, Katherine took a couple of deep, calming breaths. "I understand your feelings, Daniel. God knows I do. And when the marshal finds the killer, you and I will be there to see him hang. But I don't think it will be Logan McCloud at the end of the rope and I'm not going to tell you he was anything but polite and gracious when it isn't true." She came up beside him.

Daniel glanced over at her and Katherine reached out to rub his shoulder. "Would you rather I was dead in a snow drift somewhere?"

"No, sis, of course not. You know I never meant that. It's just..."

She saw the pained look in his blue eyes and the telltale glistening of tears. Her little brother wasn't so little anymore. He was feeling a man's anger and struggling to find a way to express his hurt without giving in to the child in him—the one who wanted to cry.

"Please listen," she said softly. He turned to face her. "Logan couldn't have been any nicer. He offered his condolences, asked if we needed anything, and even when he offered to buy the ranch, he made an extremely generous offer." The instant the words were out she regretted them.

Daniel's head came up with a snap. "There! You see? All that polite stuff was just a cover-up. The only thing he wants is to buy the ranch, like he's been trying to do for years."

And for a moment, Katherine wondered. Was Daniel right? She thought about herself with Logan last night. His sincerity, his charm, his gentleness. Was it all false? Was his motive simply to lull her into selling the ranch?

Daniel grabbed his coat off the counter and shouldered past her, heading for the front door. "When Papa wouldn't sell, they killed him. But we ain't selling. Not now! Not ever!"

The house was still. Everyone was asleep but Katherine. She heard Daniel's snoring even through the closed bedroom door. *Hope he finds a wife who's a sound sleeper.*

With a quilt wrapped around her, she settled comfortably on the divan, her legs stretched out in front of her. She was restless. The bed felt wrong—not physically, but emotionally. She wanted to curl up in a corner, somewhere where she was surrounded, where she felt protected, like a child in its mother's arms.

She was too old to feel that way, she supposed, but lately, life's problems seemed to be coming at her from all sides, leaving her feeling too vulnerable. Of course, she'd never say that to her mother, or her brother, either. For them she was strong and self-assured. It's what they needed her to be.

So here she was on the divan.

Four more hours and Daniel would be getting up. She'd be dressed and ready to go with him and the ranch hands. Her first day home after the storm they'd spent digging the sheep out of drifts. It was hard work, but she wasn't about to sit around the house. She had every intention of *working* on this ranch, not staying in the kitchen making jam.

Fortunately, Daniel hadn't argued much. He knew they were running out of time. Another pair of hands would mean saving more sheep. As it was, it would take days of back-breaking labor to find and uncover all the animals.

Bad luck always came in bunches, it seemed. So, of course, this last storm would have to come at the same time the ewes were due to drop their lambs. Those little wet newborns would have no chance at all of surviving in this cold. She took a deep breath. They needed those lambs.

Right now the ranch was in the black, thanks to her father's diligence. There was no mortgage and no loans. That was good, but they needed cash from the sale of lambs and wool to carry them through until next year. Without that money, they'd have to take a loan, and that was one thing she didn't want to do.

Don't go looking for trouble, she chided herself, it seems to be finding you well enough all by itself. Why did she feel the most trouble was in the form of a six-foot-two-inch rancher with wicked black eyes? What was this power he seemed to hold over her? No man had ever said the things, done the things, and oh, Lord, made her feel the things that Logan McCloud had.

She let her head drop back against the curved wooden trim on the divan. Her eyes drifted closed and she found a strange comfort in the memory of being held in Logan's gentle embrace.

Her tension eased. It was all going to work out. The marshal would find the killer; they'd keep the ranch going until Daniel could take over; she'd go back to her wonderful little hat shop and blessed civilization.

Logan rode at the head of the column, his horse moving slowly, struggling to make a path in the two and a half feet of snow. Behind him, the cowboys were strung out like the tail of a giant rattler.

The men talked quietly. News that the cattle were at the bluffs had traveled down the line. Overhead a red-tailed hawk circled, seeking its prize much the way Logan scanned the horizon seeking his.

Ed Bromley and a dozen of his Bar 76 hands joined the group moving southeast. Tall and rotund, Bromley was built like a bear. He pulled his piebald gelding alongside Logan's horse. "McCloud," was all he said by way of acknowledgement. Bromley's men filtered in with the Double Four cowboys.

Logan nodded his greeting. "One of my men trailed the herd to Hazard Bluffs."

The two looked at each other. Each understood the full impact of Logan's casual sounding statement. Bromley turned back to face straight ahead.

Glancing over, Logan could see the strain of worry written on Bromley's cold-reddened face. The Bar 76 had suffered major losses in the last storm and Logan wondered how much more the ranch could survive. Hell, how much more could any of them survive?

The Double Four had an advantage in size, but that also meant that they stood to lose more. In the end everyone was hit hard and there wasn't a damn thing to do about it. These storms were impossible to fight. Nature, he thought, was aptly referred to as a woman. She was just as fickle.

Until the branding in a few weeks, there was no telling what the total losses would be. With spring coming and the chance of any more snow virtually gone, Logan figured he'd make it through, but Bromley and Morris—he wasn't so sure. This storm could finish them.

He flinched at the sudden tightening of muscles in his shoulders. It damn well wasn't fair for a man to be brought to his knees without a fight.

Then he remembered his words to Katherine about this being an unforgiving country. The arrogant words left a bitter taste in his mouth when he thought about friends losing everything they owned.

Joker suddenly tossed his head and pranced sideways. Logan realized he'd tightened the reins. He loosened his control. "Easy, boy," he soothed with a pat.

When his work was done, Logan had every intention of finding Katherine Thorn again. He'd laughed more and been angry more in the days she'd been at the ranch than he had in months. She made him feel alive—intensely, totally alive. He liked the feeling.

Out of the corner of his eye, he saw another group of a dozen or so riders plodding through the snow, moving in the same general direction as they. Probably John Morris.

As the afternoon wore on, groups from other ranches joined them until there were over a hundred men from a half-dozen ranches riding southeast. It was midafternoon when they saw the first carcasses.

Cattle—frozen stiff—piled on top of each other at strange and grotesque angles. It was obvious the leaders had become stuck in low places and been trampled by those following behind, left broken and freezing while the others climbed over them.

At the fences near the southern edge of the sheep ranch it was the same story. The cattle had piled against the fence for hundreds of yards until it broke under the weight, and those behind had walked over or around those already dead.

Logan stared grim-faced at the dead cattle.

"Damn those fences," Bromley said in a tone colder than the weather. "And damn that idiot Thorn for putting them up. Whoever shot the man ought to get a medal."

The other ranchers agreed and Logan found himself silently echoing the sentiment. It was hard not to in the face of this destruction. Those fences had been nothing but trouble, and more than once he'd been tempted just to pull the damn things down and be done with it. Now he wished he had.

He reined over and rejoined the group. They were still searching for the main herd.

The men were gravely silent as they rode by. The only sound was the occasional snorting of a horse or the soft between-the-teeth whistle of some cowboy viewing the devastation the storm had left.

Logan glanced over at Bill Statler riding a few yards away. His beard-covered jaw was clenched rigidly, his expression gaunt.

They rode parallel to the fence line for another hour before Logan realized he hadn't seen a single sheep. Not one. Where were they? Could they all be dead? He scanned the treeless landscape.

Nothing.

Of course, he wouldn't miss the woollybacks, not for a single minute. But if the sheep were dead, would Katherine stay and try to rebuild, or would she go back to Philadelphia? She'd said something about a hat shop there.

The thought of her leaving caused a strange tightness in his chest. Suddenly he found himself hoping at least some of the ugly critters had survived. He shook his head in disbelief. On a day like this, a man could get himself lynched for that kind of thought, at least in this crowd.

It was nearly sunset before they saw the herd. Exhausted by the long march, thousands and thousands of steers stood or lay on the ground where they had stopped the night before. The sight cheered Logan. Maybe it wasn't going to be so bad after all. Around him, men were starting to smile.

Suddenly everyone seemed talkative, encouraged by the sheer numbers of cattle.

It was the first time he'd seen a smile on anyone's face all day. Hell, he had a payday grin on his own face.

Logan took charge of the group. He'd already been elected boss of the spring roundup, and while branding wasn't due to start for another month or so, he figured if they didn't get this herd moved there wouldn't be any branding.

"Pete, take a dozen men and start shoveling a place clear for a camp."

"Right."

"Breen," he said, turning to one of the Circle M hands, "start a picket line over there. Then unload the pack horses."

"I don't work for you, McCloud," Breen snapped back.

Logan paused and looked the husky cowhand straight in the eye. "The hell you don't. I'm boss until this roundup is finished. Everyone works for me until then. You don't like it, get the hell out."

Logan saw Breen cast a glance toward John Morris who was standing a few feet away. John frowned, but gave the man a subtle nod.

"Okay, McCloud." Breen's split-tooth smile didn't reach the cold stare in his hazel eyes. "I didn't know you was already elected boss."

"Don't let that stop you if you've got a problem, Breen."

"Naw, no problem." Breen grabbed his horse's reins from the snow and along with several others, headed off to follow Logan's orders.

Morris walked over to Logan. "I'll talk to him. He won't give you any more trouble," Morris promised.

"Explain it to him, John." Logan adjusted his black hat lower on his forehead. "If I have to explain it to him, he won't like it."

With that, Logan swung up onto his horse and rode out through the herd. Smart-mouthed cowboys were the least of his problems. Right now he had to figure out how to round up and move thousands and thousands of cattle north, to home range. There was not enough grass here and no water. Lack of both would finish off whatever the blizzard hadn't. Time was their enemy now, not the storm.

He paused, flexing his stiff shoulder and neck muscles. Around him cattle moaned and bawled. The sound was music to his ears. He couldn't remember ever being so glad to see a bunch of mangy steers. He touched his spurs to Joker's sides and started off again.

Everything was going to be all right. Now he had something to do. Now he had something to fight, and fighting was something he knew how to do. It was how he'd made the Double Four the largest ranch in this part of the territory.

When he rode back into camp an hour later, he was even more encouraged. He'd seen a fair share of Double Four brands and he was selfish enough to be pleased. They weren't out of the woods, by any means, but things were looking better.

The Double Four was going to survive this bitch of a winter and he was going to do his damnedest to make sure everyone else did, too.

# Chapter Eight

Rain poured off the wide brim of Logan's hat and cascaded in sheets down his slicker. It was almost as if the damnable liquid had some secret power to find and seep through every tiny opening, soaking his clothes and annoying the hell out of him in the process.

He shifted and tugged at the slicker simultaneously.

John Morris glanced over at him. "Looks like we're in for a long siege," he observed, glancing up at the late-afternoon sky, which was ominously gray.

Logan glanced up and got splattered in the face for his trouble. He swiped the water from his eyes and mustache. "It's also at least twenty degrees warmer than when we got here a week ago."

Besides making working conditions miserable, the rain was melting whatever snow the last five days of warm weather hadn't. While that wasn't necessarily bad, the constant moving of the thousands of cattle was turning the ground into a quagmire and effectively destroying what little grazing there was.

The two were joined by Ed Bromley and Pete.

The men gazed out over the treeless terrain. White-faced cattle covered the area like locusts on a cornfield. It was a sight to make a cattleman's heart glad. They were looking at their present and their future, all in the form of ornery steers worth forty dollars a head on the open market.

Pete pushed at his red bandana, which the wind kept flapping in his face. Glancing over at Logan, he said, "The boys on the skinning detail say the count is up to 923. Maybe a hundred or so more to go and they'll be done."

The men fell silent, their attention diverted from profit to losses. Logan understood. The sale of hides to the eastern leather market would hardly make up the price a steer on the hoof would have brought.

"And who's to know how many more are piled up around them damn sheep fences?" Bromley asked. His tone was harsh, bitter.

"I figured that when Thorn died, the family'd sell out and move on," Morris said.

"What the hell are they sticking around for?" Bromley shot back. "His wife and them kids are fools if they think they can make a go of it."

"Appears they think just that," Logan told them, remembering Katherine's adamant statement in his office. "I believe they're determined to stick it out."

Bromley looked around with a mirthless smile. He pulled a plug of tobacco from his inside jacket pocket and bit off a corner. "Well," he mused, the tobacco making a bulge in his cheek, "Thorn was determined, and look what happened to him."

Bromley was smirking a little too much, Logan thought, yet he'd known Ed six years and didn't think he was the type to kill. All talk and no action was Logan's appraisal of the man. Could he be wrong?

Logan looked through the stream pouring off his water-soaked hat. "I sure as hell don't miss Thorn, but killing's not the answer." He shot Bromley a hard look. "I'd rather try to buy them out."

Morris gave a harsh laugh. "You've been trying to do that for years and look where it's got you. Nowhere! For the price of a Remington .44 cartridge, the problem's solved."

"Was it?" Logan shot back. "They're still there."

Morris took a long time answering. "For a while, anyway."

Bromley let fly a stream of brown tobacco juice. It disappeared down between the horses. "Ain't no two ways about it. It was bad enough having sheep on the range, clouding the water holes and using up our grazing land, but now them fences is killing cattle."

Logan didn't like the way this conversation was going. He understood their anger. Just thinking about those fences made him mad as hell himself, but now there was a new problem. Katherine. She was there and determined to stay, and the fierce protectiveness he felt toward her surprised him. "It doesn't take much of a man to overrun two women and a kid. It wouldn't set well with me to find out someone had hurt one of the ladies."

Morris arched one brow with interest. He glanced over at Logan. "I saw the daughter in town right after Thorn's funeral. She's a looker. Heard she was your... guest, during the storm."

Logan's stare turned cold. "Be careful, John," was all he said. It was enough.

"No offense," Morris quickly replied.

Bromley scowled. "I don't give a rat's ass about the daughter. I'm telling you those fences have got to go, whatever it takes."

Logan twisted in his saddle. "Like hired guns, Ed?" he asked, remembering the rumors.

"Maybe." Bromley shrugged.

Logan frowned. "We've got all summer to work this out. They'll probably give up and leave by next fall anyway, and the problem will take care of itself."

Bromley shook his head in disagreement. Rain streamed off his tan hat and soaked into the collar of his wool jacket. "There's one thing nobody's mentioned yet."

All eyes turned to him. "When Thorn put up them fences, it also closed off the headwaters to the creek. In a dry year, that creek is the only water for a helluva long way. If they decided there wasn't enough water to share..."

Hired guns, water rights, sheep in the heart of cattle country—Damn, Logan thought, it was a mess and Katherine was right in the middle.

Logan and the rest of the men were already in position when the first shafts of light broke over the eastern horizon. Rain, lighter than yesterday, continued to fall, turning the ground to a brown slush the consistency of river-bottom mud.

Logan stood up in the stirrups and gave one final look around. He was starting north with the herd—all of it. There were too many cattle and too few men. But it had to be done.

He gave a loud whistle with his fingers and hollered, "Move 'em out!"

The cowboys, scattered over half a square mile, answered with shouts and whistles and yells. The startled cattle surged to their feet and the men quickly moved to force them into a group and head them back to home range.

In a matter of a few hours the cattle were strung out in a thin, scraggly line, the strongest steers in the lead, the weaker ones behind. Soon the herd stretched out for miles in an almost unmanageable column.

Logan rode back and forth along the line, helping where he could, or just shouting instructions to his crew.

All day and into the night they pushed the cattle without stopping. Meals—antelope jerky and water—were taken in the saddle. There was no time to stop. By the second day, physical exhaustion and hours without sleep took their toll. Reactions were slow, tempers were short.

Some of the men managed to sleep in the saddle. Most, like Logan, did without.

Every muscle in his body hurt. He was tired right down to the bone, and he couldn't help wishing he had someone waiting for him at the end of the trail—someone to rub the ache in his shoulders and welcome him home. Someone just for him. It was a pleasing thought, one he'd been having a lot lately.

Overhead, ink black vultures circled in the sky like prophets of doom. The ground was littered with the bodies of dead cattle. It was going to be worse around the Bar T fences. He'd seen the snow-covered mounds last week.

Logan pulled his bandana over his nose to try to filter out the stench of rotting carcasses. They'd have to be burned. It was too late to skin them.

"It's enough to break a man's heart, ain't it, boss?" Slim said, dropping back to ride alongside Logan.

Logan didn't answer. It wasn't a question that required one. It was worse than heartbreaking, it could be the ruin of more than one of them. Had he been too optimistic?

It was late, about four, Logan guessed, when they neared the junction of Double Four range and the Thorn ranch. Logan started to notice the bodies of sheep. He wondered how badly the storm had affected the Thorn family.

"Boss," Slim called, riding up to Logan. His bright red shirt was spattered with mud. "I sure am glad we're almost there. Tomorrow noon, for sure."

"Tonight is more like it."

Slim thumbed his tan hat back off his forehead. "How'd you figure? We still gotta cross White Creek a couple of miles up ahead, then make a bend around the Bar T—"

"We're going straight through," Logan said flatly.

Slim's brown eyes widened in surprise. Then a smile spread across his weathered face. "Okay. Whatever you say. I'll tell the boys."

Half an hour later the first of the steers crossed White Creek without a problem. Logan made his way forward as the herd drew closer to that damned barbed wire fence Thorn had put around the Bar T. Then he cut through the herd. "Slim, you and George ride ahead and pull that fence down. Make sure you push the wire down into the mud so the cattle won't get tangled."

"Well, let's get her done, George." Slim spurred his chestnut forward and George nudged his bay and took off.

Logan reined over and rode back to the head of the column. The fence was about a mile farther on.

Logan reached it and the two cowboys a few minutes before the herd did. "You men cut straight across and head for the northwest corner of the Bar T. Pull down the fence. Cookie and the chuck wagon will be at the usual place about five miles beyond."

"Consider it done," George answered.

"Slim," Logan shouted to the retreating riders, "if you see any sheep, herd them out of the way. Don't hurt them, just move 'em far enough away that the cattle can get through."

Slim gave a wave, then he and George took off at an easy lope.

Logan waited at the fence as the first of the cattle came through. "Keep them moving, boys." This shortcut would save them a day. The sooner they finished this drive the better he'd like it.

For the next thirty minutes he sat astride his horse, watching as the bawling herd moved through the opening in the wire. He twisted in the saddle to check the angle of the sun sinking behind the Laramie Mountains. Turning back, he noticed a rider approaching from the northeast. Another followed. With a slight pressure of his leg, he turned Joker around and faced the oncoming riders, who were still about a mile away.

He took off his Stetson and rubbed his hand across his tired eyes, then settled his hat snugly on his forehead. Instinctively, his hand dropped to the Colt that hung low on his hip.

He heard the cattle moving behind him, but his attention was on the riders. The men would take care of the cattle. He would take care of trouble.

When the first rider came within a hundred yards, Logan recognized Daniel Thorn. To his surprise, the kid lifted his carbine and fired. The shot landed in the dirt inches from Joker's feet.

Joker reared and bucked.

"What the—" Logan hit the ground with a jolt that rattled his teeth. "Bloody hell!" he roared, coming quickly to his feet.

Cattle scattered in twenty different directions while two of the closest cowboys reined up near their boss.

Logan heard the familiar sharp click of Winchesters being cocked, but he didn't look at his men. He was already up and moving toward the kid who had reined to a stop ten feet away.

Logan was mad—damn mad, and the kid was about to be on the receiving end of all that anger.

Daniel glared at him, eyes contemptuous and hostile. "Now, look, McCloud—"

Without a word, Logan grabbed the carbine from Daniel's hands and hurled it away. Then, in what seemed to be one motion, he reached up, tangled both hands in the kid's shirtfront and hauled him out of the saddle.

"Logan, no!"

He heard Katherine's voice about the same instant he heard the kid's body hit the ground with a thud. His men laughed.

He was about to teach the kid some manners when Katherine stepped right in front of him.

"Logan! Stop, Logan!"

"Get out of my way, woman. I'm going to give this brother of yours a lesson he won't soon forget. He could have stampeded this whole damn herd, not to mention getting a few of your precious sheep trampled in the process."

His eyes were so sharp with fury that Katherine was momentarily startled out of her own rage. He was right about the stampede, she conceded, but the need to protect Daniel outweighed her fear of Logan's anger.

Logan took a step toward Daniel. Instinctively, she placed both hands on his chest to try to hold him back—as if anything could stop him once he made up his mind. "Don't you dare touch him!''

Daniel scrambled to his feet. His face went from surprise to rage. "Shut up, sis!" he shouted. Humiliation churned in his eyes. "I can fight my own battles. And you, you son of a bitch, get the hell off my land."

Logan put his hands on Katherine's shoulders and shifted her out of his way. Not a muscle moved in his face. Hands clenched at his sides, he advanced toward Daniel until he felt Katherine's hand close over his arm.

"Logan, don't!"

Logan glanced over his shoulder, some of his anger fading when he saw the apprehension in Katherine's eyes. She had every reason to be worried about her brother, he thought. He had fully intended to beat the living hell out of the kid, but he couldn't do it now, not while she was watching.

Brows knit in anger, he glared at Daniel. "Boy, the next time you draw on me, you'd better kill me, because next time I may not be in such a forgiving mood."

He gave Katherine a look that said he was dead serious.

She suddenly realized her hand was still on his arm. His breathing was rapid, harsh, and she knew he meant every word.

Logan glanced over at the two cowboys still sitting astride their horses, their rifles in their hands. "Get those cattle moving again," he snapped while he grabbed his hat from the ground and slapped it on his head. "Now!" he shouted when they hesitated. The two turned and rode away.

Logan started for his horse. This discussion was over, he thought.

Katherine had other ideas. Now that she'd managed to defuse the situation between Logan and her brother, she had to let Logan know he couldn't run roughshod over her, her brother or her land.

She glanced at the gaping hole in the fence and got angry all over again. "What are you doing here, Mr. McCloud?"

He had his reins in his hand when he turned back to her. "My job," he answered in an unflinching tone.

"Your job!" She was incredulous. "Since when is your job tearing down my fences?" She took a step toward him. "Who gave you the right to trespass on my property?"

He hardly seemed to hear her. "I have twenty thousand head of starving cattle to move, that gives me all the damned rights I need."

Daniel moved up to stand beside his sister, his retrieved carbine held loosely in his left hand. "McCloud, no one gives a damn about you or your cattle," he said disdainfully. "That's *your* problem. This is the last time I'm going to tell you to get off our land."

Logan dropped the reins to the ground again and started back toward Daniel. Katherine thought he looked as dark as Satan and twice as powerful. Rage filled his eyes. "I'm going through here because it's faster," he ground out, his voice brittle. "And because this has always been open range. And because I *hate* these fences. If I had my way, I'd tear them *all* down."

Katherine refused to cower. "This is Bar T land whether you like it or not and we're here to stay—sheep, fences and all."

He stared at her for a long minute. "I'm going through here," he repeated quietly.

Too quietly. It unsettled her nerves. Still, she wouldn't back down. She looked at him more closely. He suddenly seemed more tired than arrogant. Though she wished she didn't, she understood his plight. They were both ranchers. Both had suffered from the storm. She softened, just a little.

"This time, Mr. McCloud, I'll *allow* you to use our land," she said rather magnanimously. "I feel I owe you...one."

Logan swung up in the saddle.

She turned and strode briskly toward her horse. After all, he had saved her life and she always paid her debts.

Quickly mounting, she reined over and faced him. "Stay away from the sheep and replace the fence posts after you cross. If there are any problems, I'll hold you personally responsible."

He had already started away when she turned and called after him. "This makes us even."

Logan twisted in the saddle. "I'll tell you when we're even, sweetheart!" he shouted back, and rode off.

Katherine drew in a sharp breath. He was too far away to hear her angry reply. She glared at Daniel. "Don't say a word," she warned. With a silent curse, she jerked the reins and turned her horse toward home.

# Chapter Nine

Katherine wiped the sweat from her eyes with her sleeve. The soft flannel was sticky with a strange mixture of lanolin and blood. Glancing down, she realized blood covered nearly the entire front of her faded green shirt and denim pants.

They'd been docking lambs since three in the morning, and judging by the way things were going, this wasn't going to be a one-day job. No, she thought wearily, looking at the pens full of ewes and lambs, this would take days, probably very long days.

"Come on, sis," Daniel chided as one of the ranch hands slid another lamb, rump down, in her direction. "You can't slow down yet."

*Slow down, my foot! I'd like to stop, quit, pack it in and never see another sheep as long as I live.*

They'd been putting in sixteen-hour days since the storm quit. Six hundred sheep and nearly a hundred newborns had been lost, almost one-fifth of the herd. The survivors they'd driven down to the birthing pens near the ranch. She and Daniel couldn't take chances on losing any more of the lambs.

"Ma'am?"

She heard a voice and realized Will Murphy, one of the hands, was speaking to her.

"Sorry," she mumbled. She dabbed blue paint on the fuzzy white belly of the lamb in front of her.

Harry, Will's brother, grabbed another lamb and plopped it down on the foot-wide board Daniel had nailed to the top of the fence. As Harry dragged the lamb along, Daniel quickly sliced the little critter's ear, whacked off the tail and castrated it.

Katherine's job was branding, and while it was the least gruesome, it was the most messy. By the time the struggling, bawling lambs got to her, they were a bloody sight indeed.

So it went, hour after endless hour. There was no relief, either now or in the near future. They still had to drive the herd south for the shearing.

She rubbed the muscles in her shoulders, then headed for the outdoor stove. Her back muscles screamed in protest as she lifted another bucket of blue paint and went back to work.

Three days later, the end was in sight. They'd be finished with the docking today, Daniel had assured her. Dawn was just breaking as she strode across the yard, prepared to take her place at the fence.

It was shortly after the lunch break that she saw Marshal Dorn ride into the yard.

She watched him tie his bay next to Daniel's piebald by the front porch and walk toward them. Clean shaven, unusually tall and barrel chested, he looked every inch a marshal.

"Daniel," she prompted, "looks like we've got company." Daniel looked up from his work, then glanced over to the men working with them. "Take a break."

He and Katherine climbed over the fence and met the marshal in the middle of the yard.

"Ma'am," Marshal Dorn said, his tone firm but polite as he doffed his sweat-stained brown Stetson. He greeted Daniel with a nod. "I'd like to speak to you and your ma."

Katherine looked hard at the serious expression on the marshal's weathered face. "Mama's in the back, hanging wash. Maybe you'd better talk to us first."

Daniel wasted no time in coming to the point. "It's been two months since my father was killed. Did you find the bastard who did the shooting?"

The marshal turned. "No," he said flatly, "I didn't. And the way things look, I'm not going to." He hesitated a moment, then continued. "I've come by to tell you that I'm closing the case."

"What?" Daniel snarled, his eyes narrowed to slits as he glared at the marshal.

Katherine felt a tight, hard knot twist in her gut. "You mean you're giving up? A man is murdered and you're not going to do anything about it? You're just giving up?" Her tone was disbelieving as emotions, raw and painful, wrapped around her.

Dorn looked a little taken aback. He gazed at her from beneath his bushy brows, then drew a deep breath. "I've talked to everyone within twenty miles of here and no one saw or heard nothing—"

"Now there's a real surprise for you," Daniel interrupted, his tone thick with disdain. "Cattlemen don't turn in one of their own."

Katherine felt a cold edge of fury slice through her at the thought of her father's killer going unpunished. "I can't believe this. What kind of country is it when a man is murdered on his own land and the law doesn't do a thing?"

Her fingers curled into tight fists.

The marshal appeared unperturbed. "I know this is a hard thing to take for both of you." He glanced from Katherine to Daniel and back again. "But there's nothing else to go on. I got no choice but to close the case. If something turns up..."

Katherine turned away. She snatched her hat from her head and slapped it against her denim-clad thigh. Just like that, a murderer went free. It was incomprehensible. It was intolerable.

She turned back and glared hotly at the marshal. "Now what? Do you suggest we pretend it never happened? Maybe we could pretend my father...the dearest man that ever..." Her throat clogged with tears. "...that he isn't..." It was too much. Tears slid down her cheeks. She swiped at them, angry at her weakness. Her skin was awash in a mixture of her tears and blood. Bile rose to her throat.

The bright spring day grew dim around her. All she could see was blood—days and days of blood.

She turned and ran to the porch, where she mounted Daniel's horse.

Daniel started after her. "Sis, wait!"

She hardly looked at him. "I need some time. I'll be back later."

Daniel held the gelding's bridle. "Sis, I—"

"Not now, Daniel." Katherine jerked on the reins and took off out of the yard at a full gallop.

She didn't know how long she rode or where she was going. She only knew she couldn't stand any more—no more dirt, no more blood, no more pain.

When she spotted White Creek near the southern boundary of their property, she rode into the shelter of the budding cottonwoods and dismounted. She couldn't seem to stop her tears.

She'd been sure the law would bring the killer to justice. All she wanted was to turn the ranch over to Daniel and go back to Philadelphia.

She paced the edge of the creek. Her boots sank slightly into the soft, moist soil. *What am I doing here, in a bleak and harsh land where, if the weather doesn't kill you, the people do?*

She trembled inside, she was so afraid, and angry and tired. Throwing herself down on the sweet grass, she cried.

"No, I'm not going to Cheyenne," Logan told Mary Rosa firmly. "You of all people should know that. I'm only here now to pick up a couple of clean shirts and some supplies.''

"You always go to the Johnsons' party," Mary Rosa said coming back from the pantry. She put the mason jars of stewed tomatoes on the counter by the sink. "People will be mighty disappointed...especially Melissa," she added with feigned innocence.

"God sakes, Mary Rosa, are you that anxious to marry me off?" Frowning, Logan looked across the kitchen at her.

"Melissa and you were pretty close for a while there and—"

"And never mind. My love life is my own business, thank you very much." Logan's frown deepened.

Mary Rosa wiped her hands on the front of her pristine white apron and leaned back against the kitchen counter. "You sound like a man with interests somewhere else. Like a certain sheep-rancher's daughter."

"I've gotta get going," Logan answered dryly.

Mary Rosa smiled at his discomfort.

"For a man in such a hurry, I see you had time to take a bath and help yourself to some chicken stew."

"Sure," he teased, his smile returning. "I'm the boss. I get some benefits, don't I?" He carried his dish over to the sink. Living in a house full of women had trained him well.

Dropping the white china in the pan of soapy water, he gave her a wink. The last two weeks had gone well—as well as possible. The drive had finished without a hitch. That little go-around with Katherine was forgotten, though he had the feeling it wasn't the last time he and Daniel would go at it.

Still, he had gotten his way and he'd been over his anger—most of it—by the next day. Hell, he admired the lady's stand.

But taking that shortcut hadn't helped much with losses. They were high. About three thousand head, near as he'd been able to figure. Coupled with the two earlier storms, well, it was going to be rough on the smaller ranches. The Double Four, being so large, was faring better than most.

Logan's real concern was the cattle that had died against the fences. There was a lot of grumbling among the ranchers. Talk of tearing down the wire and running the Thorns out was escalating. So far it was *only* talk but—

"Hello in the house!" a male voice called from the direction of the back porch.

Logan started across the kitchen. He'd only taken two steps when Bob Dorn poked his head around the half-open door.

"Bob, you ol' son of a—" Logan broke off, grinning at his aunt.

A bright smile spread across Mary Rosa's face as she moved toward the door. "Don't stand on formality around here, Bob. Come on in," she cheerfully admonished the waiting marshal.

Logan welcomed his old friend with a handshake. "Nice to see you, Bob. Have a seat. You want something to eat?"

"Sounds mighty fine." The chair scraped on the clean pine floor as Bob pulled it away from the kitchen table. Sitting down sideways in the chair, he hooked his arm over the back and glanced at Logan. "I'm on my way up to Fort Laramie to pick up a couple of prisoners they're holding for me." He tossed his Stetson on the chair next to him.

Mary Rosa served him a bowl of stew and some fresh cornbread, then took her usual place on the other side of the table. "The fort's a day's ride from here. You make a wrong turn?" she teased.

The marshal looked up from his stew. "Why, no," he answered with great seriousness. "Ma'am, I'd ride a week outa my way for some of your cookin'."

Logan saw the color rise in Mary Rosa's cheeks. These two were worse then a couple of kids. It was embarrassing. Logan stopped listening. If Bob had come to spark Mary Rosa, he thought, this was no place for him.

He went to his room and grabbed a couple of clean shirts and some socks from the wardrobe cabinet, then headed back toward the kitchen to let Mary Rosa know he was leaving. He chuckled. She probably wouldn't even notice.

As he rounded the corner of the doorway, something in the conversation caught his attention.

"I sure didn't mean to upset Miss Thorn like that."

Logan stopped at the mention of Katherine's name. He walked over to the table and sat down, the rolled shirts still tucked under his left arm.

"What's wrong with Katherine?" he asked.

The marshal looked puzzled for a moment. "Oh, you mean Miss Thorn," he corrected with an understanding nod.

Logan's mouth turned down in a frown. A feeling of dread prickled through his body. Something was wrong and he wanted to know what.

"Get down to it, Bob," he snapped.

Bob didn't seem to notice. "Well, I stopped by their place to tell them I hadn't found out who shot their pa and the way things is going . . . well . . . I'm closing the case."

Logan let go of the breath he suddenly realized he had been holding. She wasn't injured. He relaxed a little. The news was probably hard for her to understand, but in truth, he hadn't really expected the marshal to do more. How could you find a killer whom no one had seen?

"You said she was crying," Mary Rosa prompted. "She doesn't seem the type to cry easily. I would've expected her to be mad."

"Oh, at first she was real angry. Demanded that I keep on looking . . . you know. And I will, of course, it's just that I figure it's best to tell people straight out what's going on instead of gettin' their hopes up."

"At least she has her mother there. A woman *needs* comforting sometimes," Mary Rosa said pointedly.

"Yes, ma'am, except all of a sudden Miss Thorn, she took a notion to ride out. She climbed on her brother's horse and took off, hell bent for leather."

"Where did she go?" Logan asked.

Bob shrugged. "Don't know. She was headed south last I saw of her."

"Alone?"

"Appeared so."

Logan didn't like the sound of that. Even in daylight, this wasn't country for anyone to be riding around alone in. A muscle flexed in his cheek. That woman was determined to get herself into trouble. And he was determined to stop her.

"Look," he said abruptly, "I've got to get going... back to the branding. Bob, you're welcome to spend the night in the bunkhouse if you like, and Mary Rosa will give you dinner and breakfast before you head out."

"Thanks," Bob said, obviously pleased.

Logan slammed the back door and took the three porch steps in one leap. He stuffed the extra shirts in one of his saddlebags, then mounted up and headed south.

An hour later he was skirting the edge of the Bar T. No sign of Katherine. He reined to a stop near the spot where they'd had their little confrontation a few days ago. Meadowlarks sang a melodious tune and the late afternoon breeze was clean and sweet.

He stood in the stirrups and scanned the area. Nothing. This was stupid, he chided himself. What the hell was he doing out here? Katherine was probably long since back at her house. Besides, what was he going to do if he did find her—tell her he was worried? Well, he was. Or maybe tell her he'd been thinking about her for days, and nights, and that he needed to see her again.

This really was crazy. He shook his head, and had started to turn back when he heard a sound. He paused. Joker heard it too, his ears pricked up and he answered with a whinny.

Logan glanced in the direction of the trees along the creek bed. He could just make out the shape of a horse in the shadows of the cottonwoods. He glanced at the damned barbed wire fence. No way Joker could jump something he couldn't see, even if it was only four feet high.

Dismounting, he ground-tied Joker's reins. With one hand braced on the post, he swung over the wire and started walking toward the trees, three hundred yards away. If it was Daniel or one of the Bar T hands down there, he was going to have a fight on his hands explaining what he was doing on their land again.

He was near the edge of the trees when he saw her. She was sitting on a small rock, her back toward him. Her hair hung in a braid down her back. She didn't move, so he guessed she hadn't heard him approach. Lord, the lady sure took chances. He could have been anyone.

"What the hell are you doing out here alone?" he demanded, his earlier concern replaced with anger at the risk she was taking.

She jumped up and turned toward him. It was then he realized she was clad in her undergarments—some sort of white frilly things.

"And where the hell are your clothes?"

# Chapter Ten

"That's none of your business," she retaliated. Ignoring her state of undress, Katherine shouldered past him. She was too tired to be bullied and too emotionally drained to fight back. All she wanted was to be left alone. Was that too much to ask?

"Wait a minute!" Logan caught her wrist and turned her toward him.

"Let me go!" Katherine easily twisted free of his grasp and started away again. "What I do, where and when are no business of yours," she snapped. "Besides, you're trespassing again, McCloud." She stomped over to pick up the blood-stained clothes she'd rinsed and spread out to dry a couple of hours ago. "Maybe I should've let Daniel shoot you that day, after all."

"Not bloody likely," he growled. "Dammit, Katherine, I want to know what you think you're doing out here, alone, for God's sake. What if something...someone..." He folded his arms across his chest and glared at her, his eyes sparking with anger.

Katherine glared right back. He could get angry all he wanted. He didn't own her. All she'd wanted was a little peace. You'd think in the middle of nowhere, she could be alone for an hour or two!

A quick glance told her Logan showed no indication of leaving. He looked as dark and immovable as the Black Hills.

Katherine snatched up her denim pants, yanked them on and headed for a nearby cottonwood to retrieve her shirt from a low-hanging branch.

She tugged on the thread-bare flannel, but it caught on the limb and refused to budge. She reached up with both hands and tugged.

She glanced back at him. "Why won't you understand that all I want is to be left alone?" She heard the rip the same instant she felt the fabric give. Still, it didn't release.

Logan came up beside her. He unhooked the material from the branch and wordlessly handed it to her.

Katherine stared at the tattered shirt. She felt as if the very fabric of her life was dissolving in the same way.

All her confidence had evaporated under days of back-breaking work and sleepless nights of wishing things had remained unchanged—wishing her father was still alive and she was back in her wonderful little hat shop in Philadelphia. *Why* did things have to change? It wasn't fair!

Tears, fresh and hot, slipped down her cheeks. Her hands curled into fists. Her nails dug into her palms. Damnation, she was sure she'd cried herself out by now.

She spun away and fussed with trying to put the shirt on, but the tear had effectively shredded the front and made all her efforts useless. She swallowed the lump in her throat. She had to get out of here.

She took one step and slammed into Logan's broad chest. She hadn't even heard him come around to stand in front of her.

She tried to look away, but he caught her face in his hands and looked at her with those fiery black eyes. "I'm tired," she admitted with a weary sigh.

His tone was hushed. "I know." He kissed her forehead.

It felt so nice, his touch on her skin. "I'm exhausted from the problems—"

He lightly kissed her cheek. "I know."

"I'm tired of the sheep—"

"Me, too," he answered with a half smile, and kissed her other cheek. "And you miss your father," he added pointedly.

Pain, sharp and real, sliced through her. "Yes! Dear God, yes," she told him, knowing *that* was the real source of anger for her. "I want him back..." Uncomfortable sharing her feelings, she tried once more to move away, but Logan grabbed her shoulders and held her. He gave her a long, slow look.

"I understand, darlin'," he told her in a voice filled with concern. "Believe me, I do. It's been eight years since my father died and I still think of that Texas cowboy every day."

She could see the compassion in his eyes. He made it too easy, too safe, for the hurt and anger she'd controlled these past months to seep to the surface. If she ever let go, ever acknowledged the feelings, would she be able to control them again? She was terrified at the thought. Who would help her put her life back together? If she allowed herself to fall apart, who would help her family?

She closed her eyes and struggled to regain her composure. "I feel so..."

"Empty," he supplied, and she nodded.

He gave her a little smile and lightly kissed her cheek again. "Oh, Angel," he murmured, holding her face once more, "I wish I could give you the answers you want. I *can* tell you that after a while, all you remember are the good times, and the memories become a comfort, not a hurt."

Katherine leaned her forehead into the curve of his broad shoulder and let her arms loop around his waist. He smelled like leather and sunshine. Her hands splayed against the soft chambray fabric of his shirt and the hard muscles beneath it. He was strong, warm and alive. For a moment she just stood there, allowing the steady beating of his heart to soothe her.

"It gets easier," she heard him say against the top of her head. Then he leaned back slightly, one hand curved around her shoulder, the other pushing a strand of hair back from her face. Looking into her eyes, he promised, "Time helps . . . and people. People who care about you."

She closed her eyes, suddenly very aware of how gentle and soothing his hands felt against her skin. The anger and fear inside her started to dissolve, replaced with a calm, sure feeling of security. She turned her face slightly, pressing her cheek into his callused palm. Did it make her weak, this need in her to be comforted?

Logan looked down into Katherine's tear-washed face. A knot formed in his chest. He hated seeing her like this—so terribly alone. He wished there were some magic words he could utter to change her life and the hurt in it.

He offered her the only thing he could. "I'm here for you," he said simply.

For Katherine, the words were like salve on an open wound, easing the rawness. "I'm glad you came, Logan," she replied softly. And it was true. She was glad he was here. It seemed he was always there when she was in need.

"Are you, Angel?"

"Yes." Her lips turned up in a glimmer of a smile.

He arched one dark brow. "Even if I am a . . . cowboy?" He traced the edge of her ear with the tip of one finger, thinking how beautiful she was and how much he wanted her.

"You're not an ordinary cowboy," she contradicted.

His hand moved around to cradle the back of her neck, tilting her face upward. His gaze drifted from her eyes to her lips and back again. "Why, thank you, Angel." His tone was hushed. "I try never to be ordinary—in anything." He lowered his head.

The sensation of his mouth on hers was startling in its intensity. His lips were warm, enticing, inviting. His fingers massaged the tendons of her neck and his chest brushed her breasts.

Tiny prickles of heat skittered along her nerve endings, shutting out all other feeling, all other thought. It was everything she remembered and more, so much more. She couldn't move. She didn't try.

Logan was barely aware of her fingers digging into the tops of his arms. He felt more than heard the tiny moan that escaped her lips. He slipped his arm around her waist and pulled her carefully against him, then let his hand drift lower, to the base of her spine. The denim fabric of her pants was cool to his touch as he held her tightly against him.

She felt so good in his arms, so right. He didn't want to frighten her, but right this minute he needed her as much as she needed him.

"Let me help you, Angel. Trust me and I'll make the world go away."

His mouth slanted across hers, teasing a hunger in her that he knew was there—waiting. Slowly, relentlessly, he thrust his tongue inside, tasting her, savoring the sweetness he'd remembered all these weeks.

A heated rush turned Katherine's knees the consistency of warm syrup. Her whole body seemed alive with the sweet rapture that he was creating. For just a moment, instinct warned her against this force, this enticement, but before she could act, he renewed his sensual assault, raining light kisses along the bridge of her nose and the tip of her chin. Resistance dissolved like ice in the sun.

"Katherine," he murmured huskily. "My sweet, Katherine. I've missed you. I've wanted to feel you in my arms again."

With the pad of one finger, he traced the outline of her cheekbone and the edge of her jaw. Everywhere he touched, her skin felt heated, tingling.

Katherine's eyes fluttered open. All she could see was his face, tan from days in the sun. She saw his smile, that warm, lazy smile that made her shiver in its promise. His eyes were as dark as sable and just as soft, and they appeared to have the answers to all her unspoken questions.

Feather light, his mouth brushed across hers again and left her wanting more. His fingers worked her hair loose from its braid and let it cascade over her shoulders and across her breasts.

Logan sifted her hair through his fingers. He loved her hair, the feel of it, the rose scent of it.

"Beautiful Angel," he murmured. "So little joy in your life...so little pleasure. Let me show you the pleasures...."

He took her mouth again, and for Katherine there was no thought of resistance. There was no thought at all. His tongue moved in a ritual as old as time and it was an invitation her body couldn't refuse. When her tongue slipped inside his mouth, she heard him groan. He tensed and pulled her tighter against him.

Katherine trembled, every fiber of her being raw and aching with wanting. She clung to Logan, feeling the straining muscles of his broad back beneath her fingers. The more she touched, the more she wanted. Her nerves were on fire and a demanding desire she'd never guessed existed pounded through her body.

His mouth caressed her throat and she arched back, welcoming his kisses. Logan's breath fanned her heated skin. She wove her fingers into his hair; it was soft, like silken threads.

Deftly, Logan slipped the torn flannel shirt from her shoulders and tossed it aside. He let his hands play across her shoulders, down her bare arms and up again, delighting in the soft, satiny feel of her against his work-roughened hands. His heart pounded painfully in his chest and he had to remind himself to breath. Dear God, she set him on fire.

He nuzzled the tender skin beneath her jaw, then teased the back of her ear with his tongue. The shudder that passed through her was slight, but he took encouragement from it. Slipping the straps of her camisole from her shoulders, he reached for the satin ties of her bodice, surprised to see his fingers shake.

Reason, faint but insistent, filtered through to Katherine. She tried to form the words, but by the time she did, the first of the ties had fallen away. "We can't," she whispered weakly.

Her voice sounded feeble even to her own ears, drowned out by the drumming of her heart. The only thing that she could focus on was Logan's handsome face, his dark, dark eyes, fiery with passion, and his smile, lush and seductive.

"You take my breath away," he murmured as he tugged on the last ribbon, letting it drift from his fingers. Her camisole fell open. He pushed the straps down her arms and let the fabric fall away.

She was magnificent. Her wild silken mane fell over one shoulder, partially concealing one breast. As she looked at him, uncertainty was clear in her sapphire eyes and he thought perhaps she meant to turn away. Wrapping his fingers lightly around the tops of her arms, he told himself he wouldn't die if she did.

But desire coursed through his body and his heart beat against his ribs like a wild-horse stampede. He wasn't totally sure he *would* survive.

"Let me," he said in a voice raw with passion, then took her small hands in his large ones. He lifted them to his mouth, kissing and licking each palm in turn, then each individual finger, before he draped her arms around his neck, kissing the inside of each elbow.

A delicious shiver ran down Katherine's spine. She was mesmerized, caught in the black fire of his eyes. He was promise and temptation, and she wanted him. Dear God, how she wanted him.

His gaze never left hers while his hands glided up her arms to her shoulders, then drifted down her bare rib cage and curved under her breasts. His thumbs caressed each nipple again and again, sending shockwaves of pleasure clear down to her bare toes. Her nipples puckered and hardened into tiny aching nubs and a spiraling warmth built in the core of her, reaching, reaching.

"It's heaven," she breathed, thinking nothing could feel as wonderful as this.

"I know," he confirmed, thinking of the other delights he wanted to share with her.

He lowered his head, blazing a moist, heated path down her slender neck and across her chest. His mouth touched her nipple in a gentle suckling kiss that turned her insides to molten lava. He nipped at the overly sensitized skin, then laved the spot with his tongue.

Katherine arched back. Her fingers thrust through his hair, pulling him closer, demanding more of this pleasure-pain that she was just now coming to understand.

He kissed the top of her breast and the deep valley between. He wanted to devour her, inch by delicious inch. Excitement built in him like fast-moving thunderclouds on the open plains. He nibbled at her ears and the sensitive corners of her mouth. He wanted every part of him touching every part of her.

Katherine was hot, as if fire, not blood, were coursing through her veins. A throbbing ache coiled tightly between her legs, making her cry out with driving, desperate need.

"Logan. Please..." she moaned against his lips. The longing was too great, the pleasure too intense for her to bear. But instead of pulling away, she wrapped her hands around Logan's neck and pulled him closer, her body refusing to relinquish the powerful sensation he was creating in her.

Logan released the buttons on her trousers, and in one motion pushed them and her pantalets to her bare ankles. He leaned back, desperate to see her, all of her. His gaze traveled the length of her slender shoulders, high firm breasts, gently rounded hips and long, long legs. How he loved long legs. He reached to stroke her thigh.

Katherine moved to cover herself. He didn't stop her. With the tips of his fingers, he lifted her face toward him.

"Look at me," he gently ordered.

She did.

"You're beautiful." He took a slow breath. "I've never wanted any woman as much as I want you." Lifting her hands, he placed them palms down against his chest. With gentle pressure he held them there while he looked directly into her eyes, waiting, willing her to feel as he did.

He got his answer in a slight curving of her lips. It was enough. He scooped her up in his arms and carried her to the fresh green grass by the side of the creek. He dropped to his knees, then lowered her to the ground. He made quick work of removing his clothes, then moved to cover her with his body, reveling in the feeling of her heated flesh against him.

She felt his weight for an instant before he propped himself on his elbows, the hard evidence of his manhood pressed against her abdomen. For a moment she was frightened.

*This can't be happening,* the distant voice of logic called. *I can't* let *this happen....*

But her body was consumed in desire and refused to listen. Her breath came in shallow gulps. Logan's mouth devoured hers, his hand stroking her from hip to breast. The mat of hair on his chest prickled the skin of her breast. Slowly, she draped her hands over his bare shoulders. His skin was smooth against her shaking fingers. She let her hands move cautiously down his back, exploring the corded muscles there, feeling the strength of him as her hands glided to his waist.

Logan watched the play of emotions on her face as she inched her way along his body, and he wondered if she had any idea of the excitement she was building in him. As her touch became bolder, surer, white-hot desire coursed through him. He couldn't get enough of her, of seeing her, touching her, tasting her, loving her. He wanted all of her— her determination, her pride, her anger and her tears.

His mouth sought her bare nipples once more, this time sucking and licking until she moaned with the pleasure of it.

He shifted his body to one side. His hand glided slowly over her ribs and the gentle swell of her abdomen, and lower, seeking the soft golden hair at the junction of her thighs.

Logan drew two fingers across the warm, heated entrance to her, feeling the slick wetness there. Katherine gasped. It excited him to watch her, knowing she was experiencing passion for the first time, selfishly glad it was with him.

"There's so much I want to show you, to give you," he whispered against her lips, stroking her wetness lightly.

Katherine held her breath as if to hold on to the exquisite sensation that spread through her. It was like being drenched in sun-warmed honey. She could never have imagined the sensual paradise that Logan created with his touch and word and kiss.

"Feel the fire, Katherine," Logan said softly against her flushed cheek as he stroked her core once again, much deeper this time. "I'm on fire, too."

Her eyes flew open and she saw Logan's face, damp and flushed with passion. His voice was raw, husky. "Say yes, Katherine. I need to hear you say it."

Katherine knew what he was asking, what he was offering. In some far distant corner of her mind, a feeble voice said she should stop this madness.

Instead, her arms slipped around his shoulders. Her mouth sought his. A muffled sound escaped her lips as he moved to cover her again. His knee pressed between hers, forcing her legs apart. She felt him poised against her. The entire focus of her world centered on the hot throbbing demand between her legs. Her pulse beat frantically in her ears and her body strained toward him.

"Yes," she said, knowing she should stop him, knowing she didn't want to. "Yes, Logan."

"Yes," he repeated. It was his last coherent thought before need consumed him. He eased into her waiting body and buried himself in the sweetness there. He felt her go rigid beneath him and he lay still, giving her a chance to accept him.

His hand curved around her waist as if to reassure her, to tell her he'd never, ever, hurt her again.

When he felt her relax he began moving inside her, gently, deliberately. He took his time, wanting to please her. Slowly, he withdrew, then slid in with exquisite care, letting her lush warmth wrap around him. She was everything he'd ever imagined, every erotic fantasy he'd ever had.

Katherine welcomed him, feeling as though the greatest wonder in life was opening to her, showing her the enchantment that man and woman can give each other.

And all the while, he whispered words of promise and temptation against her ear. He stroked and fondled, kissed and enticed until, wet and lush, she clung to him and copied his rhythm, seeking release to this sweet torment.

Logan strained to maintain control until she was ready. He moved with slow, powerful strokes and felt her first tiny tremors. He glided fully, deeply into her once more.

Her nails dug into his shoulders "Logan..." she pleaded, arching against him, writhing beneath him.

"Angel," he murmured against her ear, then gave in to his own driving need. He pulled her close, wanting to feel her release with his own. He increased the rhythm, taking them both higher and higher.

Katherine was in a pleasure-driven agony. Desperately, her body sought that which her mind didn't understand. Clutching him, she met him stroke for stroke, and suddenly she felt her body find the heaven it was seeking. A feeling too intense to name, shuddered through her in wave after wave of pure, blinding, blissful ecstasy.

Breathing labored, Logan poured himself into her lush warmth. The world around him dissolved, melted away. Nothing, no one, had ever made him feel this glorious, this complete.

She *was* extraordinary. She'd met him with a passion that equaled his own. In a heartbeat he knew he'd found what was missing in his life—Katherine Thorn. And he wanted her.

Forever.

He rolled over on his back and easily lifted her on top of him. Bodies slick with perspiration, they lay there in the warm, dappled sunlight, wrapped in each other's arms.

Katherine's thoughts were muddled. How could she have known the power, the all-enveloping force that had claimed her body and touched her soul? She was terrified by the change in her.

Still wrapped in his arms, she opened her eyes. He was looking at her with an expression she couldn't read.

"I'll make arrangements with the preacher," he said quietly. "We'll be married right away."

## Chapter Eleven

Her heart skipped a beat. The man who'd just rearranged her world the way an earthquake changes the path of rivers had asked her to marry him.

For a long moment she just stared into his soft, smiling eyes. She tried to imagine waking up every morning to find Logan, warm and sleepy, lying next to her—his hair rumpled from sleep, his lean, powerful body stretched out against hers. Her heart rate took off like a jackrabbit.

"You want to get married?" she repeated numbly.

"I want to do a lot of things, Angel." He kissed her chin while his hand stroked her bare back.

Katherine felt suddenly mortified at her nakedness and the way she was sprawled on top of Logan's equally naked body. More than that, she was thunderstruck by what she'd just done.

She squirmed and got up, needing some distance to think. With as much calm as she could muster, she walked to where she'd left her clothes, all the while trying to pretend Logan wasn't staring at her bare behind. There was no help for it, so she stiffened her spine and proudly squared her shoulders.

The late-afternoon sun cast flickering shadows on her clothes, still pooled on the ground where she'd stepped out of them with hardly a hesitation. Good Lord, what kind of woman was she? For a moment she was filled with shame and self-reproach. She'd never meant things to go this far. While she could blame Logan for enticing from her a passion she'd never guessed existed, *she* was the one who had said yes. Worse yet, she'd enjoyed every minute.

Her fingers trembled as she pulled on her pantalets and bodice. She heard Logan moving around behind her and guessed he was getting dressed also. He was humming some abstract little tune, pausing now and then to talk about wedding plans.

"I never considered marriage," she told him honestly.

He chuckled. "Not ever?"

"Well, not in the near future." And certainly not to a cattleman, even if he was the handsomest man she'd ever seen.

Tying her satin ribbons, she glanced over her shoulder at Logan. His seductive smile left no doubt that he wanted her, at least the way any man wants a woman. Lord knew he made her feel desirable. And more than that, he made her feel safe—something she felt nowhere else, with no one else.

She fastened the buttons on her denim trousers and pulled on the torn shirt which she tucked in. Her back was still toward Logan when she plopped down on the ground to put on her socks and boots.

She heard him talking, his voice coming closer.

" . . . You'll sell the ranch to me, of course, and—"

"Now wait a minute!" Katherine surged to her feet and spun around to face him. "Did you say 'sell the ranch'?" she asked him carefully, letting her mind focus on the plans he was making instead of her own daydreaming.

He moved toward her. "Yes. You'll sell the ranch to me and I'll take care of your family."

But it was her family, not his. And it was *her* responsibility to take care of them. Could she just turn everything over to Logan?

"What about Daniel?"

She saw Logan's eyes narrow a little, but he didn't falter—much.

"He can live with us if you want him to," he said in a less-than-enthusiastic tone, "but I think boarding school in the East would be a better choice. I know a couple of good ones we could—"

"Send Daniel away?" Sadness washed over her at the thought of being separated from her brother when they'd just been reunited after so long. "Daniel doesn't want to go to school. He wants to run the ranch."

Logan frowned. He reached out and pushed the hair back from her shoulder.

"We'll work it out...somehow."

"I doubt it."

"Why not?"

"Because Daniel thinks you're involved with my father's murder."

Logan stilled. His hand rested lightly on her shoulder. Very softly he asked, "Do you?"

She looked into his questioning gaze. "No."

"Thank you, Angel." His hand traveled back and forth across the top of her shoulder tracing the outline of her collarbone beneath the flannel. "Now, about the ceremony, I can send for the preacher from Cheyenne—"

"What about my mother?"

He looked momentarily confused. "She'll come to the ceremony...I hope. Afterward, we'll have her sell the ranch to me and she can live with us, if you'd like. I can add to the house without any problem, so she'd have her own room, and—"

"She doesn't want a room. She wants her own home. It's all she ever wanted and now she's got it."

"Well, I don't think it would be wise for her to stay out there on that little place all alone. I'm sure when we tell her about our plans, she'll understand."

How could she tell her family what she'd done? Her indiscretion would change not only her life but theirs as well. How could she tell them she was breaking all her promises to them, destroying all their plans?

She looked at Logan for a long, long minute, trying to sort things through in her mind. She and Logan had given in to desire, but it was just that, nothing more. Could she turn her back on everyone dear to her and spend the rest of her life with Logan just to absolve one moment of lust?

She knew there could be only one answer. "I can't marry you, Logan."

Logan's expression turned serious. The grin slipped from his face. "Why not?" His fingers tightened ever so slightly on her shoulders, then he let go, dropping his hands back to his sides.

She had to end it. She stepped away.

"Look," he began carefully, thinking perhaps it was embarrassment or uncertainty that colored her words. "The first time is always—"

She spun around to face him, her jaw set, her lips drawn into tight lines. "The first and *last* time."

A riot of tension started to form in his gut. He was offering her his world, his protection, a way off that damnable sheep ranch, and she was turning him down flat.

The silence lengthened between them like an ever-widening ocean. He loved her. He'd made love to her. And now he was offering her marriage. "Would being married to me be so terrible?" he found himself asking, trying to understand what he'd done wrong. He reached for her.

"Don't touch me!"

Logan stood stock-still. He watched the emotions play across her face, which was pale except for the slight trace of pink in her cheeks. He knew. She was serious.

The truth of it cut into him like a knife. That quickly, all his joy was gone. The flame of passion that had warmed him moments ago flickered and died, leaving a cold emptiness in its place.

"Perhaps, under the circumstances, you should reconsider your decision. I'm offering to marry you," he told her, unable to keep the sharp edge from his voice.

"Just like that?" she snapped back.

"No... well, yes, dammit."

She shot him an icy stare. "No."

"What else do you expect me to do? I can't change what's happened, though right this minute, God knows, I would if I could," he said with a gentle sigh.

His words hit her like a slap in the face. He regretted making love to her. Making love, now there was a misnomer! You couldn't *make* love, and Logan obviously didn't love her. And she absolutely didn't—couldn't—love Logan. It would turn her world up side down, not to mention end all her dreams and hopes for her future.

Katherine snatched up her hat, shoved her hair under the crown and started toward her horse. "Allow me to release you from any and all obligations you may feel," she said as she walked.

Logan stalked her steps. "What if you're pregnant?"

She whirled around to face him. She'd never given that a thought. How could she have been so unthinking? But then again, in Logan's arms she never could think clearly. "I'm not," she told him, hoping that saying it would make it so.

"You can't be certain, at least not for a while. If you are, I damn well want to know."

Katherine gave him a curt nod and started to turn.

"Woman, don't try to dismiss me. You might intimidate other men with that distant manner and haughty stare, but not me. I know you." His mouth turned up in a cold smile. "I know *every* inch of you."

Katherine's head snapped around. "I said it's over, and if you ever mention this to me or to anyone..."

Something flashed in his eyes—hurt or sadness, she couldn't tell. Whatever it was, it was quickly replaced with a hard gleam. "Well, now, thanks for telling me. Here I was planning on putting an announcement in Sunday's edition of the *Cheyenne Leader*," he retorted, his voice thick with sarcasm. "Logan McCloud and Katherine Thorn had sex and then the lady promptly turned down his offer of marriage."

"Dammit, Logan, you can't ask me to choose you over my family!" she cried.

His tone was quiet. "Have it your way, sweetheart."

The sun was just coming up over the horizon, casting a pale pink glow in the cloudless sky. The slam of the tailgate on the chuck wagon announced that breakfast would soon be ready. Logan didn't care.

Around him, men sat up, stretched and yawned. Even as they rolled to their feet, they were starting to grumble and complain about everything from Cookie's food to life in general. Typical cowboy stuff, Logan thought, throwing back his blanket and getting up.

Of course, he hadn't been asleep yet. Not that he hadn't tried. He'd tried damn hard, but sleep required him to put Katherine out of his mind, and that was something he didn't seem to be able to do. At least not right now—not since she'd refused him.

He grabbed his bedroll, folded it and tossed it into the back of the supply wagon. Cookie was making coffee. That's what he needed—a mug of coffee, black and thick enough to float a horseshoe in.

There was a late-April chill in the air, and Logan briskly rubbed his arms a couple of times as he closed the distance to the chuck wagon.

"Morning," Cookie said, looking up from the pan of bacon he was stirring.

Logan scowled. "Coffee," he muttered, not wanting to make small talk.

Cookie handed Logan a gray metal mug, a small dent in one side.

Logan bent and poured his own coffee.

"Mornin'," Pete said with a grin.

Logan groaned inwardly, sipped his coffee and turned away. How the hell could people smile before at least three cups of coffee?

"Sleep well?" Pete asked, walking over to stand next to him. The steam from his mug turned to white mist in the clean air.

Logan nodded. It wasn't true, but he had no intention of discussing his restlessness with Pete or anyone else.

Draining the last contents from his cup, he retrieved his narrow leather chaps from a hook on the side of the wagon. He let the cup balance on the edge of the unpainted wheel while he fastened the sweat-stained leather around his thighs.

Heading back for a refill of the eye-opener, he started giving orders for the day. He was roundup boss and he had a job to do. All the ranches pooled men and resources for one large branding operation instead of each trying to do it separately. It made more sense, since the herds often intermingled on the open range. Trying to separate them was too much trouble.

"Pete, I want six fires going today instead of four." He glanced back over his shoulder. "Send two-dozen men out to keep pushing the strays in toward the branding area." He took another swallow and looked over the rim of his cup. Pete was helping himself to bacon and biscuits.

"Pete! Are you listening to me?"

"Sure," Pete said casually before he bit off a piece of biscuit.

Logan drained the contents of his cup once more, adjusted his hat more securely on his head and headed for the remuda. When none of the other men seemed to be following, Logan turned back. "Well, let's go. We've got work to do and I don't want to be out here all summer."

All faces turned in his direction. Even Pete paused in mid-chew. He gulped. "Can't it wait? The men haven't had chow yet."

Logan was being pushed by personal demons. He wanted to be busy. He wanted to work so he'd have something to think about besides the scene that kept repeating itself in his head.

Katherine wild and passionate in his arms, more lush and seductive than he'd ever imagined. Him proposing to her, and Katherine turning him down—flat.

He shook off the image and focused on the men, who were all staring at him expectantly.

"Twenty minutes," he told them gruffly and continued on to the remuda.

Logan had Joker saddled in less than two minutes. He led him away from the rope corral and was about to swing up in the saddle when Pete's voice stopped him.

"Looks like we got company." Pete's gaze turned toward the south and a lone rider on a black gelding. He tossed his empty plate down and walked over to Logan. "Why is it I never like seeing strangers?" he muttered, staring at the approaching man.

The rider came to a halt. "Mornin' to you folks," he said with a southern drawl. A thin coating of dust covered his dark brown shirt. He lifted his black hat and wiped his forehead with the crook of his elbow.

"Mornin'" Pete returned.

"Chow's on," Logan said, eyeing the sandy-haired man. "Take a plate, if you're inclined." Western hospitality required as much, no questions asked.

The man nodded and swung down. The gelding pawed the ground restlessly, and the rider soothed the horse with a pat.

"I appreciate the invite," the man said. His gaze moved from Pete to Logan. "You're McCloud, ain't you?"

"That's right," Logan acknowledged. The man didn't look familiar. For that matter, he didn't look like a cowboy, not dressed as he was in buckskin pants and knee-high moccasins.

The stranger hesitated. He regarded Logan with eyes pale and cold as a winter sky.

"Name's Jake Faraday," the man told them directly.

Someone gave a low whistle. Obviously Logan wasn't the only man who had heard of Faraday. That about summed up Logan's reaction as he looked hard at the lean man standing in front of him.

What the hell was a gunfighter doing in Clearwater, especially one with Faraday's reputation? Logan was acutely aware that all conversation around them had ceased. Even Pete was at a loss for words.

Hearsay had it that Faraday had killed twelve men. Logan didn't always believe rumors, but the man *had* made quite a name for himself working for Colonel Dodge and more recently providing protection for mine shipments in Colorado.

There'd been rumors around town for months that some of the cattle ranchers were planning to bring in a fast gun. Had some damn fool actually gone and done it? Perfect, Logan thought, his already simmering temper moving up to a slow boil. This could push a bad situation right into a disaster.

"I've heard of you." Logan glanced at the Smith & Wesson Schofield hung low on the man's left hip. "Gun for hire."

"I've done that," Jake answered directly. He'd done a lot of things in the fifteen years since he'd gotten out of a Yankee prison. He'd worked cattle and horses, discovered he was no good at gambling and was very good with a gun. A year with Mosby's Rangers had taught him well.

McCloud raked him with a stare that was none too friendly. Jake wondered if he'd made a mistake. He'd been tempted to lie about who he was, but it was only a fleeting thought. He had his own code of ethics and it didn't include lying.

Logan's tone was brisk when he asked, "Who told you to look for me?"

"Big Jim Poteet. He said if I was ever up this way you was the man to see for a job." Jake's gaze never wavered. He'd hoped to find work here. The kind that didn't require him looking over his shoulder every minute. He was tired of always being alone, of sitting with his back to the wall in every saloon. Hell, at forty-one he was tired of saloons.

"Big Jim, huh?" Logan arched one dark brow with interest. He knew and respected the manager of the Red Rover Mine. The McClouds were half owners in the gold-mining venture. "How is it you know Jim?"

Jake straightened and hooked his thumbs over the top of his gun belt. "I did a little work for him awhile back."

The killing kind, Logan thought. "I don't need a fast gun," he told him flatly.

Jake felt his heart sink but he kept his expression blank. He shifted his weight to one hip. He needed this job. It wasn't by accident that he was in Clearwater. "A man does what he has to to stay alive, Mr. McCloud. He don't always get a choice about it."

That gave Logan pause. There was something intriguing about Faraday. He didn't fit the gunfighter mold. The few he'd met tended to be flashy dressers and big talkers, preferring work with a gun over the hard, dirty work of ranching.

Logan looked at Faraday a long moment, then walked over and circled the big black the gunfighter had ridden in on. He ran an experienced hand over the withers, then across the flanks.

Ducking under the horse's neck, Logan said, "Nice animal." You could tell a lot about a man from the way he treated his horse. This one had been well cared for.

"Me and Jeb been together a long time," Jake volunteered with a touch of pride. He reached into his pocket and took out the makings for a cigarette. He sprinkled tobacco in the paper, rolled it and struck a match on the well-worn handle of his gun.

Logan paused. "You ever work cattle?"

Jake took a drag on the cigarette. "Worked for the Hales for a while."

The Hale brothers had a big spread down in the Texas Panhandle. A man had to know what he was doing to work for them. "How long?" Logan asked.

"Two... three years, thereabout."

Logan considered that statement. Something about Jake Faraday seemed genuine. More than that, he liked the way Jake made no excuses for who or what he was. Logan liked to play his hunches, and right now he had the feeling that Jake Faraday would be a good man to have around. Besides, this way he'd know where Faraday was and what he was up to.

"Okay," he decided. "I'll give you a try. The usual pay. You take your orders from Pete. He's foreman for the Double Four."

Jake straightened. "You can check on me if you want."

Logan walked back to his horse and swung up in the saddle. "No need," he said looking down. "I'll know soon enough."

Jake smiled, softening the sharp angles of his clean-shaven face. "Thanks," was all he said, but Logan had the feeling that was a lot coming from a man the likes of Faraday.

It was turning out to be quite a day, Logan thought, turning away and riding out through the herd. Right now, he needed to be moving, working, anything but sitting still. Very soon the men had the branding fires going. Irons were heated and the day's work began.

Logan took the job of roper. He cut the unbranded calves from the herd, roped them and dragged them to the fire to be branded and ear-notched. The whole procedure took less than five minutes, but they had thousands of calves to brand. As it was, they'd be at it for weeks.

After a couple of hours, the hard work cooled some of Logan's earlier anger. That was something, at least. Still, the ache in his gut was cold and sore, like he'd been kicked by a Missouri mule, and he had the feeling all the hard work in the world wouldn't make it go away.

Where the hell had he gone wrong? he asked himself over and over and over.

There was never any answer. At least, none he could understand. Dammit, he'd offered her marriage, his name, his life. He'd never asked a woman to marry him before. And when he finally did, she turned him down. That made him angry all over again.

Glancing up at the sun, he could tell it was close to noon. The men would stop soon for chow. He thought he'd skip the meal.

He wanted to be alone. A man needed privacy when he sulked and that was exactly what he was doing. He'd been wrong—totally and completely—about Katherine.

Sure, he knew they were an unlikely pair, but he hadn't cared. He'd figured he could work it out, the same way his father and mother had made a marriage work for over twenty years.

He sighed, feeling the loss. He'd been so sure that he and Katherine belonged together. He could feel the electricity every time they were in the same room. He'd thought Katherine cared for him. She'd given him her most precious gift, then calmly turned and walked away as if it meant nothing at all—as if *he* meant nothing at all.

The worst of it was that he still loved her and it still hurt like hell.

Katherine put the scissors down. She took a deep breath, then let her eyes flutter closed. With the tips of her index fingers, she rubbed her temples, trying to ease the ache that had plagued her all day.

"You all right, dear?" Sarah looked up from the dress material she was cutting on the kitchen table. "Let me get you some ergot drops—"

"It's okay, Mama," Katherine assured her, still rubbing her temples. "I spent too long working on the books this morning, that's all." She glanced up. The light streaming in the front window momentarily caused her to squint. "I was straining to read the numbers. Papa's handwriting wasn't the best.''

''I know,'' Sarah confirmed with a slight smile. She picked up her scissors and started cutting the muslin fabric again. ''Is everything all right—with the accounts, I mean?'' The metal blades made a rhythmic *clunk-thump* as they moved across the pine kitchen table.

''Everything's fine,'' Katherine assured her. ''If the price of wool stays up, we'll do just fine.'' Barely, she added to herself. There wasn't enough money to replace the nearly one-fifth of their flock that had died in the winter storms. But there was nothing she could do about that now. If they scrimped and saved, maybe by spring...

She sighed inwardly. They were on the edge of disaster. It was always the same, she thought as she rubbed her eyes, then forced herself to concentrate on the dressmaking. That, at least, brought back a lot of *good* memories—warm, cozy, childhood memories. Lord knew, she needed those right now.

''This is going to be a beautiful dress,'' Sarah said as she snipped the last corner of the fabric. ''I'm so glad you got the muslin when you were in town.'' She held the material up, admiring the tiny blue flowers on delicate green vines that patterned the white cloth. ''Reminds me of all the years when you were little and I'd make a dress for you every spring.''

''I remember. You always said it was for church, but I knew how much you loved to sew.''

''Was I that obvious?'' Sarah's lips turned up in a smile. ''I tried to be careful. Money was always so dear, but you were growing like a weed.'' She chuckled. ''And Daniel, too.''

Sarah stroked the soft white fabric. ''This reminds me of the material I used when you were twelve.''

Katherine returned the smile. ''Only that had pink flowers, like rose buds, I think.''

''That's the one. I'm surprised you remember.''

"It was my favorite and I nearly cried when it got too small."

Sarah chuckled again. "I let that dress out until I thought the seams would surely give way if you breathed hard. I never was able to find more and, of course, we weren't near the town where we'd bought it."

"We moved a lot then."

Sarah nodded suddenly feeling sad at the memory of so many towns, getting work anywhere they could, trying to save some money to get a place of their own again. The worst was the children were never anywhere long enough to attend school and though Sarah had taught them reading and ciphering she couldn't make up for the lack of friends.

Oh, she'd asked Charles to settle down several times, but he always said it wasn't the right place or they needed more money. And after a while, she stopped asking. It wasn't a wife's place to question her husband.

Besides, Charles had been a fine, hard working man, whom she respected, if not truly loved. He'd married her when she was beginning to think no one would ask, well, least ways, no one since . . .

She shook off the image of her first love, her first heart break. Goodness, she hadn't thought of him in years.

When Charles came along, she was already twenty-one, long past marriageable age in a farming community like Marysville. Most of the men were off fighting in the Confederate Army, the rest said she was too headstrong, too willful.

Maybe she was, but she knew Charles Thorn was her only chance and all she had to do was mend her ways, learn to bite her tongue. She did and was rewarded with a kind husband and two wonderful children.

She'd made the best of what life had to offer and had no regrets—not any that she had control over, at least.

"Mama?"

Sarah blinked. Her gaze focused on Katherine. "Sorry dear." She fussed with folding the pieces of cloth. "Daydreaming," she mumbled.

Katherine chuckled, then pointed to the navy cotton with thin white stripes she'd bought for her mother. "What about this?"

Sarah's mouth turned down in a small frown. "I appreciate you thinking of me, dear, but I'm in mourning and black is more fitting."

Katherine reached over and touched her mother's hand. She'd purchased the material on an impulse. She knew black was required for the first year, but the rules of etiquette didn't seem to apply west of the Mississippi. Besides, she was tired of seeing her mother in one faded dress after another. "Papa always liked you in blue."

Sarah gave a small shake of her head. "Folks will talk."

"People will say you're a kind, respectful woman who's never done anything to bring shame on her husband."

Sarah felt the tears well up behind her eyes at her daughter's kind words. She fingered the fabric, cool and smooth against her skin. "He did like me in blue, didn't he?" It wasn't her favorite color, pink was, but she'd never said so. Whatever Charles liked, she had told herself *she* liked.

"You need a new dress," Katherine added.

Sarah spread the cloth on the table. It was very dark navy—almost black. No one could say it was the least showy. "All right," she decided.

They started to work again. Katherine felt better. It was good to see her mother smile. Standing here in the small house, watching her mother, Katherine knew she'd made the right decision yesterday.

How could she have possibly looked this sweet woman in the eyes and calmly asked her to give up the home she treasured, just because her daughter had been foolish and indiscreet? How could she have asked Daniel to give up his dreams because of her?

She had never intended things to go as far as they did. She'd been so tired, and Logan's voice and hands worked such magic. Remembering made an exquisite tingling slide up her spine. Her fingers trembled as she tried to cut a straight line.

She paused, took a deep breath and glanced over at her mother, who was intent on what she was doing, thank goodness. For a long time this morning, Katherine had actually worried that she somehow looked different—that her mother would take one look at her and instantly recoil in shock. It was stupid, she realized, but she felt forever changed. She also felt ashamed of her weakness, of her selfish behavior, of her total thoughtlessness.

She'd been thinking only of herself. Actually, she hadn't been thinking at all. Once Logan's lips touched hers she had been lost, all her resolutions forgotten in a haze of desire. What was this feeling, this magic that Logan worked on her?

If she closed her eyes she could see herself lying naked in the sun, Logan's lean, powerful body entwined with hers as they joined in the ultimate act of passion.

Oh, God, could that have been her? The scissors dropped from her shaking fingers with a heavy thud. She quickly picked them up. Through her lashes, she looked at her mother, who shot her a questioning glance but blessedly said nothing. Could she possibly suspect?

No one must know. Even if it meant living her life alone. She'd made one mistake; she wouldn't compound it with another. She'd made the right decision—the only decision she could have made, and still be able to live with herself.

No one must ever know.

The front door banged open and Katherine visibly jumped. Daniel stormed in with all the fury of a swarm of hornets.

"They're dead. Every damned one of them!"

"Dead?" Katherine looked sharply at her brother. Her headache returned full force. "Who's dead?"

Sarah surged to her feet, her face drained of all color. Her hand covered her throat. "My Lord, Daniel, what's happened?"

"Just what I said," he shouted. "At least three dozen sheep are dead." Daniel paced back and forth near the kitchen table. "Damn that McCloud and every stinking cattleman from here to Cheyenne."

Katherine felt her own anger rise at her brother's behavior. She was in no mood for another one of Daniel's tirades. Her head hurt and this shouting wasn't helping, nor was the loss of any more sheep.

Taking a deep breath, she gazed into her brother's angry face. "Before you start accusing anyone of anything, maybe you'd better tell me exactly what it is you saw."

"Exactly what I saw," he repeated, mimicking her voice in a way that intensified the throbbing behind her eyes, "is dead sheep lying twisted and broken at the bottom of the ravine just north of here."

"It's possible they walked off the edge, isn't it?" Katherine returned hotly, rubbing her temples with the tips of her fingers.

Daniel made a derisive sound in the back of his throat. He snatched off his hat and slapped it repeatedly against his thigh. "Sure, it's possible they walked off the edge," he informed her sarcastically, "and it's possible Papa shot himself in the back."

Sarah gasped and sank down in one of the chairs.

"Daniel!" Katherine felt her blood turn to ice at the mention of her father's brutal death.

Daniel threw his hat down on the table and wrenched out of his plaid jacket, tossing it on the divan a few feet away. In a calmer tone he said, "Why won't you see that someone is doing everything they can to drive us out? Why do you insist on pretending nothing is going on?"

"I *do* see," Katherine answered. "I see that Papa is dead and that it's up to the three of us to keep this ranch going. I see that you're so determined to confront Logan McCloud and blame everything that happens on him that you don't stop to think what the repercussions might be.

"What's your plan? To ride over to the Double Four and shoot Logan dead? Assuming you could, of course, before he killed you."

A knot of hatred formed in Daniel's gut at the mention of the cattle rancher's name. Logan McCloud was responsible for all their troubles, one way or another. It was time McCloud knew that Daniel Thorn wouldn't be bullied or scared off. His mouth tightened into a hard line. "I don't care. I—"

"Exactly, you *don't* care," Katherine interrupted. Her anger boiled over and the words came bubbling out. "So with you lying dead somewhere, Mama and I will sell the ranch and go back to Philadelphia to live." She glanced over at her mother, who was silent, pale. "Of course, how Mama will ever get over losing both you and Papa is beyond me."

Katherine took a step closer and stood just inches from Daniel's face. "If somehow you managed to kill McCloud, of course, the rest of the ranchers around here wouldn't object at all. They'd probably just come in here and hang you." She paced away, too agitated to keep still, then promptly came back at him, pushing at his chest with the tip of one finger. "Now, you tell me which way it's going to be, because I want to start getting ready for when they bring your body home like they did Papa's."

"Katherine, for the love of God!" Sarah cried as tears slipped down her thin face.

"I'm sorry, Mama, but Daniel's got to get his temper under control if he's ever going to run this ranch."

Daniel dropped down into a chair. He hated it when Katherine got that holier-than-thou attitude. "I'm telling you, McCloud is responsible for all of this. Those sheep didn't walk off a cliff by themselves. Someone herded them off. If it wasn't McCloud, he damn sure knows who it was. You can bet nothing goes on around here that the head of the Cattlemen's Association doesn't know about."

"Logan is not the problem here, Daniel, you are," Katherine fired back at him. "You've got to stop thinking with your temper and start thinking with your brain. You're the one who was so adamant about keeping Papa's legacy going. Well then, work at it. The most important thing right now is getting the flock to the shearing pens. We need that money for winter feed. We can take care of the rest by moving the flock, or having the men keep a more watchful eye out."

Daniel took a deep breath. He knew she was right, at least about the shearing being important, but it filled him with bitterness, this helpless feeling. She just didn't understand. He was the man of the family and a man had to protect what was his, no matter what the cost. He sighed inwardly and decided he'd give in this time. But Logan McCloud wouldn't get away with this, nor would he get away with murder—marshal or no marshal.

Katherine looked at her brother's angry face and she could almost hear him thinking. She knew he wasn't going to let go of this grudge he felt for Logan.

She took a deep breath. What else could go wrong?

Six weeks later, she had her answer.

# Chapter Twelve

Katherine rested her forehead against the top rung of the corral, waiting for the rolling in her stomach to quit. Her heavy braid fell over her shoulder, baring her neck to the warm June sun. Her hands clenched the rough bark of the slender cottonwood pole.

Around her, meadowlarks sang as though they didn't have a care in the world. Why should they? They didn't have to explain to their families the awful, selfish mistake they'd made.

Her stomach rolled again and this time it wasn't due entirely to morning sickness, but to shame and limitless guilt over what her mistake would cost her and those she loved. How could she ever expect them to understand? She'd done something no decent woman would, and worse yet, she'd done it with a man who was diametrically opposed to everything she'd pledged to do. She'd lose her mother's respect and her brother's.

She wanted to scream. She wanted to kick something. She wanted to rant and rave and curse like a drunken cowboy. Good God, sometimes she hated being a woman!

This morning she'd realized she was going to have to go to Logan and ask him to marry her. She was going to have to humble herself and admit that all her brave words had been for nothing. It galled her to know that she had no choice. Even in a territory as progressive as Wyoming, where women could vote, own property and get a divorce, people still looked with disgust at a pregnant, unmarried woman. And the child was labeled illegitimate or worse. Prejudice was something she understood all too well as a sheep rancher in the middle of cattle country, and a woman in business.

But Katherine was an adult. She made choices fully understanding the risks. A child didn't have that opportunity and she wasn't about to make the innocent suffer for her mistake.

She took a deep breath, stiffened her spine and marched toward the barn.

In a few minutes, she had her horse saddled and was headed out of the barn. She couldn't have felt any more grim if she was going to her own execution.

Daniel was just coming out of the house when she rode across the yard. He waved and hollered, "Where're you going?"

She didn't want to lie, but now was hardly the time to blurt out, "I'm pregnant and I'm going over to tell the happy father." So she waved and pretended not to hear him. She'd face him—later.

First, she went to the Double Four and learned that Logan was out branding cattle. Mary Rosa said she thought he'd be home in a few days and Katherine was tempted to wait, but she decided against it. If she waited she'd only have to get her nerve up again. Better to get it over with now.

So, she thanked Mary Rosa and, following her directions, headed for the roundup camp.

All the way there, her heart was beating faster than a hummingbird's wings. She tried to figure out some way to get around this, some way to not have to tell Logan. There wasn't any, unless she was willing to leave Wyoming. But she couldn't do that. After all, Logan was the father and he did have a right to know.

But it was his only right, she decided. For weeks she had berated herself for the impulsive act she had committed with Logan. It had taken equally as long for her to banish all the longings and erotic images that had tormented her thoughts and her dreams. Now, however, she was in control of her emotions she assured herself as she reined to a stop on a small rise.

Before her, scattered as far as the eye could see, were cattle. Half a dozen fires dotted the landscape and she could see men roping and branding the calves.

Slowly, she rode toward the area where the men were working. The sounds of their shouting filled the air. Antelope, grazing among the cattle, scattered as she came closer. The cattle paid only cursory attention.

Scanning the cowboys, she spotted Logan immediately. Tall and broad-shouldered, he stood out from the crowd. He had a calf roped, and his horse kept the lariat taut while men on the ground branded the poor critter.

Katherine winced at the calf's bellowing. The acrid smell of burned hide caused her stomach to roll again. Instinctively, she swallowed hard, forcing down the bile. She wasn't about to make a fool of herself in front of all these men. Thank goodness Logan hadn't seen her yet. She was frantically trying to remember the little speech she rehearsed on the way over.

Men stopped their work and stared as she rode between the branding fires. She felt the heat, like the flames of Hades, against her arms below the rolled-up sleeves of her calico blouse. So this is how the sinners feel, she thought. And a hundred yards away was the devil himself.

Only this devil wore a chambray shirt that was molded to his broad chest. Dark blotches of perspiration circled his collar and stained the areas under his well-muscled arms. Dusty brown leather chaps were wrapped tightly around his legs clear to the ankle, revealing a pair of worn brown boots. Sun glinted off his spurs. Wind ruffled the brim of his black hat and she watched him adjust it lower on his forehead, a familiar gesture.

He hadn't done a thing, hadn't even looked in her direction, and already Katherine's nerves had flared to life, singing with anticipation.

Then she saw him gather his rope and loop it over his saddle horn. He wheeled around and faced her, not moving, just waiting as she closed the distance between them.

Their gazes met and locked. Knowledge and desire filled the space between them like heat lightning.

And as she looked at him, a simple truth surpassed all other thoughts. She wanted him—as much as she had that day on the creek bank.

Logan watched her. He'd known she was there even before he saw her. It was like that between them, magnetic. When he couldn't stand not looking at her, he'd turned.

Her hair was all but invisible under her tan hat. She was wearing that brown split riding skirt, the one that outlined every curve and left nothing to the imagination. Of course, for him it didn't take imagination. He *knew* those curves, had memorized every luscious inch of her. His fingers trembled slightly as all the extravagant memories, the ones he'd lived with, lost sleep over and never quite banished from his mind, came flooding back.

His muscles tensed and blood started to heat inside him, pounding in his neck. Silently, he cursed himself, helpless to stop the longing that welled up in him.

Katherine halted next to him. She gripped the reins so tightly that the stiff edges seemed to cut right through her gloves into her fingers. She drew a deep breath and cleared her throat. "I need to talk to you." The words came out in a rush and not at all the way she'd planned.

Logan lifted one dark brow in seeming disinterest. "Talk?" he repeated.

Katherine straightened. "About a personal matter." She glanced around at the staring cowboys. She didn't like creating a scene. She could almost feel their eyes on her and hear them wondering what a sheep rancher's daughter was doing out here in the middle of a roundup.

She was uncomfortable and wanted to say what she'd come to say and get it over with.

Logan nudged his horse and circled around behind her, coming up on the other side. "Let's go," he said and loped off in the direction she'd come.

Katherine followed. He pulled to a stop and positioned himself between her and the cattle. He thumbed his hat back off his forehead, revealing his face, handsome even stained with sweat and dirt, yet different. The smile was gone, she realized. The soft sable eyes were sharp and hard like obsidian.

Katherine steadied herself. The reins were a lifeline and she clung to them. Her gaze never wavered from his. "I've come to..." She faltered. It took all her strength to meet his eyes. "I've come to tell you that I'm going to have a baby."

It seemed an eternity before Logan reacted and then he didn't speak at all. He laughed—a cold, hard laugh that held no amusement.

"Pregnant, sweetheart?" he finally said, his smile taking on a bitter curve. "What happened to 'I'm not'?" He knew she was hurting, but dammit, so was he. He leaned forward, resting his arm on the saddle horn. "So what do you want?"

Katherine flinched at his harsh tone. Anger boiled up in her. Perhaps it came from the humiliation at having to confess her plight, or perhaps from knowing she'd failed in her promises, but it was there and she used it.

"Nothing, McCloud," she told him curtly, her pride overriding her good sense. "I'll let you know when the blessed event occurs so you can pass out cigars."

"Like hell!" he growled, grabbing a handful of her horse's mane to stop her from turning. "You've had things your way, sweetheart. Now we'll do things the right way. *My* way."

Katherine glared at him, at his hand restraining her horse. Anger and desire slammed together inside her, mixing and tumbling, until without even realizing what she was doing, her arm swung back and, with all her strength, she slapped him across the face.

The shock, though cushioned by her glove, vibrated through her. Arm still poised in the air, Katherine was stunned by what she'd just done. Disbelieving, she stared at her hand as if it weren't part of her. Never in her life had she been a violent person. Never had she even contemplated striking another.

Her gaze flew to Logan, who was frozen, staring at her. She could see the reddened imprint of her hand on his face. His eyes were dark, his expression tight.

"Logan, I . . ." Her hand reached for him, as if to take back the blow. He straightened abruptly. Saddle leather creaked. She let her hand drop to her lap, unable to change what she had done.

"Is this what it's come to between us, Katherine?"

Katherine trembled inside and out. She thought every tendon and muscle in her body would shake apart with the force of it. Her hand wrapped around the worn leather of her saddle horn, seeking support.

Her voice cracked when she said, "I'm sorry." Tears started to well up behind her eyes and she blinked them back.

She could see a muscle flex in the jaw she'd just slapped. His expression was so dark, so ominous, yet it held her with its power.

His voice was strangely quiet when he spoke. "No matter what we feel, there's a child to be considered—*my* child," he said with deliberate emphasis. "I'll not let it be born a bastard."

Katherine nodded, afraid to trust her voice.

"Whether you like it or not," he continued, "we're going to be married. Right away."

Katherine cleared her throat. "All right, Logan. I'll marry you," she said, knowing his honor demanded no less.

"Monday," he confirmed, knowing she was trapped.

*   *   *

The cabin at the Bar T was small, Logan thought as he stopped in the doorway and allowed Katherine to precede him inside. But a quick glance also showed everything to be neat and spotless—certainly a difficult feat in range country. The sharp scent of lye and the gleam on the pine-planked floor told him it had been freshly scrubbed. It was second nature for him to stoop down, remove his spurs and stamp the mud off his boots before entering. It was good manners that made him remove his hat.

Sarah Thorn looked up from the green-and-white flannel shirt she was mending. Logan didn't miss the way her pale blue eyes widened in surprise. And though she straightened abruptly, she didn't order him off the place. Not like her husband had the last time they'd met.

In a tone that sounded more carefully polite than truly warm she said, "Mr. McCloud, this is a surprise." Her gaze flicked to her daughter. "Katherine, is something wrong?" She pushed the shirt aside and rose, her black skirt covering the tops of her equally black shoes.

"No, Mama," Katherine quickly replied. "Everything's all right."

Everything wasn't all right and Sarah knew it. Not with Logan McCloud standing in the middle of her parlor. His chambray shirt and brown chaps were covered with a thin coating of dust, and his chin showed several days' growth of beard. The expression in his eyes was dark, tired. No, Sarah thought, sad. Uneasiness tightened her throat.

Logan's voice was calm when he spoke. "I apologize for coming by unannounced, Mrs. Thorn, but there's an important matter I wish to discuss with you."

"Daniel's not here, Mr. McCloud, so if you've come to talk about selling the ranch, I—"

"It's not the ranch I've come about." Logan raked one hand through his hair in an agitated gesture.

The edge of the chair pressed tight against the back of Sarah's legs. "What then?" she asked anxiously.

"Mrs. Thorn, I've asked Katherine to marry me and she's consented. The wedding will be Monday. We'd like you to be there."

If he'd said sheep could fly, Sarah couldn't have been more stunned. For a long minute she simply stared at both of them. *Katherine and McCloud?*. Words failed her.

She glanced at her daughter, pale and tense, standing next to this man whose mere presence filled the room. "Katherine, maybe you'd best tell me what the devil's going on."

Katherine didn't return her mother's gaze when she replied quietly, "I'm going to have a baby."

The words hit Sarah like a blow. All the air rushed from her lungs. She sat down heavily in the chair. "Oh, my God," was all she managed while she absorbed the news. She clasped her hands tightly together in her lap, trying to still her sudden shaking. "If Charles were here he'd kill you for this, Mr. McCloud. Daniel still might."

"I hope, for his sake, he doesn't try," Logan said flatly.

Sarah was stung by the implication and the blandness of his tone. She didn't doubt for a moment his ability to carry out his threat.

"This is the first time we've met face to face, Mr. McCloud. I can see now that we have all underestimated you, and my daughter has suffered for it." She raked the rancher with a hostile stare.

Katherine rushed to her mother's side and dropped to one knee, covering her mother's icy hands with her own. "I'm so sorry, Mama," she said, tears slipping down her cheeks.

Sarah's heart ached for her daughter. She stroked Katherine's hair, much the way she had when Katherine was a child, tearfully coming to her mother with some terrible problem. Only then Sarah could soothe away the trouble with a word, a smile, a kiss. Not now. Nothing could change this. "Oh, Katherine, how could you have let this happen? You're not a child. You must have realized the possible consequences of your actions."

"I know, Mama. Can you ever forgive me?"

Tears welled in Sarah's eyes and she had to swallow down the lump that clogged her throat. She continued stroking Katherine's silky golden hair.

She glanced at McCloud, standing just inside the door. His gaze was focused on Katherine. There was a look in his eyes, soft, almost wistful, and startling in its longing. It gave Sarah pause.

She cupped the side of her daughter's face in one hand. "Katherine, this isn't how I'd hope things to be for you, but you're my child and I love you. If you don't want to marry this man, just say so and we'll work something out—no matter what people think."

Katherine gave her a trembling smile. "Oh, Mama, thank you." More tears slipped down her cheeks. "But I've thought it through and—"

"It's settled," Logan broke in.

Sarah's protective instincts came to the fore and she shot him a look colder than the bottom of a hundred-foot coal shaft. "I'm talking to my daughter. I don't want her spending her life in a loveless marriage." *Like I did,* she thought, and not for the first time felt sad because of it.

"Katherine," Sarah started gently, deciding there was one question that had to be asked. "Do you love him?"

The silence in the room was nearly palpable. Sarah glanced at Logan. He kept his expression schooled, and yet there was that look in his eyes again, just for an instant—hope, or perhaps longing. It was gone so quickly she couldn't be sure. But she was certain that McCloud was intently focused on the answer.

Katherine's head came up slowly. Firmly, she said, "We both want what's best for the child."

"And he won't be born a bastard, Mrs. Thorn," Logan added just as firmly.

There was that adamant tone again. He was claiming his child; Sarah respected him for that. And Katherine had not said that she didn't love the man. For that matter, would Katherine have given herself to a man she didn't care for?

Unlikely, Sarah thought, knowing her very determined daughter.

"Mama, I love you for what you're saying, but what happened between Logan and me... He did not force me to do anything against my will," Katherine said in a rather defensive tone that almost made Sarah smile. "Logan's an honorable man and I intend to fulfill my responsibility...to the child. Don't worry, everything's going to be just fine."

Could she really be defending him? Logan wondered. Had he misunderstood? Two hours ago she'd been less than enthusiastic. Hell, she'd struck him, but now... He looked hard at her tear-streaked face. He could see the pain of her confession in her eyes. Instinctively, he wanted to shield and protect her. His boots scraped on the floor as he moved closer, letting her shoulder brush the top of his arm. The back of his hand brushed the back of hers.

Sarah didn't miss the protective gesture, the gentle look in Logan's black eyes, or especially the way Katherine acknowledged his closeness with a ghost of a smile. In that instant, Sarah knew. This wasn't the best of starts, that was for sure. But these two cared for each other, perhaps more than they realized.

"Katherine," Sarah sighed. Her hand trembled as she stroked her daughter's cheek. "I want what's best for you. I want you to be happy."

"I'll take good care of her," Logan said quietly, firmly.

Sarah's grudging respect for the man grew. He shouldn't have made love to Katherine without benefit of marriage, and yet he was here. He was resolute about marrying. What's more, there was something in the way he looked at her daughter, all soft and rich. Someone had looked at her like that once, a long time ago.

Softly, she said, "I've always trusted you, Katherine, and I'll not change now."

At that moment, Katherine had never loved her mother more, or felt more guilty, more sad, about her own actions.

But she owed it to her mother, to the child and to Logan, not to whine or complain about her situation. She squared her shoulders and said, "I'd like you to come to the wedding. Will you?"

"I'll be there, and I'll explain things to Daniel for you, too," Sarah added, giving Katherine a kiss on the cheek.

Katherine smiled and returned the kiss, grateful for her mother's understanding and help. When she glanced at Logan, standing close beside her, the back of his hand brushed the back of hers again, this time in a delicate gesture that sent warm sparks skittering up her arm.

He looked at her with those fathomless black eyes and his voice was a hushed whisper. "I'll send for the preacher this afternoon. Monday at ten we'll be married."

Katherine tried to smile, as much for her mother's sake as her own. Logan was living up to his obligation. She should be grateful, and yet she thought this wasn't how she'd imagined announcing her marriage. She had always envisioned words of love and promise, hearts filled with joy, people smiling.

It was not to be.


Three days later, Katherine was standing in the parlor of the Double Four. The sofa had been pushed back a little and the Reverend Holland stood with his back to the empty fireplace. Tall and exceptionally thin, dressed in black, he was the picture of a preacher, even down to his snow-white hair and kindly smile.

Right now, Katherine needed all the kindness she could get. Not that anyone had been mean to her. Quite the contrary. Mary Rosa was her usual bubbling self, all smiles and orders, mostly to Pete. Where to put the furniture, where to put the bunches of Indian paintbrush and wild poppies that decorated the tabletop, even the placement of the burnt-sugar cake on the table had to be just so.

The parlor windows were open and an early morning breeze fluttered past the white lace curtains and ruffled the hem of Katherine's dress. She glanced down at the simple creation her mother had fashioned from the white muslin. Katherine had never suspected when they made the dress that it would first be worn at her wedding.

She glanced over at her mother, who was standing slightly behind her. She looked lovely in her navy-and-white-striped dress. Sarah gave her a smile that warmed Katherine's heart. It was reassuring.

"Now," the reverend started, "Mr. McCloud, you stand right here." He pointed to a spot on the polished pine floor as if there were an *X* there. Logan stepped into place, looking darkly handsome in his black suit and rust-colored silk tie.

"Miss Thorn," the reverend continued, pointing to another invisible *X* next to Logan, "if you please?"

Numbly, Katherine did as directed. Inside she was shaking so hard she thought her knees would surely give out before this ordeal was through. She took a deep breath, then another. Calm, she told herself, be calm. It has to be this way.

Pete flanked Logan as his best man and Mary Rosa stepped up beside Sarah.

"All right, let's begin," the reverend started.

Katherine heard all the words, but they seemed to come from far away. Concentration was impossible. She kept thinking about all her failures, her broken promises. How would she ever make this right? Was there any way she could make Daniel understand?

He'd been angry when they'd told him about the wedding. He'd called her traitor and hadn't spoken to her since. His refusal to come to the wedding broke her heart.

"Do you take this man to be your lawfully wedded husband, to have and to hold, to love, honor and obey, until death do you part?"

This was it. The moment, the one word that would change her life forever. Her hands, cold and clammy, gripped her bouquet of wildflowers.

The reverend smiled and patted her forearm. "Now, don't you be nervous, dear," he told her gently. "Take a deep breath and say 'I do.'"

Katherine glanced over at Logan, standing so impassively beside her. His dark gaze bore into hers. Softly she said, "I do."

Logan let out the breath he'd been holding. If she'd tried to change her mind...well, he wasn't going to let her. Neither of them had a choice and they both knew it.

"I do," he said at the appropriate moment.

The reverend smiled as he pronounced them man and wife.

The deed was done.

## Chapter Thirteen

Alone, Katherine felt as still and lifeless as the lace curtains that lay motionless against the closed parlor windows. Around her were the scattered remains of her wedding day. A half-eaten cake lay on the cherry serving table, surrounded by five wine glasses, all empty except hers—the French champagne had tasted bitter in her mouth. Was it supposed to taste like that? She shook her head.

What did she know of champagne? She scanned the elegant room. What did she know of wealth, or, for that matter, what did she know of marriage?

She heard Logan's voice through the open front door. He was giving some instructions to one of his ranch hands. Any minute now he'd walk through that doorway—Logan McCloud, her husband.

A small sigh escaped her lips. It seemed life was conspiring against her these days, heaping obligations and responsibilities on her one after another in some perverse test of endurance. A month ago she would have said her family took all her time and energy. As of ten this morning she'd added a husband to the list of obligations. She felt as if she were being torn to pieces.

Logan's boots sounded on the pine planks of the porch. She took a deep breath and forced her clasped hands to loosen. Logan walked in and shut the door quietly behind him. Across the room they simply stared at each other, neither. moving. Her fingers felt cold, even to her. Muscles along the top of her shoulders slowly tensed like an ever-tightening vise.

"Alone at last," Logan muttered, breaking the awkward silence. He continued to lean back against the closed door. The late afternoon sun was blocked by the porch, casting the room, and Logan, in shadows. "The place seems almost too quiet with everyone gone." His voice was soft, husky.

"Almost," Katherine repeated, suddenly very aware of the fact that she and Logan were totally alone. She could feel his gaze on her as surely as if he were touching her. The knot that had formed in the pit of her stomach that morning seemed to have doubled in size.

"Nice lunch, don't you think?"

"Very," she replied, forcing herself to make small talk when she really wanted to crawl into a corner and hide from the world. And from Logan.

Logan crossed the room and stopped beside her. He leaned his shoulder against the mantle and stood looking at her with eyes so soft, so sensuous, her heart took off like a scared fawn running from a cougar. A sigh escaped her lips. He smiled, obviously enjoying her discomfort.

"Stop it, Logan."

"What?" he asked innocently, but his smile broadened just a touch, enough that his dimples showed and his eyes sparkled and her knees liquefied, just like always.

He hadn't touched her or said a word, and already she was succumbing to his enchantment.

He actually seemed happy, she thought for a moment, then quickly dismissed the idea. *You're crazy,* she told herself. This was a marriage of necessity, of business. There was no love for either of them, and that was just fine with her. Love complicated things, and Lord knew things were already complicated enough.

When he caressed her cheek with the backs of his knuckles, things got a lot more complicated. "You're beautiful,

Katherine. Your skin is soft and flushed. I like to see you this way.''

As though it were the most natural thing in the world, she instinctively turned into his touch, then abruptly straightened and pulled back. He drew her in too easily. She needed to keep her wits about her, to remember that it was his power that had gotten her into this fix in the first place.

She swallowed hard, deciding small talk was safer than none at all. "I wish I could have talked Mary Rosa out of going to San Francisco. I know she was being nice, but, well, she's a joy and... Maybe we should have gone with them to the stage?"

"Mary Rosa has been making her own decisions for a long time." Logan's fingers traced the edge of her jaw. "Don't worry about her. Pete will make sure she gets off all right after he takes your mother home."

His gaze flicked from her eyes to her mouth and lingered there. Nervous, she licked her suddenly parched lips.

His gaze darkened and his tone dropped slightly. "Would you like more champagne?"

"No." She stepped around him and walked to the window. The sun was dropping behind the mountains. A couple of hours and it would be night. Her wedding night, she realized with a jolt.

A man expected certain things on his wedding night. Logan was making it clear he was no different than any other man. Would he be a warm and gentle lover? She knew the answer. Just thinking about it made her body come alive with anticipation. A throbbing pulse raced along her nerve endings.

She drew in a ragged breath. Logan had a way of surrounding her, of overwhelming her senses until she was saturated with him and the desire he stirred in her. That was what terrified her. It would be so easy to give in, forget everything and everyone else, forget plans and promises, but was it right? She honestly didn't know.

Logan came up behind her. He stroked his hand down her neck, then along her shoulder. "I've missed you."

Katherine took a deep breath. It didn't help. Logan's pulling her back against his chest didn't help, either. She could feel the heat of him through the muslin of her dress. The clean, fresh cologne that he used assailed her nostrils. His cheek rubbed against her ear. He turned her into his arms.

Instinctively, her hands rested on his shoulders. The wool of his suit was soft under her fingers. Her hem brushed the tops of his boots and she fought against the desire that he ignited in her.

It took all her strength to stand her ground against the sensual assault. Panic rose in her and her eyes widened as she saw him lower his face toward hers.

Before she could speak, Logan's mouth covered hers. His arms wrapped around her waist and shoulders, molding her firmly against the hard length of him.

Katherine didn't fight the kiss. How could she fight something so wonderful? Lord help her, she wanted it, the touching, the kissing, the intimacy. On some primitive level, deep down inside, where thought ceased to exist and there was only feeling, she wanted Logan McCloud. And she hated herself for the wanting, and in some way, him, too, for making her feel things she'd never known existed.

Like a drowning person she made a desperate grab for safety. With more will than she thought she possessed, she wrenched her mouth from his and twisted free of his embrace.

Logan took a half step toward her and stopped. "Why, Katherine?" She could see the muscle flex in his cheek. The same cheek she'd slapped three days ago. "Why do you keep trying to deny what you feel?" he demanded, his voice raspy. "Every time we're in a room together, every time we're within a mile of each other, it's there, this, this, electricity that sparks between us."

"No!" Katherine clenched her hands. "How can I make you understand?" she countered. "We're married. You've gotten what you wanted—a woman to warm your bed and a name for your child. It cost *you* nothing. It cost *me* everything—my family, my promises, my dreams." Her voice rang with desperation. "What I did was wrong! For the rest of my life I'll have to pay the price. I gave myself to you like the cheapest whore, without thought, but not again. Never again!"

The room was deadly silent. It was as if the whole world held its breath. Not a shutter rattled, or a beam creaked, or a bird sang.

Logan's gaze raked over her. Her cheeks flushed in anger. Her chest was heaving. Her hands knotted in tight fists at her sides. He took it all in and said, "Yes, Katherine, I understand."

He closed the distance between them, firmly taking her shoulders in his grip. His expression was serious. "I understand that you'd like to believe what happened between us was some sordid little affair, a casual roll in the hay. It wasn't. It was more, much more." His lips turned up in a mocking smile. "And you know it." His voice dropped in timbre. "Don't you, Angel?"

Katherine shook her head in frantic denial. It was lust, nothing more. It couldn't be more!

She closed her eyes. One hand reached out for support and grasped the edge of the smooth, hard surface of the pine mantle.

When she opened her eyes he was there, filling her vision, swamping her senses. She stiffened her spine and forced her hand to release the mantle. She needed no support, of any kind. She stood very tall.

"I'm your wife. I'll fulfill my duty to you. All my duties." She said each word clearly, distinctly, coldly.

"Duty, is it?" Logan smiled then, a slow certain smile, his eyes filled with a knowledge that came from their shared intimacy. "You can deny it until the moon turns purple and falls from the sky, but it won't change. I'm in your blood, lady, now and forever. God help me, you're in mine.''

It was as if all the oxygen had suddenly been sucked from the room, leaving Katherine suspended in time and space. There was no heartbeat, no pulse, no breath. There was only Logan's eyes and touch and husky voice, and the terrifying fear that he was right.

She backed away from him, one deliberate step at a time, and with each step the panic increased until she reached the hallway. Then she did the unforgivable, at least for Katherine Thorn—she turned and ran, slamming the bedroom door behind her, as if she could barricade herself from the truth as easily as she could the man.


Logan yawned and stretched. "Ouch!" His neck muscles knotted. Late last night he'd fallen asleep in the high-backed chair in the parlor. "Damn," he muttered, rubbing the sore spot at the top of his right shoulder. What the hell time was it?

A quick glance at the mantle clock gave him his answer. Seven! He surged to his feet. His black suit jacket, which he'd used for a blanket, fell to the floor and tangled around his boots. He bent to pick it up.

"Ouch!"

Tossing the jacket on the sofa, he rotated his neck again. Why hadn't Mary Rosa called him? Oh yes, she was away. And Pete probably hadn't come by, knowing a man ought to have a little privacy on his wedding night...morning. He squinted at the sunlight pouring through the front windows, then rubbed the sleep from his eyes.

Helluva wedding night, he thought, frowning and stretching stiff muscles in his arms and back. He'd spent what was left of yesterday working in his office, then had had a cold supper—he hated cold suppers—and one too many glasses of whiskey. Several times he'd started for the bedroom, but he'd always stopped short. In some convoluted way he'd thought it would appear that he was crawling back to her and he damned sure wasn't about do that.

*So, great, McCloud!* Instead he'd fallen asleep in the chair. He should have at least made it to the guest room, for God's sake. Now he had the sore muscles to remind him of his mistake.

Hell, no, it wasn't his mistake, it was hers. Katherine was being totally unreasonable. Duty, was it? Just what a man wanted—a clenched-jaw wife willing to *submit* to her husband in the bedroom.

But that was then and this was now, and he'd had enough. It was time they had a talk. A very, very long talk. Today they were going to clarify her "duties."

A quick look told him the bedroom door was still closed, but it wouldn't be for long. He turned on his heel and started down the hall. His boots echoed on the bare pine of the hallway. Pausing at the door, he shoved his hands through his hair to straighten it. He tucked his shirt in more neatly and pledged to ignore the pain in his neck. He wouldn't give her the satisfaction of knowing he was in the least way inconvenienced.

He started to knock, then changed his mind. This was his house and she was his wife, dammit, and she might as well start getting used to the idea. He twisted the brass knob, pushed open the door and stepped inside.

"Katherine, I . . ."

His gaze scanned the room.

Empty! Where was she? Had she packed and gone home to mother already? The open wardrobe dispelled that notion. Then where the . . .

He spun on his heel and headed for the kitchen. Of course, she'd probably come to her senses and was making breakfast, he thought with smug relief. The fact that no sound or food smells emanated from the kitchen didn't deter him.

Half a minute later, standing in the doorway of the empty room, he wasn't quite so smug. There wasn't even a sign she'd been there. No cold coffee in the pot, no dishes in the sink. If he didn't know better he'd think he'd imagined getting married yesterday.

Where was she? Maybe she was outside somewhere. He started across the kitchen when a piece of brown paper on the table caught his eye. He took two long strides and snatched it up.

The delicate handwriting was deceptive cover for the contents of the note. There was no salutation, not even his name. Just a curt message.

Gone to Bar T. Back by dinner.

K.

That was it? She'd gone back to the Bar T like she was going off to open her hat shop! "Back by dinner."

Like hell!

Muscles in his chest tightened and his heart rate shot up. He stomped back toward the bedroom, tugging off his shirt as he went.

He slammed open the door of the wardrobe, nearly wrenching it off the hinges. It banged back and hit him in the shoulder, making him jerk. "Ouch!" he roared as that stiff muscle in his neck throbbed painfully.

He yanked off his boots and suit pants and grabbed his denims and a burgundy-colored cotton shirt. He pulled on the pants, tugged on the shirt, trying to button both at the same time. Thirty seconds later, he was out the bedroom door and moving down the hall in a hop-skip while he pulled his pant legs down over his boot tops.

If she thought she could pretend nothing had changed, well, she had another think coming. He crossed the kitchen in four long strides, grabbing his gun belt and, of course, his trail hat on the way out.

The kitchen door banged shut behind him as he went to the barn. The clear day and warm sun were in direct contrast to his mood.

Shouts of men repairing the corral caught his attention, but only briefly. He answered the men's waves with a cursory one of his own but he didn't stop. He had one thought and one thought only—to get his wife and bring her home. If she thought she could run roughshod over him she was dead wrong, and the sooner she found out the better.

He marched into the barn and down the long center aisle. Straw crunched under his angry stride. The big gray barn cat scampered out of his way. He grabbed the latch on Joker's stall, and was about to swing open the door when he halted in his tracks.

What was he doing? Was he going after her like some lovesick school boy? Was he going to plead with her to come home? Not likely. Was he going to drag her kicking and screaming from the place? It was a provocative image but hardly appropriate—humiliating was more like it.

He let the latch drop back into place and braced both hands on the gnarled wood of the stall gate. He'd like to choke her. Of course, he wouldn't. He'd never raised his hand to a woman in his life, but this one, this one... Eyes narrowed, a deep frown on his face, he turned and walked out of the barn. He'd wait until the lady returned. Then she'd find out she'd met her match in Logan McCloud.

Katherine slapped the reins on the horse's rump. The buggy creaked and rattled as the big chestnut picked up his pace. She was late. That is, later than she'd intended to be.

"Gid up," she urged the horse. The sun was a bright red ball casting the Laramie Mountains in purple shadows.

Stretching, she eased the tired ache in her shoulders. And she *was* tired, emotionally much more than physically. A day spent arguing with Daniel until he finally relented, plus last night's unpleasant little scene had taken their toll. She shook her head.

All night she'd sat up, waiting, expecting Logan to come barging in. But he hadn't. So why was she disappointed?

She wasn't, she assured herself. She was surprised. That's what that feeling was—surprise.

The stone pillars of the Double Four came into view and she turned between them, pulling to a stop by the barn.

One of the ranch hands spotted her and came to help.

"Name's Slim, Missus McCloud," he said with a polite smile and a tip of his sweat-stained hat.

"Thank you, Slim." She accepted his hand and climbed down. "I appreciate the help. Would you mind putting the buggy away for me? I seem to be a little late and—"

"Be my pleasure, ma'am. You go on about your business."

The hem of her dark brown skirt caught the dust as she walked to the back door. Was Logan in the house?

Maybe he was out working. She'd make a hurried dinner. She paused, smoothing her hair back where it had come loose from its braid as she stared at the half-opened back door. He was in there, waiting, she just knew it. And he was going to be angry. She took a deep breath, willed her stomach to stop knotting up and marched into the kitchen.

Just as she expected, he was there, leaning against the edge of the sink. He looked tall and powerful and dark as a thundercloud.

"Don't start, Logan."

He slammed down a half-empty glass of buttermilk sloshing its contents on the counter. "*You* started it this morning with that charming little love note."

She ignored him long enough to throw her hat and gloves down on the kitchen table. She was feeling pretty stormy herself.

"Say what's on your mind."

Logan lifted away from the pine counter, arms folded across his chest. "You, dear wife. You're what's on my mind."

"I'm flattered," she said curtly as she walked past him and into the pantry. A moment later she reappeared with a jar of green beans and a slab of bacon. She went around him, put the things down on the counter and lifted the stove plate.

He grabbed her shoulders and spun her toward him, the metal falling against the stove with a loud bang.

She tried to twist away. His grip tightened.

"Logan, I'm trying to make dinner, if you'll just—"

"I don't care about dinner, dammit. What's the big idea?"

She tried to twist away again. "What idea?"

"That's it!" Wrapping his hands around her waist, he lifted her like she was made of feathers and plunked her down by the table. He dragged out a chair. "Sit," he ordered, none too gently.

She obliged. No sense tormenting an angry bear.

He paced back and forth. "No more games, Katherine. You are my wife, a McCloud. You are not a Thorn anymore and your first obligation is to me." He paused to stare directly at her.

Silently, she returned his gaze with one equally determined, equally stubborn.

He pressed on, a day's worth of tirade stored up inside. "You *will* be here in the mornings when I get up. If you *need* to go somewhere, you will *tell* me and I'll make arrangements to take you or have someone else take you. Your days at the Bar T are over, do you understand me?" He emphasized the last words as if he could force the demand into her brain.

Katherine's cold stare never faltered. Slowly she rose to her feet. "Are you finished, McCloud?" She didn't wait for an answer. "Now you let me tell you something. I don't take orders from you or anyone else." She took a half step forward. "I am not your slave or your bond servant. I will go where I please, when I please." She took another half step forward, until she was inches from his chest.

"I went to the Bar T today to see my family and to do whatever I could to help. I see no reason why I should break my promises to them, just because I—" She jerked her chin up. "Just because we're married."

"Damn right, we're married," he snarled, his eyes cold. "You came to me, if you remember, sweetheart. I expect—"

"Expect all you want," she hurled back at him, stung by his rebuke. "I'm telling you how it is."

"No, I'm telling *you* how it is. A man deserves a hot meal and a warm smile when he comes in the door."

His patronizing attitude set her teeth on edge. "I'll keep your house clean. I'll make breakfast for you in the mornings and dinner at night, if that's so all-fired important." She raked him with an insolent stare. "But you're a big boy. You ought to be able to cook for yourself," she added sarcastically.

"I can," he retaliated. "That's not the point and you know it."

"I don't know it. I'm not going to abandon my family and that's final."

She moved past him and went to the cupboard. She pulled out a frying pan and a saucepan and slammed them on the stove. "Dinner in twenty minutes."

"The hell with dinner!" he thundered and slammed out the back door.

## Chapter Fourteen

Four days later, Logan had had enough. They were sleeping in the same bed, but only because he refused to let his *wife* move into the guest room. She'd given in on that point, at least.

Of course, that long-sleeved, high-necked nightgown she wore made her intentions, or lack of them, very clear. The darn thing had more material in it than a nun's habit. And the way she kept her back to him and hugged the edge of the bed . . . well, it was a miracle she didn't fall out.

It was killing him to lie there every night, feeling the heat of her body, wanting to touch her, but he could be as stubborn as she. So much for honeymoons!

The afternoon sun beat down on him. Even the breeze was warm. He reined in, snatched off his hat and wiped his brow with the crook of his elbow, then clapped his Stetson back in place. Touching his spurs to Joker's sides, he headed for the next watering hole he'd planned to check. He couldn't help glancing east. Katherine was out there somewhere, at the damned sheep ranch.

Oh, sure, she fixed his breakfast every day just like she'd said she would. And right after he left, *she* left—just like she'd said she would.

She took the buggy instead of riding her horse. That and her refusal to eat breakfast were the only outward signs of her pregnancy.

They barely talked, and didn't touch at all. The whole situation was aggravating in the extreme. He'd clamped his jaw down so many times to keep from starting another argument that his back teeth were actually starting to ache.

Something had to change and it was up to him to change it. He wanted his wife. He wanted Katherine. He was damned determined to have her—and not some rigid submission, either. He wanted her warm and willing. Hell, he wanted her anxious, even eager. More than that he wanted her to give in to her feelings and admit what she felt.

Seduction was his plan. Surrender was his goal, but not here. There were too many other forces pulling at them. Well, at her, anyway.

As he rode, an idea began to formulate in his mind. Thursday night at dinner, he sprang it on her.

"I'm going to Cheyenne on Saturday. I want you to come with me." His tone was casual, easy, at least as much as he could make it considering his frustration of the past few days.

"I can't."

Logan had expected her refusal. He put his fork down on his plate. Days of arguing hadn't gotten him anywhere. He was trying a new approach—cold, calm and rational.

"Why not?" he asked, the knitting of his dark brows the only outward sign of impatience.

"Daniel and the hands are moving the flock to the north pasture. I promised to help."

"On horseback?"

"On foot."

"I see." He considered this for a moment. She was as skittish as a spring colt, and he was going to gentle her. Determination was not her exclusive domain. "Your brother does have help, though."

Katherine's gaze narrowed. "Yes," she conceded.

There was a certain apprehension in her voice that he didn't fail to notice. A little uncertainty on her part was good. It gave him an edge and he took it.

"You feel strongly about your obligations." He fixed her with a hard stare. "That's correct, isn't it?"

Her eyes narrowed a bit more. "You know I do."

"Well, it seems to me you've lived up to your obligations to everyone but your husband."

Her glare turned as cold as a Wyoming winter. "I never said you—"

"One subject at a time," he interrupted, not wanting to be distracted by a discussion of sex. He was distracted enough just thinking about it. Discreetly, he wiped his sweaty palms on his denim-covered thighs. Stay with the plan, he told himself.

"I'm going to Cheyenne on business," he repeated. "I want my wife with me."

"If it's business, why do you need me?"

"People will wonder why my new bride chose to remain at home. There will be gossip." He shifted slightly in the kitchen chair.

Katherine made a sound in the back of her throat that could have been a chuckle or could have been a derisive groan. Her mouth turned up in a wry smile. "When the largest cattle rancher in this county suddenly marries a sheep rancher, there's gossip."

"True. But being seen in public together should go a long way in stopping the rumors." He tossed his calico napkin on the table next to his plate.

For long moments she didn't speak, but her gaze, cold and suspicious as it was, didn't waver from his. He liked a lot of things about her, but right now her stubbornness wasn't one of them.

"Katherine—"

"You're right."

"What?"

"You're right."

Her shoulders visibly slumped. She pushed her half-eaten dinner away and for a moment she stared down into her lap. Her voice was quiet when she spoke. "I feel sometimes there aren't enough hours in the day or enough of me to go around." She looked at him, her eyes filled with sadness and something he'd never seen in her before—defeat.

It tore at him. "It's not a war, you know, Katherine. It's just you and me trying to make a future for ourselves and find some happiness along the way."

There were unshed tears in her eyes when she abruptly stood and placed her napkin on the table. "I'll be ready Saturday morning."

He stood. "So will I," he replied, watching her walk gracefully from the room. "So will I."

The stage for Cheyenne left from in front of Mr. Hockbaur's general store at nine. Logan and Katherine were the only passengers.

Logan took the seat next to her instead of the one opposite. "I like facing forward," he supplied to her questioning stare. Then he crossed his legs, one black-booted ankle resting on the other knee.

Katherine tried to make herself comfortable on the straight-backed red leather seats. It wasn't easy. Logan's sitting shoulder-rubbing tight against her didn't help.

She glanced at him out of the corner of her eye. His profile was all sharp angles and flat planes. Just looking at him, feeling his warmth—well, it was too bad this stage couldn't move as fast as her heart.

She squirmed and created a little space between them. He squirmed and filled the gap. She sighed, and out of the corner of her eye she thought she saw the corners of his mouth lift up behind his mustache.

Well, there was no hope, so give in, she told herself. She'd had a long talk with herself Thursday night and she'd been forced to admit that Logan was right. He was her husband, and though he'd not been as gracious as she had hoped when she'd told him of her situation, he had still married her when he didn't have to—not legally, anyway.

She owed him and she was going to try to make this marriage work. But it was hard to revise her entire life in a matter of days. Nevertheless, she had decided this morning to wire the bank in Philadelphia about selling the hat shop. She really hated to do it, but now that she was pregnant and married, going back seemed out of the question. Besides, there was nothing like burning a bridge to force a person to make the best of a situation.

She was lost in thought when the driver called a loud, "Gid up!" The stage took off with a lurch that sent her sliding from her seat. Logan grabbed her, pulling her tightly against his shoulder. She looked up, her face only inches from his. His breath was warm against her cheek. She forgot to move or speak, so spellbound was she by the inviting look in his soft, sable eyes.

A cloud of dust filled the coach, choking her and bringing her to her senses. She waved her green linen handkerchief in front of her face, trying to clear the air. "Sorry," she mumbled as she straightened.

"I'm not," he returned with a definite tone of amusement in his voice and that lopsided, lazy smile of his.

Tiny tingles skittered across her skin, the prickly kind that seemed to start at the neck and work their way down. It wasn't an unpleasant feeling, but it was different this time, the sort of feeling you get when a storm is brewing. But the sky outside was bright and blue and cloudless.

Just nerves, she told herself as she settled back.

Logan felt her squirm against him. Even through all those petticoats and the tan linen traveling suit she was wearing, he could feel her body. At least he thought he could, and it was enough to start his senses throbbing. He swallowed hard. Stick to the plan.

So far things were going fine. It was a simple enough plan. The best schemes usually were, he thought rather immodestly. He'd used her own convoluted sense of responsibility to get her to come with him to Cheyenne, and he'd managed to do it without an argument. *That* was one for the record books.

Cheyenne, he'd determined, was neutral territory. Away from the sheep and the cattle, with no distractions and no place to run, they could concentrate all their energy on each other. Right now he had more pent-up energy than a prairie fire.

He was a man in love, after all—totally and completely. Oh, he'd told himself loving Katherine wasn't a wise choice. He'd even made a mental list of all the reasons it wouldn't work, couldn't work, and it was a good list. But it didn't change a thing. Because, God help him, there was no logic to love.

So he'd decided to court Katherine and had planned it all out in his head. Days of picnics and long rides, evenings of theater and restaurants, and nights . . .

The nights he was still a little worried about. He'd firmly promised himself he wouldn't rush her, but he wouldn't give any quarter, either. He wanted her and he was going to have her.

It was seduction, just as lush and sensual, opulent and erotic as he could make it. When the lady's senses were fully aroused, then . . . He swallowed hard again and glanced out the window. Wouldn't this stage ever get to Cheyenne?

Late that afternoon, the coach rumbled down Sixteenth Street and skidded to a halt in front of the Inter-Ocean Hotel.

Logan climbed out, then reached up to help Katherine down the two wobbly folding steps. "Welcome to Cheyenne, the Magic City of the Plains."

"Thanks," she mumbled, gaping at the imposing, three-story stone structure looming up behind Logan. "Is this where we're staying?" she asked and missed the bottom step. Logan grabbed her around the waist and set her firmly on the cement sidewalk.

"We're staying at my house," he told her as he went to take the bags from the stage driver.

Katherine looked startled. "Your house?"

"Yes." Logan scanned the street, obviously looking for someone.

"What do you mean 'your house'?" She tugged at his arm.

"Just a minute, Angel." He craned his neck. "Jack!" He waved to a man perched on the driver's seat of a parked carriage.

Leaving the bags by the curb, Logan looped her arm through his in a possessive gesture and started down the block. Katherine had to hurry to match his long strides.

The tall, lean man jumped down from the carriage. "Logan," he called, grinning. "It's about time you came into town."

"Jack, you old horse thief," Logan returned with a handshake. "It's good to see you, too."

Katherine stood awkwardly by, watching the two men.

Quickly, Logan turned to her, reached an arm around her shoulder and pulled her close against his side. "Katherine, this is Jack Holcombe. He and his wife, Sally, take care of our place here in Cheyenne."

Katherine nodded. "Mr. Holcombe."

The man yanked his dark brown Stetson from his head and stammered, "Pleased to meet you, Mrs. McCloud. When Logan wired that he was bringing his wife, well, Sally's just gone plumb crazy. Been baking and cleaning all day, getting ready." He slapped his hat back on his head. "Now, you climb on up in the carriage," he told her. "Won't take two minutes to get the bags in the back and we'll be home in ten."

Logan pulled the door open and helped Katherine in. "I'll give Jack a hand and be right back."

"Wait, Logan, I—" Too late. He was gone. Katherine sank down on one of the fine-grained black leather seats. They were soft and well padded, like sitting on a feather bed. After the stage ride, her bruised bottom appreciated the difference.

She also appreciated that this was no ordinary carriage. It was huge. The black-and-silver carriage with its matched team of grays standing in harness was as elegant as any-thing she'd ever seen, even in Philadelphia. It bespoke wealth and prominence, and she was acutely aware of peo-ple looking as they went by.

She felt awkward, uncomfortable and suddenly con-scious of just how wealthy Logan was, something she'd never considered until just this moment. No wonder he could offer such a high price for the Bar T.

The carriage rocked slightly as Logan climbed in beside her. "Home in a few minutes," he said, adjusting his black hat low on his forehead.

She saw Jack climb up in the driver's seat. A sharp snap of the reins had the team pulling smartly away from the curb.

Keeping her voice low, she asked, "Why didn't you tell me you had a house here?"

"You didn't ask," he replied.

She sighed in frustration and sank back against the seat. "I'm hardly likely to ask across the dinner table, 'By the way, do you have a house in Cheyenne, New York, Paris or Timbuktu?'"

Logan cleared his throat, or chuckled, she wasn't sure which. Then he twisted in the seat and faced her. "The an-swer to your question is yes, I . . . *we*," he corrected, "have a house in Cheyenne and a brownstone in New York. I stay at my cousin's when I'm in Paris and I've never been to Timbuktu, but if you think you'd like to see the fabled city, we'll go."

Her eyes widened in surprise. "You're kidding—aren't you?"

"Nope."

"Good heavens, Logan, I knew you were rich, but—" She flounced back against the seat again, arms crossed over her chest. "—I didn't know you were . . . *rich!*"

She saw Jack's shoulders shaking. At least he had the good manners not to laugh out loud.

Logan, however, did laugh. "Why, Angel, I do believe you're a snob. The cattle business has been very lucrative the last ten years. What do you suggest I do, have Logan McCloud, Rich Person printed on business cards?"

"Well, certainly—" she twisted back to face him once again, but she suddenly envisioned Logan walking down Ransom Street, handing out cards to everyone who went past while merchants streamed out of shops to follow him. The more she thought about it, the funnier the image became, until she simply burst out laughing. So did Logan.

Jack turned around, looked puzzled, smiled slightly and went back to driving.

Katherine dabbed at her eyes with the corner of her handkerchief. "I'm sorry, Logan. It's not your fault you're rich."

Logan grinned. "I appreciate your understanding. For a minute I thought you were going to ask me to give it away and—"

He was cut off by the whistle of the east-bound Union Pacific. Katherine covered her ears against the ear-piercing shrill. The steady clang of the bell only added to the noise, which lasted less than a minute. It was enough.

Just as they turned down Ransom, the noise stopped.

"Business section," Logan told her, glancing around. Stores and restaurants lined both sides of the street.

"Impressive."

Katherine was enthralled with the sights and sounds and even the smells of the city. What a pleasure this was! Like an excited child, she took in every detail, from the store windows to the fashions the ladies on the streets were wearing.

They turned on Eighteenth Street. The sun peeked from behind a cloud, warming her face.

"So what do you think of my city?" Logan asked with a touch of pride in his voice. "Cheyenne will give those eastern cities a run for their money any day."

"It's spectacular," she told him honestly. "I might have to revise my opinion of Wyoming. How many people live here?"

"About twenty-five thousand, last I heard. Even got some British royalty. Well, I don't know if they're royalty exactly. There's a couple of earls and a, a . . ." He shook his head. "Something else. I don't take much stock in titles. You'll meet them."

"Royalty?" Katherine stared at him, her eyes wide.

Logan chuckled. "Sure. I told you cattle was lucrative. They've got ranches west of here."

That was a surprise. Imagine, royalty in Wyoming. Who would have thought?

She was still mulling that over when they turned onto Ferguson and left the business section behind. This was clearly a residential neighborhood, if you could call houses as big as hotels residential.

The horses' hooves made a steady clip-clop on the hard-packed earth. Halfway down the block, some ladies in a front yard waved and called to Logan. He returned the wave. "Melissa Johnson and her mother," he said, identifying the two women.

Katherine was just about to ask how far away his house was when Jack pulled to a stop.

"Well, this is home," Logan said brightly and crossed in front of Katherine before stepping out of the carriage. "At least, it is when we're in town."

Katherine joined him on the cement sidewalk. Home?

She stared wide-eyed at the stone-and-brick structure in front of her. This wasn't home; this wasn't even a house. The Bar T had a house. This was a mansion.

Good Lord, the yard alone took up half a block. There was a stable in back of the three-story house, and the entire area was surrounded by a lilac hedge. "It's enormous."

"My father built it for my mother." He looked at Katherine, who was still staring at the house. Jack was already carrying the bags up the brick walkway.

"Katherine, don't you want to go inside?"

"I'm not sure," she admitted, feeling like a child about to sneak into the circus without paying.

Logan chuckled. "Come on. It's only four walls and a roof, you know."

She made a derisive sound in the back of her throat. "Sure, and Pike's Peak is just another pile of rocks."

Logan laughed at that remark and took her by the arm. Together they started up the walk. Katherine felt a little less sure of herself than she had when they left Clearwater, but uncertainty was nothing new to her.

Hiking up her skirt, she climbed the two white-painted steps and crossed the porch. Before she knew what was happening, Logan scooped her up in his arms. "It's traditional for a man to carry his bride across the threshold," he told her, pushing open the door and walking in.

"Logan, put me down. Someone will see, and I'm . . . my goodness."

Never in her wildest dreams could she have anticipated the grand sight that greeted her. The foyer was bigger than the entire house at the Bar T. Dark paneled walls gleamed, the planked floor was waxed to a fine polish, and the curved staircase almost begged for a lady in a sweeping gown to come gliding down. A four-tiered, crystal chandelier hung from the center of the ceiling.

The sheer elegance of the place took her breath away, and for a moment she forgot she was still in Logan's arms, until he lowered her feet to the floor, that is.

Suddenly, it was the room that was forgotten as she stared into Logan's fathomless eyes. She was pressed against him, length to length. His hands rested lightly on her waist while hers lay on his chest, where his suit jacket hung open. Through his cotton shirt, she felt his heart beating, felt his chest expand with each breath, felt the heat of his body.

As always, she was lost in the world he created. He didn't move. Neither did she. As a matter of fact, she wasn't sure she was breathing.

Carefully, with a slight hesitation, he lowered his head and kissed her. It was just the barest of kisses—a tasting, really. Then he did it once more.

Her lips were warm and pliant, and for the first time, Logan felt they really had a chance. He took a half step back, his hands still touching her waist.

"Welcome home, Mrs. McCloud," he said softly.


"Here we are," Sally said as she escorted Katherine into what the housekeeper referred to as "the blue room."

It was blue, all right. It was also the most beautiful bedroom Katherine had ever seen, complete with a cherry-wood four-poster bed covered in royal blue satin. Matching drapes hung at the three windows and a plush oriental rug in shades of pale blue and green covered the floor. It was the kind of room every woman dreams of having someday. Totally impractical and gorgeous.

"This can't be Logan's room," Katherine remarked.

"Goodness, no." Sally laughed, and pushed at a loose strand of carrot red hair that perfectly matched her freckles.

The sound of men's voices preceded the arrival of Logan and Jack with the luggage.

"What are you doing in the guest room?" Logan asked from the doorway, a scowl replacing his smile. He let the trunk slip from his shoulder with a floor-shaking thud. "My wife will share my room."

"Of course." Sally grinned and blushed right down to the neckline of her bright yellow dress. "Logan, you're the boss, but that room of yours is as dark and plain as a dungeon. I was thinking maybe Mrs. McCloud might like something a little more..." She made a sweeping gesture. "You know, ladylike, especially on a honeymoon and all."

His room wasn't frilly, that was for sure. "Is this all right with you, Katherine?"

"It's beautiful," she murmured from her place near the foot of the bed.

Logan smiled. He didn't care where they slept as long as they slept together. Glancing toward the door, he said, "This is it then, Jack. Bring in the other bags."

Jack shouldered past and put the two carpetbags down near the wardrobe. Turning to his still-grinning wife, he told her, "Come on, woman. Let these folks alone." He started pushing her forcefully toward the door.

"If you need anything—" Sally started.

"They need to be left alone." Jack pulled the door closed behind them.

Logan hefted the trunk and carried it the four steps to the wardrobe. He put it down more carefully this time, then undid the two brass buckles on the leather straps. Pushing open the lid, he glanced back at Katherine.

"If you're tired, I could help you unpack or ask Sally to."

"I'm fine." She came to stand next to him, her black kid shoes sinking into the carpet. "I can manage by myself."

"I know," he said softly, sadly. "Why don't I go downstairs and see what's for dinner? If you want to rest awhile or, well— Last door at the end of the hall...you can freshen up," he stammered. "Whenever you're ready to come down, I'll give you the nickel tour."

He gave her a quick kiss on the cheek. He was across the room and halfway out the door when he stopped. "I'll be in the library—bottom of the stairs, double doors on the left."

She nodded. Logan closed the door with a small snap.

As Katherine started to hang her dresses in the wardrobe, she paused and scanned the room once more. It was luxurious, like waking up to find you were a princess in a fairy tale. She shook her head in disbelief. She always knew that people lived like this, but she'd never actually known any.

She did feel just a pang of jealousy. Not for herself, but for her mother. They weren't poor. No one with a family like hers was poor, but she would like her mother to have some of the finer things to make life a little easier.

Soon, she promised, hanging her last dress on a wooden hanger. She closed the wardrobe while making a mental note to ask Sally for an iron, then put her underthings in the two top drawers of the bureau. The carved cherry wood felt cool and smooth against her fingers.

Moving her shoulders, she tried to ease the tension that had settled there from months of work and worry, fear and guilt.

The bed looked inviting. Walking over she tested it with her hand. Soft and fluffy and *really* inviting, she thought, her hand sinking in the down comforter. If she crawled in she'd stay there for a week, at least.

*Since when do you look for the easy way out?*

Since now, she answered her conscience. Didn't she deserve some rest, some time for herself, some happiness?

Now there was a word she hadn't used in a while—happiness.

With a sigh, she walked around the bed and out the bedroom door. She wasn't exactly *unhappy,* she thought, searching her mind for the correct word the way someone searches a closet for something lost. The odd thing was, this closet was nearly empty, as if she'd packed all her feelings away with her wool clothes.

She ambled slowly down the hall, the hem of her tan skirt skimming the pine green carpet.

Oh, she felt angry a lot these days, more than she wanted to. And when she was with Logan, he stirred up unique feelings, special feelings, ~~sensual,~~ demanding feelings. He overpowered her, made her lose control. But what confused her most was that she liked being out of control with Logan.

It was more than physical, she decided as she reached the top of the stairs. She paused, giving in to the restlessness she felt. Instantly, she thought of Logan. Why? It seemed to happen a lot at odd times, when she was sad or lonely or fearful. Somehow thinking of Logan seemed to ease whatever was bothering her.

Now they were bound together by marriage and by their impending parenthood. Quite honestly, she hated morning sickness. She'd spent enough mornings retching to last a lifetime. She'd heard it didn't last long and she fervently hoped that was true. The poor little fellow inside must be wondering what the devil was going on.

*Little fellow.* This was the very first time she'd thought of the child inside of her as something other than "it" or "baby"—something distant, almost impersonal.

She stood at the top of the stairs looking out over the foyer, struck with the reality of her situation. In about seven months, she would give birth to another living human being, a child who would require love and kindness, direction and discipline, to grow into a strong, able adult.

What would it be like for a child to grow up in a house like this? ˙

Her hand rested on the oak banister, waxed and gleaming. In her mind she saw the child of her thoughts, a little boy...

"Katherine."

She was surprised to see Logan standing at the bottom of the stairs. His head was cocked to one side.

"Are you all right?" he asked quietly. "You've been standing there awhile."

"I was thinking."

He climbed two stairs, closing the physical distance between them, wishing it were as easy to reach her heart. "What were you so lost in thought about?"

She didn't move, and looked at him with a melancholy smile that made him a little anxious.

"I was thinking that a little boy would love to go whooshing down this railing."

His anxiety eased and he smiled just a trace, taking another step. "I suppose a little boy would." His tone was hushed and an image of a very specific child came to his mind. A child he wanted more than he'd ever thought possible. "What does this mischievous cherub look like?" he asked carefully.

Her hand glided back and forth on the banister, testing the surface. "The one I'm thinking of has ruffled black hair."

Why was it becoming hard to breathe in here? Logan climbed three stairs, his boot steps muffled by the dark green carpet. "And?"

"And an impish grin."

Logan climbed another stair, his heart pounding as if he had climbed a thousand. "What else?"

She looked at him then. "He has big dark eyes. You know, the kind that can melt a mother's heart."

Logan climbed one more stair. His hand slid along the banister until the barest tips of his fingers touched hers.

"Whose little boy would he be, this black-haired charmer?" he asked, his voice a husky whisper.

"Yours," she told him.

"Ours," he corrected as his hand covered hers.

"Ours," she agreed with a wistful smile.

He said a silent prayer of thanks, forever grateful for the child to come.

Hand in hand they descended the stairs. He wanted to talk more about the child and the future, make plans for a nursery. He wanted to tell her he loved her. But he couldn't do any of those things, not yet. It was too soon. Instead, he said, "I'll take care of everything for you from now on." It was as much as he'd risk right now.

"I believe you promised me a tour," Katherine prompted, feeling very calm and comfortable. She continued to hold his hand.

"Yes, ma'am, I sure did," he confirmed, lacing his fingers through hers.

He smiled and kissed the tip of her nose and was pleased when she smiled back. He liked seeing her smile, especially when it was for him alone.

## Chapter Fifteen

Katherine rubbed the sleep from her eyes and sat up in bed. She was alone. The rumpled bed covers and the depression in the other pillow were the only evidence that Logan had spent the night next to her. He must have come up late, she thought.

She hadn't even noticed, probably because of the glass of wine she'd had with dinner, or this incredibly soft bed. Whatever the reason, she'd slept better than she had in a very long time.

Tossing back the covers and swinging her feet over the side, she stood and glanced at the clock. Half past ten! Someone should have awakened her. Pouring water in the blue porcelain basin, she quickly scrubbed her face and arms, then walked to the wardrobe and took out her navy skirt and a calico blouse. No sense getting dressed up until she knew what Logan's plans were for the day.

She tried to put her hair up in combs, but it didn't want to cooperate, so she gave up and simply braided it, tied a bright yellow ribbon around the end, then headed out the bedroom door toward the stairs.

The oak banister felt cool beneath her hand. Halfway down the stairs she halted, suddenly assaulted with the memory of Logan standing two steps below her. In her mind, she saw his face turned up to hers, his eyes softer and deeper than ever before. A warm, easy feeling moved through her.

*Logan, what are you doing to me?*

It was all so confusing. She liked things to be clear and direct. This wasn't. She wanted someone to tell her what was happening, what to do.

With a sigh, she continued to the bottom of the stairs, then crossed the foyer. The heels of her black kid shoes clicked on the bare pine floor.

A bouquet of fresh white-and-yellow daisies on the mahogany entry table caught her eye. She stopped to admire them, thinking nothing brightened a room, or a person's spirits, better than flowers.

It was then she noticed the house was quiet. Where was everyone?

A familiar warmth prickled up her spine and she turned toward the library doorway. Logan was there. Dressed in a forest green shirt and black pants, he was as handsome as ever. Katherine had the strange impulse to go to him, to touch him and to be touched. Refusing to acknowledge what she didn't understand, she shook off the notion, almost successfully.

"Good morning," he said softly. His lips turned up in that lazy smile of his. Her impulse got a little stronger.

"Good morning," she replied, her voice unsteady. "I'm sorry I slept so late. I—"

"Needed the rest," he interrupted, closing the distance between them in four long strides. His gaze never left hers. "You look beautiful this morning," he added, brushing her jaw with his knuckles. He lightly kissed the place his fingers had touched.

His face was only inches from hers. For a long moment they just stood there in the foyer. His breath was warm on her cheek, his gaze heated with a knowledge that came from their shared intimacy.

His hand came up to push an imaginary wisp of hair back from her face. His voice was a husky whisper. "You know,

Angel, waking up and finding you asleep next to me is enough to make me like mornings."

It was the kind of remark shared by a husband and wife. Which they were, Katherine reminded herself. It was also the kind of remark that left her a little breathless, a little unsure.

She swallowed hard and took a definite step back, which only seemed to make Logan's smile broaden.

"How about some breakfast... or luncheon?"

"Neither," she quickly replied as her hand covered her stomach, trying to still the sudden convulsing at the mention of food. "Later would be better."

Logan's smile faded. "I think I'll take you to see Doc Hiller while we're here. Maybe he can give you something to help."

He looked so concerned, so anxious, that Katherine was genuinely touched. "I've been told morning sickness is usual, and as long as I don't eat before noon, it seems to be fine. Please don't worry. If I thought there was something wrong I'd tell you," she assured him. "Now," she continued before he could press the point, "what would you like to do today?"

The question was such a leading one he almost told her. *Spend the day in bed with you.* But he didn't. Things were going well and he was determined to stay with his plan.

Seduction, slow and gentle.

"Well, Angel," he said quietly, "as much as it pains me to say so—" and the pain was increasing every minute he stood here looking at those luminous blue eyes of hers "—this is a business trip and I have to be gone today."

Katherine nodded, not sure whether she was grateful or disappointed that he would be absent.

"I'll be in meetings most of the day, but if you want to shop, I could—"

"No, actually, I'd just as soon spend some time here, if you don't mind. It isn't often I get the chance to be alone." To think, she added to herself.

"I don't like leaving you," Logan continued, "but my attorney's going to Denver tomorrow and I need to meet with him before he goes. . . . Family business."

"I understand," Katherine said. "You could send a telegram for me, though, if you have time."

He arched one dark brow. "A wire?"

"Please. If you'll give me something to write on."

Logan escorted her into his library and handed her a sheet of pale yellow paper. He pushed back the draperies, providing more light to the dark room, while Katherine went around his desk and wrote out a brief message. She didn't bother to fold it before she handed it to him.

Logan's eyes narrowed slightly and he shot her a questioning look, wondering if she meant for him to see the contents.

"It's to the bank in Philadelphia. Go ahead and read it, if you like."

He did, then looked at her in surprise. "You're selling your millinery shop?"

"Yes."

"Why?"

She casually shrugged her shoulders. "Well, considering that I'm married and about to have a baby, I think the likelihood of my returning to my business is rather remote."

There was a tone of sadness in her voice that tugged at him. "Perhaps there's someone who could run it for you," he said halfheartedly, torn between wanting to ease her regret and being glad she'd chosen to break her ties with the past.

He folded the paper and slipped it into his shirt pocket, a less than subtle indication of his preference.

Katherine's expression was as gloomy as the day outside. "There's no sense prolonging the inevitable. Unless, of course, you're planning to sell the Double Four and move with me to Philadelphia so I can return to my work."

Looking across the desk, Logan laughed disbelievingly. "You're not serious, of course. As soon as the baby comes, you'll—"

"Be busy, I know," she said for him with a shake of her head. She strolled over to the window. "No, Logan, I'm not serious about selling the Double Four, but it is interesting, isn't it?"

"What?"

"How everyone…" She glanced over her shoulder at him. "How *men* always seem to think that all any woman wants to do is be a wife and raise children. No one ever thinks that all a man wants is to be a husband and raise children."

"It comes naturally to women," he said, and suddenly felt like he was standing on thin ice.

"Logan, you can't seriously believe that there's some biological difference that makes women born knowing how to cook and clean and care for babies. This may come as a surprise to you, but I hate cleaning, I'm a mediocre cook at best and if I didn't have my mother to rely on, well, I wouldn't have the faintest idea about raising children."

Logan just stared at her. "Seriously?"

"Seriously," she confirmed. "I'm learning as I go, and because I like a challenge, because I want this baby, I'm determined to be the best cook and housekeeper and mother there ever was. But being in business was easier and much less frightening, and the rewards were, if not greater, certainly more obvious."

"How do you mean?" he asked, intrigued by her candor.

"I mean being wife and mother, well, it takes a long time before you know if your work is successful—about fifteen years," she said with a rueful chuckle. "With my shop, I was in complete control. I was responsible only for myself, accountable only to myself. If I made a decision on Monday, odds were by Friday I'd see the results, good or bad, and I could adjust my actions accordingly. Besides, having a shop gave me an identity. I was Katherine Thorn, Milliner. Now..." she looked out the window at the sprawling, grassy yard.

Logan was coming to understand just what marriage to him had cost her and just how much her family meant to her. The words she'd spoken on their wedding day came back to haunt him. *It cost you nothing. It cost me everything.*

He took a deep breath and let it out slowly, trying to formulate his feelings into words.

"Katherine, what you're saying is true. Men do attach their identity to what they do, how successful they are. And yes, I guess it's also true that we don't expect women to have the same feeling about that sort of thing, though right this minute I can't think why," he said honestly. He closed the distance between them, coming to stand next to her. "But please believe me when I tell you that you don't need a millinery shop, or a sheep ranch, or even being Mrs. Logan McCloud. None of those things can add to or take away from the person you are."

He cupped her delicate face in his hands, thinking she'd never looked more alluring or more vulnerable than at this moment. His voice dropped a little deeper. "Don't you know how extraordinary you are? You are the brightest, most beautiful woman I've ever known." He traced the curve of her cheek with his thumbs. "You confuse me. Sometimes, Lord knows, you anger me. But always, Angel, always you fascinate me."

He lowered his head and took her mouth in a tender kiss, willing her to know that he understood her anxiety and ached for all that she'd missed by growing up too early. Her lips were warm and yielding beneath his, and when he lifted his face, she was looking at him with eyes bluer than Jackson Lake, but not nearly as cold. Not cold at all, as a matter of fact. He was heating up himself.

*Don't scare her away. Not now. Not when things are going so well.*

Softly, he said, "May I take you out to dinner tonight, some place special, with music and dancing? I feel I owe you a real waltz."

Katherine was drowning in the nearness of him, in the joy his tender words gave her and especially in those black, liquid eyes of his. Her arms just naturally glided across his shoulders and twined around his neck.

Her heart beat a slow, heavy rhythm as she thought of the night in his parlor when they had danced to Strauss. "I didn't bring evening clothes," she said.

He smiled behind his mustache. The glint in his eyes was definitely wicked. "Evening clothes are not a requirement. Say you'll come with me and I promise to make this a night we'll both remember for a long time to come."

Sensual images flashed through her mind and feelings, lush and sultry, heated her blood. "Yes," she said, and wondered if she were agreeing to more than just the dinner.

Logan adjusted his black silk cravat in the mirror, rather pleased with the complicated knot. Not bad, he thought, considering he hadn't worn evening clothes in over six months—not since he'd left San Francisco last fall. He made a quick appraisal of his black frock coat and matching double-breasted waistcoat.

His hand brushed against the velvet box making a small bulge in his breast pocket. Reaching in, he shifted it to the side. "Better," he murmured, checking his appearance once again.

Upstairs, a door slammed. Looking up, he caught a glimpse of Sally before she disappeared back into the guest room—now his and Katherine's room.

What on earth was taking so long? Katherine had been ensconced in that room with Sally ever since he'd gotten home an hour and a half ago.

He sighed. Fortunately, his evening clothes had been in his own room or he'd probably be standing here naked.

The grandfather clock bonged once, then played half its tune. Eight-thirty. Where was she? He paced across the foyer then back again, finally stopping in the open front doorway. The moist night breeze against his face did little to calm him.

He was filled with anxiety—the floor-pacing, heart-pounding type. He'd hardly been able to keep his thoughts on business today. His mind was on something else—someone else. When Katherine had looked at him this morning with those sensual eyes of hers, it had made his chest hurt, he'd wanted her so much. And every time he looked at her mouth he thought of temptation and sin and sex, and he stopped breathing all together.

Dear Lord, how he loved her. And that's what this seduction was about. He wanted her to admit that they were destined to be together.

He wanted her in all the ways a man wants the woman he loves. He wanted her to love him.

He *wanted* his wife.

A restlessness moved through him and he turned, knowing she was there.

"I'm late," she confessed, hurrying down the steps while tying the ribbon on the black opera cape, the one Sally had asked to borrow from the wardrobe Logan's sister kept at the house. "There were some...difficulties with the dress."

Logan looked at her. All that honey-colored hair was piled high in soft curls and feathery wisps framed her face, making her eyes seem bigger than ever. Her skin looked pale next to the black satin she wore. Only the teal-and-gold beaded train of her dress showed beneath the cape.

She looked like an angel—his angel.

"Ready?" Logan inquired.

"Ready," Katherine confirmed. In evening clothes, Logan seemed as dark and tempting as the devil himself.

Two minutes later they were comfortably seated in the covered buggy. Katherine carefully tucked her dress around her legs, protecting it from the bright yellow wheels. When she looked up, Logan was watching her. She met his gaze, expecting him to speak. He didn't.

"What?" she finally asked, feeling awkward. "Is something wrong?"

"Everything is exactly perfect," he said with a slow, lazy smile that didn't quite reach his dimples—thank goodness. Anticipation about spending an evening alone with Logan already had her shaking inside like an earthquake.

Logan dragged his gaze away and gave a quick slap of the reins. The sorrel moved smartly away from the curb.

The moon, obscured by the clouds, occasionally peeked through to fill the night with pale rays of silver moonlight. The buggy lantern and light from the houses illuminated the hard-packed earthen street.

"I arranged for a table at the Inter-Ocean," he told her over the steady clip-clop of the horse's hooves.

"Not the Cheyenne Club? I thought that was the best place in town."

Logan chuckled. "No women allowed. Besides, the hotel has a small band and I'm looking forward to holding an angel in my arms."

His face was cast in shadows, but his tone was definitely husky. It was enough to start a slow heat building inside her. Muscles tensed as she remembered how strong his embrace could be, how he could set her on fire with only a look.

Ten minutes later, they pulled up outside Cheyenne's leading hotel. Logan helped Katherine from the buggy and escorted her inside.

Her kid shoes sank in the rich Brussels carpet and she paused. "Logan, this is..." her gaze scanned the polished wood-paneled lobby "...incredible," she finished somewhat lamely as she took in the red velvet drapes and matching chairs.

"For the wilderness, you mean," Logan teased. Taking her elbow, he escorted her toward the dining room. He waved to a Negro man standing near the front desk. "Evening, Barney," Logan called as they walked. The man returned the wave.

More quietly Logan said, "Barney Ford, builder and owner. Not bad for a runaway slave, do you think?"

Before she could answer, they stepped into the equally elegant dinning room, complete with flowered wallpaper and low-burning gas lamps.

Just as Logan had promised, there was a small band. The piano, violin and cello trio was playing "Aura Lea." Next to them a small dance floor was unoccupied.

The tables, however, were not. As a matter of fact they were nearly all full, Katherine noticed. Candles flickered on each, refracting their light through the crystal glasses or off the gleaming white china.

Logan stepped up behind her. Katherine didn't fail to miss the slight murmur that went through the crowd when he walked in. Nor did she miss the heads that turned in his direction and the coy smiles on several of the ladies' faces.

"Good evening, Mr. McCloud," the chubby maître d' said in a deferential tone. "Your table is waiting," he added with an awkward bow that pulled at his slightly tight black suit.

"Thank you, John."

The man's gaze quickly moved to Katherine. "If you'd give me your wrap, I'll have it put away until you're ready to leave."

Standing behind her, Logan lifted the cape from her shoulders and handed it to the man. When he turned back his gaze scanned the room. His brows knitted. At least a dozen men were making no secret of staring—leering—at Katherine.

That was when he glanced over at her and got a look at his wife.

"Katherine?" he mumbled, doing a little staring himself. He was startled, no doubt about that.

His gaze drifted across her slender shoulders, pale and delicate against the blue-green cap sleeves of the dress, then down to her creamy white breasts revealed above her plunging neckline. His gaze returned to her blue eyes. Quite simply, she took his breath away. The only thing he could think to say was, "Stunning."

# Chapter Sixteen

"Stunning?" Katherine blushed. She'd never thought of herself that way. She glanced at Logan and was rewarded with one of his lazy half smiles, the kind that made her palms sweat and her fingers tremble. Only this one also made her smile, too.

It was not her need to tempt Logan that had gotten her into this getup tonight. It was her failure to anticipate just how much, or more precisely, how *little* material would be left after Sally removed the lace inset from the dress's bodice.

It had seemed like a good idea at the time, she thought, an easy way to make a day dress seem more formal. Unfortunately, when she'd finally put it on, there just wasn't time to change it back. Now, seeing the way Logan was looking at her... well, maybe it wasn't such a bad idea after all.

She reminded herself not to breathe too deeply as they followed the maître'd to the table in the far corner.

"Shall I send the champagne over now?" the man inquired once they were settled. A waiter in a black suit inched past, carrying a tray of food for the foursome at the table a scant five feet away.

Logan tried not to frown as he glanced around the room. What the hell were all these people doing here? Then he remembered. That Shakespearian actor, John somebody or other, was in town, and the theater had let out about a half hour ago. The frown he was trying to hide behind his mustache grew deeper. Didn't these people have homes?

"Sir?" the man prompted.

Logan sighed inwardly. "Yes, John," he confirmed. "We'll have chamgagne now, then oysters, then we'll look at a menu."

"Very well, sir," the man said and hurried between the tables toward the doorway on the opposite side of the room.

A loud peel of laughter from a table of men drew Katherine's and Logan's attention, but only for an instant. He was determined to think only about them, to make this night unique. That's why he'd brought her out instead of staying home. He smiled and said, very quietly, "I missed being with you today." His directness didn't surprise her. He'd always had a way of saying things that took her off guard.

The silence stretched between them. Sounds of people talking, glasses clinking and china rattling all blurred together as Katherine willingly drowned in his bottomless black eyes.

Katherine looked up, startled to find the waiter standing there holding the bottle of champagne.

After Logan tasted and approved the selection the waiter filled two glasses, put the bottle in the wine bucket and left.

"To blizzards," Logan said, lifting his glass slightly. "I'll never curse one again."

"You say that now." Katherine chuckled and gently touched her glass to his, making a small *clink*. The backs of their hands brushed, sending tiny sparks skittering up her bare arm. She pulled away and sipped the champagne, letting the bubbles tickle her nose and make her smile.

Logan liked the way she smiled. It was becoming almost obsessive with him to find what made her smile. He had the feeling she hadn't done nearly enough smiling or laughing in her life. That was another thing he was going to change.

Looking at her now, his mouth went dry. Dear God, she was glorious, and she belonged to him.

"Have I told you just how beautiful you are tonight?"

Katherine blushed again. "What I feel is half . . ."

"Naked," he supplied with a wicked glint in his eyes. "And you said you didn't have evening clothes."

"I don't. This is a day dress. Sally altered it and—"

"And she did a wonderful job. Remind me to double her salary in the morning," he commented with what he hoped was his most charming smile. Evidently it worked, because now Katherine was really blushing. Unfortunately, the waiter chose that moment to arrive. He placed a platter of oysters in the center of the table and left again.

Katherine took one look at the raw shellfish and felt her stomach convulse. "No, thank you," she told Logan when he pushed the plate in her direction. No sense taking any chances on her body rejecting the slimy seafood.

Logan only chuckled. "Something else?"

She shook her head and continued to sip the sparkling wine. She couldn't help wincing when Logan actually ate one of the oysters and reached for another.

Rather than watch, she glanced around the room. Gas lamps on the walls sputtered and flickered. All the ladies present were dressed to the nines. Their bright-colored silks and satins were merely a background for their expensive jewels. And while some of the men wore suits, others wore evening attire like Logan.

No, not like Logan, she corrected, as she glanced back at this man who was her husband. There wasn't a man in the room who was like Logan, not in appearance, not in sheer male presence.

As if sensing her thoughts, he smiled roguishly behind his mustache and lounged back in his chair. "Did you find something to keep you busy today?"

*I tried not to think about you and the way you kissed me this morning,* she was tempted to say, but didn't. "Well, I read, and I helped Sally make some sugar cookies. I wasn't busy at all . . . it was sinfully lazy of me."

"But did you enjoy it?" he asked softly, covering her hand with his larger one, feeling her fingers flutter against his palm.

"Yes," she answered just as softly.

"Good. I want you to do whatever pleases you." He had a couple of suggestions along those lines and was considering telling her when the gentle sounds of "I'll Take You Home Again, Kathleen" drifted over the hum of the crowd. Perhaps a dance might be more appropriate, he decided. For now, at least.

"Shall we finish that dance?" Logan asked on a husky whisper, suddenly on fire with the need to hold her in his arms.

For a moment, the words didn't even register with Katherine, so caught up was she in the nearness of him, the feel of flesh against flesh as his thumb teased the back of her knuckles, making her heart pound.

He did that to her. From the very first time she'd seen him, all he had to do was look at her in that special way of his, or say her name, or touch her, and everything around her ceased to exist.

Never letting go of her hand, he stood.

"Good evening, Logan," a distinctly feminine voice purred near his shoulder.

Oh, hell! Logan didn't have to look to identify the speaker. He'd heard that voice purr in his ear before.

Tearing his gaze away from Katherine's, he forced a smile and turned. "Hello, Melissa. What are you doing here?"

"Why, dining with friends, of course, darling," she said with a cordial smile. She nonchalantly adjusted the lace on the bodice of her pale blue silk gown, drawing Logan's attention to her generous attributes.

It wasn't necessary, he thought. He'd seen her...attributes. All of them, that summer they'd spent together. But that was two years ago. He had not seen her since, except in passing, of course, which was good. She had become much too possessive, something he'd never wanted in a woman. Until Katherine.

"Katherine, allow me introduce you to Melissa Johnson. Melissa, this is Katherine, my wife."

Katherine nodded. "Miss Johnson."

Melissa's eyes widened slightly at the news, but she quickly recovered and gave a small laugh. "Why, Logan, you always did know how to tease me. I almost believed you," she said in a calm tone.

"Believe it," Logan confirmed rather sharply annoyed at Melissa's arrogance.

"What!" She turned a cold appraising stare on Katherine. "You got married?"

"A week ago," he confirmed.

"Congratulations," she muttered with all the sincerity of a snake-oil salesman.

She placed her hand on Logan's sleeve in what was obviously a calculated gesture. "Logan, how could you have done this without giving your mother and Mary Rosa an opportunity for a big wedding?" She made a perfect little pout that Logan thought must have required hours of practice in front of a mirror.

"My wedding is no one's concern," he said flatly.

Melissa seemed to ignore his pointed remark. She turned back to Katherine, who was standing now. She hadn't said another word, but Logan knew that stiff-backed stance of Katherine's all too well. The lady's temper was rising. So was his.

"Well, thanks for stopping by, Melissa," he said with as much congeniality as he could muster.

Melissa didn't take the hint, nor did she try to conceal her appraising stare.

"Yes, indeed," she murmured, her hand still on Logan's sleeve, "Cheyenne society will be sorely disappointed when news gets out that it's been cheated out of the wedding of the year." She arched one perfect brown brow. "You kept it terribly quiet. No invitations, no—" Suddenly a knowing smile played across her lips. Her gaze flicked from Logan to Katherine and back to Logan again. "Why, darling," she fairly cooed, "you were always so careful ... before."

*Was murder still a hanging offense?* "Excuse us, Katherine. I need to speak with Melissa privately." Logan's tone was harsh. Without waiting for an answer he took her elbow and escorted her a couple of steps closer to the corner, near a fan palm.

"It's sweet of you to want to speak to me, darling," Melissa said innocently, "but don't you think this is a little obvious? Perhaps you should drop by my house later."

"I am not being sweet, Melissa, and you know it." His expression was hard, his voice low. "Put your damned claws away."

Melissa rolled her eyes in a seductive manner. "Why, darling, you always liked my claws, usually on the inside of your thigh, as I remember." Curling the tips of her fingers, she imitated the gesture by letting her hand glide up his sleeve, stopping just below his shoulder.

"Stop it, Melissa!" Logan snarled, grabbing her hand and holding it between them.

Katherine didn't miss the action. She watched them for a full ten seconds, unable to hear what was being said. She didn't have to. She watched the way Melissa's hand never left Logan's arm, the way she stood just a little too close to him, and most especially the way he didn't seem to find any of that unusual.

It was obvious they'd known each other before. The reality hit her like a splash of cold water. Until this very moment she'd never thought of Logan with another woman.

Now she was. Now she was imagining all kinds of things. Him sitting in front of a fire with someone other than her, sipping wine, looking at *her* with his hypnotic eyes, enchanting *her* with his seductive smile, tempting *her* with promises that Katherine knew, all too well, he was lushly capable of fulfilling.

Her heart pounded heavily in her chest. Logan moved, blocking her view. A quick glance around the room revealed that she wasn't the only one watching the little scene unfolding a few feet away. Well, she wasn't going to stand here and be humiliated. She squared her shoulders and walked from the room, needing some fresh air. Lots of it.

Logan was so angry, he didn't see or hear anything except the little hellcat who was intent on ruining his evening. "Let's get this clear. I'm happily married. If that suspicious little mind of yours dreams up any questions, you damned well better keep them to yourself. Under no circumstances will I tolerate the slightest rudeness to my wife. Do you understand me, Melissa?" he ground out, his temper barely under control.

Melissa's smile faded. "You mean you married the chit because you wanted to?"

Logan took a deep breath. The impulse to strangle her was getting stronger by the second.

"Yes, Melissa. Try to get it through your head—I'm in love with Katherine. Now get the hell out of my way while I go dance with my wife."

Katherine stepped out onto the front porch. She took a deep calming breath, then another, and one more for good measure. The evening breeze ruffled the tiny curls that framed her face, much the way Logan had earlier. Oh, Lord, she was such an idiot to be taken in so completely by his charm. She squeezed her eyes closed.

And there in her mind was Melissa. Beautiful Melissa. A little porcelain doll, with a perfect figure and perfect hair, in perfect ringlets around a perfect heart-shaped face. It was enough to make her want to throw up, and this time not from morning sickness. And it wasn't jealousy!

*Of course it was.*

She was being petty and envious and it wasn't like her at all. *What are you so upset about?* she asked herself. It was no surprise that Logan hadn't led the life of a monk before he met her. And actually meeting someone whom he'd known before was bound to happen. Cheyenne wasn't that large a city.

She stared up at the cloud-filled night sky. Then it came to her. *She* was the one he'd married. He'd obviously not asked that Melissa person. That thought made her feel a whole lot better.

A man's voice broke into her thoughts. "Miss, are you all right?"

"Fine," she muttered absently. The breeze seemed suddenly cool on her shoulders and she shivered.

"Are you ill?" the man inquired with a soft but decidedly British accent. "Can I get someone for you?"

He was so solicitous, so polite, that she chided herself for her lack of good manners. Turning, she looked up at the tall, blond man, clean shaven and impeccably dressed in black evening attire.

Katherine gave him a polite smile and absently smoothed the folds of her foulard skirt. "My apologies for my abruptness, but I'm quite fine. Thank you for your concern."

"My pleasure," he assured her over the rumble of a wagon passing down the street. "May I be so bold as to introduce myself? I am Anthony Halstead, the Earl of Stowe." He made a slight bow that seemed as foreign as his accent.

"Royalty?" Katherine said with surprise.

"Not the way you mean." He moved to the side and leaned one shoulder against the stone wall of the hotel. "I would be pleased if you would call me Anthony."

"Mr. Halstead," she said with a smile.

"As you wish." He chuckled. "I thought I knew everyone in town. Are you from Cheyenne? I can't believe I would have missed meeting anyone as beautiful as you."

Katherine blushed and smiled, not immune to the flattery.

"I'm Katherine Th—McCloud."

Halstead straightened abruptly, glanced around as if searching for someone, then quickly returned his gaze to her. "Do you mean to say you are Mrs. *Logan* McCloud?"

Katherine stiffened a little. "Yes, that's correct."

Halstead arched one blond brow. "Well, well, this is a surprise. And where is your husband this evening? Surely he didn't let you come out alone?"

Katherine frowned, remembering the reason—the person, who had sent her out here in the darkness. "Logan is inside talking with Melissa Johnson."

"Ah," Halstead offered with a knowing nod. "They're old acquaintances."

Something in the way he said "acquaintances" didn't settle too well with Katherine. Did everyone in town know what she was just now figuring out? Logan McCloud's charm obviously came from long years of practice.

"Why don't we have a seat inside?" Mr. Halstead suggested, gesturing toward two red velvet chairs visible through the lobby window. "I would be pleased to keep you company until Logan is available—if you'd like, that is. Logan's an old friend and he could see us easily there."

A glance confirmed the accuracy of his statement and she agreed. Stepping into the lobby, she sat down, the velvet cool against her bare shoulders. Halstead carefully pushed her skirt aside and sat next to her. Light from the gas lamp on the wall above them illuminated his features. He twisted to face her more fully.

"I just came from tonight's performance of *King Lear*. Do you know it?"

"I've read it. Did you enjoy it?"

"Yes. The troupe was quite good, actually. The last time I saw *Lear* I was in New York," he remarked, then launched into a story about an after-theater party he'd attended where a table leg had collapsed, spilling a large bowl of champagne punch on the hostess's white silk dress. The material was rendered quite transparent, which the lady didn't seem to realize immediately, much to the enjoyment of the men present.

The story was completely inappropriate, and Katherine was about to tell him so when he screwed up his face in an imitation of the horrified hostess and hiked up his voice like an Italian soprano. Katherine laughed. She couldn't help it, any more than she could help glancing toward the restaurant doorway, wondering where Logan was. Why hadn't he come looking for her? Was he still talking with Melissa?

Muscles in her stomach clenched. No! She refused to get angry. She was going to sit here and enjoy herself. After all, that's what Logan had said he wanted her to do—feel good and enjoy herself. She forced herself to concentrate on the story Anthony Halstead was telling about his encounter with an amorous bull moose that had mistaken him for a love-sick female and proceeded to chase him up a tree.

Katherine started to laugh. As the story went on, tears actually slipped down her cheeks and she had to plead with him to stop. Suddenly she was having fun. So much so that she shared a story about crossing paths with an aggressive bull in an apple orchard back in Virginia on a day she was determined to have apple pie for dinner.

Now Halstead was laughing. His hand squeezed her bare arm. "You are delightful."

That's when Logan saw her. Cheeks flushed, eyes sparkling, she was sitting sideways on the small velvet chair, laughing at something Anthony Halstead was saying. *Anthony Halstead. The biggest womanizer in Cheyenne.* This was all he needed. He felt hostile—gut-tightening hostile.

First Melissa and now this. It had been a helluva night.

For some reason he couldn't fathom, he simply stood there and watched. Watched his wife give away smiles to strangers when he had to work all day for one.

The hostility in him grew into something cold and ugly. Logan had never thought of himself as jealous—until now.

Slowly, determinedly, he walked across the lobby, oblivious to those who offered greetings.

He didn't care. Good manners were the last thing on his mind. He wasn't interested in anyone or anything but the lady his gaze was riveted on.

"Good evening, sweetheart," Logan said politely, quietly, with a smile that didn't reach his eyes.

Halstead rose to his feet, as did Katherine.

Logan moved to stand next to her and looped her arm around his in a blatantly possessive gesture. The breeze through the open door ruffled his hair, but Logan paid scant notice. His attention was focused on the man directly in front of him. "Enjoying yourself, Halstead?" he asked pointedly.

"It's turned out to be a very...rewarding evening," Halstead returned with a casual arrogance that went with his aristocratic upbringing. "You always did have impeccable taste in women," he added, then turned his smile on Katherine. "If you ever tire of this provincial, why, please call on me...Katherine. I know how to treat a lady."

Logan didn't miss Halstead's familiarity. His wife had gotten damned chummy with the man in the ten or so minutes since she'd walked out of the dining room. His hostility grew and he instinctively took a half step in Halstead's direction, then stopped. He'd had it with rakes and conniving witches.

Giving Halstead one last look, he took Katherine's elbow firmly in his hand. "We're leaving now, sweetheart."

"What are you talking about? What about dinner?"

Logan shot her a hard look, then started away, forcing her to follow.

Out the door and two steps toward the buggy she halted. This barbarian attitude of his wasn't working with her, she thought, feeling her Irish temper start to rise.

She glared at him. "Wait. I need my cloak."

"Forget the damn cloak," he snapped. Then, feeling a light mist of rain on his face, he turned and strode briskly into the lobby, retrieved the garment and returned to drop it around Katherine's shoulders.

In the distance, lightning made a jagged path through the night sky. The first faint rumbling of thunder echoed as he helped her into the buggy, then climbed in after.

She tried to pull her hem out of his way, but was too late to keep him from stepping on it with his muddy boots. "My dress," she admonished.

"I'll buy you another," he tossed back with casual arrogance before slapping the reins against the horse's rump. The sorrel took off at a gallop. The harness jingled sharply.

The frantic pounding of hooves matched the pounding of Katherine's heart. "Slow down," she told him. He didn't. The buggy creaked as they turned first one corner, then another. The cloak slipped down behind her and she ignored it.

Lightning flashed, much closer now and thunder crashed angrily overhead. Reaching the house, Logan reined up hard, making the horse paw the ground anxiously.

Unmindful of the rain, he turned to stare intently at his wife. His hands shot out. He grabbed her bare shoulders, cool and wet from the mist, and yanked her against him. He covered her mouth with a kiss that was searing in its intensity. He wanted her, it was that simple. A man had his patience but *this* man's had just run out.

Abruptly, he tore his mouth from hers, jumped down from the buggy, hollered for a groom to tend to the horse and buggy and scooped Katherine up in his arms. He strode up the walk and into the house. Boots thudding on the polished floor, he headed for the library the way any male predator heads for familiar territory.

"Logan, stop it." She squirmed in his arms, pushing at his broad shoulders. "What do you think you're doing?"

"What I should have done days ago."

# Chapter Seventeen

Three steps inside the front doors, he halted. Outside, lightning sizzled across the night sky. Logan was doing a fair amount of sizzling himself.

The lamp flickered on the entry table, casting the room in moving shadows of gray and violet. Dampness clung to them, doing nothing to cool him while seeming to intensify the familiar smell of Katherine's rose perfume. The fragrance surrounded him, much the way she did, or at least the way he wanted her to. His mouth went dry.

Abruptly, he lowered Katherine's feet to the bare floor.

For five long seconds she glared at him while his hand encircled her wrist like a shackle. "Let me go," she demanded.

"I wish I could." He swayed against her, his arousal, hard and aching, pressing against her hip. Desire raged through him.

She writhed in an attempt to free herself, and he grabbed her other wrist. Arms spread wide, he pressed her back against the walnut-paneled wall near the bottom of the stairs.

"What, no smiles for your husband, sweetheart?"

"Logan, what's the matter with you?" she challenged, feeling more excited than afraid. Logan had never hurt her; she knew he never would.

"You were smiling enough for Halstead. What else were you doing with Halstead?"

She suddenly became very still. "I was doing the same thing with Mr. Halstead that you were doing with Melissa!" she hurled back at him.

"I don't give a damn about Melissa. You stay away from Halstead. He's a womanizer, and he doesn't care whose wife—"

"We were talking! He said you were friends."

"The hell we are." Logan emphasized each word carefully. "I don't want you near him. I don't want you near *any* other man, dammit." Anger rejected reason. "You're mine! Do you understand me, Katherine? Mine, now and always, and—oh, the hell with it!"

Ruthlessly, his mouth took hers, slanting first one way, then the other. His hips swayed against her, leaving no doubt of his intention.

When she made that little half cry, half moan deep in her throat, it was like adding kindling to a smoldering ember. Heat shot through him, scorching the edges of what little sanity he had left. God help him, he was damned close to ripping that dress off her and taking her right there on the stairs.

His kiss was brutal, stealing the breath from her lungs and sending her pulse rate soaring. Nerves flared to life and her whole body instantly opened to him as if it were welcoming home a lover—and it was. A molten rush plunged through her and centered low in her abdomen. Katherine tried to break free of his grasp, not to run away, but to wrap her arms around him and hang on.

Harshly, frantically, he kissed her jaw, nipped her neck and along her rain-dampened shoulders. Everywhere his mouth touched, her flesh was on fire. Restless, desperate to touch him, she moaned, "Logan…please…let go of me."

Logan stopped. He'd never forced a woman in his life. "Dammit," he muttered on an uneven breath.

"Logan, I want—"

"You want," he repeated harshly. "*You* want!" He shot her a hard look and released her. He raked both hands through his damp hair, leaving furrows in the blackness. "*I* want a wife. A *real* wife, someone who saves her smiles, her laughter, only for me." He glared at her and she met his gaze directly with eyes dark and luminous.

"Forget it, Katherine," he snarled and strode toward the library. "Forget everything!" He slammed the doors so hard the glass rattled. The rush of air made the lamp on the desk flicker precariously inside the crystal globe.

Logan barely noticed. In fifteen seconds he was out of his frock coat and silk tie, both of which he flung on the chair. The little velvet box slipped out of his pocket and skittered across the floor, stopping near the burgundy drapes. Logan frowned and ignored it.

He must have been crazy to let himself fall in love with her.

He headed for the liquor table and poured himself a double whiskey. With a mock salute to the empty room, he said, "Here's to women in general and a certain sheep rancher in particular." He emptied the glass in one gulp.

Turning on his heel, he hurled the crystal at the bookcase on the opposite wall. The glass shattered the same instant the library door banged open.

He looked around to see Katherine striding straight toward him. Her hair was half down around her shoulders, her cheeks were flushed and her chest was heaving too damned seductively near that plunging neckline. "I'm not up to this, Katherine. I'm in no mood to be civilized."

Neither was Katherine. She strode right up to him and without a word, pulled his mouth to hers and kissed him. Then, tearing her mouth away, she said, "Don't you *ever* do that again!"

His eyes narrowed. It took two tries to get his voice to work. "What the hell are you talking about?" he finally managed in a raspy tone.

"You," she flung at him. "Don't you ever kiss me like you did out there and then walk away. Do you think I'm made of stone?"

"Aren't you?"

"No!"

"You could have fooled me."

She deserved that, she supposed, and more, considering how she'd kept him at arm's length. He was her husband. He'd made it very clear he wanted her, and the truth was, she wanted him just as much.

She took a deep breath and let it out slowly. "Let me show you what I'm made of." She cupped the side of his face with her hand.

Her words were seductive, her invitation clear. But Logan resisted. Not two minutes ago he'd decided to end this torture, to stop this futile quest for the woman who had the power to please him and hurt him beyond anything he'd ever known. His mouth turned down in a deep frown.

Katherine stroked his jaw, her thumb skimming his mustache and along his bottom lip, while she looked at him with warm, liquid eyes.

"Katherine," he said against her fingers. "Don't play games with me. I want you. If that's not what you want, lady, you better run like hell while there's still time."

"No," she said softly and moved closer to him. Her outstretched hand rested lightly on his cotton shirtsleeve. "I'm here to stay."

Logan gave a sharp laugh. "For how long? Until tomorrow, or until an hour from now?"

"Forever."

Finally, the word he'd been waiting for. His beautiful, stubborn, determined loner was giving in. For the span of two heartbeats, he stared into her breathtakingly huge eyes while the words penetrated his brain. *You won, you fool. Don't just stand there.*

On a sudden intake of breath, he pulled her to him. His arms went around her shoulders as his hungry mouth claimed hers, letting her know there would be no turning back.

Katherine understood his message. Heart pounding, she grabbed hold of his waistcoat and hung on as she gladly surrendered to him.

The bedroom was upstairs, but Logan didn't think he could wait that long. There was a black bearskin rug on the floor by the hearth. Lifting Katherine in his arms, he crossed the room in four powerful strides.

This time when he released her, she slid down the front of him like silk over steel. His hardened arousal strained at the soft black wool of his trousers.

Feverishly, his mouth ate at hers. Desire forced him to move like a caged, restless animal, desperate for release. Shaking his head, he said, "I want you so much, and there's no way I can go slow." His voice was a harsh whisper. "The baby—"

"Is fine," she assured him.

He couldn't stop touching her. He couldn't stop kissing her. One-handed, he tore at his waistcoat and shirt. Buttons flew, fabric ripped, but he didn't care.

Katherine struggled with the delicate laces at the back of her dress. Her shaking fingers refused to function. "I can't," she pleaded.

Logan produced a small bone-handled knife from his trouser pocket. With two swipes, the dress and petticoats became a green silken pool at her feet.

The light in the room was poor but good enough to remind Logan that even in her undergarments, Katherine was beautiful. He shook his head, wanting to say something but not knowing what. She was all long legs and silken hair. All he could think about were those legs, bare and wrapped around his waist. Memories, hot and carnal, came flooding back and he knew he had to have her soon or die.

Lightning slashed across the night, illuminating the room in a momentary flash of white light. Logan barely noticed.

With shaking fingers, he reached for the pale yellow satin ribbons on her camisole.

Katherine watched him. Passion smoldered in his deep black eyes. Just looking at him increased her desire beyond anything she'd known before.

"Let me," she offered. With a trace of a smile, she pulled the three ribbons loose and let the garment slip from her shoulders and float to the floor.

She stood proudly as he stared at her. The delicate flesh of her bare breasts heated under his gaze, the nipples pulling into tight buds longing for his touch.

Logan drew in a lungful of air. Then, feet braced wide, he pulled her into him with one hand, letting her feel his hardness press against her cotton-clad belly. The other hand cupped her breast, reveling in the feel of her nipple against his callused palm just before he took the rosy nubbin between his thumb and forefinger, gently squeezing.

Katherine moaned, letting her head roll back. But the torture was delicious and she pressed into his palm, wanting more all the while her fingers were clamped hard around his upper arms.

Logan looked into her half-open, passion-glazed eyes. "I want to love you, every delicious inch of you," he muttered, then ran his tongue lightly along her jaw, pausing to suck on her chin. Lowering his head, he took one rosy nipple in his mouth, teasing and exciting it with his tongue and teeth.

Longing, more intense than the lightning outside, streaked through her. Out of control and loving every minute, she reveled in the opulent, luscious sensations spiraling through her. She wanted it all. Every touch, every breath created a demand for more. A lifetime of barriers crumbled under his sensuous assault.

Logan moved to the other side to work his erotic magic there.

"It's wonderful," she murmured. "You make me feel wonderful."

Breathing hard, he looked at her, cupped her chin in his hand and rained tiny kisses over her brow and along the ridge of her cheekbone. "I want you to feel wonderful, Angel." His tone was fire warm and cashmere soft. "I want to spend my life giving you pleasure."

With a groan, he grabbed her shoulders like a drowning man going down for the last time. "I need you now."

"And I need you," she returned in a fierce whisper.

Lush memories mixed with savage desire. Muscles straining, she swayed against him, feeling his arousal, feeling her breasts pressed against the hot skin of his chest. Her mind and body focused on one thing—satisfying the blazing passion that was consuming her, breath by frantic breath.

Lifting up on her stocking-clad toes, she kissed him hard, holding nothing back and demanding the same from him. When her tongue slipped inside his mouth, he groaned deep down inside.

Shifting slightly, Logan pulled the cord on her pantalets and pushed them to the floor, taking her stockings with them. In one motion, he scooped her up in his arms. Lightning crackled again in the night sky. Logan felt it more than saw it. His whole body seemed electric, like the storm raging outside.

He dropped to one knee and lowered her onto the thick, black pelt. She sprawled seductively on the fur, and the picture she presented was every dream he'd ever had come true.

Logan shed his boots and pants and covered her with his body. He hoped to hell she was ready because he was being driven by a need so strong he was powerless against it.

Heart pounding, he slid into her. She was hot and wet and soothed him like warm brandy on a cold winter night. In that instant he knew that she owned him, body and soul.

Katherine welcomed him, exulting in his sheer male strength. She was powerless against the violent need he created in her. She gave herself completely, anxious for the remembered rapture that came closer with each touch, each powerful stroke.

Logan struggled to maintain some control. Already the passion that clouded his brain was driving his body to move faster, harder into the warm, tight cavern she offered. His mouth tore at hers in a searing kiss. His tongue laved at the roof of her mouth and the sweet, tender flesh on the inside of her cheek.

He withdrew and reentered her, sliding over the slick, swollen sweetness of her. Her head rolled back and forth on the velvet fur, but she met him stroke for stroke. She was close.

On a raspy breath, he whispered near her ear, "Let me love you."

Tears clogged her throat. She wrapped her arms around his bare shoulders and pulled him hard against her. She couldn't get enough of him.

And on that thought, she felt the first tiny tremor.

He changed the rhythm, faster, harder, fuller, and each time she felt the tremors increase, felt herself convulse around him.

Like a storm rushing down the Eastern Rockies, they crashed together in a merging of body and spirit that consumed them both and left them breathless. It was rapture, sweet and pure.

Katherine clung to him, her head nestled in the hollow of his shoulder. Her breath came in rapid, short gasps as she drifted back to earth. And as she did, she knew with a certainty that she loved Logan McCloud.

For several minutes afterward, Logan lay in the near-dark room with the woman he loved snug in his arms. Her body curved down the length of him like rose-scented silk.

She was warm and sleepy and Logan was content to hold her. One hand caressed her from shoulder to hip, the other toyed with her hair which was pooled on his chest like sunshine.

He let his eyes drift closed, enjoying the moment, and was dimly aware that outside, even the storm had changed. The violence had moved on, leaving only soft, gentle rain splashing on the porch roof. It was an easy sound, peaceful, much the way Logan felt.

Katherine stirred. Her arm slid up his chest and around his neck. He smiled and briefly wondered, if he locked the library doors and had food delivered once or twice a day, whether he could keep Katherine here and naked for the rest of the week.

Probably not. But it was a tempting thought.

Katherine's lips on his shoulder brought him out of his musings.

"Is it always this nice?" she asked, feeling replete and lazy and so very content.

Logan ran the tips of his fingers along her spine. She shivered, making his smile broaden. "Didn't you know?" he couldn't help teasing. "Nice is one of my specialties."

"Of course," she confirmed, moving her head slightly. Beneath her ear she could hear the slow, steady beat of his heart. "I should have known." *Just like I should have known I loved you.*

If she were honest, and she finally was, she would admit that she had loved Logan from practically the first minute she'd set eyes on him. She couldn't have made love with him on the creek bank if she hadn't loved him. But falling in love at first sight was not the sort of thing a sensible young businesswoman did. Besides, there were so many differences between them.

And yet, lying there, listening to the rain, wrapped in Logan's strong embrace with the exquisite rapture they'd shared still singing in her body, she didn't care about differences. There were problems yet to be resolved between them. But not tonight. Tonight there were no sheep or cattle or ranches—only the two of them.

"Hey," came Logan's deep, playful voice. "You awake?"

Resting her chin on his chest, she looked at him with those luminous blue eyes, dark like the sapphires in the bracelet he'd bought earlier. The one he'd failed to give her. For a fleeting moment, he actually considered getting up to find the velvet box.

But then Katherine squirmed, her leg slipping between his, her thigh dangerously close to his manhood. Instantly, desire started to build in him.

He kissed her lightly and wondered if she would understand that he wanted her so soon again. He rolled onto his side so he could see her face. She lay on her back next to him, her eyes closed, her hair fanned out around her, bright against the black fur. He brushed her flushed cheeks with his knuckles. "You really are extraordinary, you know," he murmured, thinking of the first time he'd seen her.

Her eyes fluttered open. "Thank you." She smiled, pleased that she had pleased him too. She drew up her knees, the soft fur caressing the bottoms of her bare feet.

Bending one elbow, Logan cupped the side of his face in his hand. "We made a new beginning tonight. What made you change your mind?"

Katherine stilled. This love she felt was too new to speak of yet, so she said simply, "You did."

"Me?" he said softly, then brushed the hair back from her face, tucking it securely behind one ear. With the tips of two fingers he traced her jaw and neck and shoulder and down across her breast. He couldn't stop touching her. He couldn't stop wanting her. "What did I do?"

Katherine didn't move. He was barely touching her and already her body was alive with anticipation. "You know exactly what you did. You wouldn't take no for an answer. You made me feel things—things I didn't know existed. When you're gone, I miss you. When you're here I want..."

"What?"

"More," she whispered seductively.


Katherine stretched and slowly opened her eyes. Four days had passed, four days of magic. A blush heated her cheeks and she smiled. Maybe the magic was knowing she was in love with her husband. So why hadn't she told him? She wasn't quite sure.

The sapphire-and-gold bracelet glinted on her wrist, a dozen tiny blue stones offset by diamonds. It, too, was delicate and new, like her feelings for Logan. Even when he'd fastened it on her wrist, she couldn't seem to find the words to say she loved him.

So she'd decided to wait. Surely she had shown that she cared for him, and when the time was right the words would come. After all, was it words or actions that mattered? Thinking of how much action this bed had seen in the last few days, she did more than blush, she got hot all over.

Abruptly, she swung her legs over the side and stood. Her white cotton nightdress lay in a heap on the floor. Every night she put it on, and every night Logan took it off, insisting she didn't need it. She smiled again. He was right.

It seemed strange not to have Logan here this morning, but he had gone to a Cattlemen's Association meeting. And when he returned they were leaving for the stage depot and the Double Four. Somehow, she still didn't think of the Double Four as home.

She stepped over the carpetbags Logan had left by the wardrobe and went to the washbasin near the window. Sloshing a little cool water into the blue bowl, she washed, then put on her undergarments. Her hair was a mess. Not wanting to fuss with it, she deftly put it in a braid and pinned it up off her neck.

Glancing at the mantle clock, she realized Logan would be back in less than an hour. Just what was going on at that meeting? she wondered as she finished dressing in a green skirt and yellow print blouse. Were they talking about the Bar T? Did they believe her marriage to Logan would mean the end of the sheep ranch?

It didn't matter, of course. She had no intention of encouraging her family to sell. The Bar T was there to stay.

With that fact definite in her mind, she set about packing. Emptying the bureau drawers, she neatly placed her undergarments in the trunk, then retrieved her dresses from the wardrobe. Logan had wanted to buy her more, but considering she'd soon be too big to wear them, it seemed foolish.

As she was folding her tan linen traveling suit, it occurred to her that in the days since they'd been in Cheyenne, they'd never once talked about sheep or cattle or ranches or families. She couldn't believe it, but it was true. She and Logan had been so involved with each other, they really had shut out the rest of the world.

It seemed that in Cheyenne, fairy tales could come true. But what about back in Clearwater? She'd be living on a cattle ranch with a man who had given no indication he'd changed his mind about her family's right to be where they were.

No! She wasn't going to think that way. Things were going to work out, somehow. For the sake of her child, her marriage and her family, she would find a way. She simply *wouldn't* think otherwise.


Seven men sat in the elegantly paneled conference room of the Cheyenne Club for the quarterly meeting of the Wyoming Cattlemen's Association. They were meeting an hour earlier than officially announced, because one man, Logan McCloud, was notably absent.

At the conference table, Ed Bromley droned on and on about sheep and sheep ranchers.

"Tell 'em, John," Bromley prompted.

"What?" John Morris asked from his place by the open window.

"Tell 'em how many steers you lost this winter."

Morris frowned. "A little over half my herd, mostly because of those fences." His tone was hard.

"It's them stinking sheep ranchers," Bromley snarled. "I lost nearly eight thousand head this winter." He scanned the group with his gaze. "Ain't a man here who didn't lose cattle."

"Yep," Tucker commented.

Amos frowned. "Damned right."

The others nodded and mumbled their agreement.

"We'll never survive another winter like this one with them fences there." Bromley sat back in the dark wooden chair. "Somebody's got to do something if we're ever gonna get rid of them folks. I thought our salvation had come when some straight-shooting cowboy plugged old Thorn." He frowned and ran a hand through his thinning brown hair.

"Sounds like you'd buy this guy a drink or two if you knew who he was," Morris coaxed.

"The hell I would," Bromley snapped. "The damned fool should've finished the job and run them folks out of there while he was at it. I'd still have them eight thousand head if he had."

Morris's eyes widened a bit as he scanned the faces of the others. "You boys feel the same?" He sauntered over and sat down.

"Ain't sorry Thorn's gone, if that's what you're asking," Amos said flatly.

"Yeah," Starker and White offered in unison.

Morris rested his forearms on the edge of the table, his fingers clasped together. "Sounds like you boys wouldn't mind if someone took a notion to stir things up a bit. Maybe make things a touch unpleasant for 'em over at the Bar T."

"How unpleasant?" Kyle asked.

"Oh, I don't know," Morris returned with an innocent stare. "I just heard they've already had some trouble, sheep run off and such. Could be someone is taking matters into his own hands."

Bromley twisted in his chair and faced Morris more directly. "Any idea who?"

Morris shrugged. "Can't say."

"Why bother guessing. I'm with Ed on this one. If we want it done then let's do it." Kyle tugged at his starched collar and cleared his throat. "What about hiring that gunfighter Faraday away from McCloud? He could take care of things once and for all. I'd be willin' to chip in a few hundred."

"Yeah," Amos agreed. "I heard he's got himself a reputation for not asking too many questions when money's on the line." There were a few mumbled agreements.

"Are you kiddin'?" Bromley snapped. "After the winter I had, I ain't got money to spare."

"We've gotta do something," Morris said. "If we don't in a year's time there'll be sheep all over this country and not a blade of grass left for cattle."

"Damn those sheep!" Bromley slammed his fist on the table. "If eating the grass ain't bad enough, they walk right through a watering hole, muddy the thing, and *we* have to dig new ones."

Amos frowned. "Speaking of water, the creeks that feed my ranch and yours, Morris, and yours, too, Kyle, run right through the Bar T."

Bromley surged to his feet, his chair rocking precariously on two legs before settling back on all four. "Dammit, we can talk till pigs fly, it ain't solving the problem." He started to pace again his hands clasped behind his back.

"What are you suggesting, Ed?" Kyle prompted.

"I'm suggestin' that we don't wait for somebody to do our work for us. Let's go in there and pull them fences down, run them sheep out and the Thorns with 'em."

"They ain't gonna go easy, Ed," Kyle commented. "Could mean gun play."

Bromley spun around. "So?"

"I'm not a killer, Ed," Amos told him. "As bad as I want them gone, I ain't willing to kill them folks to do it." He squirmed uneasily in his chair. "Bob Dorn's a tough marshal. Men get hung for murder in this territory."

"You willing to lose your place?" Bromley flung back, then he dropped down in his chair, the wood creaking from the assault. "Ain't a jury of cattlemen in this territory would convict a man for killing a sheep rancher."

"Maybe, maybe not. You wanna tell a jury you pulled the trigger on a couple of women and a kid?" White asked flatly.

Kyle shook his head. "Not me. Besides McCloud ain't gonna like this, Ed. Especially since he up and married the Thorn girl. I don't know as how I'd like to have Logan for an enemy."

Bromley glared at them. "What's the matter with all of you? We," he said, thumbing his chest, "*we* are the Wyoming Cattlemen's Association and if *we* want things run a certain way, then, by God, that's the way it's going to be. Logan McCloud can like it or not. It don't matter. He's got to go along."

"Do I?" came a deep growl from the doorway.

Bromley jumped up as if his chair were on fire.

All heads turned toward the man dressed entirely in black who filled the doorway. Where he had come from and how long he had been standing there was the question on everyone's mind.

Logan paused long enough to take in the hostile glares. He'd been tipped off to this clandestine meeting from a note sent by one of the staff here. It took only a second to realize the men were up to no good.

Walking slowly into the room, he squared off in front of Bromley. "You want to tell me what the hell is going on?"

Bromley visibly straightened. "Sure, I'll be glad to tell you. We're making plans to run them sheep ranchers out."

"That so?" Logan's eyes narrowed. Inside, a hard knot of fear formed in his gut, but he kept his voice calm and asked, "Just what are you planning, Ed?"

"We ain't quite decided," Bromley returned with a sneer.

Logan didn't move. Blood raced in his veins. His right hand slowly curled into a hard fist. "You're talking range war, Ed."

Bromley puffed out his chest, seemingly pleased that he was standing up to Logan. "Call it anything you want," he said in an arrogant tone. "We say the sheep go, and if it takes another killing—"

Logan didn't even think. He just grabbed Bromley's jacket front and shoved him against the table, bending him back until he was nearly flat on the hard mahogany.

The sneer slipped from Bromley's face. He grabbed Logan's wrists, trying to break their hold. Through clenched teeth he snarled, "Don't take it so hard, McCloud. We promise not to chase off that little filly you're playing around with."

For a heartbeat, Logan didn't move. He barely breathed. His jaw clamped down so hard that pain radiated down his neck. With deliberate slowness, he managed to release his hold. He even made a show of straightening Bromley's shirtfront before he stepped back. Bromley came to his feet with a smug grin for the others.

That's when Logan hauled back and let his fist slam into Bromley's face with a jaw-breaking force that sent the man sprawling on the smooth pine floor.

Bromley lay there, stunned. Logan closed the distance. He hauled Bromley to his feet and swung on him again. Bromley's head snapped back, blood spurting from his nose and mouth. He threw one punch. Logan dodged it easily and retaliated with a savage blow to Bromley's gut. The rancher doubled over and clutched his belly, his low moan the only sound in the room.

Logan slammed him against the wall, grabbed a handful of shirtfront to hold him, then threw a left to the belly. Bromley cried out and slid down the wall. He slumped in a heap on the floor.

"Stop it! McCloud!" Morris shouted. "Dammit, you'll kill him!"

He grabbed Logan, trying to hold him back but Logan broke free. His breathing labored, he stared at the whimpering man curled on the floor.

Logan dragged in a couple of deep breaths. Instinctively, he flexed his hand to ease the cramping, then sucked on the raw knuckles and spit out the blood.

Kyle and Tucker rushed to help a groaning Bromley to his feet. One eye was already swollen shut and his nose was obviously broken.

Logan watched. "Today's your lucky day, Bromley. I'm not going to kill you."

"For God's sake," Morris snapped. "Bromley's out of line talking about your wife, McCloud, but dammit, he's right about the sheep ranch. It's killing us, and one way or another it's got to go."

"Yeah," Kyle said curtly, while handing his handkerchief to Bromley.

"We *all* got a right to speak our minds, just like you, McCloud," Tucker added. The others nodded.

Logan stood his ground, and for a very long moment he merely stared at them. He forced his muscles to relax. In a voice that was deadly cold, he told them, "If you do anything stupid, if you do anything to the Bar T, and if *anything* happens to my wife because of it, I'll come looking for every mother's son of you and I'll kill you on sight."

Every man there believed him.

He turned and strode from the room without a backward glance.

# Chapter Eighteen

The lone rider sat on a black horse three hundred yards away behind the little cabin on the Bar T. His dropped-brim black hat shaded his eyes, and his right hand instinctively rested on the well-worn handle of his Smith & Wesson Schofield. For the last twenty minutes he'd been staring at the house. A few chickens pecked at the ground in the backyard and on the clothesline, white bed sheets fluttered in the breeze. There was no other movement, no other sign of the inhabitants of the faded clapboard house.

His horse shook its head vigorously against an annoying fly. The bridle jingled and the reins slipped in his ungloved hand.

Overhead, a red-tailed hawk circled and soared on the warm currents. It, too, was watching and waiting. But it was looking for prey.

This man was looking for something else. He was looking for his past.

He was looking for the way home again.

"Ouch!" Sarah dropped the lid on the stove with a sharp clank. She stuck her two burned fingers in the her mouth and hurried to the pump. After a couple of jerks on the squeaky handle, cold water spurted out onto her fingers. "That's better," she said to the empty room, then tucked an errant strand of graying blond hair behind her ear.

She went back to the stove, and this time made a point of picking up a faded green kitchen towel before she lifted the lid. Giving the chicken stew a quick stir, just to keep it from sticking, she dropped the lid of the blue-speckled pot back in place.

She glanced toward the small window by the back door. She could see the laundry waving in the breeze. The sun was shining brightly and there wasn't a cloud in the sky. She sighed. It was one of those days that made a body want to be outside doing something, even if it was only taking in the laundry.

She was all alone at the ranch. Daniel was out checking the fence line. Sarah frowned, remembering him carrying his Springfield when he left. He'd been carrying it every day since some more sheep had been killed. On that fateful day, too, one of the hands had been wounded, and all the men had up and quit.

She took a deep breath and let it out slowly. The men's quitting had come as quite a blow. Oh, she understood. It wasn't their ranch, so why should they be willing to die for it?

And that's what really bothered her. Was Daniel willing to die for it? Moreover, was she willing to let him? Five months ago, when Charles had been killed, she'd decided it was a coincidence, that the act had been done by a stranger passing through. But there had been too many incidents since then, and she was afraid it was going to get worse.

She leaned back against the sink. She wished she knew what to do. In truth, she'd lain awake nights trying to decide, and in the end it was always the same. Charles had built this ranch for Daniel. He would have wanted Daniel to have it. "A man needs something of worth, something to be proud of," Charles had said. But Charles had never expected this kind of trouble.

Maybe they *should* sell. Maybe she should force Daniel to go with her to... where? Besides, Daniel was past the age when she could force him to do anything. It was possible that she could sell the ranch without his consent, but then what? He'd never forgive her. But was *not* selling worth the risk?

She let her eyes flutter closed. Round and round like a cat chasing its tail, her head was spinning with questions that had no answers.

The wind rattled the shutters on the front windows and Sarah jumped. Her gaze darted to the loaded Greener over the mantle. When she realized it was just the wind, she laughed. No denying it, she was a little edgy.

Abruptly, she grabbed up a wicker basket, tucked it hard against her waist, and went out the back door. A dozen or so chickens in the yard scattered at her approach.

Putting the basket on the dirt at her feet, she released the first bed sheet from the clothesline and let it slide into the basket. She was about to do the same with the second when she suddenly had the feeling she wasn't alone anymore. And this time she *knew* she wasn't imagining things. How could she have left the gun in the house?

She whirled around. Eyes wide with alarm, she looked at the man standing less than ten feet away. "No," she gasped. Her voice seemed to come from someone else.

The man stood ramrod straight, his tall, lean frame projecting an air of alertness, of wariness. He looked half-savage, dressed as he was in knee-high moccasins and buckskin pants, his royal blue shirt tucked in at the waist. A gun hung low on his left hip and his thumb hooked over the edge of the belt.

His face was hidden in the shadow of his black trail hat. When he thumbed it back off his forehead, she looked at his eyes, pale blue eyes . . . familiar eyes.

"It can't be," she breathed. Her knees turned the consistency of warm water.

"I've missed you, Sarah," he said softly, his gaze locked with hers.

Sarah just stood there, motionless, speechless, as if every muscle in her body was no longer connected to her brain. It seemed that time had stopped and then begun to run backward. Years ticked away, faster, faster, and suddenly she was eighteen again, in Virginia again. "It can't be you."

He took a step toward her, his moccasins soundless on the dry brown grass. "It is."

Jake.

Her mind told her it was true and her heart confirmed it. Joy rushed through her. It was Jake, her first love, her only love, here.

He was a scant five feet away and she took a small step toward him. He looked different, harder and colder. The years had done that. It didn't matter. Nothing mattered.

He looked wonderful.

She stared at him and his gaze never left hers. Tears slipped down her cheeks and she wiped them away with the back of her hand, briefly wishing she was wearing something pink and satin and young-looking. Her heart pounded so hard she thought it would explode in her chest.

After twenty years, Jake was here.

She swiped at the tears again. "How?" She searched his face with her gaze, memorizing every line, wondering about the scar on the bridge of his nose and the deep creases around his mouth. "I thought you were dead."

"I think I was, until just this minute," he answered quietly. Then he smiled. She was exactly as he'd remembered, as young and as beautiful as the last day he'd seen her. It was that vision he'd kept all those nights lying awake in the Yankee prison and all the long years afterward.

By the time he'd come back to Virginia, the war was over and she was married. Her father had told him—told him she'd made a good choice. Jake had promised not to interfere, though it nearly killed him not to. So he'd had to be content with keeping track of her from a distance.

But that was all changed now. She was here. Willow thin and dressed in black, to him she was still Sarah of the bright blue eyes and musical laughter. She'd laughed so easily in those days. Even now if he closed his eyes he could hear the sound, feel it ease his tension.

"I couldn't stay away." His voice was thick and he ached to touch her, yet he was uncertain. Time changed things. "You look beautiful . . . as always, Sarah."

She loved him for the lie and instinctively pushed at her hair. "You look thinner." It was silly. He looked magnificent, as young and handsome as he had that summer of '62 when he had left with his regiment. Her mouth went dry, her knees getting more wobbly by the second.

"Where have you been?" she asked in a breathless whisper. "Why didn't you come for me?"

"I did," he replied simply. "You weren't there." Jake's heart was beating a slow, heavy rhythm. Inside, his nerves were warming, as if he was coming to life after a long, long sleep.

Sarah stilled. "But it was more than a year, Jake, without a word. I thought you were dead. They told me you were dead." Her voice cracked with the pain of the memories.

"I wasn't," he said softly, simply. "You married."

"Yes." *Charles asked me when I thought no one else would. And a woman needs a man to take care of her.*

"Have you been . . . happy?" he asked then wondered why. It was killing him to think of her happy with another man.

"Happy? I guess I've been happy. I've got two fine children to show for the years."

"That's nice, Sarah." His voice was filled with the anguish of chances missed. He forced himself to concentrate on the words and not on the longing that was heating inside him.

"Your husband died, I heard."

Sarah hesitated. She cocked her head to one side. "How, Jake? How did you hear? How did you find me after all this time?"

The corners of Jake's mouth turned up in a rueful smile. "I've kept track."

Sarah straightened. The breeze tugged a strand of hair loose from the bun at the back of her neck. "Kept track? You mean you've known where I was all these years and you let me go on thinking you were lying dead on some battlefield in an unmarked grave, or worse yet, scattered to the—Oh, Jake, how could you?" Tears clogged her throat.

"You were married, sunshine. It wasn't my place...."

Sarah looked at him with sudden understanding.

Jake forced a smile as he silently cursed Charles Thorn for being lucky enough, or smart enough, to stay clear of the war. Dammit, those should have been *his* years, *his* children, but a damned Yankee ambush had changed all that.

He just kept looking at her, devouring her with his gaze. "I should go, I guess." But he didn't move. The thought of leaving her again cut into him sharper than any knife. "Are you all right?" he asked. "I'll be around for a while if you need anything." His voice was husky.

"I'm glad," Sarah whispered. Just being near him made the familiar feelings return—the passion, the yearning—just as clear and strong as if they had parted yesterday.

He gave her a little smile. It was the best he could do when he wanted to touch her, to hold her, to make her his again. But he had no right, not after so many years.

Jake took a half step back, grateful his legs supported him. He tugged his hat lower so she wouldn't see the despair in his face. "It was good seein' you, sunshine." He started to turn. *I'll always love you.*

"Jake."

She closed the distance between them. Her hand on his arm was warm and set off a stampede of emotions in him. She looked up at him with tear-bright eyes and a tenuous smile. He didn't have to think. He wrapped his arms around her and pulled her against him. His heart started beating double time, his nerves sizzling and lighting up inside him like a bonfire.

His mouth covered hers. She tasted like sweet coffee and peaches. He took her face between his hands and his fingers splayed in her hair, pulling it loose from its pins. He rained tiny kisses over her forehead and eyes and cheeks and took her mouth again in a kiss that claimed her as his, now and forever.

Sarah clung to him. He held her so tightly she could barely catch her breath, so she shared Jake's. She reveled in the feelings that washed through her. It was all there, the longing, the need, the love—all there in his arms and his kiss.

When they came up for air, Sarah smiled. "Welcome home, Jake."

The words were simple, but they were the most beautiful three words Jake had ever heard. Like a living presence they touched him deep inside and healed twenty years of hurt. "After so much time, I was afraid you wouldn't remember," he told her honestly.

She stroked his face with her hand. "Oh, Jake, you've been with me all along, safe—" she covered her heart with her hand "—in here."

Jake lifted that same hand to his lips and tenderly kissed her palm. His gaze drifted to her face and he smiled. In a soft tone he said, "I heard someone once say that home is where the heart is. I've waited half a lifetime to come home."

For the next two hours they sat at the kitchen table and talked and drank an entire pot of coffee. They talked on and on about people and places they'd known and experiences they'd shared. Like two people new to love, they never let go of each other's hand.

It was long past dinnertime when Daniel opened the front door and stepped in. "Sorry I'm late, Ma. Is there any—"

Jake quickly released Sarah's hand.

Daniel stopped midstride and stared. *What the hell?*

He thumbed his hat back but pointedly didn't let go of his rifle. "Ma?" His eyes narrowed. "What's goin' on?"

Sarah rose, her chair scraping on the raw wood planks of the floor. "Daniel, this is—"

"Faraday," Jake said, turning to face Daniel fully. "Jake Faraday. I'm an old friend of your ma's."

Good Lord, Daniel thought, recognizing the name. His eyes widened in surprise. He was startled, no doubt about that, and intrigued, for a moment. Then he decided it was better to act indifferent until he found out what was going on. He made a show of tossing his hat in the chair, his father's chair, by the fireplace.

"I didn't realize my mother had any friends around these parts, us being sheep ranchers and all," he said curtly.

Jake toyed with the coffee mug he held lightly between his fingers. "I knew Sarah before she married your pa."

Daniel's gaze flicked to his mother, who was in the kitchen ladling up a bowl of stew. "That so?" He pulled out a chair at the end of the table and sat down. He never thought of his mother knowing anyone else or even having a life outside of their family. Somehow the idea didn't sit well with him.

He glanced over at Jake. "Well, next time you're in Wyoming, be sure to look us up." The statement was rude and blunt, but he didn't care. There'd been enough changes and surprises this year to last a lifetime. He didn't want any more.

"Daniel, for heaven's sake, what's got into you?" Sarah said brusquely as she walked over to the table with the bowl of stew. "I haven't seen Jake in over twenty years and it's a real joy to see a . . . friend." Her voice was soft and wistful. She cleared her throat and shot Daniel a hard look. "So you just behave, you hear what I'm telling you?"

Daniel had the good manners to look sheepish. Lord, he was tired, and he wasn't sure what bothered him most, finding a man in the parlor or having the man be Jake Faraday. What did it matter? He took a spoonful of stew, then another. He hadn't eaten since breakfast and he was damned hungry.

Sarah turned her attention to Jake. "Are you staying in town?"

"I'm workin' over at the Double Four."

"Then we're neighbors," she told him. "My daughter, Katherine, just got married to Logan McCloud."

Jake nodded. "I hope she'll be very happy."

Daniel's head came up with a start. "Happy? With *him?*" He shook his head. "I can't for the life of me understand why she—"

Sarah frowned. "It's none of your business, Daniel. Katherine's a grown woman and she made her own decision." *Like I made mine.* And for a minute she felt sad, very sad, thinking of the years she had missed with Jake. Not that she hadn't respected Charles; she had. But Charles had been a sturdy wool coat and Jake was sun-warmed cashmere.

She'd worked her whole life—she'd earned cashmere.

The silence in the room was almost deafening.

Jake stood to leave. "Well, Sarah, I guess I'll be movin' on." He clamped his dropped-brim black hat on his head. "Like I said earlier, if there's anything you need..." His voice took on a husky tone. "If I can help... well, I'll be around."

At his words, Sarah thought her heart would surely break in two. How could she casually walk him to the door and say good-night?

"Jake, wait." She touched his arm and was rewarded with a gentle smile that made her pulse race.

She glanced at Daniel, who was staring hard at them. Her chin came up a notch and she looked back at Jake. "All our hands quit. There was some trouble. Someone killed a bunch of our sheep and wounded one of the men. That leaves just Daniel and me to keep things going and—"

"And we're doing just fine," Daniel said abruptly.

Sarah frowned but continued. "We need someone to help, and if you could—"

"We don't need anyone," Daniel broke in again. "I take care of my mother just fine."

Jake's mouth turned up in a knowing smile. "I can see that you're doing a fine job." He glanced from Daniel to Sarah and back again. "Maybe I'd better go."

He had taken two steps toward the front door when Sarah said, "Wait for me on the front porch, would you, Jake? Daniel and I need to talk a minute."

"Sure."

The instant Jake closed the front door, Sarah marched up to Daniel and said, "Let's get something straight around here. *I* own this ranch, whether you like it or not. Up till now, I've chosen to let you run it your way, but we need help and Jake's offering. I trust him and I say we're hiring him." Her blue eyes narrowed in a challenge.

"Fine," Daniel said curtly. "Just fine. You want him, you hire him. But if it turns out he's workin' for McCloud and is only here to..."

"What?"

Daniel surged to his feet. "Never mind. Do whatever you want."

For the first time in a long time, Sarah did just that.


Logan walked home from the Cheyenne Club the long way. He needed the time to let his temper cool down. No sense getting Katherine upset over something she couldn't control.

Besides, he'd taken care of things—*this* time. He stopped at the corner and waited for a freight wagon to rattle past with its load of feed sacks. Dust and a few kernels of corn spilled on the hard-packed dirt street.

Logan skirted behind the wagon and briskly crossed the street. He paid scant attention to the warm July weather or the sparrows that scattered in his path. His thoughts were back at the Cheyenne Club and that bastard Bromley.

The fool was talking range war. *Range war.* The words played over and over again in his head like a litany.

Logan didn't give a damn about the Bar T. He would, however, gladly put his life on the line to protect Katherine.

As long as the ranch and her family remained, Katherine would be drawn there. And when trouble came, she'd be right in the middle of it.

His steps slowed, then stopped, and he gazed with unseeing eyes into the distance. He had to find some way to get rid of the Bar T, and soon, without risking his tenuous relationship with Katherine. But how?

He was still frowning when he turned up the brick walkway of his house and climbed the porch stairs. He made a quick check of his black jacket. There was a little blood on the lapel and he rubbed at it with his hand, hoping Katherine wouldn't notice.

Logan nearly collided with Jack in the doorway.

"Sorry," Logan said, standing aside to let Jack pass with the trunk. Katherine and Sally followed right behind. Logan slipped Katherine's arm through his and the three walked to the front gate. They said their good-byes and climbed into the carriage.

Katherine sat close, her shoulder rubbing against his, her green skirt partially covering his thigh. She seemed distracted.

"You're very quiet," he said, talking under the creak and rattle of the carriage wheels.

She looked at him, her eyes soft. "I hate to see it end."

Logan took her slender hand in his. The sapphire bracelet sparkled in the sun. "It isn't ending, Angel." Lightly, he kissed the backs of her knuckles. "We're just getting started. There's so much we have yet to see and do."

The corners of her mouth turned up in a smile that made his heart pound a little harder.

"I thought we'd already done it all," she whispered. Her cheeks flushed hot pink.

He arched one brow in surprise at her suggestive teasing. "Not hardly, darlin'. . . not hardly." .

Ten minutes later they pulled up in front of the Inter-Ocean. The stage was there and loading. A couple of men were already seated inside the coach. Logan helped Jack and the driver put the luggage in the boot.

"Howdy," a male voice called.

Logan looked up and smiled. Katherine turned and was surprised to see Marshal Dorn striding toward them. His badge caught the sun and glinted momentarily in Katherine's eyes, making her squint.

The marshal greeted Logan with a handshake, then tipped his dark brown Stetson to Katherine. She answered with a sharp nod, feeling a chill as she remembered the last time she'd seen the marshal, in the yard of the Bar T.

"Well, Logan," the marshal said, "I heard you got yerself hitched."

"Yes," Logan stepped closer to Katherine. "I believe you already know my wife."

"Miss... I mean, ma'am," the marshal said with great formality. "Much happiness to you."

When she didn't answer, Logan shot her a look. Seeing her stern expression, he hurried to fill the silence. "I would have come around to see you, Bob, but the time seemed to go by so quickly. We're heading back to the Double Four now. How did you hear about the wedding?"

The marshal grinned. "There ain't nothing goes on around here I don't know about."

Katherine scowled. "Really, Marshal?" she injected in a sarcastic tone. "That's good news. You've found my father's murderer, then." She didn't wait for an answer before turning and climbing into the coach. With unseeing eyes, she stared at the green cloth of her skirt, imagining instead her father's black-draped coffin being lowered into the cold, hard earth. Somewhere out there was a murderer walking around free. She shivered, feeling suddenly cold and very much alone.

When Jack stopped by the open coach door to wish her a safe trip, she managed to mumble her thanks.

Logan climbed into the coach, slamming the door behind him. He sat down next to Katherine, briefly glancing at the two men occupying the opposite seat. As quietly as he could, he said, "You ought to give the marshal a chance. He's a good man trying to do a difficult job."

Katherine choked back the tears that clogged her throat. "I did give the marshal a chance. Now it's up to me."

Logan felt his blood turn cold at her words. "No," he corrected on a harsh whisper. "It's too dangerous for you and—" His gaze flicked to her abdomen and back to her face. "Trust me to look into it."

There was no way in hell he was going to let her go off looking for a killer, though short of locking her in their room, he didn't know how he was going to stop her if she was determined.

He saw her chin come up a notch and thought she meant to argue. He wanted to say more, but not in front of these two strangers, who were watching and listening intently. He sighed inwardly. Was there some grand plan today to make his life as complicated and as frustrating as possible?

Right now, she looked so sad and so far away. Logan reached over and took her hand in his. Lacing his fingers through hers, he pressed her hand against the side of his leg.

Katherine didn't draw away. She knew Logan was right. Hunting for a killer was dangerous. If anything happened, if the baby was hurt because of her vow, she would never forgive herself. She glanced over at Logan, so strong and powerful sitting next to her. She loved him and now she'd have to learn to trust him.

"Under the circumstances…" She gave him a small nod. Logan squeezed her hand in grateful acknowledgment.

It was late afternoon when the stage rumbled and rattled to a stop in front of Hockbaur's General Store. A grinning Pete, who'd been leaning on the hitching rail straightened and waved.

Katherine recognized the Double Four buckboard and Pete's chestnut tied to the back. She exited through the closest door with the stage driver's assistance, followed by Logan, who greeted Pete with a handshake.

"Welcome home, Missus McCloud." Pete grinned and snatched his well-worn tan Stetson from his head. His glance flicked from Katherine to Logan and back again. His infectious smile broadened. "I was gonna ask if you folks had a nice time." He nonchalantly untied his horse from the back of the wagon. "But judging by the look of you both, well, I can see it ain't necessary."

Katherine blushed at the implication.

Logan tried to frown, but it was difficult when he was so happy. "Never mind the inquisition. Just help me with the luggage."

Pete laughed and slapped his hat back on his head. In a mocking, conspiratorial tone, he leaned toward Katherine and said, "He sure can throw them five-dollar words around...can't he, ma'am?" He was laughing as he gave her a hand up onto the wagon seat.

The man's good mood was infectious. Suddenly, Katherine wasn't as anxious as she'd been about coming back to Clearwater. Yes, she was feeling better by the minute.

Logan tossed the carpetbags in the back and climbed in next to Katherine. The seat springs creaked under his additional weight.

The afternoon sun was warm. Logan shrugged out of his black suit jacket and tossed it on top of the trunk, then loosened the top two buttons of his shirt. It felt good to be back in the place he loved with the woman he loved.

Logan gave her a brief smile, then slapped the reins on the rumps of the two sorrels. Pete swung up in the saddle and followed behind.

The wagon rattled and lurched with each little bump in the road. "We'll be home in an hour."

"Home," she repeated softly, looking out over the treeless grassland.

The steady clip-clop of the horses and the song of a meadowlark filled the silence between them. Shifting the reins to one hand, Logan put her hand on his knee and held it lightly in place with his elbow while he grabbed the reins again. He gave her one of those lazy, sensual smiles that curved up behind his mustache and made her blush. The man was incredible. How could everything not be all right when he looked at her like that?

They pulled into the ranch yard around dinner time. The stone-and-log house looked the same, like a fortress, and for a moment she wished it were strong enough to hold back the entire world so that she and Logan could continue the fairy-tale existence they'd shared in Cheyenne.

Katherine waited in the parlor while Logan and Pete carried the bags into the bedroom. She smiled and nodded as Pete crossed the room and walked to the open front door, his spurs jingling as he walked. "See you folks later," he said, closing the door behind him.

A loud squeak drew Katherine's attention to the open bedroom door. She guessed Logan was opening the window in his room—their room, she corrected. They'd slept in his big bed before they'd gone to Cheyenne, but they hadn't shared it, in the usual sense. For just a moment, her heart raced. Heat rose in her cheeks and she covered them with her hands.

"Hey," Logan's happy voice called. "Get in here, woman. I'm not unpacking all by myself."

She shook her head and, smiling, went to help him. It *was* good to be home.

They made quick work of unpacking. It would have gone quicker if Logan had helped instead of occupying himself with pulling the pins from her hair.

"I like it down," he told her when she objected. "It looks like sunlight on a wheat field."

Katherine smiled, gave him a quick kiss and slipped away to the kitchen to start dinner.

She got the steak and onions started while Logan retrieved jars of stewed tomatoes and corn from the pantry. He put both on the counter next to the stove, came up behind her, and nibbled on the side of her neck.

"Stop that!" she demanded playfully. "Do you want me to get burned? This stove's hot."

"I'm feeling a little hot myself," he murmured. Lifting her hair out of the way, he licked at the sensitive skin on the edge of her ear.

Katherine shivered, then let her head roll back against his shoulder. He knew her too well now, all the ways to tease and tempt her. Dinner was forgotten as Logan's arms slipped around her, one hand cupping her breast through the cotton blouse.

Logan rubbed his cheek against hers. "Why don't we eat dinner later . . . much later?"

"It'll spoil."

"Let it."

"It's practically the middle of the day." Propriety demanded some hesitation, she decided, but not too much. Her nerves were already pulsing with anticipation.

He turned her in his arms and reached back to push the pan off the heat. With a wicked look, Logan hooked his hands under her arms and slowly lifted her toward the ceiling until his arms were fully extended. She felt silly, suspended there in midair, with only Logan as her strength, her support. But she also felt free and alive and excited, like the child she'd never been.

"Say it," he demanded with a grin.

Katherine rolled her eyes to the ceiling and pretended not to understand. She could feel the muscles in his arms quivering. He shook her gently. Her black kid shoes brushed against his black pants, leaving a gray dust streak.

"Say it," came his teasing demand again. "Say you want me. Say you want me to take you to bed. Say you want me to make love to you."

The invitation was direct and her body's response was instantaneous. In a husky tone, she said, "I want you to—"

"Katherine Thorn, you in there?" A male voice came in through the open front windows. "Katherine!"

"Damn," Logan muttered.

"Logan," she admonished. "It's Daniel." She wiggled, her hands squeezing his broad shoulders through his white shirt. "Logan, put me down. It's Daniel," she repeated happily, forgetting the provocative invitation she'd been about to accept. Maybe Daniel was coming to put past differences aside.

Logan lowered her to the floor. Ignoring his frown, Katherine went to open the front door.

"Hi," she called to her brother, who was still seated on his chestnut gelding. "Come on in. Dinner will be ready soon. Can you stay?"

"Not hardly," came Daniel's cold reply.

Katherine couldn't help sighing. So much for her hopes of a friendly reunion. She heard Logan's steps behind her. She felt his reassuring touch on her shoulder and at the same instant saw Daniel straightened abruptly in the saddle.

If looks could kill...

Katherine broke the silence. "All right, Daniel," she said as pleasantly as she could. "If you won't come in, why are you here?"

"Why, I come by to see the newlyweds, of course." The words were polite, but the tone wasn't. Katherine wondered if Daniel would ever accept her marriage to Logan.

Logan moved in front of Katherine. In a flat tone, he said, "If you're here for a friendly visit, you're welcome to come in. If not..." He let the implication drag out.

Daniel's eyes narrowed beneath the brim of his Stetson. "Look, McCloud, I came over to see my sister, if you don't mind."

Logan started to step forward. Katherine stopped him with a touch and a look.

She walked down the porch steps. "I'll be right back," she said over her shoulder. There was something in her brother's tone that bothered her.

Daniel dismounted as Katherine walked up to the hitching rail. Softly, for her ears only, he said, "I'm sorry, sis. I didn't mean to lose my temper like that, it's just that..." He slapped the reins lightly against his open palm and cast a sideways glance at Logan, who was still on the porch. "Why'd you have to go and marry him, anyway?"

"Because . . . I love him," she said softly, and she meant it. "And I'd appreciate it if you'd remember that."

Daniel made a small derisive sound in the back of his throat, but he didn't say anything else. She was his big sister and he loved her no matter what, though her marrying McCloud was a hard pill to swallow.

The breeze swirled her skirt around her legs and she and Daniel turned their backs to keep the dust out of their eyes. Katherine pushed her skirt back in place.

"What's been going on since I left?"

Now that he was here, Daniel hesitated. He didn't want to worry her, but he needed to talk to someone. "It's like this, sis. While you were gone, someone decided to use our herd for target practice—"

"Daniel, no." She clutched his arm. "How bad is it?"

"We lost about fifty," he said flatly with a shake of his head. Things just seemed to be going from bad to worse. Trying to hold on to the Bar T was like racing with a herd of stampeding horses, and he had the feeling he was about to be trampled. He was worried that he was in over his head, but he wouldn't say so. A man never admitted a thing like that. So he'd come to his big sister seeking . . . advice.

Absently, he continued toying with the reins he held in his hand.

"What else?" Katherine prompted.

"Will Murphy was shot. . . ."

Katherine visibly paled. "Is he . . ." Her hand covered her mouth.

Daniel grabbed her arm to steady her. "He's all right, but he quit. All the hands quit two days ago."

# Chapter Nineteen

"Oh, no," Katherine said with a sudden intake of breath. Logan walked up beside her and she looked at him. His expression was stern, his bottomless black eyes unreadable. She continued to look at Logan while she spoke to Daniel.

"Tomorrow," she said softly, hoping Logan would understand her strong sense of commitment to her family. "I'll be there in the morning."

"No," Logan said, moving between her and Daniel, "you won't be going anywhere."

Blue eyes locked with black and for a long minute neither spoke. Katherine turned on her heel and strode back into the house. She wasn't going to discuss this further in front of Daniel, but she *was* going to discuss it. She was pacing back and forth in front of the sofa when she heard Daniel ride away. She stopped and stared at the front door, waiting for Logan.

He closed the solid pine door with a soft click. "I can see you're not going to let this go."

"That's right."

His boots thudded on the polished floor as he walked over to the sofa. Stopping behind it, he braced his hands on the curved wood trim and looked at her. "I'm not going to argue with you, Katherine. You can't go over there and you know it."

"I know no such thing," she retorted, starting to pace again. "Give me one good reason why I shouldn't go."

Logan sat down on the sofa, the leather creaking under his weight. He leaned forward and rested his elbows on his knees. Quietly, firmly, he said, "It isn't safe."

"Hmmph." She kept pacing, her range getting larger. This time she walked to the lace-curtained front window and back. "When was it ever safe? Good Lord, Logan, someone murdered my father." Her hands suddenly turned cold and clammy at the memory and she kept walking. "My family is in trouble. My brother and mother can't do it all."

Abruptly, Logan stood. "Your mother doesn't have to work. No one has to be in any danger. All this could be solved with the stroke of a pen on a bill of sale."

"Are we back to that again?" Her tone was incredulous. "Daniel wants the ranch. It's the only thing my father left him. He's not willing to give it up, and my mother and I are trying to help him." She started to pace again. Her pulse rate increased by half.

"You're not helping him," Logan said flatly. "The truth of it is that damned ranch has been nothing but trouble from the beginning."

"That's your truth, not mine!"

He took a step toward her. "Katherine, you're pregnant."

She whirled to face him, her balled fists shoved into her still-narrow waist. "I'm pregnant, not dying. And you know full well I'd *never* do anything to injure this child. But there's no one left at the ranch now except Daniel and my mother. And Mama will try to do more than she can to make up the difference. It isn't fair!"

"And just what do you think you're going to do? I won't have you out riding horses, herding sheep!" His tone was sharp, his expression dark.

Katherine took a step toward Logan. They stood face to face less than three feet apart. "I didn't say I was, but I can do what any other rancher's wife does while she's pregnant. I can do laundry, feed horses, muck stalls, feed the chickens—''

"The hell you will. You're not any other rancher's wife," he said, crossing his arms over his chest. "You're my wife and I won't have you working like a damned mule."

"Do you expect me to sit here for the next seven months reading *Godeys* and crocheting doilies?''

A muscle flexed in Logan's cheek. "Your brother doesn't need *my* pregnant wife, he needs half a dozen men. And I can assure you he isn't going to find them, not around here, not anytime soon. This is just more proof that the damned sheep ranch doesn't belong here."

"It does belong here! You've got more than enough men. Why can't you send some of your men to help, until Daniel hires some?''

"Cowboys on a sheep ranch, now there's a thought." Logan shook his head. "If I asked them, and you're assuming Daniel would accept the help, they'd quit before they'd have anything to do with a sheep rancher."

"But they've all been friendly to me—''

"Damn right they have. You're my wife."

That statement gave her pause. It wasn't her the men were deferring to, it was Mrs. Logan McCloud. She should have realized that people accepted her simply because no one would go against her husband. Logan had the presence to command and the money to back him up.

She turned her back, not wanting to see him. "I hate this, Logan." Her hands curled into tight fists. She wanted to hit something, to scream. "I don't know how to be helpless."

Logan's hand closed over her shoulders and he turned her toward him. She put her balled fists lightly on his chest, her forehead resting between her hands. The steady rise and fall of his chest was somehow reassuring.

Her eyes drifted closed. She was tired, very tired. Softly, quietly, she said, "I have to go, Logan. I have no choice. They're my family." Slowly, she lifted her head to look at him. His dark eyes searched her face. Oh, how she wanted to drown in their depths, to surrender to him. Instead, she said, "Please understand. They need me."

He sighed. "I know." His stare turned hard. "I'll only let you go if you agree to take someone with you. I don't want you there alone, no matter what." He paused and took her face in his hands, his thumbs hooked under her chin. "I want your word, Katherine."

"I promise." She covered his hands with her own and wished there was some other way around this dilemma, this divided loyalty she felt between the family she loved and the man she loved.

"Thank you for understanding," she added quietly.

"I don't, but I'm trying."

And he did try. For the next twenty-three days he tried—hard.

Logan headed for the horse trough and the cool water that waited there. The August sun was hot. He stripped off his shirt and splashed water on his face, neck and chest. It was too little, too late. Ah, what the hell! He bent over and dunked his head and shoulders in the water.

Standing straight again, he wiped the water from his face with the palms of his hands and shook his head, sending water spraying in all directions.

As he wiped his face once more, he couldn't help looking up at the gate to the Double Four. A quick glance at the clear afternoon sky told him it was late, at least four o'clock. Where was she?

Be patient, he told himself.

*Why?* another part of him argued. For weeks now, he'd been trying to be patient, to be understanding.

He'd been so understanding, he'd pretended it didn't hurt his pride to ask Pete to escort Katherine to the Bar T each day. He'd pretended he didn't notice the sly looks and rueful head shakes from the men when she drove out each day. He'd pretended it didn't bother him when she came home later than she'd said she would because something had come up.

Yes, he'd tried hard to understand—damned hard. Trouble was, no matter how he sliced it, he didn't understand. And that bothered him as much as what was happening.

He'd always thought of himself as a progressive, a supporter of women's suffrage and women's rights. His mother was certainly no simpering wallflower.

But this—this was different, his male pride said. This wasn't his wife involved in some civic organization or church betterment league. This was like having a wife who worked.

Hell, she'd even spent the last two nights over there because her mother was down with a summer cold. He wasn't complaining because he couldn't take care of himself—he could. It was the situation that made him angry. It wasn't right. He was the man of the family, dammit. He could take care of his wife and family, and he plain didn't want her out working like a hired hand—not when she didn't have to, not when she was going to have his child. A man could be liberal only to a certain point.

If there had been no way around the situation it would be different, but he'd offered to provide for Sarah and Daniel, and he'd offered to pay twice what the place was worth. But they were determined to hang on, like a tick to a cow's ear and twice as annoying.

Water trickled down his back and chest. Well, his body was cooler. Too bad his temper wasn't.

Grabbing up his shirt, he used it like a towel on his neck while he headed for the house. As he walked, his spurs left small furrows in the dirt, and with each step he got a little more short-tempered.

Slamming in the back door, he stopped short. Not a sound. In the whole house, there wasn't a damned sound. Not exactly what a man wanted at the end of a hard day.

He took a long, deep breath, filling his lungs. His eyes drifted closed. What he wanted was Katherine, here, smiling, waiting, wanting.... His blood warmed. His breathing slowed as images, sensual and provocative, filled his mind. He grabbed the pine counter for support.

Dear God, what had happened to him that he couldn't be without her? She was there, inside him, in every breath he took, every decision, every plan, every dream for them—for her and for his child.

Tonight. She was due back tonight and they'd talk, he assured himself. It was time *she* did a little understanding.

He was halfway through the parlor when he heard horses in the yard. A glance through the lace-curtained window at the group of men dismounting out front told him there was trouble.

Sighing, Logan pulled on his sweat-stained shirt but didn't bother to button it or tuck it in. A sharp knock announced his unexpected guests. He crossed the parlor and opened the door.

Not waiting for an invitation, Kyle and Amos marched right in. A half dozen of their ranch hands waited with the horses out by the hitching rail.

"Well?" Amos demanded as Logan closed the door with a firm click.

"Well, what?" Logan asked as he turned to face them.

Amos looked incredulous. "Well, what do you intend to do about it?" He paced over to the sofa and back, his boots leaving footprints on the dusty wood floor. "We ain't lettin' him get away with it! I'm telling you right now—"

"What the devil are you talking about?" Logan asked curtly, his gaze flicking from one man to the other.

Kyle looked surprised. Amos stopped pacing.

"You don't know?" Kyle prompted.

Logan's temper was on a short fuse. "Know what? What the hell are you talking about?"

"Water is what we're talking about," Kyle snapped. "The Thorn kid has damned up Snow Creek and White Creek where they cross his property."

Logan went still, a warning bell sounding in his head. He'd kill the kid with his bare hands for pulling a stunt like that when the country was on the verge of a drought.

Still, caution was the watchword. Keeping his expression schooled, he asked "When?"

"Yesterday or the day before, as near as we can tell." Kyle walked over to the liquor table and helped himself to a double whiskey, which he downed in two gulps before turning to glare at Logan. "What the hell difference does it make when he did it? We're on our way over to pick up Ed, then we're going over to the Bar T. We're gonna settle this here and now."

"We'd like you to come along," Amos added.

"Not likely."

Amos frowned. "Since when did you become a sheep lover?"

Logan visibly straightened. He took a half step in the little man's direction. "Since I'm trying to stop a range war and keep you damned fools from doing something stupid," he flung back at them. This humiliation was going to cost the Thorn kid every inch of hide on his body.

"Saving our ranches ain't stupid. *You* got water, *you* don't have to worry." Kyle and Amos closed ranks.

"It's obviously a mistake." Muscles tensed along Logan's spine. "I'll talk to Thorn and straighten it out," he told them flatly. Was he really defending the damned sheep ranch? The words left a bitter taste in his mouth.

"Look, Logan. We'd like you in on this, but either way, we're going. Them folks can leave peaceful or not. It's up to them, but they're leaving!"

Logan stopped dead still. "And if I say they're not?"

The two men looked momentarily startled. "How are you going to stop us?"

Logan's right hand curled into a fist. "I can put nearly a hundred men in the saddle in less than an hour."

"Your men won't ride to protect a sheep ranch."

"My men ride for the brand," Logan said, his tone hard and cold. "And *I'm* the brand. They'll do what I tell them to do."

"We ain't going to give in on this one, Logan. We need that water and we're gonna have it."

Logan walked to the front door and yanked it open, blatantly dismissing the men. "I'll take care of it. You'll get your water."

"When?"

"Forty-eight hours."

"Forty-eight hours," Kyle agreed quietly. "Then we do it our way."

Logan watched the two men storm out the front door. He slammed it behind them nearly hard enough to rip it off its hinges.

Now he was protecting the damn sheep ranch. But no more!

Tonight this thing was going to end once and for all.

## Chapter Twenty

"Katherine, you're working too hard," Sarah said, walking into the parlor. The sleeves of her black dress were rolled up to the elbow. She reached up and tucked the last couple of pins into the bun at the nape of her neck. She joined Katherine at the sink and started scraping the remains from lunch off the plates into the wooden slop bucket on the floor.

"Mama, you're hopeless," Katherine sighed with a shake of her head. "You're supposed to be in bed." She wiped the perspiration off her forehead with the crook of her elbow. "I'll take care of these dishes."

Sarah sneezed loudly and grabbed for a white handkerchief tucked in her pocket.

"Bless you," Katherine offered. "Now, you see?"

"Never mind. I was in bed all day yesterday and half of today. It's more than enough. I don't like you working so hard in your condition." Sarah cleaned another metal plate and stacked it on the counter with the others.

"A few dishes won't kill me," Katherine corrected and reached in to wash the first plate. She jerked her hands back. "But this hot water might."

She gave the pump handle a couple of squeaky tugs and cold water poured into the dishpan. Dipping her hands in again, she said, "Better."

Sarah picked up a yellow cloth from the counter and walked over to wipe the table clean. "It's not just dishes. It's also laundry and feeding the stock and gathering the eggs and mucking—"

"I'm only doing the same things that you did when you were expecting. Besides," she continued, "since you've been sick, Jake's been staying here and he's been a big help."

Sarah glanced over her shoulder at Katherine. Softly, she said, "You like Jake, then?"

The corners of Katherine's mouth turned up in a smile. "I like any man who helps with the laundry."

Sarah grinned. "Jake's not the kind to stand around and watch." She paused, her back to Katherine. "You never asked me about Jake."

"Well, I knew you wouldn't have asked him to stay if . . . you didn't feel strongly about it."

Sarah nodded, her eyes narrowed. "He's a good man, Katherine."

"I'm sure he is." Katherine paused. "Seeing him must have come as quite a shock when you thought he was dead all these years."

"A pleasant shock," Sarah corrected.

Obviously very pleasnt, Katherine thought, considering the looks and smiles she'd seen them discreetly exchange. "Will Jake be staying?"

Sarah stopped mid-motion. She turned back to face Katherine fully. "Jake has asked me to marry him. I've said yes."

Somehow, Katherine wasn't surprised. She'd suspected as much. Love was practically written all over them. Her mother had actually blushed when Jake looked at her at lunch a couple of days ago. And she'd seen them talking privately, intently, several times. It was as if no one else existed when they were together. Katherine knew that feeling very well.

She wiped her hands on her dark blue apron and walked over to her mother. "You're sure he's the right one for you?"

Sarah smiled and nodded. "He's the only one."

"Then I'm glad you found each other," Katherine said sincerely as she gave her mother a warm hug. She understood what it meant to love someone—the only one.

She was going home. After two days and two very long nights at the Bar T, Katherine was going home. The steady clip-clop of the horse's hooves seemed to imitate the rhythm of the words—going home, going home.

The late afternoon sun warmed her face and heated her skin through the royal blue cotton of her dress. It felt good—soothing, comforting. The same way that going home felt.

She reined to a stop at the top of a small knoll. Her escort, riding alongside the buggy, did the same. The stone gates of the Double Four were visible about a quarter of a mile beyond.

"Something wrong?" Jake's voice startled her.

She glanced over. "No. Nothing," she told him cheerfully. "I appreciate your seeing me home, but you don't have to go any farther. I can—"

Jake shook his head. "The other day I told Pete I'd see you home safe and sound and I'm doin' just that."

Katherine looked at the man sitting astride the big black gelding. She'd come to know and like him quite well in the last few weeks. And now that her mother and Jake were going to be married, well, she was genuinely happy for them both. With Jake at the ranch, Katherine could stop going over there so often as soon as Daniel could hire some more help. She could stay home with Logan, spend lazy mornings in bed with Logan and—

"You ready?" Jake's voice brought her out of her musing.

"What?" She chuckled at her daydreaming. "Sorry. Look, I'll be perfectly fine from here on."

She glanced at the Double Four and was suddenly very anxious to be there.

A meadowlark sang in the high grass and a gentle breeze swirled dust on the road ahead. She threaded the stiff leather reins more securely through her gloved fingers. "Now, Mama's promised to take it easy, but I know her and she won't. She'll probably start fixing the roof on the barn or some such." She chuckled again.

Jake smiled. "I'll make sure she don't go doing too much, even if I have to nail her shoes to the floor."

Katherine laughed. "And they said chivalry was dead," she teased. Jake snatched his hat from his head and made a sweeping bow. She laughed again and Jake did, too. Yep, she decided, she liked this man a lot. No matter what his past, her instincts said he was a good man and that he genuinely cared for her mother.

Katherine was still chuckling as she slapped the reins on the rump of the gray mare. The buggy started off with a lurch. "I'll be over in a couple of days," she called over her shoulder.

"I'll tell your ma."

She gave a backward wave, but she was looking forward—toward home.

All the way along the road she kept thinking about Logan. He'd been so patient and understanding. Tonight she was going to make it all up to him. A slow smile turned up the corners of her mouth. Maybe she wouldn't wait until tonight. She felt the heat in her cheeks, heat that wasn't from the sun.

She was turning into the gate as a group of riders wheeled away from the front of the house and rode off toward town. Shading her face with one hand, Katherine tried to see if it was Logan and some of his men. Strangers, she decided, squinting her eyes against the sun.

Driving past the barn, she stopped in front of the house. She'd put the horse and buggy away later. Right now she just wanted to see Logan, to have him smile that lazy smile that made her spine shiver.

She climbed the three steps and walked into the house.

The parlor was empty. A layer of dust thick enough to write your name in coated all the furniture. She felt guilty. Mary Rosa had kept the place gleaming. But there just wasn't enough time, and she was too tired most nights to do more than wash the dishes; some nights not even that.

Well, first thing tomorrow she'd get the place spruced up and shining. After all, Mary Rosa and Logan's mother were due home in three weeks. She wanted to make a good impression.

"Logan," she called out. "Are you here?" No answer. Maybe he was in his office. He'd never hear her from there. She started down the hall and then she heard a sharp noise, like a door slamming, coming from their bedroom.

She hurried on and stopped in the doorway. Logan was standing near the foot of the bed, his hair slicked back as if he'd just raked his hands through it. He was tucking a flowing white shirt into the waistband of his denim pants when he looked up. Black eyes locked with blue and for an instant neither spoke, just stood motionless, staring. The silence stretched tight, like a strand of barbed wire.

Katherine felt heat rise in her cheeks and she tore her gaze away. "Well," she started lamely, "here you are. I thought maybe you weren't home." She walked past him to sit in the oversized chair by the window.

"*I'm* always here," he said sharply.

Katherine sighed inwardly. "Well, I'm here, too," she said, forcing a cheerful tone. "Mama is better and I wanted . . . I thought I'd come home and take care of a few things."

Logan stepped over to the foot of the bed and sat on the carved footboard. "I see. Am I one of those few things you dropped by to take care of?"

Katherine's brow knitted in a frown. "Please, Logan, let's not argue. I'm in such a good mood. Things are going very well over at the ranch. Jake . . . Mr. Faraday has been a real help. Mama's on the mend. And Daniel, well, Daniel's been so busy working, I've hardly seen him."

"Would you like to know what dear Daniel's been doing?" His tone was gruff.

Katherine grew still. Logan's jaw was set and his black eyes were hard as Wyoming coal. She could see the rapid rise and fall of his chest, see the way his fingers curved white-knuckle hard around the edge of the mahogany footboard.

"All right," she said wearily, "just what has Daniel been doing?"

"While you were playing Miss I-Can-Fix-Everything, Daniel was out damming up the creeks that supply the water to the lower ranches. Seems he's made a few folks downright annoyed." He shook his head in mock surprise. "And *I* was forced to defend him." His tone left no doubt about his anger.

Katherine bristled. No matter what else she was feeling, the ranch was always a sore spot with her. "I'm so sorry you were put in such an unsavory position. I'll be sure to tell Daniel to send a thank-you note first thing tomorrow." She matched him in tone and temper.

He glared at her, the power of his anger evident. "Dammit, Katherine, I'm not going to sit here and exchange sarcasm with you. Daniel's in big trouble. That water isn't his."

"I'll speak to him."

Logan shook his head. "No, you won't. *I* will. I intend to speak to your mother tomorrow. All this has got to stop. So far that ranch has been nothing but trouble. Your father's dead because of it, cattlemen lost large portions of their herds because of it, men have been wounded because of it, and now this. That ranch has to go. That's what I'm telling your mother, and I hope to hell she has more sense than you and Daniel."

Katherine practically sprang out of the chair. His words touched off a stampede of emotions she'd been denying for months. "Sell the ranch, sell the ranch! That's all you ever say and I'm sick to death of hearing it. We're not selling the ranch and that's final."

Logan took a step toward her. She refused to be intimidated by his size or his menacing expression. "You're my wife. I have an obligation to protect you and the baby. I can't do that as long as the ranch remains. From now on, you're staying here." He took another step toward her. "Do you understand me?"

Logan waited. He was not going to relent this time. He was not going to change his mind. He was determined to argue for as long as it took to make her see it his way. Her safety was too important.

But Katherine didn't argue. Instead of anger, he saw sadness in her deep blue eyes. It took him by surprise. He'd come to expect fire and temper and even arrogance, but not this.

In what was barely more than a whisper, she said, "I can't go on like this."

He was tempted to touch her, to take her in his arms and console her, to tell her that he didn't mean it. He couldn't. They had to resolve this once and for all.

"I said your mother could live with us. Daniel, too, if that's what he wants."

Katherine shook her head. "It always comes back to this, doesn't it, Logan? No matter how we try to avoid it, we can't. I cannot turn my back on my family. They deserve to have a little place in this world. God knows they've earned it as much as anyone. And it's for that reason I can't ask them to give it up and come live in someone else's home, on someone else's charity."

"It's not charity."

"It would be." She gave him a wry smile. "So it comes down to this, to me being torn in half. All you want is for the ranch to be gone. All they want is for it to stay."

Logan felt a coldness start low in his stomach and spread slowly through his body. "What, exactly, are you saying?" His words were almost inaudible.

Her tone was grave. "I'm saying that this situation is untenable. I can't be in two places, live in two worlds." She started past him. He grabbed her shoulder.

"Where are you going?"

"I'm going back to the Bar T. My family needs me...more than you." Her tone was so hushed, so sad, it tore at him.

"You're wrong, Katherine. I do need you—more than I can say." His expression mirrored her own sadness.

She started for the door.

"Katherine."

Tears welled in her eyes, blurring his features. She loved him. She loved him more at this moment than she'd ever thought possible. But this wasn't a fairy tale and sometimes love wasn't enough. "We didn't marry for the best of reasons...all things considered. We were only fooling ourselves that this would ever work out." She walked into the hallway and he followed.

"Katherine."

She halted and turned back to face him. "If you want a divorce, I'll agree. The baby, of course, you can—" Her voice broke. One tear slipped down her cheek, then another. She brushed at them with the back of her trembling hand.

Turning abruptly, she hurried toward the front door.

"Katherine! Dammit, Katherine, don't do this."

She walked out the door and closed it firmly behind her. Logan just stood there. He felt dazed, like he'd been slammed in the chest with a fence post. He couldn't believe this was happening. In a fleeting moment, he wondered if he should have told her he loved her.

Ah, hell, it wouldn't have made any difference. She was determined to go and this time he was too proud to stop her.

* * *

Katherine wiped her eyes with her sleeve, took a deep, calming breath and climbed down from the buggy. Without knocking, she walked into the cabin at the Bar T. Her mother, Daniel and Jake were in the middle of supper. Normally the delicious aroma of baked chicken and cornbread would have made her hungry. Tonight it upset her already queasy stomach.

All heads turned in her direction.

She felt awkward, uncomfortable. What she wanted was a dark corner to curl up in, but she forced a smile instead and tried to sound casual.

"Hello, Mama," was all she said. Her hands curled into fists as she fought back the urge to cry again.

Sarah stood and quickly came around the table. "Katherine, for heaven's sake, are you all right? I thought you went home. Is something wrong?" She put her arms around her daughter and gave her a hug. It was nearly Katherine's undoing.

"Everything's fine," she lied.

"Of course, it is." Sarah's tone was skeptical and she eyed Katherine carefully. "Now, you come on over here and sit down." She pulled out the chair at the end of the table. "You want something to eat?"

Katherine's stomach rolled over again and she shook her head.

"Daniel, make your sister a cup of tea," Sarah said with authority.

"Sure thing."

Katherine didn't feel well at all. The argument with Logan had started her head pounding like there was a herd of buffalo running through it, and her stomach kept knotting and unknotting. She tried to force a smile, but a slight curving of her lips was all she could manage.

She was beginning to think coming here hadn't been a good idea, but she was in trouble, hurting. She thought of Logan, who had always been there when she needed comforting and strength—but he wasn't now, not tonight, maybe never again. So she'd come home, instinctively looking for the only other person she could trust enough to understand. "Mama, I thought I'd stay a few more days, if you don't mind."

Jake leaned closer, forearms resting on the table edge. "But you said you wouldn't be back for a couple of days."

Sarah shot him a sharp look and nodded discreetly toward the door.

He arched one brow in understanding. "Come on, Daniel," he said, sliding his chair back and standing. "You can take care of the tea later. I think your sister and your ma need to talk. Why don't we check on the horses?"

Daniel looked up from pouring the hot water. He set the kettle down on the counter with a loud thud and looked at his mother and then at Katherine, whose tenuous smile confirmed that she did indeed want to be alone with their mother.

Jake lifted his hat off the peg by the kitchen door and started across the parlor, his moccasins making no sound on the wood floor. Daniel grabbed his own Stetson and followed, closing the front door with a small click.

Sarah pulled out a chair and scooted forward until she was knee to knee with her daughter, her black skirt touching Katherine's blue one. She took Katherine's hand in hers. "Now we're all alone, and something's got you upset, so why don't you tell me about it? It'll make you feel better." She smiled reassuringly.

It was the smile more than anything that pushed Katherine over the edge. Tears welled up in her eyes and clogged her throat. Her stomach clenched, and suddenly the words and the tears poured forth together. "Oh, Mama, I—" she gulped in some air "—don't know what to do."

"About what?"

Katherine wiped at her face with the edge of her cotton sleeve. "Logan...he said we have to sell the Bar T...." She gulped in more air, trying to calm her voice. "He tried to tell

me, I can't help anymore..." Katherine wiped at her eyes
again. "He said—"

"All right, dear. Try to stop crying," Sarah said calmly.
"I understand. You and Logan had a fight."

"Not just a fight. I wouldn't walk away from a fight. It's
the ranch. It's Logan." Katherine shook her head. Her
stomach kept clenching and unclenching and the tears kept
flowing, forcing her to talk in gulps. "I can't live like this!"
She shook her head again, adamantly.

Sarah leaned in and gathered Katherine in a hug. "It'll be
all right. I promise," she said softly as she rubbed Katherine's back in a soothing gesture. "Do you love Logan so
much?"

Katherine pulled back and answered with a shaky nod and
hurt-filled eyes. "Yes, Mama, I love him. I wish I didn't,
but I do and that's what makes it so confusing." She started
sobbing again.

Sarah took a deep breath and let it out slowly. "Katherine, I want you to listen to me carefully."

Katherine nodded.

"Logan's right."

Katherine couldn't believe her ears. "But—"

"Logan's right. You said you love him, and judging from
what you're telling me, he loves you. He's worried about
you, and that's good. Your place is with him, not here."

Katherine's eyes widened in surprise. "Mama, don't you
understand? Logan wants me to stop coming over here."
Her tone was incredulous. "I can't just turn my back on you
and Daniel."

Sarah shook her head, her brow creased in a frown.
"Katherine, it isn't all or nothing, but you're trying to make
it that way. *We* are your family. Logan is your *future.* "

"No," Katherine argued. "Logan's the one who's trying
to make it all or nothing. He's the one who's insisting—"

"Don't you see?" Sarah continued in a patient tone. "He
wants you to make a life with him. You're his wife first, my
daughter second and Daniel's sister third. I left my family

and made a life with Charles. Someday Daniel will do the same, though I'm sure he doesn't see that now. All of us having our own lives is how it's suppose to be. It doesn't mean we care less about each other." She covered a cough with her white handkerchief.

"But the ranch—"

"Ah, the ranch." Sarah gave an understanding nod. "The ranch is Daniel's dream not yours. And no one has the right to expect you to give up your future—not even your brother."

Katherine's tears slowed as she tried to absorb her mother's words. *Her* future. Hers, what she wanted—not what she thought she should do or was obligated to do, but what she *wanted* to do.

The answer came swiftly. She wanted a life with her husband and child. Still, that all seemed too easy, too selfish.

She shifted in the chair. "Daniel's trying so hard. I can't ignore him," she said firmly.

"You're not ignoring him. He's making demands that you can't keep. It was all right before, but now that you're married—well, he doesn't understand." She looked straight at Katherine. "You have to decide who's most important in your life. Everything and everyone else comes after. It doesn't mean the rest of us are left out, we just have less of you. You have to believe we'll understand and keep right on loving you."

"Oh, Mama," Katherine said softly as she took her mother's hand in hers. "How did you get to be so wise?"

Sarah chuckled. "I'm a mother. All mothers are smart, didn't you know? Just remember, love first."

"Are you putting your love for Jake first?" Katherine asked carefully, not wanting to pry, just trying to understand.

Sarah gave a small sigh. "Katherine, sometimes life can seem very long. The days can be empty and the nights cold. It's a miracle that brought Jake back to me...so yes, I guess I'd say I am putting my love for him first."

"And Papa..."

Sarah's smile faded. "Oh, dear, make no mistake, I loved your father. He was faithful, a good provider. He was good to you children and I know he loved you both very much. I respected him."

"But he didn't make you feel special," Katherine supplied.

Sarah nodded. "My feelings for one don't take away from the other. Do you understand the difference?"

"I do," Katherine said, acknowledging the special chemistry that she and Logan shared. "I'm glad for you, Mama. But Logan and I...there are so many problems. I'm not sure that love is enough."

Sarah smiled patiently. "Katherine, love is all there is. If you care enough, want things to work out enough, then the love will see you through."

As much as she wanted to believe her mother's advice, a niggling doubt remained. "What about the ranch, Mama? Logan hasn't changed his mind, and neither has Daniel."

Sarah dabbed at her cold-reddened nose with a handkerchief. "I know. With all that's happened I'm worried about Daniel's safety if we stay in Clearwater."

"But with Jake to help—"

"I know all about Jake's... abilities with a gun, but he's only one man. He can't be everywhere."

"Are you seriously thinking of selling?"

"I'm thinking that maybe you should go home and talk things through with your husband. Then, in a couple of days the five of us should sit down and see if we can't find a solution to this."

Sarah stood and held out her hand to Katherine. "Now, in the meantime, I think you ought to be heading back to the Double Four. I'll ask Jake to ride along with you...what do you say?"

Katherine reached up and took her mother's hand. "I say yes." She smiled. Suddenly she felt confident again, anxious to go home, anxious to tell Logan how very much she loved him and how sorry she was that she'd given up on the two of them.

With renewed determination, Katherine stood and headed for the door. Sarah followed. Katherine was on the bottom step when Sarah's voice stopped her.

"Now, I'll expect to see you, both of you, back here and smiling in a couple of days," she said gently as she stepped out on the porch. "It's going to be a nice night, don't you think?" she added, noting the first of the evening stars faintly visible in the sky.

"A very nice night," Katherine replied with confidence. As she turned, the breeze swirled her skirt around her legs. She caught her foot in the hem. Panic rose in her as she felt herself slip. Wide-eyed, she made a frantic grab for the railing. She missed. With a bone-jarring thud, her shoulder slammed into the hard-packed dirt a fraction of a second before her head did. Blackness engulfed her.

"Jake!" Sarah rushed down the three stairs to her daughter's side. "Jake, hurry! Hurry!"

Gently, Sarah turned Katherine over. She was breathing, but unconscious. Her blue dress was still twisted around her legs. Already a bruise was forming on her forehead over her left eye. Her chin and cheek were scratched but there was no bleeding, at least none that Sarah could see. *Dear Lord, please let her be all right.* She took Katherine's face between her own shaking hands. "Katherine, child, speak to me. Please, honey, say something." Tears clogged her throat.

"What happened?" Jake's voice startled her. He was on his knees beside her. The night breeze lifted the brim of his hat and he yanked it lower on his head.

"Oh, Jake. She fell, coming out the door." Sarah patted Katherine's face again then turned to Jake. Tears slipped down her cheeks. "She's not moving. Oh, God, what if—"

Jake didn't wait for her to finish the sentence. He scooped Katherine up in his arms just as Daniel skidded to a halt next to them. Jake carried Katherine into the house. Sarah followed close on his heels, as did Daniel.

"What happened?" Daniel demanded. "Will she be all right?"

Inside the bedroom, Jake gently laid Katherine on the pale yellow quilt covering the bed, then turned to Daniel.

In a tone that brooked no discussion, he said, "Daniel, ride for town. Tell the doc to come. Then go to the Double Four. Tell McCloud to get over here." He glanced at Sarah, who was kneeling beside Katherine, cleansing her face with a cloth from the washstand.

Daniel stared at his sister, then turned a fearful gaze on Jake. "Is she—"

"Go, Daniel," Jake cut him off.

Daniel spun on his heel and was halfway down across the parlor when Sarah's voice stopped him.

"Daniel," she called from the doorway, "tell the doctor that Katherine's expecting. That'll make him move faster, I hope."

Daniel froze in his tracks. "A baby?" he repeated numbly.

"Yes," Sarah confirmed, her voice sharp with worry. "Now get going and ride like a life depended on it."

Maybe one did.

## Chapter Twenty-one

The Pink Lady Saloon was the last building on the north end of Main Street. Every so often Joe Bailey, the owner, slapped a coat of whitewash on the place, but right now it showed more raw wood than paint.

Lights shone brightly through the large plate-glass windows that ran the length of the front. Anyone passing by could see right in, spot a friend and mosey in for a sociable drink or two. That was the idea, and it had been working just fine for the last four years.

Tonight was Saturday—a payday Saturday, and that meant an especially big crowd at the Pink Lady. The long mahogany bar was lined with thirsty cowboys from all the local ranches. And Joe, short and pudgy, with a dirty apron and even dirtier hands, kept the rotgut flowing.

"Yeah, yeah!" Joe hollered to a group from the Flying W as he sent a bottle skidding down the length of the bar.

The piano player started to pound out a song on the upright piano. No one seemed to notice how badly tuned the instrument was. It was loud and that was enough.

Four men from the Bar 76 wandered in and managed to shoulder a space at the counter.

The dozen or so cloth-covered card tables were already filled to capacity. It seemed a cowboy just couldn't wait to shoot his wad, and a few hands of poker was as good a way as any.

Sal and Lottie kept the men well supplied with drinks and anything else they might have a hankering for. After all, this *was* a payday Saturday and a cowboy with money jingling in his pocket, well, it was a sight to warm a whore's heart.

But there was one group of men sitting over by the front window who didn't seem interested in the card games or even the whores. They weren't even drinking the same rotgut as the other men.

No, these men were ranch owners, and they were sharing John Morris's private stock of Irish whiskey, kept at the Pink Lady for special occasions.

Morris opened a second bottle and poured another round of drinks for the five men present.

"So," he said, leaning back in his chair. "McCloud said he'd take care of things."

"That's what he said," Amos confirmed. He threw back the whiskey in one gulp, not bothering to appreciate its smoothness.

The others nodded. All except Ed Bromley, who was particularly quiet.

"And just what else did McCloud say?" Morris pressed in a sarcastic tone.

Kyle toyed with his glass. "He said he'd need forty-eight hours."

Obviously skeptical, Morris lifted one brown brow. He took a long swallow of whiskey. "You mean to tell me you're agreeable to that? You're just gonna sit here and wait." There was a tinge of the incredulous in his tone and his expression.

Starker cleared his throat. "You think he won't come through for us?"

Morris finished his drink and poured himself another. "McCloud hasn't had much luck so far, what with all his fancy talk of lawyers and such. I, for one, gave up waitin' for him." His lips drew back in a grim slash. "The way I see things, it's them or us."

"Yeah." Bromley emptied his glass in one gulp. "Mc-Cloud thinks he owns this damned county. He thinks just because his daddy left him money he can lord it over the rest of us."

From a table near the piano, a round of laughter sounded. A group of cowboys at the end of the bar were encouraging Lottie to sing for them, and the lady seemed inclined to oblige.

Morris watched the action unfold. "There must be three or four dozen cowboys in here tonight," he told them.

"Yeah," Kyle agreed, helping himself to another whiskey. "This keeps up, there'll be a brawl before long, and half of 'em won't be fit for work come Monday."

Morris seemed to consider this a moment. "You know," he said thoughtfully, rubbing his jaw, "I'd venture a guess that there's not a man in here who likes sheep."

"Who does?" Bromley said curtly.

"I'll bet if I was to ask, these boys would be more than happy to ride on out to the Bar T and help them folks move along."

Kyle's eyes widened in surprise. Then a smile turned up the corners of his mouth. "You know, I do believe you might be on to something." He glanced more carefully around the room.

Morris poured himself another drink and refilled the other men's glasses. "I'll bet that this could all be handled tonight and be over before McCloud even hears about it." He shrugged. "Can't stop what you don't know about. Once it's done..." He shrugged again.

The others seemed to warm to the idea.

"Well," Morris continued, "are you with me?"

"Damn right!" Bromley said.

"Let's do it," Kyle added.

Morris's chair scraped on the filthy wood floor as he pushed away from the table. He edged through the crowd to stand at the center of the room.

"Men!" he shouted above the noise. About half the cowboys looked up. "Men!" he repeated, this time louder. The piano player stopped and everyone turned in his direction.

Morris's expression was deadly serious. "We've got a problem here in Clearwater," he told the more-drunk-than-sober crowd. "The problem is sheep."

A low rumble of rude remarks and choice curses rippled through the smoky room.

"Not only do sheep ruin the grass and water . . . not only do the damned fences kill our cattle . . . but now that Thorn kid has gone and dammed up the creeks."

"The hell you say!" a gaunt-faced cowboy at one of the tables commented.

"I do say," Morris confirmed. "What I want to know is, what are we going to do about it?"

"Run them stinking woollies out of here!" came the answer, and everyone seemed to agree, bolstered as they were by several hours of drinking.

"What we're talking about ain't legal," Morris reminded them.

"Says who?"

"Who cares what's legal?"

"Let's get them damned critters off the range before they ruin it forever."

Morris was joined by his foreman, Steen. "I say we ride with Mr. Morris and go get them sheep ranchers out of there." He scanned the room. "What do you say? Are you with me?"

A resounding yes rattled the windows.

Morris glanced toward the table of ranchers. A slow smile turned up the corners of his mouth. "All right then, let's go do it. And when we're through, the drinks are on me."

"All right!"

"Sounds good."

About a dozen men filed past Morris and out the swinging doors.

Several of the ranchers, including Morris, took another gulp of liquid courage, then resolutely followed the others. When Morris got outside, most of the men were already mounted and waiting for him to lead them. Morris checked his Remington, then slid it back into its holster. Steen and a few other men followed suit.

"Let's go!" Morris shouted and reining hard over, he took off in the direction of the Bar T.

"McCloud!" Daniel pounded his fist on the solid pine door of the Double Four ranch house. "McCloud!"

Logan yanked the door open and stood glaring at Daniel. This was all he needed tonight. "What the hell do you want?"

"You've gotta...come right away," Daniel cried between gulps of breath. "It's Katherine."

Logan grabbed the kid by the shoulders. "What? For God's sake, what's wrong?"

"Katherine fell. Doc's on his way." Logan didn't need to hear more. He bolted past Daniel and took the porch steps in one long jump, then ran for the barn. He threw the door open with a crash and raced for his horse's stall. In less than two minutes, he had Joker saddled. He took off out of the barn at a gallop, leaving Daniel far behind.

Leaning down against the Appaloosa's neck, Logan took every shortcut he knew, praying Joker wouldn't stumble in some prairie-dog hole. The miles seemed to stretch on forever. With every pounding step, a sickening feeling seeped through him until no part of him was untouched.

The sun was nothing more than a red glow over the Laramie Mountains when he got to the Bar T. He reined up so hard that Joker nearly sat down in the dust. Logan's feet hit the ground before the horse stopped moving. He burst through the front door and found Jake waiting for him.

"Where is she?" Logan demanded.

"In the bedroom."

Logan tried to push past. Jake grabbed him by the shoulders and blocked him. "Doc's just gone in."

"I don't care about that." Logan tried to get by again. "I just want to see her. For God's sake, is she all right?" Suddenly, he stopped struggling. He couldn't keep the fear from his voice. "Is it the baby?"

Jake's expression was grim. "Don't know. She's still unconscious. Let's wait for the doc, okay?"

It took all Logan's will just to nod. Hell, he could barely breathe. He knew he couldn't move, the pain in his chest was so intense. Not that it mattered. Nothing mattered except Katherine.

Jake let go of his shoulders and Logan turned away. Tears welled in his eyes. He blinked them back.

*Katherine, I'm sorry. I never meant for this to happen.*

He took a deep breath, then another. He raked his hands through his hair.

When he turned back, Jake was pouring a double whiskey into a tall glass. He shoved it into Logan's hands, which shook so badly he downed the liquor in one gulp to keep it from spilling. Tasteless. Hell, if it had been coal oil he wouldn't have known.

He was staring at the bedroom door when Sarah walked out. Seeing her dressed in black sent a stab of terror through Logan before he remembered she was in mourning for her husband. Doc Willis was right behind her. His brown suit was rumpled, as if he'd slept in it, and his long narrow face was pulled down in a frown.

Sarah went straight to Logan and hugged him tightly. Logan returned the hug, grateful for the genuine warmth and caring. God knew he needed it.

"Is Katherine all right?" he asked both of them, afraid of the answer.

Doc Willis tossed his black bag on the scarred kitchen table. It landed with a thud. "She appears to be resting comfortably."

"Comfortably? What the hell does that mean?" Logan snapped. He started to shoulder past again.

"It means I don't know," the doctor said.

Logan turned back with a scowl.

"She's still unconscious, but she took a mighty hard blow to the head. I suggest that we keep the cold compresses on to bring down the swelling and then wait and see." The doctor gave Logan a little smile. "Come on, Logan, I've known you since you were a kid. You know I wouldn't tell you something I didn't believe."

Yes, he'd known Doc a long time and trusted him, but with Katherine...well, he wasn't sure he trusted anyone with her. Logan took a deep breath and let it out slowly. "And the baby?"

"We'll know better in a couple of weeks."

"A couple of weeks?" Logan repeated numbly, feeling the fear grow in him.

"Let's just wait, okay?"

Logan gave a curt nod. "All right for me to go in now?"

"Sure," the doctor confirmed.

Taking a deep, calming breath, Logan raked his hands through his hair once more and walked toward the bedroom, the jingle of his spurs loud in his ears.

He paused in the doorway of the tiny room, one hand braced against the cool wood of the frame. A kerosene lamp flickered on the worn oak bureau near the door. For a moment, he just stood there looking at his wife, resting in the narrow bed on the opposite wall. She looked so pale, so fragile. Her beautiful golden hair was fanned out on the pillow, and her nightgown was like a pale blue mist against the white muslin sheets.

Every muscle in his body tensed. All he could think of was that he wanted to pick her up, cradle her in his arms, and never let her go. God, how he wished it was him lying there instead of her.

His boots thudded on the roughhewn plank floor as he moved into the room. Two steps and he was beside the bed.

Her eyes were closed. As silently as possible, Logan moved the wooden chair and sat down, his denim-covered leg pressed against the side of the bed.

Without speaking, he took her slender hand in his. With the tips of his fingers he brushed her hair back off her beautiful face. So still, so deathly still. *No, don't think that.* But his eyes burned fiercely just the same and he wouldn't let go of her hand long enough to swipe at the tears that slid down his cheeks.

And so he stayed, listening to her gentle breathing, feeling the fear well up in him and thinking about all they'd shared.

*Shared? Who are you kidding, McCloud?* He'd taken and she'd given. From the first moment he'd seen her, he'd wanted her, and in his own blind arrogance he'd thought he could make everything work out. Well, now he had his answer. He couldn't.

Katherine was right. He had been asking, no, *demanding* that she choose him over her family. If he hadn't pursued her, hadn't made love to her, hadn't forced her to marry him, none of this would have happened. With each thought, the painful truth cut a little deeper. Regret was like a living thing eating him up inside.

He loved her more than he would have thought possible. But it was his love that was destroying her, and perhaps their child.

Softly, he said, "Dear Lord, if you'll only let her recover, I won't ask her to stay with me. If you'll just let our child be born..." Tears clogged his throat and he had to swallow.

As if in a trance, he reached over and turned the lamp down very low. Through the bedroom door, he heard when Daniel came home. Katherine's family was talking quietly with the doctor.

They would probably come in here soon to check on Katherine and to talk to him. Logan was in no mood to make conversation or to give the required words of encouragement. He needed to be alone. So he stood and walked out the bedroom door, closing it with a click. With barely a nod, he strode past them and out the back door. The night breeze ruffled his hair as he climbed the small hill behind the house. With each step, the fear and the guilt became burdens he could no longer carry.

Logan sank to his knees, his hands braced on his denim-covered thighs. He looked up into the starlit sky and there, in the semidarkness, he gave in to the demons that hounded him this night. Tears washed down his cheeks, and he slipped silently into his own personal hell.

"Are you sure she's gonna be all right?" Daniel asked for the tenth time in as many minutes.

"I hope so," Sarah told him patiently from her place by the sink.

"Doc's been in there a long time this time," he countered.

Sarah sighed. She tried to pour coffee, but her hand shook so badly she dropped the mug. It hit the floor with a sharp clank that made everyone jump. "Oh, Lord." She grabbed a towel and kneeled down to start cleaning up the mess.

Jake came up to her and took the towel from her hand. "I'll help you, sunshine."

She looked at his kind face. "Oh, Jake, if she's not all right... if she loses this baby..." Tears welled in her eyes. "She wants the child so much. She and Logan had had a fight, but she was on her way home to try to work things out."

He took her trembling shoulders in his hands and helped her to stand, then pulled her into his embrace.

Sarah wrapped her arms around his waist and held on, needing to feel his reassurance. She sighed and the tears slowed. "I'm glad you're here," she told him as he kissed the top of her head.

Daniel spared them only a cursory glance. He'd seen them holding hands and hugging before. Seemed natural, since they were getting married. He'd gotten to like Jake and he was slowly getting used to the idea of his mother married to someone other than his father.

That wasn't what bothered him, exactly—it was all the changes. Too damned many changes. He wanted things to be like they'd been a year ago.

Abruptly, he slid his chair back from the table. His boots beat a hollow rhythm on the bare floor as he paced the four steps to the front window and back, each time pausing to stare at the closed door of Katherine's room.

He kept seeing Katherine lying motionless on the ground. It was like the day he'd found his father's body.

Daniel's hands went cold and clammy. This was all his fault. His mother had said it was no one's fault, but Daniel knew better.

Oh, God, all these weeks he'd made her work too hard, even though he hadn't known she was pregnant. And he'd selfishly upset Katherine when he told her about the sheep being shot. None of this would have happened if she hadn't tried to help him with the ranch.

His heart pounded like a hammer striking an anvil. He forced himself to stop pacing and dragged in a couple of lungfuls of warm air. The cabin seemed small and stuffy.

"Mama, can I go see sis?"

"In a little while," Sarah said, glancing from where she and Jake were talking quietly near the stove. She paused in her conversation and walked over to him. Lifting up on tiptoe, she gave him a kiss on the cheek. It was all Daniel could do to keep from hugging her. But only kids needed their mothers to hug them.

"I'd really like to talk to her," Daniel repeated, trying to sound less anxious than he felt.

Sarah smiled tenderly. "As soon as she wakes up and the doctor says it's okay."

Daniel nodded. "Yeah, I know," he muttered.

Jake lifted his black hat down from the peg in the kitchen. "Sarah, it's been awhile since Logan went out back. I think I'll go make sure he's doing okay." He headed out the back door.

Daniel watched him go, then dropped down in the big chair by the window. He wasn't going anywhere until he saw his sister. Over the next ten minutes, he just sat there, staring at the closed bedroom door, praying his big sister would be better soon.

"Hello in the house!" a man called from out front.

It wasn't a friendly voice.

Daniel came out of the chair in one motion and tried to look out the window without moving the lace curtains.

"Daniel, what is it?" Sarah asked in an unsteady voice.

"Trouble." In the moonlight, he could see about a dozen men fanned out around the porch.

*Oh, God.* His stomach tied itself into a giant knot, and his breathing became shallow and fast. He was scared, no doubt about it, but he wouldn't let these bastards know that—not if he could help it.

He glanced around to see his mother hurrying toward him. "Get down," Daniel said sharply.

Sarah stopped midstride. She did as she was told and crouched behind the table.

"Inside the house! You've got company!"

Several of the men echoed the call.

Keeping low, Daniel made his way to the lamp by the front window and extinguished the flame, plunging the cabin into darkness. What the hell was he going to do now? He was outmanned and outgunned. Where were Jake and McCloud?

Briefly, Daniel considered going out the back to find them and . . . what, leave his mother and Katherine in here with only the old doctor? Not likely.

"Come on, Thorn! We know you're in there!"

"Stay inside," Daniel admonished his mother. He grabbed his Springfield, which was propped near the window. "No matter what happens, don't come outside."

"Daniel, wait!"

He didn't. As scared as he was, this was still his place and it was up to him to defend it. He turned the brass knob and stepped out onto the porch. His dark blue shirt and denim pants made him a barely discernible shadow in the darkness. Moonlight glinted off the barrel of the Springfield he held firmly in his hands.

"Get off my property!" he ordered with as much bravado as he could manage

"Not this time," John Morris said flatly, nudging his horse a little closer. "You shouldn't have damned up them creeks, kid. That's our water you're playing with, and out here, water is the same as blood."

"Ah, let's get on with it," one of the cowboys prompted in a slurred voice.

"Are we gonna stand here jawin' all night, Mr. Morris?" his foreman, Steen, asked in slurred tones.

Several other men mumbled their agreement.

Daniel's heart was beating faster than a Gatling gun but he didn't back down. His voice failed to work on the first try, so he softly cleared his throat and said, "I'm tellin' you for the last time to clear out...*now!*" He lifted the rifle to emphasize his determination.

John Morris glanced down from the big sorrel he was riding. "Who do you think you're kidding? You can't shoot all of us, you stupid sheep lover."

Daniel came forward, stopping at the top of the first step. Not wanting them to see the sweat on his forehead, he stayed in the shadows. "Naw, Morris, I ain't gonna shoot everyone. I'm only gonna shoot the ugly ones, starting with you."

Somewhere in the crowd a cowboy laughed. A couple of others chuckled.

Morris bristled. "Boy, we come here to say we've had enough of sheep on this range. We're gonna help you folks pack up." His eyes narrowed. Leather creaked as he leaned forward in the saddle, resting his forearms on the horn. "But if you want to press your luck, I'd be happy to oblige. It would make things a lot quicker."

"Yep," Steen chimed in, "just like your pa."

Daniel visibly straightened. "What about my pa?"

Steen swayed a little in the saddle. "Why nothin', boy, only Mr. Morris talked to him, too, and you know—"

"Shut-up, you idiot!" Morris snapped.

It was too late. Understanding, cold and hard, hit Daniel square in the gut. He didn't think about consequences. He didn't think at all.

"You son of a bitch. You killed my father!" he yelled. Wanting to get his hands on his father's killer, he dropped the rifle and hurled himself at Morris. He slammed into the rancher, tumbling him off his horse. The two hit the ground with a bone-jarring thud.

Bromley's horse shied and kicked as Daniel and Morris rolled dangerously close to its back legs.

"Look out!" Bromley hollered, and the other riders cursed and shouted while frantically trying to keep their horses from trampling the two men rolling in the dirt.

Daniel was barely aware of what was going on around him. Rage, pure and fierce, consumed him. He struggled to get his hands around the killer's neck, but Morris had a powerful grip on Daniel's wrists.

"I'm gonna kill you, you bastard!" Daniel promised through clenched teeth. Muscles in his arms screamed under the strain.

Suddenly Morris shifted and Daniel was thrown off, landing on his back. Frantically, he rubbed the dirt from his eyes and scrambled to his knees, only to find himself looking straight down the barrel of Morris's Remington.

"Now we'll see who does the killing," Morris ground out between labored breaths.

"Not so fast, John." A hard voice cut through the night. Morris froze.

Logan stepped out of the shadows at the end of the porch. He and Jake had heard the men ride up, but they had reached the house too late. Daniel was already on the porch. Logan had grabbed the Greener off the rack over the mantle and the two had circled the house, one on each side.

Wind ruffled the sleeves of Logan's white shirt as he walked toward Morris. At the same time, Jake stepped around the other side of the porch.

With an angry curse and a slap, Jake shouldered a couple of horses out of his path and moved closer to Daniel, who was still on his knees, staring wide-eyed at Morris's gun.

Jake stood sideways, his left hand on the handle of his own gun. He kept an eye on the crowd and Morris while Logan moved up close.

"Looks like we got us a Mexican standoff here," Jake said to the crowd.

Morris kept his gaze focused on Jake, his back to Logan. "This is gettin' to be a bad habit with you, Logan," he said, his gun still pointed at Daniel's head. "Just stay the hell out of it."

Logan stopped. The shotgun he held was braced tightly against one hip; at this distance he didn't need to aim. He sent a cold look to the crowd of cowboys. "You boys sure you want to buy into this?"

"No, sir, Mr. McCloud," one of the men said very respectfully. "We was just—"

"I know exactly what you were doing." He fixed his gaze on Morris again. "Now, unless you want more trouble than you ever dreamed about, I suggest you get the hell out of here."

"Yes, sir, Mr. McCloud," the man replied gratefully and began backing away. Others quickly followed.

"You, too, Bromley," Logan ordered dryly. "Take Kyle and the others with you. John will be staying until the marshal comes."

For a moment the men didn't move.

Logan took a half step toward Bromley and the others.
"Well? You think this is your lucky day, Ed?"

Jake edged back from the horses, just a bit, and slipped
his gun free of the holster. This was no time for a fast draw.

Bromley looked from one to the other, his jaw set. His
face was mottled with anger. Suddenly, he said, "I ain't going up against you and a damned gunfighter. The hell with
it." He jerked on the reins and rode off into the night.

"We ain't through with this, Logan," Amos said flatly.

"Yes you are," Logan assured them in a tone that didn't
brook any discussion.

Evidently, Amos got the message. He made a derisive
sound in the back of his throat, then turned and rode off.
Kyle, Starker and the others followed.

When the dust settled, only Morris was left, still standing with his back to Logan, his gun aimed straight at Daniel. Logan noticed Jake had turned to face Morris squarely.

The three-quarter moon lit the small ranch yard enough
to see clearly. A hundred yards away, horses in the corral
snorted and blew. And yet the yard seemed quiet.

"Drop the gun, John," Logan ordered. He'd had enough
hurt and anger this day to last him a lifetime.

Morris pointedly ignored the demand. "Are you gonna
shoot a friend in the back over a bunch of damned sheep?"

Logan sighed inwardly. "Is it true, John? Did you kill
Thorn?"

"I didn't plan it," Morris supplied, still not turning to
face Logan. "But when I heard what he was doing, I went
to talk to him. Logan, you of all people know the man was
too stupid to reason with."

"*I* didn't kill him." Logan couldn't help thinking of a
time or two when he'd been sorely tempted. "Shooting
Daniel won't change anything."

"Of course it will," Morris flung back harshly. "It'll
finish the Bar T and tell sheep ranchers everywhere they
ain't welcome here."

Logan inched his way around to get a better view of Morris. You could tell a lot by the look in a man's eyes. John Morris's were cold and hard and deadly. "You're not thinking, John. This can all be worked out some—"

"The hell it can." His tone took on a menacing quality. "I'm bankrupt—all because of Thorn and his damned barbwire. Now that the truth's out, I'm not going to prison and I'm sure as hell not going to hang. I've got nothing to lose."

"You murdering bastard," Daniel yelled. "Dammit, McCloud, if you ain't gonna kill him, give me a gun and I'll do it!"

"Daniel, don't!" Sarah cried, running out on the porch. Doc Willis was right beside her.

"There's been enough killing," Logan snapped.

Morris snorted derisively. "Not until the last sheep man is dead."

"It would be a mistake to do what you're thinking, John."

"It's my only way out now," Morris exclaimed, cocking the hammer on his gun.

Logan hesitated a fraction of a second.

Jake didn't. He leveled his gun and fired.

Katherine opened her eyes and stared at the ceiling. No easy feat considering that her head hurt like blue blazes. What had happened?

She was obviously in bed, in her room at the Bar T. She frowned. She'd been talking with her mother, then she'd started for home when . . . she'd fallen. It was coming back to her now.

Suddenly, a terrifying thought occurred to her and she threw back the covers. No bleeding, she thought with relief. Surely this was a good sign.

Angry men's voices carried in from outside. Something was wrong. Where was everyone?

"Mama? Daniel?" she called. There was no answer.

The eerie stillness of the house was shattered by a loud bang that seemed to vibrate through her body.

A gunshot!

"Mama! Mama, answer me!"

Still no answer. There was no other sound, no other shot. But then it only took one to make trouble.

She swung her legs over the side of the bed. The floor was cool against her feet. So far so good, she thought, trying to ignore the fact that the dimly lit room was whirling faster than a carousel. It took several attempts before she was steady enough on her feet to walk. She wasn't taking any chances on falling again, but she had to know what was going on.

She took the old Navy revolver from the drawer in the table, just in case, and started across the room.

Heart pounding, she leaned against the doorway. "Hello? Is anyone there?"

Silence. Panic replaced concern and she couldn't move fast enough. It was as if she were walking in sand. She braced one hand against the wall for support and willed her legs to keep going.

In a well-practiced motion Jake slipped his gun back in the holster. "I didn't want to kill him."

Doc Willis hurried over to examine Morris. A slow shake of his head confirmed what Logan already knew.

"Don't blame yourself," Logan told Jake. "Morris knew what would happen when he cocked that gun. It was suicide." Softly, he added, "Maybe it's better this way."

Daniel looked at the man lying dead a few feet away. Suddenly, revenge wasn't as sweet as he'd thought it would be. All he saw was death, yet another death. His knees nearly buckled at the realization it could just as easily have been him lying there. His palms were still sweaty. He wiped his hands on his denim pants, then took a deep breath and let it out slowly.

"Mr. McCloud, I owe you. If you and Jake hadn't been here, well . . . I was wrong about you. I'd like to apologize." He looked Logan straight in the eyes and offered his hand.

Logan looked momentarily surprised, but returned the gesture. "That was a helluva thing you did, standing up to those men. Foolish, but I can't say I wouldn't have done the same thing in your place. You're all right ki—Daniel."

"Thanks." Daniel forced a shaky smile.

"Unfortunately, this isn't going to be the end of the trouble," Logan said. "As long as the fences remain and the sheep—"

"I can't stand any more of this!" Visibly pale, Sarah started down the steps. "Daniel, we've—"

"It's all right, Ma, Mr. McCloud was right earlier when he said there'd been enough killing. I'll sell the ranch before I see anyone else dead."

"Daniel, are you sure?" Sarah was obviously startled.

"Yep. I'm not risking you or anyone else again. Mr. McCloud, if you still want to buy the place, well, make us an offer."

"Daniel," Logan started, "I'd be lying if I said I didn't want the sheep and the fences gone, but I think I might have an alternative to selling the ranch."

All heads turned in his direction.

"Let's hear it," Sarah said, coming to stand next to Daniel. She tucked a loose strand of hair securely behind her ear.

Logan glanced from Sarah to Daniel. "Okay. My idea is this. First you've got to tear down those dams you built. Then you tear down the fences and sell the sheep. That done, I'll give you five hundred head of prime cattle."

"What?" Daniel was incredulous.

"It's the only answer—a way for me to be rid of the sheep and for you to keep the Bar T. I wish I'd thought of it sooner, but all things considered, you probably wouldn't have accepted before this."

"Probably not," Daniel agreed, thinking how bull-headed he'd been. McCloud's offer was generous. It did seem like a logical way to end the trouble and still keep the ranch. His pa probably would have bought cattle himself, if he could have afforded them.

"What about it?" Logan prompted.

"I don't know anything about the cattle business," Daniel told him honestly. "You sure you want to risk your cattle?"

"Your cattle," Logan corrected. "And you'll learn. Jake's here. He's worked cattle before." Logan glanced over at the gunfighter. "You are staying, aren't you, Jake?"

"Yep," he said, smiling at Sarah. "I'm staying."

Logan nodded. "Good. In a couple of weeks I'll send over the cattle and a half-dozen hands to get you started until you can hire your own. The money you get from the sale of the sheep should be enough to keep you going through the winter."

Daniel's gaze narrowed and he seemed to hesitate. "I'll accept on one condition. You write it up as a loan and I'll pay you back with interest in five years."

"Done," Logan agreed, liking the fact that Daniel wanted to pay his own way.

The two men shook hands to bind the deal. "Thanks, Mr. McCloud," was all Daniel said.

"Logan?"

Logan turned at the sound of Katherine's soft call. Wide-eyed and pale, she was slumped against the doorframe, clutching an old Navy Colt. She looked about as steady as a newborn foal. "Katherine!" Logan rushed to her, managing to grab her shoulders just as her wobbly legs gave out. "What the devil are you doing out of bed?" he asked more sharply than he meant to as he scooped her up in his arms.

"What's wrong? What's happening?" she asked against the side of his neck.

Not wanting her to see the grisly scene into the yard, Logan ignored her question and carried her back into the house.

The family and the doctor followed close behind as he headed for the bedroom. The gun she'd been holding slipped from her hand and hit the pine floor with a clunk. He wondered briefly just what she'd intended to do with it. Defend the damned ranch, of course, and her family, he decided with more than a little admiration.

"Are you all right?" he asked putting her down carefully on the bed. Not waiting for an answer, he reached for the quilt to cover her. "You scared the living hell out of me, you know." When she didn't answer, he glanced back at her. She was staring at him with those big blue eyes. Abruptly, he straightened. "Suppose you'd fallen again?"

"I heard a shot," she countered.

"There was some trouble. It's over."

"What kind of trouble?"

Before Logan could answer, Sarah hurried into the bedroom. She skirted past Logan straight to her daughter.

"Katherine, child, I was so worried." Gently, she hugged her.

"How about giving the doctor a little room to work here?" Doc Willis politely edged Sarah aside and knelt beside the bed. "How are you feeling, young lady?"

Katherine glanced at all the concerned faces silently staring at her—her mother, Logan; even Jake and Daniel stood in the doorway. "Well, my head feels like it's about to explode and my shoulder aches something fierce, but nothing seems to be broken . . . so I guess I'd say I was okay or I will be."

The doctor chuckled. "Say, who's the doctor here?" He checked the bruise on her head, then took her pulse. Still holding her wrist, he asked, "How's everything else feeling? No pain or cramps?"

Katherine shook her head. "No. Do you think something—"

"Not at all." He cut her off with a wave of his hand. "I don't think anything. You know how you feel, what's normal. Trust your body to tell you if something's wrong." He gave her a reassuring smile. "For now I want you to stay in bed for a week, at least—until all the dizziness clears. Let some of these folks around here wait on you for a bit."

"She'll stay put," Sarah confirmed, "if I have to tie her down."

Logan started to object, to say he'd be the one to look after his wife. He didn't. Sadly, he realized he had no right.

With a few final instructions, the doctor squeezed Katherine's hand and gathered up his black leather bag before making his way out of the room.

Logan followed him into the parlor, picking up the Navy Colt Katherine had dropped minutes before. He put it down on the table.

"Doc, you're *sure* she's all right?" He needed to hear it one more time.

The doctor's graying brows narrowed. "Logan, you know I'm not one for pussyfooting around. Like I said, keep her in bed a couple of weeks if you can manage it, then make her take things slow and easy...no heavy lifting. I'll be by next week to check on her."

"I understand." Logan sighed with relief. He actually smiled for the first time in what seemed like ages. "Thanks Doc. Put the charges on my bill."

"You know I will," the doctor replied, gathering up his hat. Logan walked him to the door. Grim-faced, the doctor said, "I'll take Morris's body into town with me." He slapped his hat on his head and left.

Silently, Logan shut the door. Alone, he leaned back against the smooth wood. He let his eyes flutter closed as he fought against the fear that knotted his stomach just thinking about how close Katherine had come to disaster. If he hadn't been here when Morris arrived, or if Katherine had been here alone... Logan felt a sudden chill. But Morris was dead. That, at least, was settled. And it looked like he and Daniel had found a compromise that they both could live with. It was a time for squaring accounts, and there was one account that he was long overdue in paying back.

Katherine.

Glancing toward the bedroom door, he heard the family talking with her. Though he couldn't hear the words clearly, the tone was definitely happy. This was where she belonged—where she'd always wanted to be. God knew, Katherine had never wanted to be in this marriage, and she'd certainly never planned on having a child.

From the very first, Logan admitted, he'd thought only of himself. Well, it was time to start thinking of her. It was time to give her the one thing she wanted most—the freedom to be with her family. He loved her enough to give her that.

Resolutely, he walked into the bedroom. The family was gathered around Katherine as she lay in bed. They were smiling, talking. So was Katherine. *Dammit, McCloud, this is where she belongs.*

He stepped into the room. "Jake," Logan began. "Would you mind giving the doc a hand... outside?"

"Sure," Jake confirmed, walking out the door.

Logan looked directly at Sarah. "I'd like to talk to Katherine alone a moment."

"Of course." Sarah rose from her place beside Katherine. "Come on, Daniel, you can visit with Katherine later."

With an understanding nod, Daniel followed his mother out and Logan closed the door behind them.

The silence stretched for a long moment before Katherine said, "Thank you... for standing by Daniel... for helping."

He barely noticed her remark, he was so intent on looking at her, thinking how extraordinary she was, wondering how he was going to live without her. Of course, he *would* live, if eating, sleeping and breathing was living.

Bracing herself up on one elbow, she asked, "Are you all right?"

He almost laughed. "I'm not injured, if that's what you mean."

She cocked her head to one side as if studying him. "Mama told me what happened...about Mr. Morris, I mean. I'm sorry, Logan. I know he was your friend."

"Evidently not. At least, I didn't know him as well as I thought," he replied, the bitterness evident in his tone.

"Still, I am sorry." She lay down again and stared at the ceiling as if deep in thought.

Dragging over a chair, Logan sat down next to the bed. Might as well get this over with. Even though it was going to tear him to shreds.

"Katherine." Hearing the quiver in his voice, he stopped, took a deep breath and started again. "Katherine, when you left the ranch today, you said the situation between us was untenable." His hands turned to ice and he braced them on his knees to stop the trembling. "Katherine," he practically stammered. "I—I made a decision...a promise...a while back and now I'm going to keep it." He faced her. "You can have the divorce."

Katherine was very still. "You want me to divorce you?"

Abruptly, Logan stood. He paced across the room and back, his white shirt a stark contrast to the shadows of the room. He looked at her, his expression dark and tense.

"I've had things my way since the first moment I saw you. I blatantly ignored your feelings because I...well, never mind why. I did, and now it's come to this." He scowled. A muscle flexed in his cheek. "Get the divorce, Katherine," he snapped, then added softly, "I would like to know when the baby...to see..." He turned on his heel, paused, then started for the door.

"Logan!" she called to him, knowing that her whole future depended on what she said now.

Hand on the doorknob, he stopped, but didn't turn.

Katherine sat up. The movement made her head hurt like hell and her temper spark. "I was about to tell you that I was wrong today." She squinted to make her eyes focus. "I was on my way home to you when I fell." He still didn't turn. "Dammit, Logan, I love you. Do you hear me, Logan McCloud? I *love* you."

Logan straightened. His head came up like a mountain predator's, scenting the wind. Only this time the scent was hope.

He turned. "Say that again." He moved a step closer, carefully watching.

"I love you," she repeated, her heart beating frantically in her chest. The only sound in the room was her own harsh breathing. She wondered briefly what she would do if he turned and walked out that door.

He didn't. Instead, he took another step, his tall frame silhouetted by the flickering lamp, his face cast in shadows. "Katherine, letting you go is the hardest damned thing I ever did. I can't . . . *won't* do it again."

Her gaze never wavered. "The only thing that matters to me is you."

Logan took a slow, deep breath. "All these months the Bar T has come first with you." He was certain of his feelings, as certain as he'd been from the first, but was she?

"The Bar T is Daniel's future. Deep in my heart I think I always felt that. I always thought I'd go back to Philadelphia—until I met you."

Her eyes were bright, her smile tempting. Still, he hesitated. "You know, of course, that Daniel and I have come to an arrangement?" His pride needed her to want him over all else, not to stay merely because she felt obligated.

She shook her head. "I didn't know," she said sincerely.

The gentle look in her eyes confirmed it. In that instant he knew with certainty—she wanted him. Dear Lord, she loved him. *She loved him.* Logan's heart slammed against his ribs, and for the life of him, he couldn't seem to move or think. It was all so unexpected, like being saved from execution at the last second.

"I assume this means that Daniel gets what he wanted all along—to keep the ranch," she said softly, sadly. "What about you, Logan? What do you want?"

His ebony eyes sparked with a wicked glint. "Why, the same thing I've always wanted," he replied with a slow smile that made a shiver move up her spine. "The only thing I *ever* wanted. You, Angel. I want you. I love you so much it terrifies me. The only thing that scares me more is the thought of living my life without you."

"I can't imagine living without you." She reached out a hand to him.

He came to her in a rush and gathered her in his arms as he sat on the bed. He needed to touch her, wanted to hold her for the rest of tonight and tomorrow and a lifetime of tomorrows. She was warm and willing and one thought played over and over in his mind. *She loves me.*

Katherine wrapped her arms around his broad shoulders and held on tightly. It felt so good, so right. Her heart pounded furiously in her chest and she strained to tighten her hold. His face was buried against the side of her neck, his breath warm and rapid on her skin. She felt him shudder, felt his grip tighten around her waist.

Tears welled up in her eyes as she realized the miracle of the second chance she'd been given. "Logan," she said near his ear. He straightened and looked at her with those soft sable eyes of his.

She stroked his face with her hand. "I'm sorry. I'm sorry for ever doubting us. I'm sorry I waited so long to tell you how much you mean to me." Tears slid down her cheeks. He brushed them away with his thumb.

Logan's lips turned up in a ghost of a smile. "I love you, Angel." He kissed her so gently, so tenderly, she thought her heart would break.

"Take me home, Logan," she said quietly. "Take me home with you."

"I will." He smiled and kissed her again.

\* \* \* \* \*

# Harlequin® Historical

We hope you enjoyed your introduction to our March Madness authors and that you will keep an eye out for their next titles from Harlequin Historicals.

*Castaway* by Laurel Ames—A British shipowner gets more than he bargained for when he becomes ''heir-apparent'' of a large and zany family.

*Fly Away Home* by Mary McBride—The story of a half-breed Apache and the Eastern-bred woman who proves to him that their love can conquer all.

*Silver and Steel* by Susan Amarillas—The western expansion of America's railroads serves as the backdrop for this tale of star-crossed lovers who can't escape their destiny.

*The Unicorn Bride* by Claire Delacroix—A young woman finds herself married to an enigmatic nobleman veiled in secrets and legends in this French Medieval setting.

**Four stories that you won't want to miss. Look for them wherever Harlequin Historicals are available.**

HHMMAD

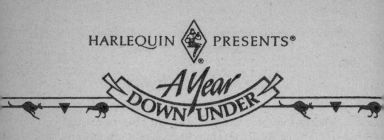

HARLEQUIN PRESENTS®

*A Year*
DOWN UNDER

In 1993, Harlequin Presents celebrates the land down
under. In April, let us take you to Queensland, Australia,
in A DANGEROUS LOVER by Lindsay Armstrong,
Harlequin Presents #1546.

Verity Wood usually manages her temperamental boss,
Brad Morris, with a fair amount of success. At least she
*had* until Brad decides to change the rules of their
relationship. But Verity's a widow with a small child—the
last thing she needs, or wants, is a dangerous lover!

Share the adventure—and the romance—
of A Year Down Under!

Available this month in
A YEAR DOWN UNDER

THE GOLDEN MASK
by Robyn Donald
Harlequin Presents #1537
Wherever Harlequin books are sold.

YDU-M